Invisible
Wallace Family Affairs
Volume III

Carey Anderson

DEDICATION

This story is dedicated in loving appreciation of the inspiration of Yussef. I know it seems hard right now sweetheart, please know that I am rooting for you to succeed

Cover design: Cover Couture

Join me on Facebook –
www.facebook.com/careythewriteranderson

Twitter - @CareyTheWriter

Blog - http://careyanderson.blogspot.com

Website – http://www.careythewriteranderson.com

Editorial – Treasures of Joy Editorial

ACKNOWLEDGMENTS

I would like to thank my baby-girl who is my life's ultimate expression of a dream realized. Thank you for sacrificing mommy time so that I could have the time to work some things out on paper.

I would like to thank my Soul Sistah #1 who has been my captivated audience since middle school. Without your love, support, encouragement, and FIRE I never would've completed Volume I or II, etc. Thank you for bringing me laughter when I couldn't get outside of my head.

I would like to thank my Sister-In-Law for taking time out of your busy family life to humor me with a read through of my latest thoughts and expressions. (SS1 & SIL THANK YOU for the trip to St. Helena where we spent the day lost in my imagination. I will never forget it, and it was exactly what I needed. THANK YOU!)

I would like to thank my dear cousin for reassuring me that my little hobby was relatable and entertaining. You are definitely a speed-reader, thank you for taking time out of your busy life to be entertained by my imagination.

I would like to thank Jamila Gomez for allowing me to mention her wonderful book of poetry. Your work is truly inspirational. A hundred years from now we will still be discussing your work.

I would like to thank last but not least Mrs. Laverne Dyes! Mrs. Dyes the day that you read my short story to my class changed my life. Thank you for giving me a positive outlet for all the angst going on in my life. You have forever changed my life, I am so thankful to have ever known you.

She was my first love, my first touch, my first embrace, my first! How was I to know that my interactions with her would forever shape the way I interacted with the world? The disappointment of our reality unseen has led me down a path of invisible pain and heartache. If you don't love me how can I understand and realize love expressed from other sources. How can I express love, the love that's in me and feel worthy of sharing it? A child without love, is a child without a future. A child without love grows into a monster.

Yussef Davis

She was my first love, my first touch, my first embrace, my first! How was I to know that my interactions with her would forever shape the way I interacted with the world? The disappointment of our reality unseen has led me down a path of invisible pain and heartache. If you don't love me how can I understand and realize love expressed from other sources. How can I express love, the love that's in me and feel worthy of sharing it? A child without love, is a child without a future. A child without love grows into a monster.

Yussef Davis

Chapter 1

We're moving again! Seems like every time I get settled, make new friends, I have to say goodbye. I feel like a nomad moving from city to city. Without any one to share my pain with I write in my journal. Sometimes I sit in my room with my headphones on writing out my feelings or writing poems until I get tired of holding my pencil or pen. I can't talk to my momma about this, she's the one doing this to me. I stopped complaining to my Grandma about it, cause it would make her mad and then she'd argue with my momma about it. Then I'd get in trouble for telling our business as if my grandma couldn't see with her own eyes. Seeing my father was bitter sweet. I was so happy to see him, and excited every time he found us. But I also knew as soon as she didn't get her way about something we were moving again. Sometimes Momma would move without a place to move to. So we would have to go home to Richmond for a couple of months. I love Richmond, the city by the Bay and my roots. When people ask me where I'm from Richmond is the only city that counts. I proudly declare Richmond California as my home.

****

"YOU ARE JUST LIKE YOUR FATHER! YOU DON'T EVER APPRECIATE ANYTHING I TRY TO DO FOR YOU! WHY WOULDN'T YOU WANT TO SPEND TIME WITH YOUR MOMMA? I'M THE ONLY ONE YOU GOT! DON'T I DESERVE YOUR TIME MORE THAN SOME LITTLE TRAMP WHO'S NOT GONNA MATTER IN TWO WEEKS?" She screamed at me
I exhaled, I hate when she acts like this. Whenever she was in between boyfriends then she was overly concerned about what I was doing and who I was doing it with.
"Momma I've had these plans for awhile. I'ma go and I'll be right back. Then we can watch a movie or whatever you wanna do."
Momma's face turned evil. "How you think you gonna tell me what you're gonna do? Little boy you don't run this show!"
She walked in my face daring me to do something. I blew out air cause I know if I reacted to her walking up on me there were going to be problems. "Fine! I won't go nowhere, I'll stay here." I mumbled, I was so mad! It's bad enough she moved us out here to the boondocks behind her ex boyfriend; I finally opened up to the idea that I'm not going back to Richmond to my Grandma, my G-momma, and my auntie. Trying to make the best out of this messed up situation one of the girls at my school invited me to her house. But oh well, I guess I'm not going so it doesn't matter. As I reached for the phone it rang. "Hello" I said
"Hey how you doing little man? Shonda home?"
"Yea, who dis?" I said
"Bernard" he said
I smiled. This fool was my ticket out of here, as long as he was calling to hook up. But I had to act like I didn't want her to go and then she'd really go. "What you want?" I said
"To talk to yo momma." He said
"For what?" I said with an attitude
"Who is it?" Momma asked
"Bernard, but don't worry I'ma tell him to call tomorrow cause we're gonna spend tonight together." I said winking at her.
"BOY!" She said snatching the phone from me. She put on a sugary sweet voice and walked away with the phone.

Invisible

I grabbed my jacket and I walked out the door. Walking to Randi's house I thought about my Grandma. I missed her so much, and all I wanted was to go back to Richmond.

I could hear Grandma's voice, "She was fast!" At least that's what she called her. She said she was always falling over herself over some no good nigga. I asked her if that included my father, and Grandma said there's something's that are easier to accept in life than others. Like my life is the end result of a booty call turned last-ditch effort to hold on. My momma liked him enough, but she was really trying to figure out how she was gonna get her hands on some money. My father was pretty big stuff, at least that's the way my Grandma said it. She said he always drove nice cars, he wore nice clothes, and his hair stayed freshly cut. I had to be about.... Let me see, I had to be about two years old when he started picking me up and taking me places. Grandma said as soon as I was potty trained it was me and him. I just remember that every time he came to get me my momma had her hand out. And if he came by talking about he didn't have no money, my momma wouldn't let him see me. My Grandma said that my father gave her money on the regular, twice a month like clockwork he brought her money. But if he didn't bring her extra whenever he wanted to see me she would act up. The messed up part is that he hardly got to see me. So when the sporadic moment presented it's self that I got to see him, I was always overjoyed. My momma was young and dumb. Grandma said they met at a club, and where my father normally didn't have breakfast with his conquest he let her stay. He said he was going through something's at the time, and for that moment my momma seemed nice enough. My parents hooked up regularly for a couple months and as my father started to lose interest my momma plotted to get pregnant. Grandma said my momma begged him for a few months to come before he actually came and found out she was pregnant with me. He was reluctant to believe that he was the father after she told him. The fact that when I was born I looked exactly like him was almost completely convincing, but my father still had to have a test before he was completely sold on the idea. Once he had suitable evidence that I was his son he was all over the fact that I was here, but my momma's gold diggerish ways began to show. Grandma said my momma has been lost for a long time, and unfortunately my relationship with my father paid the price. My parents still hooked up from time to time, and it really became like payment for services rendered. My Grandma is a very religious woman. Suddenly a single mother of two girls when her husband of many years went into a diabetic coma and died. No one even knew he was sick. Suddenly Grandma was a single mother with no work skills to provide for their family. They lost their comfortable three-bedroom home and were thrust into the ghettos of Richmond California's public housing. They had no choice but to live by the standards that welfare provides. Then Grandma's momma, my G-Momma, got sick and had to come stay with them. Grandma says she tried to influence both my momma and my auntie to rely on God to see them through and to take care of them. But I guess being young and devastated stopped Grandma's message from sinking in at first. My momma and my auntie were always running the streets. Grandma said it was only a matter of time before one if not both of her girls came home pregnant. I guess it was only right that the oldest would show up pregnant first. My momma was barely eighteen when I was born. She had all these ideas of how her life was gonna be. My momma got on welfare when I was born. This was her ticket out of Grandma's religiously based home and to a place of her own. Grandma said most times my father picked me up from her house. And I do remember being picked up from her house mostly. Probably because my momma was always moving, she never really stayed put. So that made it hard for my father to find me sometimes. I guess my Grandma felt obligated to call my father and let him know I was there. That's when he'd come for me, and then he and my mother would have some kind of a dramatic lover's quarrel. I can remember that my momma kept my hair long all my life. One day my father came to pick me up and he kept looking at me. I can't remember how old I was, but I can remember holding my father's massive hand as we entered the barbershop. A lot of people smiled at me, and they were nice. Then this one pretty lady who smelled like baby powder came over and she hugged me. She took my hand and helped me into her chair. She cut the rubber bands out of my hair then she moved it around with her hands. She put the backwards cape on me, then she took me to the other chair where she washed my hair. Then she braided my it. I remember liking the finished product, and I remember my momma being jealous. My momma tried to tell my father that he couldn't have me around Roz. Roz was always nice to me; it wasn't until then that I realized that she was my father's girlfriend. My momma asked me a bunch of questions. In the end she had to let it go. My father put his foot down. "You want his hair long, but you don't comb it. You got him walking around here looking homeless. Shut up its done!" He told her. My momma sent me outside to play, while she continued to argue. When I came back inside to pee, my parents were in my Momma's room with the door cracked. At the time I didn't know what they were doing, it looked weird but later on I found out. Even though Roz was my father's girlfriend, my momma still commanded my father's presence at times.

I rang the doorbell, I saw someone look out the window and then I could hear giggling and movement. "He's here!" I heard them whispering. Randi opened the door. "Who's at the door?" Someone called out. Randi put one finger up. Then she ran to the back of the house. Two of her friends stood there looking at me and blushing. When Randi came back she told her friends to grab their jackets and to come on. "Yussef, thank you for coming." She said blushing

"You're welcome. Where are we going?"

"The backyard, but I figured we could walk to seven eleven first and get some Slurpee's. Is that ok?" I shrugged, I felt relieved that I took a few dollars out of my secret money just in case. Whenever I see my dad he gives me money, he tells me not to tell my momma about it and to save it for a rainy day. I can't wait to see him, I hate being out here. "How long does it take to braid your hair like that?" She said staring at my hair as we walked.

"A couple hours, but that's only because my father's girlfriend can braid really fast. It would take longer otherwise." I said

"Wow!" She looked at my hair like it amazed her. "Can I touch it?"

"I don't care", I said. People always touch my hair I don't even notice it too much any more. Roz always tells me to let her know when I want her to loc it for me. My father doesn't care, but momma said I couldn't do it. I think she didn't like the idea because Roz suggested it.

"Can I touch it too?" Her friends asked. I shook my head yes, and all three of them were petting my hair like they were amazed.

When I had enough of being touched like an animal I started walking again. I blew air cause this wasn't my scene, but it beat sitting in the house. "What kind of name is Yussef?" Randi asked

The question irritated me. "What kind of name is Randi isn't that a boy's name?"

"Are you mad at me? Please don't be mad, I'm sorry." She said real fast.

Hhhhmmmm, I like this reaction. "Don't ask dumb questions!"

Randi turned red. "I'm sorry, I just never heard it before. I thought it might be ethnic." She said lowering her eyes.

I stopped walking. "Hebrew is ethnic?"

Invisible

"YOU'RE JEWISH?" One of her friend said in disbelief.

"Why else would I have a Hebrew name?" I was having fun with these dumb girls.

"Is that why your hair is so long?" The other friend asked.

"Yep! I'm gonna be like Samson when I grow up." I said with a smile. They exchanged looks; I knew they didn't know who I was talking about. I shook my head. "You guys really need to read your bibles." I said holding the door open for them.

I paid for our drinks then we walked back to Randi's house. Randi's dad worked nights, she didn't have a mom. Her big sister looked out for them at night, she was having a guy over so she told Randi she could too as long as I was gone before their dad came home.

"Where did you move here from?" Randi asked

"Richmond"

"Where's that?" Her friend asked

"On the other side of the water from San Francisco next to Berkeley."

"Is that where your father is?" She asked

"You ask a lot of questions." I said frowning.

"I'm sorry! It's just that you're the new kid. Nobody knows much about you." She said

"I didn't come over here to be drilled. I could've stayed home for that." I said

"I'm sorry! Are you bored? Do you want to leave?" She said

"Do something to entertain me!" I commanded

She looked confused. "Do something like what?"

"You like asking questions don't you." I sighed, "I'm gonna leave."

"No! Don't leave!" She looked around. "I'm sorry I don't know what to do."

"It's ok. I'm gonna go." I said standing up.

"I'll walk you to the gate." Randi said disappointed. "You guys can go up to my room, I'm gonna walk him to the gate." Her friends went inside, and we walked on the side of the house. She actually looked sad that I was leaving.

"Have you ever been kissed?" I asked

Randi's eyes got big. "Once, but it was real quick."

"Like this?" I said giving her a peck on her soft lips.

"Yes" she said looking at me with big eyes.

"What about like this?" I put my tongue in her mouth.

"Randi where's the..." Her friend stopped when she saw us kissing. Then she smiled real big, "what are you doing?"

"I'm showing her how to kiss, you wanna show her how it's done?" I said

"Is it ok with you Randi?" She said

I looked at Randi to see what she would say. She put her eyes to the ground. "I don't care."

I laughed to myself, "This girl is a pushover. She better get some back bone." I didn't even remember what her friend's name was. "Come here!" I said. This girl was ready and knew what to do. We kissed for a long time. Then I looked at Randi, "you got it?" She shook her head yes. And she did a lot better, she had some learning to do, but she'd get it. "Why don't you guys do this. Explain to Randi what she needs to do practice on each other. And when you think she's got it, I'll take it from there." Both of them gave me a funny look. I laughed, "It was worth a try!" I said still laughing.

I walked home laughing to myself. I could already hear my dad laughing in my mind when I tell him about this.

When he called himself having the birds and the bees conversation with me sometime ago he asked, "Do you have a girlfriend?"

"Yep!" I said

My father smiled, "what's she like?"

"She's pretty!" I said proudly

He gestured with his hands. "And?" I didn't know what he meant so I looked at him. "Is she smart? Is she nice? Why is she special enough to be your girlfriend?"

The only answer I had was that she was pretty. I couldn't say she had much else going for her. He said if pretty was enough my mother would've been his girlfriend. I asked him why my momma wasn't his girlfriend. He shook his head, I had this conversation with my Grandma and that's when she told me all the above. But I needed to hear it from him. He compared my momma to Roz. He said my momma was only out for herself, she was too selfish. Where Roz on the other hand looked out for him, and took care of him. Roz was always nice to me even when my father wasn't looking or around. My momma had a certain voice she used when men were around and another one she used as her everyday voice. I didn't blame him, I loved my momma but I didn't like her very much.

"You can't let everyone in up here." He said pointing to his temple. "Only the special one gets that deep." Then he asked me if my girlfriend was special enough to be up here, he pointed to his head. Or was she only special enough to be right here? He pointed to his lap. I shrugged, and then he told me I didn't have to let a girl up here, just to have her down there. Then he said if I was ever unsure of where a girl went, he said put her in my lap. The ones that belong upstairs were clear from the beginning. I asked him how would I know. He said the ones who go up here, you won't miss them, and he said they would grab my attention. Then he said the ones who belong in my lap would remind me of my mother. Then he told me no matter what to stay covered, bring my own condoms, and to always flush them on my own. He demonstrated on a banana how to put a condom on, how to take it off and when. He told me if something felt "different" to pull out and inspect my condom. He told me not to let the girl touch it cause the trifling ones will try to rip it.

We were sitting at the kitchen table while he was educating me. Roz's daughter Tanisha came in the kitchen while we were talking. She looked at me and shook her head. "Boys!" She said

"You got something you wanna add?" My father asked

"Yea! How about if she isn't special enough to have your baby don't sleep with her." My father laughed. "He's not gonna be a monk. He's gonna meet a girl he wants to give it to. Or who wants to give it to him, but there's no love connection. I'm sorry that's just the truth."

She stood there looking mad. "Teach your son to be better! Don't teach him to go around breaking hearts!"

My father exhaled, then he called Tanisha to the table. "I know you're still mad at me. I can't take back what I did, but I'm really sorry for hurting you. If I could take it back I would."

Tanisha's eyes got glassy. "You broke my heart Troy! You broke my Momma's heart. She's forgiven you, but I always looked at you like a father. You let me down."

My father stood up and hugged her. "I know, I have no excuse for doing what I did. Please accept my apology. It's me and your momma from this point on."

Tanisha hugged my father back, and then she told him to finish his stupid sex education class. When I asked my father what happened he said he let a lap girl come between him and Roz. When I asked him why, he shrugged and said for that moment he became weak, and that he almost lost Roz forever.

When I got back to my apartment I knocked on the door. When there was no answer, I used my key and went inside. I opened the door slowly; my momma and her friend were in her room with the door shut. I exhaled and went in my room and turned on my radio. I put my headphones on cause I didn't wanna hear nothing coming from her room. I really wanted to see my Grandma this weekend, and next week was spring break. I wanted to spend it in the Bay with my friends and family. I took my headphones off and I called Grandma, as usual she and G-momma were excited that I called. I told them I wanted to come out; of course they didn't have a problem with it. Grandma told me to call my father. When I called Roz answered the phone. She was always happy to hear from me. She said my father wasn't home yet but she would have my ticket waiting at the train station Friday. She asked me how I was adjusting to life in Fresno, and I told her the truth I hated it. She listened to me as I explained why. I could tell she felt bad and as much as she wanted to, she wasn't gonna say anything against my mother, but I think I said it all for her. We talked for a little while then we got off the phone. I put my headphones back on and I fell asleep. I woke up in my momma telling me to get ready for school. Her friend spent the night so she played chef in the kitchen, when normally I ate cereal or oatmeal. I showered, dressed, and endured her put on like she was the sweetest female ever. Then I left to go to school. I listened to my Walkman all the way there then I did my best to keep to myself. The girls thought I was mysterious cause I was quiet and different, the guys always wanted to challenge me. Seems like I was always dropping some fool to his knees because he was trying to run up on me. It was a way to get my frustration out, but even beating people got old. There was no real challenge out here. The kids that thought they were bad were all talk.

"I practiced last night." Randi said with a smile.

I smiled, "did you take my suggestion?" She nodded yes. "Did you like it?" I asked

"It was weird, does that make me gay?" She asked looking confused.

I laughed, "no. Girls can kiss girls and it doesn't mean anything. Next time maybe the three of us can hang out." I watched her face for a reaction.

"Ok" she said

I knew she didn't know what I meant. "Are you a virgin?"

She looked embarrassed. "Yes"

"Aren't you tired of that, don't you want to experience life." I said watching her face for a reaction.

Her eyes got big and she put them on the ground. "I don't know."

"How about your friend she seems ready. She's not a virgin huh?" Randi shook her head no. I started going through the scene in my mind. This girl would let me do whatever as long as I paid her attention. And her friend seemed to go for whatever as well. Now I would definitely do her friend, but I didn't want to take Randi's virginity like this. She is eager to please, but not very smart about her heart. I changed my tone. "Randi, look at me." She glanced up at my face and then back at the ground. "No, look me in my eyes, and don't look away." She tried but she got really embarrassed and started changing colors. I exhaled, "I can't do this!" She looked confused. "Do you want to have sex?" She shrugged; I could feel myself getting irritated. "Look! You should know that you want to do it before you do it. And you shouldn't do it just so somebody will like you. I don't want to be that guy. You're a nice girl, you need a nice guy, so you guys can have nice sex." We both laughed.

"Aren't you a nice guy?"

"Sometimes, but I'm not the guy you need to give it away to. Not today anyways. I'm gonna give you a pass for being a nice girl, but I doubt the next guy will be so nice. Make sure you're ready first."

"But I like you." She said

"Why?" I said

"You're cute, smart, and funny." She said

"You want to have my baby don't you?" I smiled at her.

15

She gasped, "no!"

"Well you need to think of it that way. I'm trying to let you down easy, it seems like you just want me to stay."

"I like you, I want you to like me." She said embarrassed.

"I'ma tell you something. If the only way you can get someone to like you is to give him your body, then you need to rethink it. If you wanna give me your cherry I'll take it, but I think later on you will be kicking yourself."

"Do you like me?" She started twirling her foot.

"I don't even know you." I was starting to feel bad for this girl. She was desperate. Thank goodness the first period bell rung and I walked with Randi inside. But you know how girls are, they see one girl paying you attention then they all start looking. I sat down and this girl walks over and sits on my desk. I don't know why but it irritated me that she sat there. "What!" I said looking at her.

"Yussef right?"

"You are?" I said not masking my irritation.

"Faith" she said with a smile

"What do you want?"

She looked disappointed. I guess I was supposed to be excited cause she was talking to me. "I want you to call me."

"For?"

She smiled, "we could figure something out."

I looked around the room cause I didn't know where this hoe came from. Randi was sitting in the corner with sad eyes. Faith gave Randi a look like she was taking over. Randi looked like she was going to cry. I got up out of my desk and sat behind Randi. She looked so surprised when I sat down. She whispered thank you, then the class started. Faith kept looking at us during the class. I didn't know what the deal was between them, but I didn't like the way Faith was conducting herself. She was reminding me of my mother. When we broke off into groups I sat with Randi, a guy named Antonio came, and of course Faith hurried. The teacher gave us our assignment. "You and Randi going out?" Faith asked

"Why you in our business?" I asked

She looked like the challenge would spur her on. "Cause there's nothing she could do for you that I couldn't do better." She said, I guess she thought she was sexy. Randi put her eyes to the ground. Moments like this I wished I was in Richmond. Faith would've been getting whooped on. I frowned at her, "why would you sink to such a cheap level just to hurt Randi's feelings? You don't even know me. All you know is you see her talking to me, and you gotta win. What's wrong with you?" I asked Antonio laughed, "You can't be from around here. Nobody talks to her like that." Faith looked embarrassed, and Randi tried to hide her smile. What I didn't realize is just about everybody was listening. Almost all the girls in that class were looking at me with wanting eyes.

This city is too easy; I'm trying to lay low. At the end of class Randi gave me a big hug and Faith stormed away. By lunch time it seemed like all the girls knew my name. Randi came and sat next to me. She thanked me for standing up for her. Before long a bunch of girls were at our table. All of them were smiling at me, I got that sinking feeling. The girls were smiling the guys were frowning. Then Randi said, "Uh oh here comes Faith's brother."

I huffed then I stood up. He was coming full of anger and leaning forward when he walked. "You called my..." As soon as he stepped in firing range I connected with his jaw. Everybody oohed when they heard it. He stumbled backwards in shock, he came back in anger again, and I saw his friend coming from the left. He was still leading with his head forward I hit him in his temple and he went down as expected. I prepared myself for his friend who at least was coming upright. I calmly waited while he ran. He gave me eye contact then he looked at his friend. School staff came and grabbed him before the friend could decide what he was gonna do. "YOU TO THE OFFICE!" The woman said to me pointing, while they helped the guy off the ground. It seemed like the whole school was watching. I picked up my backpack and the rest of my lunch. I didn't even know this guy's name, but he was pretty upset. I guess it was only right that he was upset; I mean I would be too. I walked into the office finishing my lunch. The secretary asked me if she could help me, I guess because I walked in so casually behind everyone. I pointed at the guy and I told her I was there with them. Someone rushed over to the guy with a towel to hold on the cut that opened on his eye when I hit him in his temple. The guy still looked a little confused, I watched him and his friend. Then they called us in the office. The principal wanted to know why we were fighting. I shrugged and the other guys weren't saying anything. "Nobody knows why you were fighting?" She asked

"All I know is they said here comes Faith's brother. He was charging at me, so..." I put my hands out.

She looked at him, "Reese why were you charging at him?"

"My sister came to me crying talking about he called her a whore. So I went to handle it."

"Did you call her a whore?" The principal asked

"No ma'am. I asked her why she would sink to such a cheap level."

"Give me the context around that comment." So I told her what happened in first period. "We have a zero tolerance for violence in this school."

"But Ms. Connors I didn't do anything. I don't even know why I'm here." Jermaine said

She frowned, "I thought you were fighting too." She looked at all three of us for confirmation.

"You're supposed to have my back!" Reese yelled

"There was no time." Jermaine tried to explain.

"He was coming but your staff got to us before he got a chance to decide where he was gonna be." I said

"So you two didn't fight?" She said clarifying

"With all due respect, look at him." I pointed to Reese, then Jermaine. "Obviously I hadn't gotten to him yet."

Jermaine laughed a yea right laugh. "Jermaine you may go." She said. Reese was angry that she dismissed Jermaine. Then she gave us our suspension slips. I smiled cause it prolonged my trip to the Bay. The principal lectured Reese about his sister.

When I left the office fourth period let out, Randi apologized to me at my locker. I told her there was no reason for her to be apologizing. She said she felt responsible. I told her none of this was her fault and to stop it. She kept looking at the floor, I told her if she really wanted to make me feel better she had to show me what she practiced last night and she had to hurry up before she was late to her next class. Her eyes got big as she looked at the other students rushing around us, but she kissed me anyways. I smiled and told her she learned fast. Then I told her we were even. I touched her chin, smiled and then walked away.

When I walked into the apartment my momma was knocked out in her bed. No doubt exhausted from her episode with Bernard. I tiptoed around, I dumped everything out my backpack, put the essentials I'd need for my train ride. I left a note on the table that I "got suspended, going to The Bay". Then I took off running as soon as I closed the door. I called my father from the train station. Since he didn't answer at his apartment

I called Roz at the shop. She said he was out with Malcolm. So I asked her to change the ticket to today and that I was at the ticket counter waiting. Roz was good, she got everything changed around and I made the next train. I listened to my Walkman the entire train ride. When I stepped onto the platform in Richmond, I happily inhaled the polluted air due to the local refinery. I walked along the train tracks to the Townhouses in Richmond. My Grandma's unit was downstairs and in the front. I knocked on the door and let myself in. Grandma was dressed up cause she was going to service in a little; she had the phone on her ear. She handed the phone to me and said it was my momma as she hugged and kissed me. My momma fussed cause I left without permission; I exhaled while I let her fuss. Then she asked if my father was gonna drive me home. I told her I didn't know. She told me to tell him she needed some money. I agreed then we got off the phone. Grandma hugged me again then she told me to hurry and dress so I could go to service with her and G-momma. Grandma kept a stash of clothes for me for when I went to service with them. Sometimes Auntie Summer went too, but even if she didn't go she gave us a ride there and back. I braided my corn rolls into one braid and tucked the end inside my collar.

"You look so handsome Yussef." Grandma said

"But why he gotta have that long hair like a girl? Don't you wanna look like a boy?" G-momma asked me.

I smiled, "I do look like a boy G-momma."

"If you say so. Come give your G-momma some suga."

I gave her a hug and a kiss, and then they both admired me in my nice clothes. "I think it's time to get you some more. You're growing again." What my momma doesn't know is that one time my father came a little early to pick me up from my Grandma's house. He saw me in my service clothes and when he found out that Grandma was scrapping her pennies together to buy my clothes for when I went with her to service he started giving her money for my clothes. Grandma protested and she even refused the money at first so my father took me to get a suit. She said the suit he got me was a "hot mess" she said it was too loud and didn't dignify me or where we were going at all. So then he brought her with us a couple times then he had a heart to heart with her. He told her he wasn't into religion, but he respected that she was. He told her he wanted me to show the same respect by at least looking nice whenever I went with her. My father started sending money regularly after that. When she would try to protest saying I didn't need anything new for awhile he told her to hold on to the extra for me cause we all knew if he gave it to my momma I'd never see it. Grandma showed me where she hid the money in her room and she told me it was there if I ever needed it. When I told my father about that, he shook his head and said he wondered what happened to my momma.

Everyone was so happy to see me, when we went inside my Grandma's place of worship. People made so many comments about how big I've gotten or how much I've grown. G-momma and Grandma always looked proud of me.

When we got home Auntie Summer asked all kinds of questions about momma and life in the boondocks. She told me she works in Oakland and she really likes the job. I felt so peaceful laying on my Grandma's pullout couch. I told myself I needed to come up with a plan to move back.

Invisible

Chapter 2

"I'm not staying out there! Everything is too easy out there. She got us out there only to be difficult. I don't think she even likes it all that much. Why don't you tell her to move us back?" I said looking out the window

"I don't want you out there, but it's more convenient for me that she is." My father said putting food in his mouth.

"She wanted to know if you're bringing me home." He smiled at the thought of it then he looked away. I knew what that meant. "She said she needed some money."

He nodded his head, "when doesn't she?" He thought about it for a minute. "Did you go see my mom yet?"

"Yea, I went to her house. She said she wants me to come around more. Another reason why I need to move back."

He nodded, "we're gonna get you back out here. Just working out the storyline. You wanna stay with me or your Grandma?" He asked

Then his cousin Malcolm walked in. Malcolm is my father's closest cousin; they're closer than any brothers could be. Malcolm always looks like he's figuring something out when you talk to him. He's super intelligent and not someone that you would ever want to piss off or get on his bad side. Malcolm has no patience for my momma or my auntie. He always tells my father that he lets my momma get away with too much. Especially when she starts stressing him telling him she's gonna call Roz. At that point he's willing to do whatever so she'll calm down and leave Roz out of whatever. Malcolm tells him to put her in her place, I'm always curious of what he means by that. My father normally changes the subject or something.

My father told Malcolm about the fight I had. It was like my father was there or something he told him exactly the way I told him. I was impressed by his memory. Malcolm asked me about my take on the situation. I told him that fight was the first of many, I could already tell. He asked me if I was carrying anything. I told him no, but also it wasn't necessary out there everything was too easy. Malcolm asked my father how long I was gonna be out there? My father said he'd work it out when he took me home. "Why would you take him?" Malcolm asked

"I wanna get a bigger place. I think it's been long enough and I want Roz and Tanisha to move back in but we'll need more space." My father said

Malcolm squinted his eyes at him. "How hard is it to find a place? You got excuses. If it's all that, I'll take the apartment and you can take my house."

My father laughed, "You always got answers." Then a female walked in, for whatever reason she caught Malcolm's attention. He was watching her, once she gave him the green light with a glance Malcolm started to get up. My father cleared his throat at Malcolm who then looked annoyed and returned his attention back to my father. "How's Amber doing?"

Everything in Malcolm changed, his face showed emotion for the first time ever. "Nothing's happening, she's depressed. I'm trying not to show disappointment." Then he sat back.

"Just tell her you love her. Stop holding marriage ransom go ahead and marry the girl. She probably thinks you don't love her."

He blew air, "that would be ridiculous. She knows I love her."

"She's a female, they start doubting you the moment you change up. This whole thing has been traumatic for both of you. Marry her and then name the baby after me." Malcolm didn't smile but his voice sound like he was. "I'm not naming my daughter after you."

"Fine! I guess Roz will when she has my baby." We both looked at him. "I'm gonna take your house. Then I'm firing off a baby in there. You ain't the only one with a baby itch."

I know I shouldn't have but it kind of felt like he would forget about me with a new baby. "After you get me back out here, right?"

"Of course! I gotta have my twin with me. There's some other family members I gotta get a read on, but we can keep everything moving meanwhile." My father said

"He needs to kick it with my boys." Malcolm said looking back towards the girl.

"Malcolm! Man focus!" My father said

"I'm focused, and I'm frustrated. I need to blow off some steam." He said not looking at us. "Let me know when to start packing up the house. Later!" He got up walked out the door. He stood next to his car for a minute. The girl walked out and got in his car. My father said Malcolm already knew that girl.

****

"YOU CAN'T TAKE MY SON AWAY FROM ME!" I heard momma scream all the way from outside.

My father talked to my Grandma who convinced my father sooner than later would be best to move me back to The Bay. When I walked in the door my father was shirtless and barefoot. My momma had a robe on and her hair was a mess. She was opening windows when I guess he told her that I was coming back to Richmond in a week. "He doesn't want to be all the way out here. You're the only one who likes it out here." My father said calmly

"What about me?" She whined

"What about you?" He shrugged

"The money Troy!"

My father looked at me. "The choices you make affect the rest of your life." Then he turned to her, "I'll leave something for you."

"I'm gonna need another car." She said no longer seeming upset about me leaving.

My father started putting the rest of his clothes back on. "I'm not buying you another car."

"It wasn't my fault!" She said

"Why would you let a drunk fool drive the car I bought you? You are so disrespectful!" They went back and forth for a while, and then she put on that sugary sweet tone.

"Think about it, if I have a car I can come out whenever you need me to."

My father looked disgusted. "Don't talk to me like that! You're fine out here."

She huffed, and then she squinted her eyes. "I could keep your son out here until you get me a car."

He exhaled, walked in her face. She backed up until she hit the wall. His face was mad, "you have no power here. The day you understand that is the day you might actually become grateful for the things I do for my son despite you! I could walk out of here with him right now and there would be nothing you could do! My son is moving back. You can do whatever you want, move back or stay. If you want a car, you pay for it! Don't you EVER in your life try to act like you have power to pull rank or that I should care about what you want. I don't even like you; I tolerate you for the sake of my son. Shonda so help me if you try to pull anything next week, I am not responsible for what happens to you." He took one step back, "do you understand?"

My momma was scared, her chest was moving up and down fast and heavy, but she wasn't stupid. She looked at me with a sad face. Then she put her eyes to the ground and shook her head yes. My father finished dressing then he told me to pack my stuff.

Invisible

When he left she spent the rest of the evening screaming at me and accusing me of betraying her. I didn't say anything; I let her get it out. I told myself I was almost out of here and to not worry about it.

After my momma cried herself to sleep Randi called me. She told me that Reese was mad cause I got him like I got him. She said all he keeps talking about is revenge. I laughed and told her I wasn't concerned. I could tell she was scared for me, I told her she worried too much. She told me that all kinds of guys have been flirting with her and suddenly everybody knows who she is. "And you're welcome!" I said laughing. Then I explained that she was a cool person and she needed to enjoy the ride. I told her to stop apologizing and say what she wants. But I warned her not to lose her sweetness. She was quiet for a minute, and then she asked me why I didn't like her. I tried to explain to her without hurting her feelings. So I told her I did like her, but I had a girlfriend back home in Richmond that I talked to everyday. She seemed to accept that better than me telling her I wasn't interested in being her boyfriend just because.

Two days in, from what I could tell Reese and Jermaine were at odds. Even though I had Reese down before Jermaine got there, he was blaming Jermaine for losing our fight. But since he needed Jermaine for whatever he was planning against me I saw him trying to halfway smooth things over. Day two I was walking Randi home when we saw Jermaine coming. I had to tell Randi to calm down and be cool, she was freaking out. Jermaine gave me eye contact the entire time. "What's up Yussef?" He put his hand out to shake mine.

I shook it, "Jermaine".

"So you've heard about what's going on?" He said

"No, but I figured there would be something. Reese doesn't seem like the type to leave well enough alone." I said

"He thinks he's so smart, like I wouldn't know he's plotting against me because he's mad that you got him. No one's ever got him before, he can't handle it."

"Figures" I said

"What is he planning?" Randi asked with her eyes opened extra wide.

I put my hand out, "we don't want to know that. You're doing enough by saying hey." Randi looked at me in disbelief. "Why wouldn't you want to know? Reese is mean, and you made him bleed. We could tell and get him in a lot of trouble."

"Yea, but then how would we know about it if no one said anything. It causes more trouble than it's worth." I said

"All this because his sister is loose." He shook his head. "Faith causes more problems than she does good. Most people give her what she wants just so they don't have to deal with Reese."

"I'm not most people." I said

"I hope you're still cocky when it's all said and done." He said

We walked Randi, who was now a ball of nerves, home. She was nervous so her mouth was moving at the speed of lightning. I didn't say anything; I couldn't accuse her of not caring about what happens to me. I gave her a hug, and then Jermaine and I walked and talked about sports, Randi, girls in general, etc. He seemed cool enough, but I couldn't trust that this wasn't part of Reese's setup.

When I got home my momma was in the kitchen cooking dinner. I asked her who was coming over, and she told me no one. She wanted to make me dinner before I left. "Is this some part of a game?" I didn't understand why she was doing it.

"NO!" She sat down at the table. "I've been thinking and talking to my momma. I can't say I understand but according to my momma, she seems to think I should try harder when it comes to you." She started crying, "I don't know why you wanna leave me."

Aah! There's the game, she's trying to guilt me into staying. "Thank you for dinner. Do you wanna get dressed up real nice like we're on a date?" I said sounding super excited. I put a huge smile on my face.

She stopped crying and started laughing. "That's not necessary. Just go wash your hands."

My momma only cooked when her men were coming over, so this was a never before treat for me. She made fried pork chops, Mac and cheese from scratch, cabbage, and mashed potatoes. Then she made me a chocolate chocolate chip cake for dessert. I was so full that it hurt to laugh and of course everything was funny at that point. I actually enjoyed my evening with my momma. If she acted like this all the time I could see being stupid enough to want to stay. But I know better, so I don't.

Day three was cool for the most part, one more day until Friday and I was out of here forever I couldn't wait. Reese kept popping up everywhere, I figured today must be the day. I stayed mindful of my surroundings all day. As Randi and I started to walk towards her house we got a block from the school and here came Reese and his little crew. He was with three other guys, but I didn't see Jermaine. They stood in our path like a wall. Randi instantly started crying and apologizing. I told her to go home and not to come back. I took one arm out of my backpack straps, then I put my hands in my pockets and I grabbed my keys. Randi ran past them crying and looking like she was gonna tell whoever would listen. That girl could run, I was impressed. Once she was pretty far, I looked at the three of them. I turned on my heels and I ran. I ran across the street, and of course these stupid fools chased me. I ran up three blocks and across a busy street, a car bumped one guy, but it didn't stop them. When I got to the park by my house, I stopped running. They all stopped and caught their breath for a minute. I stood there breathing normal. They looked at Reese and he told them to get me. I gave him a look like yea right. They looked at each other then they looked at me, then him. At least they were smart enough not to come forward without him. You could see Reese's irritation. Reese stood up straight and came forward, he swung at me and he just missed me. I could feel the wind brushing past my face. The other guys surrounded me, they started closing in. I had to move quickly before they got too close. I took my keys out my pocket shook them and started spraying. I turned in a circle to make sure everyone got their fair share. One by one they all fell screaming and holding their faces. I stepped over Reese and walked away. I threw the empty mace bottle into the busy street then I walked slowly to my apartment. When I walked in the door I heated up my leftovers and ate in front of the TV.

In the middle of the night I couldn't get comfortable. My chest was heavy and it felt like I couldn't breathe. Something wasn't right, but I didn't know what it was. I pulled out my journal and started writing. At about five in the morning there was a knock at the door. Momma and I stood in our bedroom doorways with the same expressions. I expected her to say it was such and such coming over, but she was as clueless as I was. "WHO IS IT!" I barked

"Tim" the guy said

I looked out the peephole and saw a white man staring at the hole. I opened the door. "Yussef, my name is Tim. I need to talk to you and your mother." I opened the door so he could come in. At first I thought it was about Reese and Faith, but he would've come earlier than this. "You're Shonda right?" He said stepping to the side so the door could close.

"Yes, what's going on?" She asked

"Please sit down." He said calmly, but you could tell if she didn't do as she was told he would handle her. Momma sat but I chose to stand. I didn't know this man or why he was here. "I have bad news." I already knew before he said. I sat down and held my

chest. It felt like I was gonna lose my air. "Troy passed away this morning." My momma started screaming. The pain I felt in my chest spread to the rest of my body. "Malcolm is in the car, I've come to take you home." He said to me.
"No! I don't know you! You can't take him." Momma said
"I know you're upset. His family needs him. We're here to carry out Troy's wishes. I would suggest you discuss any concerns with Malcolm, but let me also say today is not the day." Then he looked at me, "do you want to stay?"
"No!" I didn't let him finish his question. I needed to be with my family. I got up and started bringing the things I was moving into the living room. Mostly my clothes and journals. "I'll call you when I get to Grandma's." I said as I grabbed my last box. I kissed her on the cheek and I walked out the door as she cried. When I put the box in the trunk Malcolm got out the car. He had shades on and his body was stiff. He hugged me and patted my back. In the car Tim lowly sang along to old school R&B music. Malcolm didn't utter a word, it didn't seem like he even moved the entire car ride. When we got to Oakland we drove up a hill, then we pulled into a driveway.
"Do you want him to bring his stuff in?" Tim asked Malcolm
Malcolm turned his head towards me. "You'll stay with me tonight." He said then he got out the car and walked slowly inside the house.
Tim helped me bring my things inside. Malcolm told us to put them in the room downstairs. Tim went to the refrigerator and he told Malcolm he didn't have any food. Malcolm exhaled then he started slowly walking up the stairs. Tim said he'd be back, and then he left. Malcolm called me upstairs; there was a big picture of a woman at the top of the stairs. He was in a room on the right; it had pictures all over the wall, a TV, and a couple couches. He handed me the remotes to the TV then he sat down. I went around the room looking at the pictures. I wanted to cry looking at the pictures of my father, but I didn't see a tear on Malcolm's face, so I wasn't gonna break down in front of him and have him thinking I'm soft. I sat on the couch, turned on the TV; I didn't realize I fell asleep until Malcolm was tapping me to wake up. He handed me the phone then walked out the room. It was my grandmother, she was a mess. She started crying really hard saying that I even sound like my father. She told me Malcolm was gonna bring me over the next day. We talked for a little while longer then we got off the phone. I called my Grandma and when she prayed with me over the phone I couldn't stop my tears from pouring out of my eyes. Grandma was crying too and I could hear G-momma crying. Malcolm suddenly appeared in the doorway, he gave me the number to his house, his car, and pager to give to my Grandma to reach me. When I followed him downstairs a woman was putting something in the oven, and unpacking groceries. She saw me but she didn't speak. When she was done she put that sugary sweet tone in her voice as she told Malcolm the food was in the oven and there were plenty of groceries. Malcolm said an unenthusiastic thank you, she kissed his cheek then she left. Malcolm told me to help myself to whatever was in the kitchen. I took an apple off the bowl the woman left on the counter. I washed it in the sink then I bit into it. I looked at Malcolm and he was watching me. I didn't say anything I just looked back at him. He exhaled and his face was sad, "you look exactly like your father. Only difference is the hair." He exhaled, "prepare yourself for everyone's reactions to you especially right now."
"Do you know what happened?" I asked
"Not yet, I've got some people working on it. All I know is he was shot in the chest, and his car is missing." He read my face for a reaction.
"What are you going to do?" I asked. He didn't say anything, he looked at me. "Can I handle it?"
"Handle it?" He asked

"'Take care of it. Do it! Whatever!" I said, my tears felt like acid.
Malcolm looked at me for a long time. "I'll think about it."
"Think about it?" I asked
"Letting you do it will get in the way of me doing it." He said. The smell coming from the oven was intoxicating. It was then that I felt hungry. It was some kind of casserole with pasta, meat, cheese, and sauce. It was so good! Malcolm barely ate though, he was mostly thinking. "I can't have you out there on the frontline even if it is vengeance for your father. What are your grades in school like?"
"They're ok, I'm not a master mind." I said
"Do you want to go to college?"
"Only if I have to." I said
"Why wouldn't you want to go?" He had a confused look on his face.
"It's more school, I'm not the biggest fan of school. I'd rather just get on with my life." I could tell he didn't like my answer, but he accepted it.
"I want you to apply yourself in school. Get the best grades you can. As long as you maintain a B average in school I will finance all your endeavors. You're gonna want a car, pocket money, all that right?"
"Yes"
"You will earn them by getting your grades. You will go to school even if its only community college. You will be of no use to yourself or me without an education. If in the end you can't decide on a career path you'll work for me. But I'm gonna need you to be a jack-of-all-trades as much as you possibly can be. I can tell you're smart, I need you to apply it."
I sighed, "ok".
"Or you can keep doing like you're doing, work at McDonald's flipping burgers for minimum wage and catch the bus everywhere. You do have a choice."
Then the phone rang. Thank goodness! He barely said anything and he got off the phone quickly. He went upstairs and Tim came in the door minutes later, he wasn't smiling he had a about business look on his face. "What smells so good?" He asked
"Dinner, you hungry?" I asked
"No thank you son." Malcolm came back downstairs, he had those shades back on, but he had on different clothes. That was the first time I've ever seen him in a flannel shirt. "You sure you wanna go?" Tim asked Malcolm. Malcolm exhaled then he stood up straight and headed for the door. "He'll be back late, call if you have any questions. You got the numbers?"
"Yes, he gave them to me earlier. Can I call Fresno?" I asked
"Sure" he said then they left.
I finished eating then I went back upstairs. I called my momma; she was in tears when she answered the phone. She kept apologizing and for the first time ever I really think she meant it. She felt horrible about the way she left things between them. Their last conversation was full of manipulation and that wasn't the way she wanted their story to end. For the first time I realized that she did care about him in her own way. I still didn't break down with her though, but I was happy I called her. She begged me to let her know when the funeral arrangements were so that she could come.
I knew Malcolm left to handle whoever was involved with my father, why else would he be wearing those disposable clothes. I tried not to think about it, cause I don't know why it was making me angry. I looked at Malcolm's bar; I don't even know what I poured. But I poured a little. It was smooth and delicious. I went upstairs and stared at the pictures of my father, cried my eyes out, and fell asleep.
****
"Next week we're gonna re-enroll you in school out here." Grandma said

Invisible

"Thanks" I said unenthusiastically. Grandma tearfully hugged me for the millionth time.

My momma came downstairs with red eyes in her respectable black dress. I forgot she could look so nice. Auntie Summer hugged her again then we piled into her car. My chest kept burning in the spot that I imagined my father getting shot in. I wondered if he thought about me in his dying moment. There were a lot of people there already, everybody was crying and looking sad. Grandma told me to go sit with my Grandmother who was not doing too well. When she saw me she started crying harder, kept hugging me and kissing me. The girl who was sitting next to her looked kind of stuck when she saw me. It was like she was looking at me with my own eyes. I know most of the people here are family, but I didn't know this girl. She didn't even kind of look familiar. The girl kept peeking at me, and I was doing the same; it was like we were trying to figure out who each other was. As soon as people started moving around Bernadette my father's cousin came and hugged me. Everyone kept saying how big I got. I would try to go over Renee's whenever I could, depending on when I went I didn't get to see everybody. When I stood up the girl wasn't sitting next to my grandmother anymore. But I spotted her dreads walking out of the auditorium; she left her jacket next to my grandmother so I knew she was coming back. I wanted to know why she looked at me like all the grown ups, and why she looked more like me than anyone else here. I walked over to my momma and Auntie as they were walking out of the auditorium. The pretty lady from the picture in Malcolm's house was standing in the lobby, she locked eyes on my auntie she tried to smile but her face was really sad. She told my aunt she didn't know she knew my father. Auntie Summer introduced my momma and then they pushed me forward. The lady got the same stuck look everybody kept having today. She was getting ready to say something to me when Malcolm walked over and took her away. His face looked hard and my momma and auntie started panicking at his lack of a response to them. They wanted to leave but I wasn't ready to go yet. Then I saw her come out of the bathroom. My momma noticed my face she turned around to see who I was looking at. "Latia?" My momma said The girl slowed down and looked at my momma like she didn't know who she was. "Yes?"

"I'm sorry baby girl, you don't know me. But your father talked about you all the time." My momma said

The girl scrunched up her nose. "He did?"

"Yes, how else would I know who you are?" Momma reached for her hand, then she reached for mine. "Latia, this is your little brother Yussef."

We both held the same surprised expression; suddenly I didn't feel alone anymore. I gave her the biggest hug to cover up my tears; I could feel her tears dripping on the top of my head. We hugged for a long time, neither one of us wanted to let go. "Make sure you guys exchange information so you can keep in touch." Momma said

"I'm sorry," she said wiping her tears off my forehead.

"I can't believe I have a big sister!" I said, the hole in my chest stopped hurting as much.

"I knew of you, I wasn't sure if you were you though. But you look just like him." She said taking me in. Then she took my hand and we went back in the auditorium. We sat in the middle of a row in the middle of the auditorium. "How old are you?"

"Almost fifteen. How old are you?" I asked

"Seventeen. Where do you live?"

"I just moved back to Richmond, where do you live?"

"In Rodeo, it's the city after Hercules."

"By the Vallejo Bridge?" I asked

"No, that's Crockett. Rodeo is a little city in between both those cities. You will come visit me won't you?"

"OF COURSE! I'm so happy to have somebody to relate to in this." I said

"Did you know him?" She asked

"As much as I could. My momma made it hard." I said lowering my head.

She blew air. "Mine too!"

I don't know why that made me perk up but it did. "Really? My momma moved all over the place just to be difficult, that's why I'm just coming back from Fresno."

She laughed, "mine took me to Roseville and Citrus Heights, then Fairfield and Suisun, then Vallejo, and just recently Rodeo."

"Where's Roseville and Citrus Heights?"

"About and hour past Sacramento."

"Can I touch your hair?" I asked. I didn't wanna reach out and touch it then she get mad at me and never wanna speak to me again or something.

She smiled, "of course. Can I touch yours? It's so long!"

Her dreads were soft to the touch and I liked the feel of them. "How long have you had them?"

"A year, I can't wait for them to get as long as your hair or longer." She said

"Roz offered to loc my hair but my momma wouldn't go for it. I guess since I won't be living with her no more I could get them. I like your hair."

"Roz is the girlfriend right?" She asked, I nodded. "Do you like her?"

"Yes! She's nothing like my momma." Then we both laughed.

"Sounds like I would've liked her too." She sighed and a tear fell down her face.

"You will like her you mean. She's gonna need us as much as we're gonna need her." I said

She eyed me like she wasn't sure about that. I assured her Roz was not like our mothers. "Why do you think we were hidden?"

I frowned, "hidden?"

"Yea, hidden. We didn't even know each other. His cousin Malcolm has kids, have you ever met them?"

"He does? Who?" I asked looking around the auditorium.

We both locked eyes on this one guy. He had a serious face, dark brown skin, and he stood like Malcolm. "That one." We both said pointing from our laps at him. Then we laughed.

"I guess I never thought of it as being hidden. My momma kept moving me around; it was kind of hard for him to get to me sometimes. We can't lose contact, it kind of feels like you're the only family I got right now." I said

She hugged me, "I know! I feel the same way. Lets never lose touch ok! We have to see each other once a week no matter what, ok?" She said

"Ok!" I said hugging her back.

****

After the funeral Auntie Summer moved out. The way she packed up and moved you would've thought someone put fire underneath her. She called to check in from time to time, but I had a feeling she was out there with my momma.

"Ms. Ruby please think of it this way. Yussef is a growing boy and he needs a room. This house has enough space for each of you to have your own room, and comfortably have people over from your service group. Troy would've wanted this." Malcolm said standing in the empty living room.

"I don't know Malcolm, this feels weird. How can you afford to do this?"

Invisible

"Which business would you like to hear about first? This house was purchased legitimately. There will be no seizures of your home or raids on your property. Contrary to whatever your daughter may have told you, I am a business man." He said

Grandma looked around. "I don't know."

"I know you wanna get out of those apartment town houses." He said

"But you've already done so much for us Malcolm, first the car now this. I'm not like my daughter. I don't expect this from you."

"I know, and that's why Troy wanted all this for you. I'm just carrying out his wishes." Malcolm said, and then he put the keys in her hand. "Tell me when you want me to send the movers. I can have someone come and pack you up if you need. In addition to the actual move."

"How?" She smiled through tears.

"Have you heard of Mitigated Staffing Solutions?" She shook her head no. "It's a temporary staffing service. I can hire people from there to do it all for you."

"No I can do it for her. You don't need to hire anyone." I said, Malcolm looked at me like he could've smiled, but he didn't of course.

"Good! But I will send someone to help you move the heavy stuff, just let me know when you're ready." Then he looked at me, "I need to talk to you." He walked out the door, I followed as my Grandma and G-momma stood in the middle of the living room hugging and crying. "Why is your sister running from me?"

"She's scared of you." I said matter of factly.

"WHY!" He barked, I shrugged and pointed at him. "I don't have time to be chasing her around. I have businesses, and my own goofy family to deal with. Tell her to stop running from me, does she think I'm gonna hurt her?"

"I don't know, but you're scary. I guess for a girl with daddy issues you can be a little intimidating." I said

He started to say something but he stopped. "You've been studying." His eyes and tone smiled his face did not.

I was pleased that he noticed. "Latia's been helping me study. She's and excellent student and she's been helping me look at the big picture." I said

He crossed his arms, "which is?"

"That a solid education is the only thing I can truly own in this world. As a black man, I need to be able to understand the basics and then build on that if I wanna ever exist peacefully."

Malcolm listened then he barked again, "TELL HER TO CALL ME! SHE NEEDS TO GO TO SCHOOL!"

I smiled, "can I call you Uncle Malcolm?"

Malcolm's face didn't change but his eyes bucked at me. "Seriously! Right now you wanna joke! Timing is everything boy! Malcolm is just fine." Then he started walking to his car. "Report cards come out Friday, I expect results! Tell your Grandma to tell me when."

I went back inside, Grandma said this house was a lot like the one she had when my momma was little. We picked out rooms. The house was one story three bedrooms and two bathrooms. It had a one-car garage, and a big backyard. Grandma already had plans for how she wanted the yard done which meant I was gonna have to do it. Seeing her excitement about it, how could I not happily do it for her? This also meant that Latia and I had our noses in books trying to figure out how to do half of it. In the end seeing their faces once we had their yard put together was priceless. Grandma had her number transferred over to the house and our move went smoothly. We didn't tell my momma or Auntie about the move. We figured once they came out to visit they'd find out about the house.

We moved to Central Richmond from the South side of Richmond. All the kids in my neighborhood went to Richmond high, but I stayed at Kennedy high school, thank goodness. Kennedy was up the street from the "Drew's" barbershop in Richmond, and Roz moved to that shop not too long after the funeral. I saw Tanisha regularly, but losing my father seemed to take something from her. I liked hearing her talk about my father. A lot of the things she said helped me connect dots. Latia said it was hard listening to another female explain her father to her. I imagined if the shoe were on the other foot, I couldn't take it if Roz had a son who knew my father better than I did and all I wanted was to know him. I got it so I didn't pressure her to come around Tanisha. But I got her to go to Roz to get her dreads touched up. They hit it off and have been close ever since.

****

When I sat in Roz's chair for the five hundredth time it was different. We talked about school, the house, and her house anything we could think of. When she was done, she explained to me how to care for them. When I looked in the mirror for the first time I saw my own face. I still looked just like my father but my face changed and now I had my own look. I picked Roz up when I hugged her and told her I loved it.

"Why don't you try a boy hair style? Now I can't tell you two apart." G-momma said to Latia and me.

"This is a boy hairstyle G-momma." I said giving her a kiss.

"Goodnight G-momma" Latia sang.

We walked over to the Richmond public library. Latia was cracking her whip all the way over there on the things she was gonna have me work on. Even though I met Malcolm's requirement of a B average, I barely made it. Latia said I should strive for an A average because I deserve it. When we rounded the corner to pick a table Malcolm was sitting with someone. "Sit down" he said. Latia looked scared, I assured her it was ok. "Why are you running from me?" He asked

"My mother told me to stay away from you cause you have a short fuse."

He looked at me then her, "your mother?"

She swallowed, "yes".

"When I call, you respond, don't ever make me have to chase you down again. Have you started applying to schools?"

"Yes, but I've been trying to make sure I can get a scholarship."

"If you would call me back." He rolled his eyes. "Pick whatever school you want, your father has money set aside for you. But this is important, since we couldn't get you away from your mother like we rescued Yussef. You tell her you got a scholarship." She started crying, "my father did this for me?"

"He's been trying to get to you since you were young. Linda was a lot sneakier than Shonda. There's more, but lets start with the basics. Pick a school, call me. Let me know where you're going. We'll make arrangements accordingly." Then he stood up. "Stop running from me, if you run again I will not chase you."

"Ok" she said

We watched Malcolm and the person walk out. Latia kept crying, partially cause she knows better than to believe her mother. And partially well because our father is still kind of like the puzzle we're solving. We got a little studying in; Latia was having a hard time focusing. We walked back to the house and plopped on the couch. We told my Grandma about Malcolm's surprise visit, and she kind of understood the feeling. "Just when you're convinced Troy is one way, he did stuff to make you think otherwise."

We were debating on an ending for our evening, when my boy Mitchell called and said he was going to the carnival at Harry Ells, he told me to come. I told him I was hanging with my sister and if she wanted to go we'd meet him down there. Before I could hang up the phone she was ready. She said she needed to go have fun. Determined to show my sister a good time, I took a few hundred out of my stash. Grandma dropped us off at the school. Harry Ells was an old high school that shut down when Kennedy was opened. From time to time the carnival would be held in the back on its fields. Right behind the school the Richmond line for the Bart train service passes through. On the other side of the tracks is the neighborhood I grew up in mostly when I lived in Richmond from time to time. There's a big rainbow shaped ramp over the tracks with a ton of stairs. I pointed to the ramp, "When people talk about 'the ramp' their talking about that ramp in Richmond. Nichol Park is to the right of Harry Ells. I told her about the park cause we've passed it so many times. I asked her if she knew where she was, and if she needed to could she get back to my house from here. She said she could, it was important to cover all the what ifs in case something happened I needed to know she'd make it home ok. I paid our entry into the carnival, Latia thanked me even though I told her I was treating. Every time I paid for something she said thank you. Now that I'm used to it, it feels good but at first her manners got on my nerves. We ran into Tanisha and Amanda. They were with some of their friends; Latia asked why I didn't tell her about Tanisha's girlfriend. I didn't think it mattered so I didn't mention it.

I won the ring toss and Latia picked a little bear that she said she was gonna call Yussef. I smiled at the thought of how sentimental she was. Mitchell came over with his cousin Shannon. Shannon didn't look happy when they approached us; she kind of hung to the back. Normally she was all smiles. I introduced Mitchell and Shannon to my sister, and instantly Shannon's smile was back, I guess he didn't tell her I was bringing my sister. Mitchell was checking my sister out, and I felt fire turn in my stomach. It calmed a little when I saw Latia blush like she liked him too. I didn't feel good about it; I didn't think Mitchell was good enough for my sister. She deserves a guy who's as smart as she is. Someone who works just as hard, plus Mitchell's a player. All Latia has to do is say the word and its lights out for Mitchell friend or not. I was watching everything Mitchell did, all the sudden he was a gentleman and mister talkative. He suggested we ride some rides, when we were all in agreement, of course he asked Latia to ride with him. She agreed too eagerly, I was getting irritated. "Yussef will you ride with me?" Shannon asked

"Yea sure whatever." I said not looking at Shannon. I watched Latia and Mitchell sit down in their seat for the Ferris wheel. Latia had a mile wide smile as she sat down. Mitchell was too quick to put his arm around the chair by her back. "You getting real comfortable real fast aren't you!" I said spitting fire.

"Oh my bad! No disrespect." He said removing his arm with a smile.

The conductor secured them and then moved them up so Shannon and I could get on. "You are really protective of your sister."

"Don't all brothers protect their sisters?" I said holding her hand while she stepped up into the ride. Suddenly I noticed Shannon had a nice body on her, but I needed to focus on my sister. I don't need the distraction of this girl's booty, FOCUS!

"Not all brothers, my brother doesn't care. Mitchell does sometimes." She said turning her body to me. "Why are you so different?" She leaned a little forward so I could see down her shirt.

Now Shannon was a good girl, I was surprised she was being so bold. In class she would always talk to me, but I didn't think she was feeling me. I didn't remember her question; she was looking at me like she was waiting for an answer. "What did you ask me?" I said still staring at her pillows.

She laughed then she touched my chin, "you're cute. I like you."

"Say what girl?" I was surprised.

"You mean to tell me this whole time you couldn't tell I liked you?" She said trying to give me a little sass.

I laughed, "No I didn't."

She smiled, "I begged Mitchell to invite you tonight."

"Why?" I said taking in her face, hair, and whole outfit. She made sure everything was just so. I never thought she was interested in me.

"I've liked you for a long time. I was hoping you would consider me." She blushed

I got butterflies, probably from the wheel turning but I kind of figured it was Shannon. "Since when you get so bold?"

She blushed harder, "you weren't getting it. I had to do something."

I felt kind of stuck, "now what?"

"I don't know, you're the man. You tell me." She said

"I'm the man huh." I liked the sound of that. Does this girl go in my lap? The way she's coming at me right now, if I didn't know her I would say definitely lap girl. But from what I know of her, she could possibly be more than that. I guess we'll have to see.

Chapter 3

My heart was beating, this woman held my life in her hands. "Make a left here." She commanded. I did as I was told. She kept looking at me. She started drumming her pen on her clipboard. Like she was battling with herself. "At the light make a left." Then she crossed her legs. The sound of her pantyhose rubbing together caught my attention and I looked down at her legs. She smiled and told me the light was green. She started looking around. "Up here Parallel Park." Then she looked at me and smiled. "Yussef do you have a girlfriend?"

"Kind of" I said pulling into the parking spot.

When I put the car in park, she turned to me and started unbuttoning her shirt. I was stuck and looking around, this is the DMV's fault. "What's her name?"

"Why you wanna know, doesn't seem like you care." I said closing my mouth cause I was starting to drool.

"Cause I want you, but first I need to know that you have just as much to lose as I do. Do you love her?"

I wasn't even claiming Shannon yet, but today we were so in love and I couldn't imagine my life without her. "I love her so much I can't do this." I said making my eyes sad and putting them on the floor. "Besides, I need my license so I can finally take her on a real date and we can be alone. Then I can tell her how I truly feel in my heart. You're too pretty to even consider someone like me." I sighed a pathetic sigh.

She screamed, "ok! Ok!" She kept crossing her legs and uncrossing them. Clearly this lady was crazy, but I didn't care. I wanted my license and getting some on the side was just what the doctor ordered. "What's her name?"

"Randi, but you gotta promise she'll never find out about this. It would break her heart." I said

"Oh I promise, I just wanna be your friend. She never has to know! Now go up to this corner and make a right." She looked like she was gonna hop out the car. She had me pull into a driveway as she took a garage door opener out of her pocket and clicked it to open. The door barely closed before I had her bent over against the car. Women seemed to lose their minds over these dreads. It was so bad but good that I didn't leave the house without at least four condoms, I never knew where the day was gonna lead me. As crazy as she seemed, she was actually a lot of fun. She told me I got a passing grade one hundred percent when we got back to the DMV. Then she wrote her name and number on a napkin. "Call me, maybe we could do this again." She said going back inside the building. I put the napkin in my pocket, and then I told my Grandma I passed.

"I'm so proud of you! Were you respectful and a gentleman like I told you to be?" Grandma asked

"Yes Grandma, my manners made her very happy!" I said winking at Judy

****

"I thought you liked Shannon?" Latia said

"I do, but I want to spend time with my sister without the add-ons. We hardly do anything just me and you anymore." I said

She huffed, "you're right. How about we spend all morning and day together. Then we hook up with them at night?"

"Latia, every weekend? Shannon's not putting out, I don't wanna be around her that much." We both laughed

"I like him!" She whined

"So!"

"Please Yussef! Please!"

"When are you gonna break up with him?"

She blew air, "no time soon as long as I can help it. When you gonna break up with Shannon?"

"Let me explain something to you little girl." She giggled. "Me and Shannon are just friends. We're not boyfriend and girlfriend. We are taking our time to get to know each other. We don't talk on the phone everyday, and I'm not trying to spend every waking minute with her. It's supposed to be me and you, then them! But you getting all goofy because there's a guy involved. You're losing cool points with me." I may have said it nicely but I meant every bit of it.

"What if I end up marrying him?" She sounds all dreamy and idealistic.

I lost it. "Marrying him? Have you lost your mind? What about him says he would be a good husband? All he's done is tickle your ears with compliments, and probably said everything he can think of to try to get in your pants. And your goofy behind is sitting over here eating it all up. He's not offering you anything and here you are trying to give it all away. Wake up! Focus on school, pick a college, and your next step. If he's gonna be a man about anything, he should be doing the same thing and encourage you in that way. I bet you he don't know what he's gonna do after high school, if he even graduates." I wasn't finished but she cut me off.

"Dang Yussef! Tell me how you really feel? Why are you jealous? You're my brother, you're supposed to be happy about me finding love..."

"LOVE!!! He doesn't love you! When a man loves you he wants what's best for you. He would take his time with you! He's just trying to get in your pants."

"So you're telling me you love Shannon?" Her question suspended me in the air. Yes, I liked Shannon, but I was trying to exert self-control with Mitchell's cousin like I wanted him to do with my sister. "Just be happy for me."

"Then you be happy for me earning C's." She hissed. "Just like you tell me I deserve better. So do you!"

"Bye Yussef!" She barked

"I don't care! Be mad! Bye!" But I did care. I don't understand how someone as smart as Latia could become as dumb as our mommas over some "no good nigga" as my Grandma called them. Needless to say I didn't see Latia that weekend.

That Monday at school, I noticed the change in Mitchell. He was up to no good, and no matter what I said Latia wasn't gonna believe me. All I could do was wait for him to hang himself. He better pray he don't go over board cause I'm not responsible for what happens to him if he does.

****

"Are you mad at me?" Shannon asked

"No" I said

"It's been weeks, you don't call me. And when I call you you're never home. What's going on Yussef, please talk to me." She pleaded

"It's not even about you. It's me. I got something's going on right now."

She threw her arms around me, which I wasn't expecting; she completely caught me off guard. "I love you Yussef! I don't want us to get off track."

Aw! Her declarations made me feel all warm and fuzzy inside. "I love you too." I heard myself say. Whoa! Then she put everything she had into our kiss. I grabbed her a little tighter. "Don't kiss me like that, you could end up in trouble."

She smiled at me. "Maybe I'm ready to be in trouble."

My stomach dropped. "Um! Wait a minute, hold on. You sure you want to do this? You don't have to do this for me."

Invisible

"I'm ready. Besides I'm not stupid, the fact you haven't asked or even pushed in that direction obviously means you're getting it from somewhere else. I could take all the time I needed, and I did. Now I'm ready, and you gotta give up your side chicks."

"So you're asking me to put you before everybody else?" I asked

"Yes, exactly." She said snuggling into my chest.

I loved the way that felt. "What about you? You gonna put me before everybody else?"

"I already do." She said looking up at me.

"Even your cousin?" I asked

She had a question mark on her face. "Yea?"

"Come here," I led her out of the cafeteria to the student parking lot. We sat in my car, "I'm gonna level with you. Your cousin isn't on the up and up with my sister. It might come down to him and me. I know that's your cousin. And I'm not asking you to choose me over your family. Obviously I'm choosing my only sister over everybody. Maybe we should wait, this could get pretty bad."

She was quiet for a long time. "I love you Yussef and I want to be with you. My cousin is stupid, and if he gets in trouble then that's on him. You're my man!"

"You would put me before your family even when I just told you I'm not doing the same? I don't think that's wise Shannon."

She leaned over and kissed me. "I love you! My cousin being stupid doesn't change how I feel about you. Please don't hold against me the dumb stuff he does. I want you, I want this."

"I don't want to get you in trouble." I said

"We'll be careful, everything will be fine." She kissed me again.

After school we went by Drew's, I introduced Roz to Shannon. Roz was trying to act normal but something was up with her. I put my name down to come back in a week to get my locs tightened. As we were walking out Malcolm was walking in. I introduced him to Shannon. He was actually nice to her then he said to me. "You love you some Rubenesque women don't you!" He smiled

"What black man doesn't?" I said

"You like what you like." He started in then he stopped. "Report cards next week right?"

"Yep! I'm not even worried about it." I said

He smiled again, "that's what I like to hear." Then he went inside.

When we got in the car Shannon had a funny look on her face. "What's wrong?"

"Did he call me fat?"

I started laughing, she did not look amused. "No, he called you thick though." She crossed her arms. "You know you're not fat."

"I know, but I also know I'm not no skinny bean pole either." She huffed

"You are perfect, it was a compliment. Have you studied Peter Paul Reuben's work yet?"

"No"

"Amongst so many other remarkable features in his paintings his women were never feather weight. His women always had curves." She looked at me, "what difference does it make what he thinks about you? I'm dating you, and I love your body."

She smiled, "you do?"

"Yes!"

"This weekend right?" she asked

"Right."

****

Now it's time to get my romance on! Knowing this will be her first time makes me nervous. I don't want to hurt her; actually I'm prepared for her to chicken out at the

last minute. Malcolm sent a man to check into a room for us at the Nautical Hotel right across the street from Fisherman's Wharf in the city. Shannon made arrangements with one of her friends to cover for her for the night. She met me at the McArthur Bart station, and then I drove us to the city. Malcolm's guy gave me the room key in the garage. Shannon was very bashful and shy which was nice and endearing. She couldn't believe how nice the room was when we went up to put our bags down. Malcolm had a bottle of champagne chilling on ice and another on the dresser. He had a box of condoms with a bow tied around them on the nightstand next to the bed. I asked her what she wanted to eat for dinner, she shrugged. Since we were on the wharf we had to have seafood right? I asked her if she wanted crab. She said only if it wasn't too expensive. I kissed her and told her she could have whatever she wanted. We decided on this little restaurant called Alto's. I ordered Oysters Rockefeller, clam chowder in a San Francisco sourdough bread bowl; Shannon ordered a dish with Dungeness crab. As our waiter brought the oysters I told her they were an aphrodisiac. I laughed when I saw her taking inventory of her body after eating one. On our way back to the hotel I didn't know who was more nervous. In the elevator she buried her face in my chest, I kissed her forehead. In the room the door wasn't closed before I was kissing her. "Hold on. Let me go get ready." I didn't know what she meant, but I said ok. I put my little radio boom box on the table. I put on a CD of slow jams; I put it on repeat so it would keep the music going over and over. I poured the champagne, and put the other bottle in the ice since we were probably gonna need both bottles. I could hear water running, I sniffed myself. Maybe I should freshen up too? I downed my glass of champagne then I grabbed my lotion when she came out I wasn't gonna look at her. When I could hear her getting ready to come out the bathroom I covered my eyes. When she saw me, she laughed and asked what I was doing. I told her I needed to get in the bathroom, and if I looked at her I might not go. I got in the shower real quick. I put lotion on and put my towel around my waist. When I walked out the bathroom she was sitting on the bed drinking her glass of champagne. She had a long T-shirt on that said, "I need hugs". She looked completely nervous, I smiled at her. "I like your shirt." I said reaching for my glass.
She smiled an embarrassed smile, "thank you. I like your towel." We both laughed.
"You are completely nervous." I said.
"So are you." She said
"I'm nervous for you."
"I think I'll survive." She smiled
"That's what you say until you see it." I said
She bucked her eyes, "are you hung?"
I smile, "I'm just messing with you. I'm average, don't worry."
"How do you know that?"
"I haven't had any reports to say otherwise."
"How many girls have you had?"
"I don't know, but right now lets focus on me and you." I turned the radio up. I poured the last of the champagne in our glasses then I opened the second one. Once I noticed her relaxing, I turned the music up and had her come slow dance with me. I asked her if she was ready and she said yes, but she asked me to turn off the lights. I asked her why and she said she was embarrassed. I told her she was beautiful and I wanted to see every inch of her, plus I wanted her to see me. She liked the part about seeing me. So she got in the bed under the covers and I took off my towel then I tied my hair back. Her eyes danced all over me. I pulled back the covers and I kissed her knee, then her thigh, I looked at her as I kissed her stomach. Then I took her shirt off, and forbid her to try to hide. I told her she was beautiful and there was no reason to

hide her beauty. I put my condom on then I kissed her until she told me she was ready. I sat at the gateway to heaven for a long time. Every time she thought she was ready, she'd run from me asking me to wait. And I patiently did, she got used to me kissing her then I pressed in on her. This was definitely no man's land; the only room within her was the space I created. I was halfway in and she couldn't take it but I knew what was on the other side. I slowly but deliberately pressed in on her and she tried to tell me to stop, but it was too late to go backwards. It took everything in me to exercise self-control and not go to town on her. I waited for her to relax, I kissed her and I told her the worst part was over. Her body was tense so I kissed her until she relaxed, then the fun part started. She got in to it a lot faster than I thought she would. She laid there frozen like she was afraid it would hurt if she moved. When we were done she was drenched in sweat from her nerves. I fell asleep and a little while later she woke me saying she wanted to do it again. She blew out air upon entry and things moved along a lot faster. She kept waking me up after that which was fine, but she just laid there. The wheels in my brain were turning.

"Last call!" I said. She smiled, "nobody said a virgin could wear you out." I smiled, "you wanna drive?" Terror flashed across her face. "It's not as scary as it sounds." I put on a condom then I had her mount me. "Now you decide which way we go." She sat there frozen for a minute. She'd go then she'd stop. After minutes of this I couldn't take it any more. I flipped her and gave her one last work over. When she stood up to go to the bathroom she walked like she was in pain. "Did I hurt you?"

"It's ok" she said walking slowly to the bathroom.

I felt horrible; I think I'm over this whole virgin thing. I don't like the idea of hurting someone, and the inexperience. Yep, Shannon would be my first and my last.

****

"If I didn't tell anybody, why does everybody know?" I was hot!

"Are you ashamed of me or something?" She was missing the point.

"No, but I don't want people in our business!" I said

"I'm not ashamed of our love." She folded her arms

"The love part is fine, but now people are calling me stallion, and stuff like that. All these females keep trying to get my attention. That's what you want?"

"What females?" She looked mad.

I exhaled, "I don't need this! Don't discuss our business with other people. Now all these females gonna come out of nowhere, watch. I thought you were smarter than this!"

"Yussef! You're being paranoid, nobody wants you but me."

Ok that offended me. "Say that again."

Realizing what she said she tried to clean it up. "I mean we're the only ones concerned about what happens with us. Nobody else cares."

"Fine Shannon, you're gonna have to learn the hard way. Mark my words you did this to yourself." I said walking away.

I went in my science class and took my seat. Demario walked into class as soon as he saw me. "What up! I hear congrats is in order, you successfully broke Shannon in." He said giving me a pound

"You listen to idle gossip too?"

He stood up straight. "You trying to say it ain't true?" He pursed his lips like he knew if I denied it I was lying.

"I'm just saying those are rumors and I ain't discussing it. Virgins need not apply here." I said irritated

"I hear you. All that, stop don't! You're hurting me! You're hurting me! For the next fool to come in there and pound her out." He laughed

"I guess."

Then Latisha walked in the room. She scanned the room until she saw me. She didn't care that she had an audience. "Hey Yussef, baby how you doing?" Even her voice sound like sex. I tried to blank stare at her but her body distracted me. "I've been hearing something's about you. I need you to call me."

"Naw, I can't do that I got a girlfriend." I said as I tried to stop my eyes from going all over her body, but they wouldn't listen.

She bent over on my desk. "Yea, who's just barely not a virgin. You'll get tired of showing her everything. Take my number for a rainy day."

I was shaking my leg. "No thank you."

Demario wasn't helping anything by making noise in the background. All the sudden it sound like a stampede was coming. Some girls walked in the class, then Shannon came in the class completely upset. "Latisha what are you doing?" Shannon asked

Latisha stood up and turned around, now her butt was in my face, I told myself not to pay attention to the way it sat up just right. "Your man seems to have cold feet, but I'm offering him the opportunity to be with a real..."

Shannon charged at her, I grabbed her right before she dove on her. Shannon was trying her best to get to her; I carried her out the class. The teacher walked in the class and asked what was going on. Everyone started talking at once. "CALM DOWN! THIS IS YOUR FAULT!" I barked

"My fault? How am I responsible for what that broad is doing?"

"Are you kidding me? Cause we just had this whole conversation less than ten minutes ago."

"Were you egging her on to make a point?"

"No! Ask anyone in there I turned her down. But she wouldn't have been coming at me like that if you would've kept your mouth shut. That's all I'm saying."

"Fine Yussef!"

"Tell me nobody wants me! Females throw their selves at me on the regular! Learn this lesson young; as long as you want a man a thousand others will want him just because of you. Never take it for granted that you have someone. Cause just like you got them you could lose them! Tell me nobody wants me! IN YO FACE!"

"Fine! I'm sorry!"

"Good, now go to class before you get a hall sweep." I said smacking her butt. Shannon and her little crew ran down the hallway to her class. Latisha came in the hallway, when we were all alone. She stuffed her number in my pocket, and put her chest up against me. I walked back in the class and sat down.

****

"How's Latia doing?" Roz asked

"Haven't talked her. What's his name?" I said eyeing her in the mirror.

She froze for a minute. "Sometimes you can look so much like your daddy, I forget you're not Troy." Then she lowered her eyes to my hair. "Why do you ask?"

"You have two monkey bites on your neck." I said giving her no smile

She touched her neck. "Oh yea. I forgot about that."

"What's his name?" I said feeling angry.

"Yuri" she said lowly.

"Good guy?" I asked not masking my jealousy for my father. Even though I was starting to lose faith in whether women could actually pick good guys.

Even though Latia finally started calling me again I could tell, she wanted to discuss Mitchell with me and I wouldn't allow it. I don't talk to her as often or as in detail as I used to. I just can't know everything about her and Mitchell and not have a reaction. She's been dragging her feet about making a final decision about where she's going to school. She got in everywhere she applied now she has to choose. Something tells me that Mitchell has a lot to do with her indecision.

It seems like losing her virginity has removed a lot of her common sense. A lot of the things I love about Shannon are still there. But now she's a ball of insecurity, she seems to lack confidentiality, and it's been months and no matter how I spin it she doesn't seem to be all that into sex. I thought it was something I did, but Judy assured me that it's not me. She said some females just aren't into adventurous sex. She still thinks Shannon is Randi though. Latisha still pushes up on me at school, I'm not stupid enough to go for that, right now at least. I'm trying to be good.

"He's a good guy." I like him a lot, Roz said

I couldn't help it; I stared at her for a long time. She gave me a pleading smile. I gave her a courtesy smile, and then I started gathering information about him.

Judy gave me a DMV printout on him. He's moved around a lot, to me that's a red flag within its self. Unless it's your job moving you from place to place it doesn't speak well of a person in my opinion. I talked to Malcolm about him, although Malcolm says Roz is a grown woman. I still feel responsible for her. I went to the Mitigated office in San Francisco; Malcolm's directions were very detailed but straight to the point. The building was huge and the directory in the lobby showed Mitigated on the eleventh floor. The building was really fancy, and there were people in suits in the elevator with me. I could see the receptionist through glass doors when I stepped off the elevator. She smiled real big when I walked through the doors.

"Welcome to Mitigated Staffing Services, how may I help you?"

"Yes, I'm here to meet with Juan."

"Yes, do you have an appointment?"

"Yes, please tell him Tyrone is here." Malcolm told me to use that name, and that Juan would know who I was.

"Will do" she called Juan. "Juan will be with you shortly. My name is Marisa if you need anything at all please let me know." She said twisting in her chair.

When Juan came out the back, he got that same stuck look at first. He gave me a strong handshake and then he invited me to the back. There were tons and tons of cubicles, offices, conference rooms, etc. Like Malcolm told Grandma this was a legitimate business. We went in Juan's office, he told me to have a seat, and then he called Malcolm. "He's here... He looks exactly like him.... I know.... You want him in your office? Ok."

Juan had a picture of his dog up only, but he wore a wedding ring. When he hung up the phone. I pointed to his ring, "is that for woofy?"

Juan smiled, "you've got your father's sense of humor as well." Then he stood up, "my family is a private matter to me. So I don't put their pictures up here. It's not a rule as you'll see, but it is what I do."

Then he unlocked Malcolm's office. He told me to sit in Malcolm's chair. Malcolm had an eight by ten picture of that woman and him on his desk. Then a picture of him and his sons. Everything on Malcolm's desk had its place you could tell he was very meticulous. Juan said Malcolm was out in the field and to call him for the passwords on his computer. I moved the mouse and a picture of the same woman came up. I called Malcolm, "sprung much?" I said when he answered the phone.

"What?" His tone had no smile.

"Everything with you is about this woman. Who is she?"

"Grow some, before you start questioning me. Are you ready?"

"Goodness! You must really be in love. One day we need to kick back with a drink and just talk." I said smiling waiting for his answer.

He was quiet for a minute. "Talk about what?"

"Life! You! Me! Shoot! Everything."

He was quiet for a minute. "I guess that's reasonable."

I clapped my hands together, "what date works for you?"

"Let's see how you do on this self assigned task first and then we'll go from there!" He told me not to write any of the passwords down, if I couldn't remember call him. Which really meant memorize them when he gave them to me. He told me to report back to him what I found and no detail was too small. I didn't exactly know all the systems I was working with but I used his DMV printout as a foundation to pull from. I was going for hours, I could see people walking past and looking at me funny cause they didn't know who I was. I was quite proud of myself, I knew the names of the dogs he had as a kid. Yuri consistently associates with women who end up in the ER; I wonder why I asked myself sarcastically. This fool has a good job at the power company, but he does nothing with his money. He gets his check, deposits, and spends. That's not a bad thing, but Roz has been spending more since she's been with him. But it looks like she's getting her divorce. I gave Malcolm all the information I found. When I heard a smile in his voice I asked him how I did. He said he was impressed and that I was a lot nosier than he gave me credit for. I asked him if I earned that drink yet. He laughed at me.

Invisible

Chapter 4

BANG! BANG! BANG! "OOH!" I yelled, "I like this one!"

Malcolm brought in my target. "Good! You're getting better."

"Better? Look at that, the target is down." I said too excited.

"I meant what I said. Keep working on your drills."

"In Malcolm language does this mean you're proud of me and I've done a good job?" His eyes poked at me. "Always with the jokes."

"I'm not joking. I need to hear you're proud of me." Then I sucked up air. "What's next?"

"I have a summer assignment for you." Then he looked at me. "If you think you can handle it."

"Of course!" I said feeling excited.

"Ok more details to come soon, but make sure you're ready. You may have to leave your little girlfriend hanging for a minute." I blew air. "Trouble in paradise?"

"What paradise? I mean I love her, but I'm starting to see more and more traces of my momma in her."

Malcolm's face was serious. "Hold on." He walked over to Tim who just finished shooting. They talked for a minute while Tim put away his gun. They both had serious faces. When we got in the car both of them were quiet. When we got to Malcolm's house, he told me to have a seat on the couch. As he was pouring drinks there was a knock at the door. Tim answered it; it was another female bringing Malcolm dinner. She seemed too happy to present her dish. Malcolm said thank you and that he would call her later. Watching the way Malcolm interacted with Tim, I paid attention to how Malcolm yielded to Tim, and Tim gave Malcolm his due respect but the way a man would to his man in training. "How do you know Malcolm?"

Tim smiled, "I came home from work one day and he was pacing in front of my house. He looked so heart broken and pathetic like you do right now."

"He's Amber's father." Malcolm said

I dropped my fork. "Whoa!"

Tim smiled, "Malcolm's young but he's a good guy."

"How does this girl remind you of your mother?" Malcolm asked

"She was cool at first but now she runs her mouth too much. She doesn't look at the big picture."

"A lot of people miss the big picture half the time. How does she rebound from that?" Tim asked

"Most times she doesn't." I said honestly.

Tim looked at Malcolm. "Let that one go. Last thing you need is some dumb female trying to hang on."

"Just like that? Just cut her off?" I said.

Tim's phone rang, he told the person he was at Malcolm's. Malcolm looked at him and he told him Drew was on his way over. A few minutes later a key was opening the front door. The guy who I assumed was Drew walked in with another guy. Drew went straight to the bathroom. "Hubby" Tim said nodding at the guy.

"Tim, Malcolm, stranger" the guy Hubby said, you could tell he had been drinking.

"Sit down" Malcolm said, and Hubby did as he was told. Drew came out the bathroom; he looked like a combination of Malcolm and Tim. He was intoxicated like Hubby. "How did you get here?"

"Juan sent somebody to pick us up." He looked at me with Malcolm's cold eyes as he tried to read me. "Who are you?"

I started to say something and Malcolm put his hand out. "Who does he look like?"

Drew stared at me for a long time. "Hubby don't he look like that fool we was beefing with the other day?"

Hubby looked at me, "no".

Drew shrugged and went in the kitchen. "Who made this?" He said looking at the food on the stove.

Tim shot Malcolm a disappointed look. "Are you staying?" Tim asked

"Naw, I got a date." He made a noise like he was remembering something. "I need a background check."

"On who?" Malcolm asked

"This girl, she seems cool so far. I need to know how twisted she is before I intro her to mom's." Malcolm blew air. "Don't start! The last thing I need is relationship advice from you."

"You have some of the most classic problems with females all because you can't let that one go."

Drew stood up straight. "Last thing I need is relationship advice from you. Last I checked my momma got a man. What can you tell me?"

Malcolm was out his chair so fast, all I could think was it would've been nice to know Drew. Oh well he's about to die. "Enough!" Tim said like a father controlling the situation. As mad as they both were they both froze. Hubby was looking wide-eyed from the couch. "You guys got to stop all this arguing and animosity towards each other. That's your son Malcolm, Andrew that's your father. Stop acting like big ole kids fighting over my daughter." They were both visibly angry, but they stood there staring each other down. I wondered if Drew was actually crazy enough to go up against Malcolm. "The day you two learn to truly get along, instead of this half way stuff you do." Tim looked at them. "Sit down!" To my surprise they both did as they were told although neither one of them wanted to. I looked at Tim in amazement, who was he to command Malcolm to do anything... And he actually did it.

Tim looked at me, "sounds like you care about this girl?"

"I do, she's not completely bad. Just these little things that I'm starting to see that I don't like." I said

Malcolm sat down in an attempt to calm himself. Drew sat down by his friend, and then he said, "How's the sex?" All three of us looked at him. "A whole mess of sins can be forgiven with good sex." Drew chuckled

"And that's why he's got a crazy one that won't go away." Malcolm said then he looked at me. "Latoya Spencer."

I ran a background check on her for Malcolm. Her juvenile record was pretty long shop lifting, assault record, etc. Her father or at least the guy on her birth certificate moved on with his life. I didn't see any indication that he was a part of her life at all. Her mother's background was pretty much the same as her daughter's. I didn't like this chick on paper. "Oh", I said.

"She ain't that crazy, just a little wild." Drew said with a knowing smile.

Tim shook his head, "wild doesn't equal anything good." Then he looked at me.

"These things you're noticing if they continue to grow in the wrong direction, you will have to make a decision and fast."

"Wait a minute! How you know Toya?" Drew stood up.

Tim didn't even turn around. "Sit down Drew!" He did as he was told. "Malcolm had him run a background check on her as a exercise."

"You're with Mitigated?" Drew asked me.

I looked at Malcolm who nodded yes. So I said, "Sure."

"I'm assuming special services." That wasn't a question. "You put him on assignment yet?" He asked Malcolm

"Not yet." Malcolm said

You could see the wheels in Drew's intoxicated mind turning. "What did you have in mind?"

"Intern at Brad's office." Malcolm said

"Isn't that situation a little hot right now? Why not use a professional?" Drew said, "Is he any good?"

"Yes" Malcolm said. I wanted to stick my chest out with pride. Malcolm just vouched for me, Yes!

"Suit yourself, mine isn't life threatening." Then he looked at me. "You do know rule number one don't you?"

They all looked at me, I smiled. I was gonna shout, "that I should never ever get down from this here pole!" But they didn't look like they watched Michael's movie like I did, so I kept it to myself. "Never mess with the Boss's woman!"

"Right!"

****

Something didn't feel right. My space felt "different" if you will. I noticed it the last time we were together as well, but I told myself I was being paranoid. "I'm gonna be working this summer."

"I am too, but it seems like you've already forgotten about me." Shannon whined

"I'm here now aren't I?"

"Only cause you wanted some."

Oh my goodness if she only knew, I could do without this feature of our relationship. Maybe then I could get my girlfriend back. The one who was sweet and I could talk to for hours without arguing about something dumb. Eventually she did loosen up and get a little more into it, but it still felt more like she was doing it for me than she was actually enjoying our time together. Heaven forbid I should ask her to do anything outside of the norm; she was almost in tears when I asked her to drive the last time. Complete turn off! "How about we take a break from sex then? That way when I'm with you you'll know it's because I wanna be with you."

She gasped, "No!"

"You don't even like it anyways. It's fine really."

She squinted her eyes at me. "You trying to find an excuse to cheat with Latisha aren't you?"

"No, you're throwing accusations. I'm trying to show you that's not the case."

"Are you sleeping with Latisha?" That fast her eyes filled up with tears. I felt horrible. "No! I'm not, she keep trying though."

"Do you want to be with her?" She asked through tears.

I don't understand why she asks me questions that just make her more insecure.

"Come on Shannon change the subject. Is this really what you wanna talk about right after we finish?"

"Yes! I wanna know!"

I blew air, "fine! Fine! Fine!" I got up irritated; I put on my boxers and sat on the edge of the bed. "If I wasn't with you, I would've hit that. But she'd never be my girlfriend or somebody I cared about. I'm with you because I care about you. But you aren't making it easy."

"How am I not making it easy?"

"For one you run your mouth too much! You keep worrying about the next chick; you got me, why are you tripping? We spend more time arguing than we do enjoying each other's company and talking like we used to. I miss talking to you."

"You're always worried about Latia, and what she's doing. You put her before me, how do think I'm gonna respond."

"I can't believe you. We talked about this you said you were fine with it."

"That was before. Now I don't like it."

I couldn't believe this. I snatched up my clothes, and violently put them on. "I don't have anything else to say to you. Get dressed, I'll take you home."

She sat there crying, making me feel horrible. I was still mad, but it hurt me to know I was the reason she was crying. "I think I'm pregnant!" She blurted out.

I felt like somebody shot me. When I looked at her she was watching me for a reaction. "How is that possible?"

"When a man and a woman love each other sometimes their passion becomes too great and."

"Shut up Shannon!" I laughed, "we have always used condoms, they've never broken or come off. I'm just asking how."

"I don't know, but I don't feel right." She said

"Are you late?"

"Not yet, but I'm telling you I feel off."

"Ok" I exhaled deeply. "So we're gonna have a baby." My voice cracked.

"Uh no!"

"WHAT?" I felt like she shot me again.

"I still have to go to school, and I have my whole life ahead of me. If I am pregnant I'm having an abortion." She said matter of factly.

"That's murder! You would kill my baby? I thought you loved me!"

She rolled her eyes, "don't start! I do love you, but having a baby would ruin our lives right now. We have our whole lives ahead of us to have babies."

"You kill my baby, I can't even mess with you no more."

"What? Why? It's not even a baby yet."

"The bible says its a life from conception!"

"Now you wanna get religious. If you truly cared about God you wouldn't be here with me right now! I can't believe you would think anything else would happen."

"Get dressed!" I walked out the door slamming it behind me. I went to the Motel office and paid for the room. Then I proceeded to beat the mess out of my car. Shannon walked out to the car crying and looking pathetic. Part of me wanted to run her over, but I knew that was just the plea of my broken heart. I couldn't even look at her the same. She got in the car crying her eyes out, and I drove real slow to take her home. "You would really breakup with me over an abortion?"

"You kill me, I'm done with you. It's not rocket science."

"But we don't even know for sure yet. Couldn't we just decide then?"

"What's to decide? It's either your way or mine, and you already made up your mind."

"Yussef my momma doesn't even know I'm active. I can't tell her I'm pregnant. She'll tell my daddy and I don't want to deal with them."

"Oh I see, this is about what's most convenient for Shannon. What will make Shannon's life less complicated. Forget about me."

"That's not what I said."

"But it's what you meant. I wish I would've known this before."

"Before what?" She asked still crying.

"Before I got involved with your goofy behind. Before I told you I loved you. Before I let you in to my heart. Before!"

"I'm still me!"

"No you're not, now you're the girl who would kill my baby, and then turn around and lie to me telling me you love me."

"I do love you Yussef."

"NO YOU DON'T! AS LONG AS LOVING ME DOESN'T GET HARD! AS SOON AS IT GETS HARD YOU'RE OUT FOR SHANNON FIRST!!!" I pounded the steering wheel.

"You can't tell me what I feel!"

"No I can't. But I'm telling you what your actions have shown." I pulled in front of her apartment. "Please get out of my car! I love you, but I don't like you no more!"

"WHAT????" Shannon started screaming and waving her hands. "Yussef please! Please don't do this! I love you!"

"You better pray to God you're not pregnant, cause if you are either way you're screwed."

"Ok! Ok! I'm not pregnant. I'm not!" She said hysterically

"What?" I was too irritated to look at her.

"I was just saying that to get your attention. I'm not pregnant."

"Why would you play like that? This isn't a game Shannon!"

"I know! I'm sorry!"

I didn't believe her. "Prove it, let's go get a test right now. Pee on the stick if it says no, then we're good. Those things are normally wrong any ways."

"I don't want to, you should believe me."

I rolled my eyes, "Shannon you're not making any sense."

She kept taking deep breaths. "If I am pregnant it's not yours." Then she exploded in tears.

She shot me again, "what?" I asked above a whisper. She sat there waving her hands and screaming. "Get out!" I couldn't even yell. I was hanging on by a thread. I don't even know what she was saying, but I knew it was true. "Get out Shannon! I don't want to hurt you!" I said in a monotone. She was still talking and crying. I saw my hand grab her chin; I kept telling myself not to hurt her just to get her out of my car. "Get out!" She opened the car door and fell out. Her purse and jacket were still in the car. I threw them out the door and stood on the gas. The jerk forward closed the door and burned rubber in front of her apartment. My heart was beating so hard and I felt it break with every beat. Before I realized it I was getting off the freeway on Willow Ave making a right at the light down into Rodeo. When I pulled in front of the house I saw Latia's momma was peeking out the window. She was calling out to her telling her I was there. Latia came bolting out the door; she jumped on me as soon as she was close enough. She squeezed me tight and kissed my cheek. "Don't ever stay gone that long!" Then she grabbed my hand and pulled me in the house. "Have a seat! Have a seat!" She said too excited to see me. Then she looked at my face.

"Where you been Yussef? We ain't seen you in a minute." Her momma said with a smirk.

"Momma can we have a minute?" Latia asked

"This is my house little girl, if you want privacy you need to go outside!" Her momma said. I stood up and walked to the door. "Ooh! Somebody's mad! I thought you weren't gonna tell him?"

"Momma! Please!" Latia said desperately.

I eyed Latia, "tell me what?"

"Nothing!" She shot her mother a look that said shut up. She grabbed her shoes and then we got in the car. "My Momma's gonna keep messing with us. Lets go to the park."

As soon as we parked. "Tell me what?"

She swallowed. "Nothing! You know my momma always like to start mess. What's wrong?"

I could tell she was lying, so I stared at her. "You're lying!"

"Ok! Ok! But it's not serious. I promise to tell you later. You're already upset, let's deal with whatever is bothering you today. We'll talk about me another day. Talk to me."

"Shannon thinks she's pregnant." I exhaled

"Oh Yussef! I'm sorry what are you guys going to do?"

"Nothing! If she is pregnant, it's not mine."

"WHAT?" Latia said wide-eyed

"And what's funny is, I thought something was different. It felt different and she was doing different stuff. I guess I assumed she watched a movie or a friend told her to try something different."

"Oh Yussef I'm sorry!"

"Thanks, I can't believe I let my guard down with her. Telling her I loved her, etc. all for what? For this?"

"So you guys are done?"

"You shouldn't even feel like you gotta ask that question." I exhaled, "WHERE ARE THE GOOD GIRLS? Do they even exist anymore?"

"Of course they do, they're just far and in between cause we get messed over so much it's hard to know who to let in. I have news!" She said all excited. I looked at her waiting for her to tell me. "I'm ready to transfer to a major university."

"You must've finally broke up with Mitchell." I said sucking my teeth.

"Don't be like that Yussef. Please be happy for me."

I exhaled, "where you gonna go?"

"First I wanna try Berkeley since its right there."

"Malcolm's son goes there."

"How do you know?" She asked

"I met him at Malcolm's house. He's just like Malcolm they got some anger issues though. He don't even appreciate that he got a dad to be mad at. He walks in the door with a key slurring, and what not. But he's still on point even when he's tipsy."

"You guys gonna start hanging out?" She asked

"I don't know, what if you can't get into Berkeley?"

"I'll try Stanford and UCLA. I wanna be close to you."

"Don't stay out here on account of me. I'll come visit you no matter where you are. Go where you'll get the best education."

"What about Princeton? It's on the other side of the country."

"If that's where you go that's where you go."

Then she looked at the time. "Ooh! My girlfriend was coming over to go to the movies. You wanna go? You could be our chauffeur." She smiled

"Do I look like I wanna play chauffeur?" I snapped

"Yes! Yes you do!" She smiled at me. "Come on you need to be out anyways. Maybe our silliness will help you snap out of your funk if only for a little while. You know I will keep asking until you say yes." She smiled real big.

"Fine! But if your friend gets on my nerves, I'm out and you guys can figure your own way home."

"Deal!"

As we were pulling up to the house her friend was walking away. Latia called out to her and introduced us. Melissa seemed kind of shy at first, which was cool cause I was in no mood to be around a chatterbox. Of course they were going to see a chick flick, exactly what my bleeding heart needed to be stuck in the dark for almost two hours watching two people fall in love. I sunk down in the chair and pretended the movie wasn't bothering me. I tried to pretend like I didn't like the movie, but in the end it was cute but I refused to admit I liked it. We went to the restaurant next door to the theater to eat.

"So Yussef tell me about yourself. Latia talks about you all the time." Melissa said
"Then you should already know everything about me. You're the stranger here." I leaned forward. "Tell me about your goals, your ambition, your biggest dream ever!" We all laughed. "Somebody was paying more attention to the movie than they wanna admit." Melissa sang
"I wasn't watching that chick flick by choice. I needed to be entertained some kinda way."
"Thank you for paying for my ticket." She said
I waved her off. "Whatever." Latia smiled at me, but she didn't say anything. "Maybe Melissa can tell us." She gave me a question mark expression. "What has happened to all the good girls? All these stinking movies are perpetuating that they still exist, it ain't true."
Melissa looked at Latia for an explanation. "He just broke up with his girlfriend today. Please excuse my brother he's a little raw and uncut today."
"I'm right here!" I huffed. "Anyways, are you in school? Do you work? What do you do?"
"I'm a teller, and I go to Contra Costa with your sister."
I put my elbows on the table and rested my face on my hands. "And how many boyfriends do you have? I bet you got a whole string of boyfriends pretty girl like you."
"Are you supposed to be insulting me or flirting? I'm a little confused." She asked
I had to think about it myself for a minute. "He's just being a guy. When they're upset the whole world must pay." Latia said rolling her eyes at me. I rolled mine back.
"I don't have a boyfriend." She said leaning back in her chair. Latia shot her a look and she shot one back.
"Why?" I asked
"I don't know, maybe I'm not pretty enough or something. I don't know." She said
I frowned, "maybe you're too guarded. Maybe you don't send a vibe out like you're available. Or interested."
"I don't think so. I don't stand out in a crowd. I'm the average girl next door that no one pays attention to, until its too late." She said
"Average?"
"Did you see me when we met?" She asked
"In my defense," I looked at my watch. "I haven't even broken up wit that chicken head twenty four hours yet. Excuse me for having a little tunnel vision."
"You're excused this time." She said
"What are you guys doing?" Latia asked looking irritated
"Talking", I said
"Cut it out, you're rebounding." She said to me. "And you're taking advantage." She said to Melissa.
"How am I taking advantage?" Then she smiled at me. Latia wiggled her neck at her. "Ok, I'm sorry."
I knew I wasn't looking for a girlfriend so I let it go. The rest of the evening I tried to keep my bad mood to myself, even though I wanted to go home. I was a good sport and took them out to shoot pool. Latia shot me daggers when I watched her friend bend over. I wasn't gonna do anything, I was just looking. We dropped her friend off at her apartment building in hilltop. Then I took Latia home. I asked her one more time what she needed to tell me and she said she'd wait cause I was still too mad. I already knew it would result in me whooping on Mitchell, but I'll wait for now.
****
I looked up at the sign, "No Words"! I found this poetry club when I was wondering around Berkeley getting a good lay of the land. Malcolm told me to pay attention to my

surroundings. No my escape routes cause I never knew when I would need to get out quickly at the drop of a hat. This club was a 21 and over club, so I had Judy get a license for me under the name of Lamont Jenkins. Lamont just turned 21 and he got me in places I needed to be. When I walked into this place I was automatically in love with the atmosphere. And then on top of everything else there were live poetry readings and performances. Once I had the words I knew I had to go up on stage. I need to vent this Shannon stuff. I had to get it out. When the MC asked me for a name, I didn't want to give Lamont or Yussef. I needed a name that reflected how I felt. One that would always be me. "The Invisible Poet" the MC said he liked it. "Thank you everyone for joining us tonight. Tonight we have someone new to our stage, but I'm sure this wont be the last time. Everyone give snaps up for The Invisible Poet!"

The audience started snapping. I stood in the middle of the stage, for this moment I existed. For this moment I was real. "I HATE your family!" The audience started laughing. "I HATE your daddy for thinking she looked good that night! I HATE your momma for knowing what he likes. I HATE your daddy for blowing his top. I HATE your momma for ovulating that month. I HATE that the timing of their love was so perfect that night that nine months later you were born into this world. I HATE your father for not sticking it out, and being the first man to break your heart and dooming the rest of his kind. I HATE your momma for not teaching you what a GOOD man looks like. How to LOVE him, how to KEEP him, HOW TO BE FAITHFUL! I HATE your family! I have to HATE them because its hard to HATE you! I LOVED you and wanted our love to last forever and ever. But who could succeed when the odds were stacked so high against us. They say young love never last, but I didn't want to believe that! I knew we would last, I knew we would soar! Shot down in our prime our love is now a statistic. I gotta blame someone and I know it wasn't me. So I blame your family!" The audience gave me snaps. I walked off the stage feeling a little better. This could be habit forming.

****

"My name is Lamont Jenkins, I'm here to interview for the position." I said.
"Right this way" the receptionist said looking me up and down. She took me into a room with a bunch of other guys. "Mister MC will be with you guys shortly." She said then she left the room. Everyone except this one guy was quiet. It was like the silence tortured him or something. He kept cracking jokes. I looked around trying to figure out who was planted here and who was actually applying. Mister made all this noise walking into the room. You could tell he expected everyone to fall all over their selves because he was there.
"Ok, you all are my final applicants. As long as everything checks out with the agility portion today you've got the job and you will receive your assignments accordingly. Darius, get 'em tested and let me know who we got."
Darius stood up in the middle of the room. I knew it! Well I would've known it even if Malcolm didn't tell me. Darius then turned to mister Jokey jokester and told him the best he could do there was being a worker in the warehouse, he talk too much. I wanted to laugh at him, but I knew better. They had us do simple stuff like run, climb a fence, scale a wall, you know simple stuff. All stuff that would fall in place with a job at a small recording studio, right? "Congratulations! When I call your name please exit through the door on your right." One by one he called names and each one did a little victory dance as they walked out. There were only four of us left. They shut the door. "Now, the four of you have been chosen for things beyond grunt work. Mister will be out shortly. The four of us stood still not even looking at each other.

Eventually Mister came out with the cutest little girl. She had to be maybe four or five years old. She was holding his hand and eyeing each of us. Then she walked up to me and wrapped her hand around mines. " I like him!"

"This one, are you sure?" He asked her.

"Yes! I like his hair." She said. I smiled on the inside; all the ladies love my hair.

"Ok, go tell your auntie to bring out the stuff." He told her.

"Ok!" She said very enthusiastically as she ran back to the door.

"Which one did she say?" Darius asked walking back in the room.

"That one, he doesn't even look intimidating. Talking bout she likes his hair." Mister said irritated

"Put 'em to the test. Bring out Ricky." Darius said

Mister shook his head and smiled at me. I felt heat on my neck, I started flexing and unflexing my hands. Some big guy walked in the room and they pointed him at me. The other three guys stepped to the side. "CRAP!" This guy was big, with swollen arms. Looked like he just got out of jail. "CRAP!" He's sizing me up and I'm doing the same. The bigger they are the harder they fall, right? All those muscles seem to slow him down, right? But he still hit me in my jaw and my ear started ringing. Ok he's faster than I thought. I was moving out the way. He was getting tired trying to get me. When I saw him taking a huge breath in I punched him in the stomach, knocked him in the jaw, and as he bent over I hit him in the back of the head. He went down, I kept kicking him, and then I started stomping him. Darius touched me and I turned it off even though everything in me wanted to keep going. My jaw still hurt. Mister and Darius had huge smiles on their faces.

"I guess she can pick 'em." Darius said

"Uncle Brad! Why is he fighting?" The little girl said with her hands on her hips.

"I had to make sure he was strong enough." Mister said

"Strong enough for what?" She said

"To work for me."

"Ok so what do we have here?" The lady said looking me up and down.

"Auntie Camille look what Uncle Brad did! I told him I liked him and he made him fight." The little girl fussed.

"You did this to Ricky?" She looked like she was about to bubble over right there in front of her man.

"Camille! Cut it out!" Mister said

"I get to have him though?" She asked

"We'll see!" Mister said, "Lamont you start tomorrow."

****

I feel like a real live Joseph in this piece! Whenever she feels the coast is clear, here she comes. There's only so much a man can take. Brad be watching me too, I'm like dude check your woman! She got the nerve to look good, smell good, and feel soft every time she brushes up against me. She's so bold she do stuff in front of her man too, it's like he wanna see how I handle it. I'm starting to wonder if Malcolm sent me here to get killed.

Here she goes again! Knowing its forty-eight degrees outside and raining, why she walking around here in heels, booty shorts, and a shirt that barely covers her breast. When she walked in the door I looked at Brad like come on!

"I love looking good for my man!" She said with that sugary sweet tone, and Brad was eating it up. She said it, and then she put his head in her chest while throwing me a "do me" look! I turned my eyes.

"Who we got up next?" Brad asked

"Ricky is setting up." I said

Brad blew air, "this fool need to let it go!" He pressed the button on the intercom. Camille straddled him making him kiss her, her big ole muscular legs dangling on either side of his chair. "Uh! Ricky?"
Ricky turned around, "yea!"
"What are you doing?" Brad said
"I'm getting ready to lay down a track." He said like it should be obvious.
"Now you know you're two seconds been up, you got Malcolm to thank for that!"
"I could strike gold again, you ain't even heard the track yet." Ricky said
"This is a waste of time and money."
"Aw, come on Mister!"
"You got sixty seconds! If I'm not feeling it, I'm pulling the plug."
"I only need ten." He said overly confident.
"Fine!" Brad said leaning back so Camille could continue to kiss on him.
The music started, "uh! Uh! Uh! I'm the greatest!......I'm the best!.......ain't nobody ever done it like me...." I turned off my ears, cause they were screaming for mercy. I kept clearing my throat trying to hold back my laughter.
"RICKY!!" Brad yelled
"You said sixty!"
"You said ten, and I tell you if I waste another second listening to that my heart's gonna stop! Just stop!"
"Camille, tell me the truth." Ricky desperately asked
"It needs some work, but you will get there." She said in that sugary sweet tone.
"Stop lying to him! She is lying to you man! I'm not putting money into pushing that out. Like I said thank Malcolm for killing your career!"
Ricky got mad and threw his headphones down. He came storming out the studio.
"Yea! I wanna thank him personally!"
"Yea right! I heard about how him and his boys beat you down in high school." Brad said nonchalantly.
"Man! That was high school. Let him come see me today."
"And what? You couldn't even handle Lamont, Malcolm would make mince meat out of you!"
"Mister, let me put him down!" Ricky begged
"Nnnnooooo!" Camille accidentally screamed. Then fear came over her face.
Brad got mad and pushed her on the floor. "You still sweet on that nigga?" He yelled at her.
"I just don't want anything bad to happen to him." She pleaded, her voice was shaking.
Brad started slapping her, he hit her a good five times before he kicked her. I put my hands in my pockets, and tried to keep my face even. Ricky looked at me and smiled. "Women!" Apparently this behavior was commonplace too.
"YOU WANNA GO WORK IN HIS SHOP AGAIN? PAYING A NIGGA TO DICK YOU DOWN?" He said while kicking her.
"NO! IM SORRY! IM SORRY!" She pleaded
"SCREAM FOR ME! WORRY ABOUT ME! FORGET THAT BLACK GORILLA!"
"BRAD PLEASE!" She pleaded
Sweat broke out on my forehead. I don't know how much more of this I was supposed to watch without reacting.
Camille was on the floor messed up makeup, hair all over her head, busted lip, and red face from where he was slapping her. He grabbed her by her hair. "Don't provoke me

like this again. Next time I won't hold back!" Then he looked at Ricky, "what you got in mind?"

Camille stayed down on the floor crying. "I'ma shoot 'em!"

Brad was pissed! "You gonna shoot him!" He said sarcastically.

"Yea!" Ricky said like it was that simple.

Brad punched him in the face. "I swear you are so DUMB sometimes!"

I personally would've stopped at dumb. But who am I?

"You think Malcolm don't have guns? What you think he gonna do while you're shooting at him? Tap dance? You are no physical match for him, but you gotta get him through his weakness! Do you know what that is?" Brad asked. Ricky stood there thinking and thinking. "You are some kind of stupid aren't you!" Ricky honestly had no idea what he was talking about. Brad rolled his hands. "His...... Woman!"

"Oh right! That like skinned chick. But they ain't even together no more. She is dating that football dude. You know da one that clocked you!" Ricky chuckled, Brad punched him again.

"You are stupid! Bring me somebody with a brain!"

I was pretending like I was looking at the switchboard, anything but focusing on their conversation or Camille who was still crying and holding her face. "Lamont, go tell Darius to come here." I stepped over Camille and did as I was told. When I came back Brad told me to go to lunch. In the car I took out a post-it note. I drew a target on it, and in the bulls eye I put a number one. Then I drove to this mom and pop looking deli. When I walked in, the woman behind the counter greeted me with a smile. I ordered the house special and I told her I had a coupon. She made this fat sandwich for me, and I gave her my post-it. I sat down and ate my sandwich and she brought me chips, a soda, cake, and some candy (Apple jolly ranchers) YUM! MY FAVORITES!

****

"Lamont your work here has been remarkable! You're such a fast learner. When you finish school you'll always have a job here. Shoot, I may need you before school's out so keep your pager on." Brad said

"Thanks, that means a lot coming from Mister MC! The guys back at home are never gonna believe I shared the same air space with you let alone that you know my name." This stupid fool liked when you talked to him like that. I guess some of Shonda's ways did rub off on me dang it. I shook Mister's hand then I got in my car. I drove to the Oakland airport. I spotted Brad's men following me about six cars back. I parked in the long-term lot as close as I could to the front. Then I grabbed my backpack and casually walked into the airport. I already planted all of Malcolm's surveillance all around up and down Brad's spots. About every purse Camille owned had bugs in them. Especially since he couldn't really seem to go too many places without her. With all that I still don't know how she managed to sneak out and still see Malcolm but she did. Even Brad's little niece that he adored so much was a walking bug and she didn't know it. My job was done it was time for me to bounce. I sat at the gate for the flight to Houston Texas. When it was time to board I gave the flight attendant my boarding pass, Brad's men watched me walk down the ramp. I stood by the strollers and wheel chairs on the ramp. When they closed the door to the ramp, I went out the baggage carrier's door and hitched a ride on the luggage car. I put on a orange vest and a ID badge that said Tyrone Walker. When I got inside, I went in the bathroom. I took off my clothes even my shoes. I stamped a few tattoos on my arms, and braided my hair into one braid. Put on a green polo shirt, a A's cap, white sneakers, and some khaki shorts. I threw my braid under my collar and put on a A's starter jacket. I told myself walk like Tyrone not Lamont. I put my old clothes in the backpack and I stuck it in the lost and found. When I made it out to the main corridor Brad's guys were still hanging out, waiting for the plane to take off. I walked out the door and went over to the bus stop to wait for shuttle to the Bart station. I caught the Bart to Fremont. At the Fremont station, I got in my little bucket in the back corner. I drove my putt putt to San Francisco. I changed my clothes again, leaving this car in a tow away zone. Then I caught a "cab" to Latia's house.

She was too excited, she got into Princeton, and so we were moving her there tomorrow. Malcolm was meeting us at the Sacramento airport first thing in the morning. Melissa came by to say farewell. They kept hugging each other and crying, whatever! Melissa asked if I was still gonna be around, I told her this was my senior year in high school so I'd be around. She smiled, but didn't say anything else.

The Princeton campus was cool, a bunch of rich snobby kids in my opinion. We found her a nice apartment not too far from campus, Malcolm bought her a car. He explained her allowance to her and how her grades paid for her expenses. Latia kept crying cause she never expected all of this. Malcolm softened and hugged her tight, he assured her of how much our father loved her. Then he told her that she also had a trust fund but he'd explain more about it after she graduated. He told her he applauds her choice to come out here and stand out as different. We bought simple stuff to furnish her apartment. When we came back Malcolm flew into San Francisco, and I flew into San Jose. I took Bart home, and relaxed for the first time all summer on my couch. "Some girl named Shannon has been calling all hours of the night, and showing up randomly. She seems a little desperate, if you ask me." G-momma said

"She is desperate G-momma," I said giving her a hug and a kiss. Then I took the phone in my room. I dialed seven digits, "can I speak to Latisha?"

Chapter 5

"This is my boy Jeremy, Jeremy this is Jennay." Drew said

"Nice to meet you Jeremy." She said

"Nice to meet you." I said, turning my eyes away from her.

Like his father Drew has the finest women. Although Drew's taste seems to be a little broader than Malcolm's, I personally would've gone for Jennay. There's a kindness in her eyes, I can see that just from meeting her fifteen seconds ago. "Baby I'm gonna go run some errands, I'll catch up with you later on tonight." She said giving him what I imagine to be a soft kiss with her full lips. "It was nice meeting you Jeremy."

"You too" I said not looking directly at her.

Drew watched her walk away with the biggest smile on his face. Then he looked at me, "how do you read her?"

"She's cool, your girl next door." I said

Drew smiled real big, "I know right! I'm thinking that one is the one!"

"The one?" I was confused

"The one I give my last name to. The one!" He said all idealistic, "why does that surprise you?"

"I don't know I guess because your dad isn't married...."

He cut me off, "Malcolm is a fool! I don't understand him either! He's had my momma wrapped around his finger since they were kids, and he keeps doing dumb stuff! Her boyfriend is cool; I can tell he wants to marry her. But she's still hung up on Malcolm, which makes no sense to me! Dwayne is offering everything! Malcolm isn't and never will offer her anything, but she wanna stay hung up on him. I don't understand them, but I know my mom deserves better. I am my own person, and I strive to be better than Malcolm. I will not hold back with the woman in my life, she will know she's loved, wanted, and needed!" His eyes were focused while he rattled off this information.

And of course as soon as he finishes his speech she walks up. Beautiful flawless chocolate skin, tight little body, but evil eyes. "Drew!" She said

You could tell she was his weakness. His body kind of sunk when he looked at her, "Toya" he said.

"You wanna dance?" She moved to the music.

"Go dance with your boyfriend." You could see jealousy in his demeanor.

She smiled, "he's out of town. Come dance with me."

"Just like that? You think you can just snap your fingers and I'm just gonna run on the dance floor with you? Girl, you tripping!"

She stared at him for a minute. Then she turned to me, with a sugary sweet tone. "How about you? You wanna dance?"

Drew looked at me like he didn't care. "No thanks, I'm good." I said

"Don't worry about him, he ain't gonna do nothing. I promise you won't regret it." Her smile was even evil.

"No thanks." I said turning my body away from her.

Drew smiled at me then he looked at her. "Leave him alone, he ain't stupid enough to fall for your tricks."

She took the sugary sweet out of her tone. "You're the only stupid one?"

"It doesn't make me stupid to go for you since I know you. I know you in every possible way to know you. Sometimes I get that itch for what I know. It ain't that deep so stop trying to act like its something it's not."

"You look like you need some scratching." She gave him a knowing expression.

He stared at her for a minute, "I'm not fooling with you today Toya. I'm seeing Jennay later."

She pouted, "Fine Andrew! Some other time I guess."

Then she turned around and looked around the spot, she spotted her victim. She walked over to some unsuspecting fool. I could tell by her body language she was doing that sugary sweet voice. Drew tried not to look, but his eyes became glued to the scene. I readied myself cause I could see the drama coming. She convinced the guy to dance with her. Drew's eyes turned evil watching her dance. She was doing too much. Drew's body twitched, I told him I would be right back. Toya smiled as she saw me approaching. Now this girl is NICE to look at, but all I could see was my momma so I wasn't all that impressed. I guess her partner was going cause he immediately got irritated when she started to walk towards me. He grabbed her arm, I tried to calm him and tell him to slow down, but he wasn't listening. He got in my face asking me who was I. I tried to calmly tell him that she was trying to get him in trouble but he wasn't listening I guess all he could see was this pretty girl was talking to him and all the possibilities for the evening. Toya stood there enjoying the scene she created. This guy had been drinking and wasn't seeing what I was trying to tell him. I told Toya she needed to come sit down and stop messing with this guy's head. She played dumb like she didn't know what I could possibly be talking about. His friend came over asking what the problem was. His friend had been drinking but he still seemed a little more reasonable. As the other friend approached I could see that he was going to be the mess starter, I could feel heat on my neck. I really wasn't trying to fight today, I had a date of my own in a little bit. The mess starter came over loud and rude. He accused me of being jealous cause his friend could pull a girl like Toya. I looked at Toya and I asked her calmly one more time to come on and to stop this. She put her hands out and shrugged like she couldn't understand what could be the problem. I put my hands out and I gave up, as I walked back to the table I could already see the evilness in Drew's eyes. "She's always playing too much! I should just leave huh?" He asked me I was surprised he was asking. I personally wouldn't fool with her period, but he definitely isn't me. "Yea man, let's go. You got a date tonight, I got a date tonight, we don't need these kinds of problems." I hoped he was listening to me.

He took another swig of his drink then he agreed with me and we started to the door. The music was going and this guy was all over Toya, when she saw me we were walking out. She pushed the guy backwards cause her plan didn't work, but the guy kept coming. Naturally he didn't understand the sudden change up in her demeanor. When the guy grabbed her arm and yanked her forward Drew's body was no longer heading to the door. He was coming for the guy. The stupid guy saw Drew coming and disregarded him. One punch the guy was going down and his friends were coming out of everywhere. I didn't want to fight today! I wasn't in the mood, but here I was laying fools out. Two minutes later there were six guys on the ground and we were walking out the spot. Toya was going with Drew she was so turned on it wasn't even funny, and I was getting in my bucket. I couldn't understand why he let her play him like that. My hand was a little sore other than that I didn't have a scratch on me. I went home showered talked to Grandma and G-momma for a little bit then I got in my nice car and drove to Hilltop. Went I entered the hallway something smelled delicious, and the closer I got to Melissa's apartment the stronger the smell got. When she opened the door my mouth watered. "I thought we were going out to dinner?" I said with a huge smile as I hugged her.

"It's the strangest thing I walked into the kitchen and my kitchen asked me to move around in it. Next thing I knew I was making you dinner. I hope that's ok."

"Of course, I just didn't want you going through any trouble on account of me."

Invisible

"Its never any trouble for you!" She said blushing. Then she showed me to a table she had set like I've only seen them on TV or in stores. She went through a lot of trouble, she doesn't make much money, and she lives paycheck to paycheck. The fact that she spent her little pennies on me was nice. "Have a seat, I hope you like dinner."
"Are you kidding? It smells delicious! I know I'm gonna love it. I don't understand why you went through all this trouble just for me." I said
"Yussef, it was no trouble. I wanted to do something nice for you. You're always working hard making sure your Grandmothers have what they need, and you take care of Latia. I just wanted to take care of you." She said still blushing.
I was embarrassed. "You wanna take care of me? Why?"
"You are a sweet guy, and you've only been a little tainted by these females, I wanted to say that I see you and ask you not to change. The world needs more good guys like you." She was blushing
I didn't know what to say to that. "Ok", I honestly wasn't expecting all this. When I ran into Melissa at her bank during her work hours, and specifically waited for her teller window to exchange a dollar for four quarters. I figured I might as well ask her out when our conversation went over five minutes. I mean that seemed only right, right?
"So how's high school coming along? You ready for graduation?"
"Yea, I'm ready to get out of that place."
"How are things going with your girlfriend?" She asked going back to the kitchen.
"I don't have a girlfriend." I exhaled
"You guys didn't get back together?" She asked sounding disappointed.
"Heck Naw! She's always trying to get me to talk to her." Shannon follows me around school begging me to forgive her. I don't say anything; I do my best to completely ignore her. She knows how much it upsets me when she cries, and so all she does is follow me around killing me with those tears. When she found out I hooked up with Latisha, she lost it, they fight almost weekly. Everybody seems to know who she cheated on me with, but I didn't care to know. Whenever someone talks about it, I'd tune them out. I didn't want to hear about it, I just wanted to get out of high school. She broke my heart, and I refuse to continue to live this pain again.
"You don't want to try to work it out?" She asked while sitting the bread and salad on the table.
"What's to work out? She broke my heart, oh well."
"I remember the first time I got my heart broken, it's kind of hard to recover from huh." I nodded in agreement. "The trick is to still be yourself, don't change who you are because that person messed up. I know that's easier said than done, but it's important to keep in mind."
"I'll try, but I can't promise no guarantees. It's hard when you think a person is one thing and then you find out that they're something else."
"Can I ask what happened?" She said handing me a plate with a steak and pasta dish on it. So, I told her my story. How I knew Shannon but thought she was too squeaky clean for me. How I didn't push her while we were dating, actually my mind didn't drift to physical fantasies that would actually be carried out. I was prepared for her to be a good girl through out the duration of our relationship. I admitted for the first time, how devastating it was to hear her allude to the fact that she cheated on me. Melissa asked me why she would tell me that she thought she was pregnant if she knew it wasn't my baby. I told her best I could figure is that she thought I would pay for the abortion. She was completely surprised when I was against the idea. "People who play games get played, and she played herself. " I looked at her with a question mark cause I didn't understand what she meant. "She figured that you would accept that she was

pregnant and that you would cough up the money for the abortion. Otherwise why would she tell you? I don't know why she was against your idea of taking a break from sex if she knew she was gonna need that procedure in the near future. I think she knew that as a nice guy you wouldn't press her about getting physical. She tried to play you and she got played."

I sat back in my chair, "girls be plotting on a whole other level. My quote unquote good girl doesn't exist huh?" Thinking about it made that broken heart pain come right back. I shifted in my seat to try and act like I wasn't affected by this conversation. "Anyways, so yea we're not getting back together. Let's change the subject."

She looked around the table with a smile as if she was satisfied with the meal she prepared. It smelled great. "Will you bless the food so we can eat?"

Her request made me smile, only my Grandma and G-momma made such request of me normally. Dinner was delicious, and she even had wine for us to drink with our meal. We sat at the table talking for hours and it was nice to have a female to talk to outside of my sister. We cleared the dinner dishes, and then what did I see sitting on the kitchen counter? A sweet potato pie, she laughed at my reaction. The pie was ok, it wasn't as good as my Grandma's but I appreciated the gesture so much. I thanked her for all the trouble she went through for me. She kept assuring me that it was no trouble at all and that she was happy that I appreciated all her hard work cause that made it worth it.

Her apartment was really small, when you walked in the door the kitchen was immediately on your left. It was very small, but it had an open nook to the dining room slash living room, which was small as well. Melissa had a small two-chair table in there. There was a built in bookshelf that she had books mostly from school and little knick-knacks for decoration on. Then she had a small loveseat along the right side of the wall, which wasn't really a wall. It was kind of accordion like, you could pull it back and you'd be in her bedroom. Across from the couch was a TV, which sat on top of a broken TV. Her bedroom had a door; I guess if you kept the wall closed you could still have the illusion of a one-bedroom apartment. She said her apartment was considered a junior one bedroom or studio apartment. She said it was cheap enough that she could afford it on her own, but nice enough that she could call it home. She asked where I was going to go to school, and I told her I applied to Berkeley and a few other local schools because I didn't want to be too far away from my Grandma and G-momma. She told me that over the summer that she and Latia spent a lot of time over there with them while I was away with my summer job. She said my Grandma even talked them into going to service with her a few times. I asked her what she thought of going to service. She said she liked it, but she loved history so whenever the bible is discussed she's all ears. I liked that answer. I looked at the time and it was almost midnight. Although I was having a good time, I figured it was time for me to go. Last thing I needed was for Latia to be mad at me talking about I was taking advantage of her friend. ALTHOUGH I definitely felt she was digging me. I didn't know what I wanted to do with that. I would be lying if I said I wasn't still pissed off at Shannon, and being pissed off like that probably wasn't healthy. I yawned, "it's getting late. I think I should go."

Melissa had a disappointed look, "really you're gonna leave?"

"You want me to stay?"

"Uh yea!"

"Ok, well I didn't want to assume that it was ok for me to camp out on your couch and then you be like", I put my hands on my hips and wiggled my neck mimicking a girl's voice. "No this nigga did not just assume it was ok for him to stay over just because I made dinner for him."

She laughed, "I do not sound like that."

"That was you, but just how girls period sound sometimes."

"I told you that I appreciate you. I wouldn't turn on you like that without being provoked." She smiled

"Tell me something," she raised her eyebrows. "Why did Latia say you were taking advantage that night we met?"

She had a question mark on her face, "advantage?"

"She said I was rebounding and that you were taking advantage."

She smiled an embarrassed smile, "all Latia does is brag about you. She's very proud of her little brother. I would always warn her that if you were as great in person as she made you sound that I was not responsible for what happened. She made sure she told me when you started dating Shannon as a way to say backup. She was saying that I was taking advantage of the situation, I had all that background information on you already, and you had just broken up. She was right, you needed some space."

"So do I still need space?" I said watching her face for a reaction.

She smiled then she looked me in my eyes, "you're not even legal yet."

"I'm almost eighteen, I won't tell if you don't. Shoot you already liquored me up. You trying to seduce me?"

"You are not tripping off that wine, I know you drink harder stuff than that." She said

"Yea, but that wine was relaxing." Then I sat back, "you think Latia will be mad?"

"Well she knows you were coming over tonight. You wanna call her?" She asked reaching for the phone.

I dialed Latia's number, "its two o'clock in the morning over there. She's gonna be mad." Melissa smiled, as she watched my mouth.

"Hello?" Latia said very groggy

"Hey sis its me." I smiled

"What's wrong? What happened? Is everybody ok?" She said trying to wake up.

"Everybody's fine, I just wanted to get your permission about something."

"What time is it?" She said sounding irritated. "Yussef you do know its two o'clock in the morning don't you!"

"Yea, real quick though…" I said with a smile

She sighed real hard real loud, "WHAT?" she barked. "Are you still at Melissa's?"

"Yes. Yes I am." I had the biggest smile on my face.

She sighed again even louder. "I CANT STAND YOU GUYS! WHATEVER YUSSEF I DONT CARE! DONT EVER CALL ME IN THE MIDDLE OF THE NIGHT JUST TO TELL ME YOU'RE ABOUT TO GET SOME. I DONT NEED THOSE KINDS OF DETAILS IN MY LIFE!"

Melissa covered her mouth while she was smiling. "I just wanna make sure you're cool with it. Last thing I need is for you to be mad at me."

"Goodbye Yussef, you better pray I can go back to sleep!" Then she hung up on me. We had a good laugh at Latia's expense, but I wasn't gonna touch her friend without her being ok with it. "So now what?"

Melissa looked excited. "Let's watch a movie."

I sighed, "you've only got chick flicks."

Then she smiled, "chick flicks set the mood. You want to watch a chick flick with me. Trust me." Then she turned on her TV and VCR. She put on a movie then she changed out of her clothes and put on a short nightgown. I took off my socks and shoes and set them over by the table where my jacket hung on my chair. When I took off my shirt she exhaled. "Oh my God Yussef!"

I smiled, and tried to pretend I didn't know what she was talking about. "What?"

"Look at your body!" she said looking all over me.

I liked her appreciation for all my hard work. "Now show me yours." I said expecting her to be shy. She smiled and she hesitated for a minute, then she stood up and took off her gown. She still had her bra and underwear on, but she was beautiful. I liked the way she didn't act like she was gonna die because I was looking at her. "You're beautiful!" I took off my pants and put them with the rest of my clothes. I sat on the couch next to her in my boxers and I looked at her again then I turned my attention back to the movie. Right when the movie got interesting she kissed my neck. Is Melissa a lap girl?

In the morning she kept smiling at me, but she had that dreamy look on her face. I told her I had to get home to go to service with my Grandma and G-momma. She told me next time she wanted to go with me. I told her she could go, but I don't know about with me cause my Grandma might have a fit about it. I told her she should call my Grandma and tell her she wants to go. Let Grandma come up with the idea to have me pick her up. She smiled and said ok, I thanked her for last night.

Driving home I was kind of perplexed about where to put her. My father said if you don't know where to put a female, she goes in your lap. But I liked Melissa more than a lap girl, but I don't know if she's someone that I let in my mind or the inner part of my heart. For my own sanity I decided to let it ride. After service I was in my room hanging out, thinking about things, writing poetry. I heard the phone ring then G-momma called me. She handed the phone to me shaking her head.

"Hello?"

"Hey baby how are you doing?"

I hadn't heard her voice in so long I stalled for a minute. "Shonda?"

"Since when do you call me by my first name?"

"Since I haven't talked to you, seen you, or anything in years! What do you want?"

"Eeewwllll! You don't talk to me like that. I just wanted to see how you're doing I was thinking about you." She said

"All the sudden you're thinking about me? You must need something!" I barked

She made a frustrated sound. "Look! I'm sure I've dropped the ball on being the mother of the year. But can we start over?"

"Start over? What do you want? Don't play this game with me! I don't have time for this!"

"YUSSEF! I DONT CARE HOW MUCH TIME HAS PASSED IT DOESNT CHANGE THAT I AM YOUR MOTHER! YOU ARE SO DISRESPECTFUL, IS MY MOMMA LETTING YOU TALK TO HER LIKE THIS?" She screamed

"No! This is a special tone reserved for you, WHAT DO YOU WANT?" G-momma looked at me. The look on her face told me I was in trouble. My momma hung up in my face. She didn't get to the reason for her call; I knew she would call me back.

"Why are you talking to your mother like that?"

"I'm not gonna act like I'm happy to hear from her when I'm not. I've been out here almost four years and she hasn't called to check on me or anything. She calls all the sudden out the blue and I'm supposed to be excited! I HATE HER!"

"YUSSEF!" G-momma stomped her foot and clapped her hand at me. Her nostrils were flaring so she was mad. "Stop talking like that immediately, that is still your momma."

"G-momma, I'm not stupid. She's only calling cause she wants something and I'm not gonna play her game. She has to be desperate to be calling me."

"If you know that why would you make it difficult for her? Even if she hasn't been good to you, you are the bigger person. Be good to your momma, who knows that could be the seed that motivates her to be a better person."

"G-momma, she views kindness as weakness. She doesn't appreciate kindness, she will just try to use your kindness against you."

"You think I don't know who your momma is? I've known her longer than you. But I'm talking to you and about how you're allowing her to change you. You don't let her ridiculousness change who you are. You don't deserve the reaction of the person you're allowing her to make you become. Now, I'm not gonna lie. She did deserve you responding to her like that. And she's probably over there crying on Summer's shoulder telling her she doesn't know why you would react to her like that. All I'm saying to you is that there is a way to get your point across without sinking to her ignorant level. I can't tell you how, cause you gotta find your own way. But there's a way."

"Yes G-momma," I said giving her a kiss. I was just happy she didn't smack me upside the head. It didn't hurt, but I didn't like it when she did it either.

The phone rang again; G-momma gave me a look when I tried to walk away with it. I exhaled, "Hello"

"Yussef, I'm sorry." My momma said

"For?"

"Everything. I know that's kind of a blanket apology, but it's the best I can do in this moment." I guess she was waiting for an apology in kind and when I didn't give that to her she blew air. "Do you have a car?"

"Yes"

"Can you come see me?" She asked

"WHY?" I forgot I was still standing in front of G-momma. She shot me a look, "why?" I said calmer

"I haven't seen you in a long time and I'd like to lay eyes on my son. Do I need a better reason than that?"

I blew air, "I don't know. I work and I got school."

"Please baby, I need to see you.," she begged

"Fine! Do you still have the same number?" I asked unenthusiastically

"Yes, its the same number and same apartment. Please let me know when you can come."

I could feel heat on my neck, but there was no one here to fight. When I got off the phone with her I felt alone. I called Latia but she wasn't home. Feeling like this I would've called Shannon and talked to her until I felt calm again. But I HATE thinking about her! I didn't want to call Melissa; I still didn't know where to put her. I could go screw Judy until I was too tired to think about anything. But I didn't feel like dealing with her quirkiness in this mindset. UGH! I told G-momma she wanted me to come see her, G-momma gave me sad eyes but she didn't say anything. I went in my room took out my journal and I wrote a quick poem trying to get this feeling out of my head and down on paper. I liked what I wrote but the feeling was still there. I picked up the phone, and my fingers dialed on their own. "What's up?"

"You busy?" I said

"Nope, just kicking back before class tomorrow. You sound upset?'"

"Got a lot on my mind right now."

"You wanna slide through?"

"Is it cool?" I asked

"Yea, come on. Jennay is here, but she'll be leaving in a little bit."

"I'm on my way." I hung up the phone, and hopped in my bucket.

"Jeremy!" Drew said opening the door for me. "Come in."

I gave him a pound, "Hey Jennay." I said walking in the door.

"Hey" she said reading my face.

"You need to relax!" Drew said reading me as well. "Babe, can you go get the box for me?" He said to Jennay all sweet and lovingly. She disappeared into his room; she came with a stationary box. He handed it to me.

I put the box on my lap and then I sat on his couch. The heat on my neck hadn't gone away, but I didn't know if I wanted to open the box either. "You got anything to drink?" I said putting the box down.

"Yea, help yourself to everything in the cupboard above the frig." Drew said

I grabbed a glass and a nice shot of something brown. I sat back on the couch. Jennay was packing up her books, etc. "Thanks again for dinner babe." She said giving him a kiss.

"Drew! You cook?" I couldn't believe it.

"Yes he does, and he's good at it too." Jennay said proudly.

"At home we all had to pitch in. You don't cook?" He said

"Not outside of the basics." I said

"You should try it, the ladies love it!" He said sarcastically

"We do!" Jennay said putting on her jacket.

"I'll be right back, I'm gonna walk her to her car." Then they disappeared. He was gone about twenty minutes, and then he came back with a mile wide smile. "Ok, what's up?"

"You and your moms get a long?" I asked

I could see the wheels in his mind turning by the question. "We're pretty tight actually." He said walking to the kitchen. I could hear him pouring a glass of his own.

"What's Malcolm's mother like?" I asked

"I don't know, I think she's dead. He doesn't talk about her. What about you?" He said taking a swallow.

I blew air, I sat up. "She's wicked!"

Drew raised an eyebrow, "wicked?"

"Selfish, self centered, you name it! I haven't seen her or heard from her since my father passed away." The irritation settled over me, "then she calls me today."

"What did she want?"

"EXACTLY! What does she want? She wants me to drive all out the way to come see her. And she's kind of making it sound urgent." I took another drink.

"You gonna go right?"

"I guess!"

Then he smiled, "when was the last time you got laid?"

"Last night" I said matter of factly.

"That was a whole night ago. You're over due! I promise once you release the frustration you'll know exactly what to do. And you won't be stressed about it."

I smiled, "you could have a point."

"You wanna go out, make the rounds or you got somebody in mind?" he asked

"Can I use your phone?"

****

Everything seemed smaller than I remembered it being. What a difference a day makes, or almost four years for that matter. I knocked on the door, and she answered it. She looked genuinely happy to see me; she gave me a hug and stepped to the side so that I could enter. Her eyes went straight to my hair. "When did you loc your hair?"

"Not too long after I got out there." I said

"Momma doesn't care?"

"I normally pull them back for Service when I go." I said looking around the apartment. Nothing was the same in there, all the furniture was different, and the door to my old room was shut.

She motioned for me to sit on the couch. "Thank you for coming all the way out here to see me. How long did you wrestle with yourself about coming?"

I sat down, "until you answered the door."

She laughed I didn't. She stared at me for a minute. "Sometimes I swear looking at you has always been a trip to me. If I didn't watch you come out of me, I would wonder if they gave me the right baby."

"G-momma says she can see you more in my face with my hair like this. She even says I have girl hair." I said with a smile in my voice but no smile on my face.

"Yea, but all I see is your daddy." Then she started crying. "I couldn't face you!" I watched her for a minute. I didn't know if this was a game or if she was for real. "Its all my fault! We could've been a family, but I was too busy trying to be fast! I thought I knew it all, and before I knew it my life and consequently your life spiraled out of control. Do you see your family now?"

I could feel heat on my neck. "I go see my grandmother from time to time, but every time I go all she sees is her dead son. We don't have anything to talk about, so it gets hard none of them know me. I do see Malcolm from time to time, but he's my last connection to that side. Without my sister I would be so lost! If I'm supposed to feel sorry for you right now I can't!"

"I understand", she said through her tears. "Nothing justifies what I've done to you. I wish I could take it all back."

"Why are you saying all this now? What's going on?"

She held up her left hand. She had an engagement ring on her finger. "His name is Scott. I want you to meet him."

"You could've told me this over the phone." I said completely irritated.

Then my Auntie Summer came bouncing in the door. I could tell by the look on her face she had no idea I was coming out there. "OH MY GOD! OH MY GOD!" She said rushing to give me a hug. I stood up and hugged her tight, picking her up off the floor a little. "Who told you, you could grow up and become a man?" Then she touched my hair, "your hair has always been so soft! I bet the girls be all over you!" Instantly my mind shifted to Shannon, and I fought to hold my smile. "I do alright."

"To what do we owe the honor?" Auntie Summer said throwing her bag in my old room without even looking to see where it landed.

I pointed to my momma, "she begged me to come out here, just to tell me she's getting married. She could've told me that over the phone."

"YOU'RE GETTING WHAT?" Auntie Summer didn't look happy, "please tell me you're not marrying Scott?"

My momma's tears came back full force as she held up her hand. "Please be happy for me!"

"NO! I won't, he's scum!" Auntie Summer spit.

"What's wrong with him?" I asked throwing my hands in my pockets.

"He hits her for one, he talks down to her. He's not a good guy." Auntie Summer said with tears pouring out of her eyes.

I guess I was supposed to feel some kind of way about that. Just like Brad and Camille, I didn't like seeing it, but they're relationship is their business. "She's a grown woman, if that's what she wants for the rest of her life, that's what she wants." I said Auntie Summer looked at me in disbelief. Then she turned her back to me and faced my momma. "Shonda, a man that hits you doesn't love you. Please don't do this!" I knew my auntie was coming from a place of love and concern for her sister. But I was coming from a place where I've only seen her run game on guys. Push guys to their limit, and it sounds like she found one who doesn't take her mess. I couldn't be in that caring space with my auntie. It would hurt me more to know a man was raising his hand to her.

She looked around my auntie, "will you meet him? He's going to come over after he gets off work."

I looked at my watch, "what time will that be? I don't want to head back too late."

"In a few hours. Meanwhile can you take me to the store to get a couple of things for dinner?"

Auntie Summer huffed then she went in her room. She came out of her room in time to go with us to the grocery store. I wasn't crazy enough to drive my nice car out here. But I drove one that I knew would make the trip there and back. My momma seemed impressed with the car all the same; auntie Summer just seemed worried about her sister. I followed them around the grocery store pushing the cart. Then I heard a familiar voice, it was coming from the other aisle. I told my momma I'd be right back. I walked around the corner and I slowly strolled down the aisle. She was talking to her sister about their cracker options. She saw me but didn't pay any attention. When I got close I spoke in her ear. She jumped really hard then she looked me in my face. She screamed and threw her arms around my neck. Her sister stood there looking at us like we were crazy. "Where did you go? You vanished into thin air!" she said kissing my cheek

"I went back to the Bay."

"Are you back?" she asked

"I came out to visit my momma and auntie, but I'm going back."

She opened her purse and pulled out a pen and paper. She wrote down her number, "Call me! We need to catch up."

"Ok, its good to see you." I said with a smile

Randi looked at me with stars in her eyes. "I can't believe I'm looking at you right now. I thought I'd never see you again."

I gave her another hug; "I'll catch up to you later."

At the house I talked to Auntie Summer and my momma catching up with them. I didn't tell them we moved, I didn't tell them I worked for Malcolm. I didn't really share all that much about myself. I listened and talked about whatever information they gave. Right before it was time for Scott to arrive, my momma got in the shower. She put on a nice dress, and she came out looking very nice. Auntie Summer shook her head in irritation. She called me in her room, I felt betrayed by my old room. It somehow became very girly and I saw no trace that I had ever lived in this room. We chatted for a while; I was in her room when Scott finally showed up. Scott was average height, average build, average brown, average appearance; everything about him was average nothing to write home about. When I shook his hand he did not give me a manly grip it was almost like touching a girl, STRIKE ONE! He didn't give me eye contact; he looked around the room but not even in my face, STRIKE TWO! I decided to cut him some slack; after all he wanted to spend the rest of his life with my momma. I didn't know if he knew what he was signing up for, but it wasn't my life. Auntie Summer put on her gym clothes and left. We ate the early dinner quietly, Scott wasn't trying and neither was I. My momma would try to spark conversation but neither one of us was going for it. I looked at my watch, if I left now I could be back in the Bay before eight. "I hate to eat and run, but I got to get back."

"You have to leave so soon?" Momma said

"Yea I got stuff to take care of. But I'll pop up some day soon. Just warning you now that I won't call first." I said looking at Scott.

My momma weakly smiled. "We need to come out that way, Scott needs to meet momma and G-momma."

Invisible

"You will need to call them first, they be running the streets these days." I gave her a hug and a kiss. "I would shake your hand again Scott, but that will just irritate me. So...." I shrugged, "keep your hands off my momma and we won't have any problems." He frowned; I looked him in his eyes. "But you strike me as the kind who don't understand or heed warnings until you've been handled." Scott looked away. I winked at my momma. "I'm out!" I walked out the door leaving it unlocked on purpose. I drove up the street to the seven eleven to use the phone. I called Malcolm's cellular phone, he told me he was at his restaurant slash lounge Shylight in Berkeley. I looped back around to the apartment. I left my jacket in Auntie Summer's room on purpose. I figured he'd act ugly with her on account of what I said, I wondered if he would be stupid enough to go off right now about it. I could hear them fussing as I walked up to the door. I slowly turned the knob; this fool didn't even secure the door. I slowly pushed the door open as he pushed my momma on the couch. He was reaching back as far as he could he was about to knock the stuffing out of her. "Please do it! Oh how I wish you would!" I said chuckling to stop myself from getting angry. Scott's eyes got real big, and he tried to straighten himself up real fast. "I said I wouldn't call first, guess you thought I meant another day." I stepped in the door and gently closed it. Scott stood there trying to catch his breath and trying to figure out what I was gonna do. "Momma you alright?"
"I'm fine baby, we were just having a spat." She said trying not to piss Scott off.
"A spat?" I said chuckling again. Then I walked up on Scott. "I don't like you. I warned you didn't I?" Before he could respond I chin checked him, and then I hit him in the face. He fell on the couch holding his nose. "Now the question is, when I walk out this door when will I return? Thirty minutes, an hour, middle of the night, etc. Who knows! If you can't keep your hands to yourself break up with her. Don't keep putting yourself through this, I don't want to have to kill you." Then I walked in the room and picked up my jacket. My momma was getting ice for Scott's nose, which was swelling up, and his eyes were red. Momma thanked me with her eyes and I walked out the door.

Chapter 6

"Explain this report to me" Drew said

"What do you mean?" I leaned forward on the table to look at it.

Drew sat back and he smiled a frustrated smile. "I mean, I know. I know she's a flirt. That's actually something that I like about her, but what do you mean by she was flirting with Thaddeus? And the rest of them, what does this mean?"

"Jennay likes attention. She doesn't try that stuff with me cause she knows I know you. But whenever there's a guy around she has to do something to get their attention. I don't think she does it to start anything. Its who she is." I could tell Andrew was trying to chew back his jealousy.

"Maybe I shouldn't have told her who you were to see how far she takes things." He said

"Drew I don't think it goes anywhere. She's just a flirt. She flirts and then its over. Even when she doesn't think I can hear her she's excited talking about you." I said

"Do you think she loves me?"

"I know she does. Its all over her, she happens to need attention as well."

Andrew got irritated, "I pay her attention!"

"You know what I mean." I had to be honest with him. "But you know you are kind of all over the place. You got Jennay in one hand, and Toya and everybody else in the other."

He exhaled, "you're saying that the flirting is getting worse."

"It has picked up a lot of steam, especially after that girl confronted her at that game. Dealing with Toya is one thing, but all these girls is a bit much."

"I know, about a month ago she started crying in the middle of the night. I felt horrible. She went off on me real bad. I've been trying to be good ever since."

"Don't you hate it when they start crying? Especially the ones who you know are not criers." I said

"She told me she's not gonna keep putting up with me hurting her like this. I don't want to lose her."

"So you dealing with her flirting is a compromise?" I asked

"She has to know you're gonna tell me, and she obviously doesn't care. But this behavior has only gotten worse since my nonsense started picking up. I can't end up like Malcolm!"

"How come you measure everything by him?" I asked

"Do I?" He smiled

"Yea, everything keeps coming back to him. Like you measure your life by the things that are happening in his." Then my pager went off. "Can I use your phone?"

"Sure" he said focusing on my report.

"Somebody page?" I said when the person said hello.

"Jeremy are you with Drew?" Jennay whispered.

"Yes" I said looking at Drew

"I need you to come get me, but you cant tell him." She said her voice was shaky.

"Now you know I cant do that." I said staring at Andrew waiting for him to realize I was looking at him. He looked at me and listened. "Where are you? What's going on?"

"I did something stupid, and I have no one else to turn to. But if he has to know I will walk home." She said

"Where are you?" I said

"Vallejo" She said

Invisible

"Now you know you're not walking from Vallejo to Berkeley. If you're calling me you know he's gonna know about it. Tell me where you are and I'll come get you." I said, Andrew frowned at me.

"I'm at a payphone right off Georgia St exit. I'll walk back to the exit so you'll see me when you get off the freeway." She said in a defeated tone

"I'm on my way." I hung up the phone. Andrew had a question mark on his face as he stood up. "Jennay is stranded in Vallejo. She didn't want you to know, she said she did something stupid."

"What does that mean?" He growled

"I don't know, don't shoot the messenger." I said putting my hands up.

When we walked out the door Tanisha was coming home. "Hey Yussef, hey Drew." She said

"Hey!" Andrew growled. She looked at me and asked me with her eyes what was wrong with him. I pointed at him to say she already knew. She nodded and went inside her apartment. I took out my keys to drive, "I'M DRIVING!" He said

"I don't know if that's such a good idea. You gonna be able to drive without reflecting your anger in your driving?" I said. Drew threw his keys to me and then he got in the passenger seat.

Drew didn't a say a word the whole car ride. When we pulled off the freeway at the Georgia Street exit, Jennay saw the car and started walking, almost running. Andrew ran out of the car. I pulled over on the side of the street and put the hazard lights on. Jennay was dressed like she had been on a date. Drew didn't have to say a word to me; I could see what was happening. They paced back and forth arguing for a good hour to a hour and a half. I sang along to the songs on the radio while I waited. "Get in the car and you better not say nothing!" Andrew barked at her holding her door open. Then he told me to drive, when we got to the first corner he told me to turn right. Then he told me to slow down and turn off the headlights, so I did. "That's his car right there! Park the car!" He commanded. "STAY IN THIS CAR!"

"Andrew," she was in tears, "please!" she pleaded.

"What did you think was gonna happen? Next time you'll think it through wont you." He said getting out the car. He didn't have to look back he knew I was with him. He walked up to the door and knocked on it. Craig answered the door; Drew knocked him out with one punch. I could see him holding himself back from doing more. He cursed then he pushed past me and got in the car in the backseat with Jennay.

I kind of felt bad for Craig. But he knew Jennay belonged to Drew. He knew exactly what he was doing, and then he left her stranded. He should be happy that's all Drew did, I've seen him do worse.

****

"Get on," I said handing her the second helmet.

"You do know how to ride that thing?" She asked

"How would you explain me sitting in front of your house? If you're too scared just say so. I'll go by myself." I said

She screamed a nervous scream. "I CAN'T BELIEVE IM DOING THIS!" Then she put her helmet on. She did a silly dance then she sat on the back of the bike. She wrapped her arms around me tight. I popped a small wheelie and she screamed squeezing me harder. "I will go back inside right now! Don't do that!"

I laughed out loud. "I had to do it one time. I'll be good now." I sat reaching back to pat her butt. When she didn't say anything I did it again.

"Ok!" She said squeezing me again. She screamed again as we took off.

We made good time out to Santa Cruz, it normally takes about two hours to get out there from Richmond, but we made it just under an hour and a half. We detoured a little to check into our room at the Hinton Hotel and drop off our backpacks with our things for the night. Then we rode down to the boardwalk. I told Randi we'd meet her at one o'clock at the Giant Dipper Roller Coaster entrance. We had an hour to kill so Melissa and I got on the Sky Glider, which takes you from one side of the park to the other. It moves real slowly and you can look down and spot people. I pointed Randi out to Melissa, and then I saw a group of familiar looking faces. CRAP! Camille was there with her niece, I didn't see Brad but that didn't mean he wasn't there. I saw Darius though. CRAP! Immediately I started looking for exit plans, and how I was going to get out of here. Melissa was too excited though, and I couldn't think of a good reason to leave other than Brad would literally kill me if he found me there. "This sun is beaming down on me." I said fanning myself.

She started nodding her head, "yea and I didn't bring any sunblock."

"Sunblock? All black folks need is cocoa butter and we good. But I think I need a hat. What about you?" I said

"Yea, that sounds good." she smiled then she snuggled into my arm.

When we got off the ride I went to the first vendor I saw and I got two hats, I always carried rubber bands for when my hair got too hot. So I banded my hair and tucked the tail in my shirt. Fortunately I started noticing all the other brown skinned dreaded fools around the boardwalk, so maybe I stood a chance. Right on time Randi and her friends showed up to the coaster. I introduced Melissa, and then Randi introduced us to her friends. Since I was a little distracted keeping an eye out for Brad I didn't pay attention to the things that were coming out of Randi's mouth exactly, or when she touched me more than she should've, or when she asked me if Melissa and I were a couple and I didn't respond cause I was distracted. Melissa kept shooting me looks and I honestly didn't know what was wrong with her. We rode a few coasters then we ventured out to the beach. I relaxed a little being off the boardwalk. Melissa was not as happy as I thought she should've been. That's when she told me about the stuff I wasn't paying attention to. My brain was functioning on high alert, and she wanted me to slow down to worry about this trivial stuff. "Randi and I never dated." I said putting my arms around her.

"But she likes you?" Melissa pouted

I shrugged, "I don't know I can't speak on that. I know she used to, but that was in junior high school. Girls don't carry torches that long."

She blew air, "you don't know women. I've liked a guy from elementary school through graduation."

"Is that the guy who called you the other night?" I smiled and squeezed her a little tighter

"Could've been, you didn't seem too concerned though."

"Why should I be?"

"Why wouldn't you be? You are my man aren't you?" I didn't say anything; I didn't know how to answer that. I didn't want her to think I didn't care about her. But I wasn't thinking about putting a claim on anyone or having them claim me for that matter. "Yussef!" She wanted an answer.

"We don't need a label, we're kicking it."

"Yes we do, especially if you think you're getting some tonight. I need to know what we're doing here?"

"We're kicking it, I just told you. You need something more than that?" I said trying not to feel irritated.

"I thought you wanted to be my man." She said trying to hold back her irritation

"Melissa, I like you. I like you a lot; I mean you're here aren't you? But I'm not ready to be in a relationship right now. I got too many other things going on to give you the attention you deserve in a true relationship."

She removed my arms from around her. "You're kidding right?" She turned to face me.

"No I'm not." I said feeling like crap for seeing the sadness in her eyes and knowing it was my fault.

"Yussef!" She walked us even further away from the group so we could talk privately.

"I really care about you."

"I care about you too."

"Then why can't we be together? We have the foundation." She said crossing her arms.

"I'm in no hurry to get my heart broken again." I said

"Why would you think I would hurt you?"

"Like you said, I don't know who was calling you the other night. I don't want to be concerned about stuff like that. If we were truly in a relationship something like that could've gotten yours and his necks broken. I don't have the tolerance for those games."

"I didn't tell him to call me, he called out of the blue."

"So" I said waiting for her point.

"You are that insecure that you would lose it over a phone call?"

"Have you given me any reason to feel like my heart is secure with you? You've cooked for me, and we talk. But I see your head turning when we're out. At least when I'm with you, I'm with you."

"Caring about you doesn't make me blind." She said

"Me neither, which is why I don't think we're ready to be in a relationship. Seems like you got some oats to sow or something."

"I'm the only one?" She asked

"No, which is why I say we're kicking it."

"Relationships are what you make them. There's nothing that says we can't have what we have but still claim each other." She said

"Why would you want that?" I asked

"Cause we both know tonight I'm looking forward to having you blow my back out. Why else would I agree to come all the way out here to hang with some people I don't know. And we both know tonight is not the last time I'll be waiting for you. I wanna call you my man, and hear you call me your woman. I want the title."

"The title seems like crap under these circumstances." She laughed I didn't. I wasn't kidding. "Fine Melissa, if it will make you feel better, go ahead and claim me. I can't promise that I will always do the same though."

She smiled real big as if I just asked her to be my girlfriend. "Kiss me!" I took one more glance around us, and then I kissed her. "I can't wait to get you back to the room!"

"How much longer you wanna stay?" I asked her

"You lead the way." She smiled

I took her by the hand. "Yussef you remember that girl Faith don't you?" Randi asked.

"How can I forget her? She caused so many problems."

"She's pregnant with her second child." Randi said waiting for a reaction from me.

"Are you surprised?"

"Not really, she barely knew my name and she was throwing it at me." Melissa wrapped her arms around me. "How long are you guys going to be here?"

Randi and her friends all kind of spaced out looking at us. I looked at Melissa and she shrugged cause it was weird to her too. "You trying to leave Yussef?"

I glanced around the beach again, "Yea. This won't be the last time I see you. You got my number."

"The plan was to stay out here as late as possible, and then go our separate ways, or not." she said looking me in the face.

"We'll see each other again, it's just not the day to be hanging out on the boardwalk for me." I said looking around the beach again. "I stayed to sundown, I think that's doing good."

"You promise we'll see each other again?" She said as if Melissa wasn't standing right there.

Melissa looked at me like I better get her. "Randi stop playing," I bucked my eyes at her. "We will see you guys another time." I bucked my eyes at Randi again, and then I turned towards Melissa "let's go."

"Bye Yussef!" The group sang

"Bye ladies," I said not looking back.

"Obviously they weren't expecting me to be here!" Melissa hissed

"Yes they were, I told Randi specifically that I was bringing you. Maybe I'm just too irresistible." I smiled

Melissa rolled her eyes, "whatever".

I could feel heat on my neck as I carefully walked up the stairs. Brad's crew could've left already for all I know. Melissa squeezed my hand, "I gotta pee, and I think the bathroom's this way." She said pointing to the left.

I saw a sea of people and I didn't want to go that way. "Yea, but it's gonna be crowded over there remember the line we saw earlier. There has to be another one this way." I said pointing to the right.

"Can you ask somebody? I don't want to go all that way and then find out there is no bathroom and then I'm in a tight doing the pee-pee dance in line." She said

I smiled, "the pee-pee dance? What does that look like?" I said messing with her.

"Keep stalling and you're about to find out." She said

I asked one of the workers sweeping up trash if there was a women's bathroom out this way. The worker explained to us where the bathroom was over to the side down the stairs. I hesitated for a minute when I saw Ricky and a few of Brad's men sitting over to the side at a table. They looked like they were waiting for Camille and her niece to come out the bathroom, which was around the corner. Ricky was running his mouth about something so they weren't paying attention to too much else. I casually walked past them and around the corner closer to the bathroom. Melissa and I kind of stopped as we saw Camille and Darius in a passionate embrace. It looked like they got caught up in the moment and all that mattered was their kiss. Melissa smiled at me and I motioned for her to go around them. I went in the men's room. My heart was racing; Malcolm needed to know about this. I didn't understand how Darius could be so dumb. He was Brad's number one guy; I guess he didn't know about rule number one. Heaven forbid that I should ever be that dumb, no female was worth all that.

I washed my hands and I listened as I heard Camille talking to her niece. She said they were going to have dinner and then go back to their room. I needed pictures, but I needed to figure out where they were staying. Their voices started trailing off, all the sudden I was in work mode. When I came out the bathroom Melissa was coming out at the same time. She smiled and said she felt better. When we came around the corner I saw Camille and her many men walking ahead while she held her nieces hand. I strolled along holding Melissa's hand. I'm sure I looked casual but inside I was screaming CRAP! I needed to figure out how I could get away for a while to find them. The wheels of my brain were turning. When we got to the parking lot Camille was waiting with her niece and Darius. Ricky pulled up and there was another car behind him. We got on my bike; I decided to let it go. I wasn't on the clock. I sat on the bike for a few minutes teasing Melissa with my tongue. Once I figured they were completely gone, I set off for our hotel. When we got up to our room I asked Melissa if she was hungry. She said she was, I told her we could have dinner downstairs in the restaurant. There was a bunch of people there so that had to be a good sign about the food. "Too bad you can't drink yet, I think it would be fun to have cocktails with dinner." Melissa said

"I have an ID, we can have cocktails." I said

She smiled real big, "no you don't?"

"You gotta call me Lamont though." I took out my wallet and I showed her my driver's license and credit card for Lamont Jenkins.

She held the ID in her hand doing all her teller checks to verify that it was real. "This is real!"

"I know it is. How you think I got this room?"

"I guess I didn't think about it. So is Lamont your alter ego?" She asked like she liked the idea.

"Sometimes." Then I pulled her close. "Who you wanna sleep with tonight? Yussef or Lamont?"

She raised her leg and rubbed it against me. "I'm curious, show me what Lamont kisses like." I kissed her hard and passionately. "Oh mother may I sleep with Lamont tonight? Will Yussef get jealous?" She said

"Maybe, but I'll talk to him." We both laughed.

When I took my kit in the bathroom to wash my face, I debated whether or not I would need anything. I decided to bring it just in case. It felt good to let my head breathe outside of that cap, my head applauded when I took it off and took out the rubber bands.

The waiter showed us to our table. We weren't sitting five minutes when Camille's niece came bouncing up. "HI LAMONT!" She was so excited. I smiled at her even though inside I couldn't believe I missed them. "Who is she?"

"Friend of yours?" Melissa said smiling at her.

CRAP! "Who are you here with?" I asked as if I didn't know.

"My auntie." She said pointing at Camille, Ricky, and Darius.

I waved then I stood up. "Just go with whatever I say ok."

Melissa smiled and said "ok".

Darius came over he shook my hand giving me eye contact the whole time. "You're back early aren't you."

"I had to come out to see her." I said pointing to Melissa.

"Hello I'm Darius." He said reaching out to shake Melissa's hand.

"Melissa" she said. I didn't know if I wanted her to give him her real name but oh well, it's done now.

"Is Melissa your girlfriend?" The little girl said as she put her hands on her hips while she looked angry.

"You're still my number one girl." I said gently flicking her chin.

She smiled and blushed at me, and then she frowned at Melissa. We all laughed.

"So how long you gonna be out here?" Darius asked, I could tell he was making a mental note.

"Just the duration of my break, then I go back." I said

"You should swing by the house Monday. We got something going on that we could use an extra man for." Darius said staring me in my eyes.

"I see!" It was serious whatever it was. "I'll be there!" CRAP!

"Come on Lil miss missy let's let them enjoy their meal." He said taking her hand. "It was nice meeting you Melissa."

"Likewise." She said still smiling.

"Monday!" He said to me walking away.

"See you then." I said.

Melissa smiled at me, "I see why you hesitated earlier, and you've already got a girlfriend Lamont."

"Yep! The best of the best." I smiled.

When our waiter came Melissa ordered some girly drink and I ordered a Hennessy double. I watched Camille and party walk out of the restaurant and get in the elevator. Perfect they were staying in the hotel. Then Melissa asked our waiter where the nearest bathroom was as she brought her another drink. The waiter told her then Melissa excused herself. I was now happy that I listened to myself and brought my kit. I pulled the bottle of pills out. I opened the capsule and dumped half the contents in Melissa's drink. Then I stirred it with her straw. When she came back she went to town on her drink, I told her to slow down cause I needed her alert for what I was about to do to her. She switched to water after she finished her drink. We had nice conversation; all the while I was looking to see if anyone was watching us. Melissa yawned and I told her to stop that cause yawning was contagious. She smiled and said it had been a long day. We finished our meal even had dessert. Melissa kept yawning, "listen, if you're too tired we could always wait until the morning." I said giving her a knowing smile.

"I'm greedy, I want dessert and breakfast." She said

I shrugged, "suit yourself."

I paid for dinner then we made our way to the elevator. Ricky came out of the gift shop with a few knick-knacks. "Lamont your lady is nice!" He said giving me a thumbs up.

"Thanks" I said with a big smile, Melissa blushed. Ricky got off on the fifth floor. "Who's unnoticed now?" I said, she blushed again. I pulled her in for a kiss; I could tell the sleeping pill was starting to affect her. Her arms were heavier around my neck. She was determined to stay awake, so I did what I had to do to knock her out for the night. She couldn't remember which name to call out; it turned her on when I covered her mouth so I went with it. I laid there waiting for her breathing to get heavy, once it did; I tried to wake her up. Even slapped her a little bit, I kind of liked that. Then I paged Malcolm. When he called back I asked if the line was secure, when he said it was I told him about the whole day. I told him I was going to see if I could get some pictures. Malcolm hesitated; he told me I was naked out here. I told him I was strapped and I always carried my kit he gave me. I asked him where Amber was. He said she was in LA at the moment. I asked him if he thought they were gonna go for her on Monday. He said it was possible, he told me to come by Shylight tomorrow.

I washed up, threw my clothes back on then I went down to the fifth floor. I walked down both ends of the hallway with no real indication of which room was Camille's. I went downstairs to the lobby trying to think of a way to trick them into giving me Camille's room number. There was no one at the desk. I walked around the counter and whoever was supposed to be manning the desk didn't lock their station. Yay for me, too bad for them. I entered Camille Caruthers and she was in 503. I entered Darius McKnight and he was in 505. I made room keys for both rooms. Then I took the screen back to the main screen. When I got to the elevator I saw the guy coming back to the computer, he didn't look concerned. I listened to the door at 503 and it was silent. I put my key card in and it unlocked. I cracked the door and waited for a reaction. I could hear snoring. I went in slowly and I held on to the door until it glided shut. This room had an adjoining door to 505, the 503 side was open. There were two beds and Camille's niece was snoring peacefully in one bed. I took pics of her sleep and I made sure to capture the empty bed next to hers. Then I heard Camille calling out to Jesus and anyone in the heavens who would hear her. It sounds like she was exploding over there. I couldn't tell if the movement was still in the bed or if they were up. So I stepped inside the armoire closet with the door cracked and waited. They were at it for a long time; I guess they had been waiting a long time. When they were done, I could hear them talking declaring their love for each other and fantasizing about both of them leaving Brad. Then there was a knock at Darius' door. Camille ran naked back into her room, shutting the adjoining door behind her. I snapped pictures of her as she pranced around the room with such a guilty look on her face. It was Ricky asking him a dumb question. When Ricky left Darius boldly walked in the room naked. I was surprised at his boldness considering there was a sleeping child in the bed next to them. They quietly went at it again. I got pictures of him hitting it from the back, the front, sideways, her riding, they didn't use one condom. When they were done, they said their "I love you's" and then he went back to his room. Baby girl stayed asleep snoring the whole time. Eventually I could hear Camille's breath as she slept harder, and Darius was calling hogs from his bed. I bet he was sleeping well tonight. I slid out the room undetected and looking at the pictures in my camera. Say what you want about her age, I wasn't even certain about that. Camille's body was banging! I put my camera in my kit, undressed and climbed into bed.

I woke up to Melissa pawing at me, she looked all rested and refreshed. Where I had been up most of the night, still it was a nice way to wake up and then go back to sleep. As we were leaving I saw Camille and her niece having brunch. They looked so happy and peaceful together. Melissa and I waved good-bye to them, and then we stopped a few blocks up and had our own brunch. I could see Ricky lurking outside the restaurant. If Darius didn't have his head up Camille's butt (pun intended) he would know sending stupid Ricky wasn't a good move. I just needed to make sure it didn't look like I was trying to shake him.

Melissa said she wanted to finish the weekend with Lamont. When I asked why, she said Lamont didn't care he just did what he wanted to do. She said Yussef was kind and loving. I asked her if all girls went for the bad boy. She said not all girls and definitely not all the time.

I could see Ricky dancing out the corner of my eye. I paid our check then I waited for him to come inside to go to the bathroom. As soon as he entered I grabbed our backpack and told Melissa to come on. We pulled off before he came back. I decided to come back up the coast. When Melissa kept squeezing me I knew she was going crazy about the water so I pulled over at a beach. It was a beautiful site to see, moments like that I thank God for letting me see them. Melissa started pawing at me, right then I realized I left my last condom at the hotel. She said it was ok cause she was on the pill, but I immediately shut down. Melissa didn't try to hide her disappointment but I didn't care. I wasn't gonna do it. We got back on the bike and made our way down the coast, we stopped at a corner store and wouldn't you know they had condoms, but the beach by that part wasn't really secluded. So we backtracked to that same spot. My jacket only provided a small space to move around on, but I wasn't trying to get sand up my butt. Now that Melissa was happy and completely satisfied we continued down the coast. We made it to Shylight after five almost six. We sat at a table over to the side not in the main view. I told Melissa I was going to the bathroom, and then I knocked on Malcolm's door. "Hey Uncle Blackie!" I said with a huge smile. Malcolm looked at me unamused by my humor. "Glad to see you're still alive." Then there was a knock at the door. Our waiter brought me my backpack. I took out my kit, then I showed Malcolm the pictures, he actually smiled at the pictures of Camille. His face returned to normal when Darius entered the pictures. "She's always looking for love." He shook his head. "Let me think of what to do with these." He put the camera in his desk. "Are you equipped to meet with him tomorrow?"

"I guess." I said

"You guess? Or you know?" Malcolm asked looking me in my eyes.

"I was looking forward to kicking back tomorrow." I huffed

"Spoken like a true kid. As a man you do what has to be done when it has to be done no whining about it. Put a trace in your shoe, and a wire somewhere. I wanna make sure I know where you are at all times in case I need to get you out of there."

"Ok" I said feeling ungrateful.

Malcolm looked at his monitor. "Who do we have here?"

It was Mitchell, and he was talking to Melissa. Her body language said she was uncomfortable. "That's Mitchell, Latia's ex."

Malcolm's eyes turned evil. "I don't like him. This isn't gonna end well I can tell. When he gets froggy take him out back." Malcolm said returning his attention back to his desk.

When I walked out the office my waiter took my backpack and I walked up to the table. "Mitchell"

He looked surprised to see me. "Yussef?" Then he started laughing.

"Something's funny?" I asked looking at Melissa.

She shook her head no. "Shannon put a hurting on you didn't she." He said still laughing.

Ok, now I could feel the heat on my neck. "I'm trying to understand what's funny."

"You and your sister are a couple of the stupidest somebody's I know."

I looked around the room, why is this fool pushing me like this. He has to have backup and not know where he is. He's in my house right now! I run this! But I gotta be cool! Malcolm said take him out back, and he's going. I'm beating him for my sister, and because he shares a bloodline with Shannon. "You're too weak to even come to me after everything happened."

I looked at Melissa and her eyes got big. "Mitchell please! He doesn't know!"

"I don't know what!" I barked all this secrecy was on my last nerve.

Mitchell smiled with satisfaction. "She didn't tell you!" He got excited, and started jumping up and down pumping himself up.

A guy walked over, "The owner has asked that you take this out back." He said putting his hand on both of our shoulders.

"Cool! Why don't we do this. Melissa," he pointed at her then me. "Fill him in, I'ma wait for you out back. I've been waiting for this for a long time." He laughed again following the guy.

Melissa sat there shaking her head. "Yussef we're having a nice dinner please stay with me. He's crazy!" She was scared and her chest was moving up and down real fast.

"I'm not gonna ask you again!" I barked.

"He got Latia pregnant on purpose." She looked at me shifted in her seat and swallowed. "When she told him, he went off as if he didn't do it on purpose. He told her to get rid of the baby, when she refused he broke up with her." I was already livid, but she had more to share. "He showed up at her house unannounced and beat her up." She had tears in her eyes. "He beat her so badly that she lost the baby."

When I looked up Malcolm was standing behind Melissa. His eyes were red and evil, he handed me brass knuckles. Then he handed me leather gloves. Melissa had no idea who Malcolm was, I told her to stay at the table. All I could see was red; Malcolm didn't say anything he walked with me. When I walked out the door Mitchell had two guys with him. Mitchell smiled at me, the heat from my neck traveled through my body. When my fist connected with his jaw I saw and heard the crack. Malcolm stood on the wall as I beat this idiot up and down the alley. At one point I saw movement around me, but all I could do was focus on Mitchell. All I saw was red, and when I started to feel tired I came back to myself. Mitchell was this bloody blob at my feet. His friends were laid out as well; Malcolm was back on the wall with his hands in his pockets watching me. When I looked at him he nodded at me like he was satisfied with what I did. Then he opened the door, I stepped in the door. The guy who told us to go out back was standing there. Malcolm told him to go sweep up. When we walked down the hallway I heard three distinct pops.

Chapter 7

"Hello?" I said very irritated

"Yussef?" She was crying

"Yea!" Even more irritated

"Have you seen Mitchell? It's been a week and no one's seen him or heard from him."

"Shannon! Why are you on my phone? I don't talk to your cousin, don't ever call me again!" I barked

"Can we please have this conversation? We'll be graduating and moving on with our lives." She pleaded

"Why call under the guise of looking for your cousin? You're always playing games."

"I didn't think you would answer the phone, or come to it. I've been trying to call you this whole time."

"For what?" I guess she figures I'm gonna take her call to hear how sorry she is? How she never meant to hurt me? She can keep saying that but it changes nothing. I hate her and there's nothing she can say or do to change that.

She was quiet for a long time. "Can you come pick me up?"

I took the phone off my ear like there had to be something wrong with it! "Why?"

"I need to apologize to you in person. This talking over the phone stuff isn't working." She thinks if she opens her legs all will be forgiven. It doesn't work that way, and I don't know what I'll do. I got mad at myself for wanting to see her. I got mad at myself for wanting my old girlfriend back. I miss the way we used to be, when we would sit and talk about nothing for hours. I hate how complicated and traumatic this whole thing got. I miss my faithful girlfriend. But I'm not falling for this, and it could be a setup. The person that I thought she was, she has proven not to be. "No Shannon! I'm not meeting you anywhere. The only reason I answered just now is cause I thought you were someone else calling. I don't want to talk to you; I don't want to see you. I'm done with you, so stop calling me! Stop acting like you know who I am!" My voice cracked and that pissed me off. Then I heard the honking outside. It sound like she started to cry, I hung up the phone. I tried to shake the mood she put me in, but it wasn't working.

Hubby was driving and Drew looked the way I felt. "What up?" Hubby said

"Nothing. You?" I said

"My step father used to live out here. You know any Mason's?" Drew asked

"Not that I'm aware of."

"Everybody's in a funk. What's going on with you Yussef?" Hubby asked

"Nothing, my ex called me. I hate her, you know.... What's going on with Drew?"

"Toya's pregnant or at least she was." Drew said sounding defeated.

"But you know that's not you." I said not understanding why he's sulking.

"She said she wasn't sure. When I looped back around to come up with a plan she already got rid of it."

"Ok" I said not understanding the mood.

"Tell him what your solution was. Tell him!" Hubby said like he was rubbing it in.

Drew exhaled, "you make it sound stupid."

"Cause that's what it was. I never thought a smart person could be so dumb. I swear Drew when you go dumb you go completely dumb. You better hope your momma don't find out." Then he laughed, "I bet you discussed none of this with her, huh?"

"Shut up!" Drew said

"What was the solution?" I asked

"I bought her a ring." Drew grumbled

"YOU DID WHAT????" I couldn't believe it. "What about Jennay?"

"Right! You better hope she don't find out about this." Hubby said laughing.

"So I take it Toya said no?" I asked.

"She thinks ole boy is going to the NFL, she's holding on to him for dear life." Drew grumbled again.

"Poor Ms. Amber! If my girl wasn't so nice, and Ms. Amber wasn't dating that fool on TV. I'd cheer her up when she finds out about this."

"If you don't stop with your pathetic crush on my momma!" Drew growled

"Hey, it's not my fault. She ain't old enough to be your momma, and she doesn't look like NOBODY'S momma. You just better be happy I found Nicole otherwise you'd be calling me daddy."

"Yea right, you'd fight Malcolm for her?" Drew said

"I'd do like her current temporary stand-in for me. Get in good with Tim so he could keep Malcolm off me." Then he laughed.

"Why are you laughing and talking nonsense?" Drew said

"Cause you stupid! And your momma is fine! You know I'ma call you on it."

"First you need to decide if you crushing on my momma or heartbroken over Sasha! If Sasha wouldn't have dumped your dumb behind, I bet you Nicole wouldn't seem as nice."

Hubby's foot got a little heavier on the gas, "why you always gotta bring Sasha up?" He said angry.

"Why you always gotta bring my momma up?" Drew said mocking his tone, "its funny how you try to act like you're not still feeling her."

"Whatever!" Hubby said irritated

"Yea whatever!" Drew said

We parked in the Drew's parking lot in Oakland. We walked around to the back. Everybody was there. "Who we got here?" Someone asked Drew while giving me eye contact.

"This is Yussef, Malcolm brought him on. Yussef this is my uncle Malachi." Drew said then he walked away.

"Hey how you doing." I said shaking Malachi's hand.

He stood there reading my face for a minute. He was definitely Tim's son. "I'm good, nice to meet you."

Then Tim came over; he put his arm around me like I was a son. I took a deep breath, I didn't wanna go all female, but this moment was definitely staying in my memory bank. I see why Malcolm is so attached to this guy; he's got a way about him that brings you in like you belong to him. "Come meet my brothers."

Tim and his brothers all looked like they were related. Jeff looked most like Tim, but Frank wasn't much different except he was a big guy. I shook their hands giving each of them eye contact the entire time. Then Tim introduced me to a couple of his nephews Jeff and Joseph. I ended up talking to them for a minute. The rest of the people there were Mitigated staff.

Malcolm went over the information they got from Brad. I told him how they're plotting against him but they will resort to hurting Amber to get at him. Tim said that Amber understands why she needs to be covered but she's not aware of this plot. He asked that she maintain as much normality as possible. Malcolm's kids would have someone on them at all times as well. Drew was over in the corner trying to keep it together, but he was having a hard time. Malcolm looked irritated with him; Tim went over and took Drew out. When the meeting was over Malcolm kept looking at Andrew, but there was no sympathy in his face. "Where's your girlfriend?" He asked him.

"She's at home studying." Andrew said

"No she's not. She had a conversation with Toya not too long ago and she looked pretty upset." Malcolm said

"Why do you have somebody on her?"

"Any road that leads to you or your brothers is covered. Did you listen to anything we just talked about?"

Andrew closed his eyes and swayed for a minute, when he opened them, his eyes they were red. Malcolm looked at him but he had no sympathy for him. Malachi took Andrew away, Malcolm went back to talking. Malachi and Andrew sat on the couch. Malachi was talking with his hands; Andrew's head was hanging low.

Malachi came back to Andrew's place and the four of us proceeded to get completely messed up. One of his brothers called and Andrew told him everything. In the morning as Malachi was leaving Jennay came over with fire in her eyes. Even though my body screamed at me for moving, I threw up the peace symbol and I left. Hubby was crawling out, but he was moving too slow for me. I knocked on Tanisha's door. She looked at me then she looked up at Drew's door, we could hear Jennay going off. She shook her head in disappointment. I laid on her floor then she brought me a huge glass of water. "How involved is Toya?" She asked me.

"It's about Toya." I said

She sat on the floor next to me. "That girl ain't nothing but trouble. She always has been. I can't even be around Drew all like we used to cause of her. Sasha don't wanna come back out here, partly cause she don't wanna deal with her."

"Who's Sasha?"

"His cousin, we were like sisters for the longest." Then she got up; she brought a picture of them when they were younger.

"Look at you dressed like a girl." I said

"I am a girl!" She said snatching her picture back.

"I know, but there you look it!" I said smiling

"I look like a girl now." She said

"You know what I mean." I said

"No I don't, what are you trying to say?"

I sat there confused. She was standing in front of me in men's boxers, sports bra, and a wife beater. Her hair was braided as usual, but she never wore a feminine style or anything. She didn't carry herself like she wanted to be acknowledged as a girl, so I just looked at her. When she kept waiting for my response I scratched my head. "I'm confused. Do you want to look like a girl?"

"Doesn't matter, I'm a girl!"

"Yes, you are a girl, that's undeniable." Then I swallowed, "why am I in trouble?"

She smiled, "you're not in trouble, just don't try to assign some weirdness to me. I'm a girl, girl feelings, girl thoughts, girl needs. Don't forget it!"

"Don't get mad at me." I put my hands out. She smiled and nodded. "Why don't you date guys?"

She turned her eyes up, "it's a long story, and more than I have the capacity to dig into right now. But I had a boyfriend before, and he was really good to me too. Maybe we were too young or whatever, but here I am."

"That was really vague but deep all at the same time."

"So you're gonna go visit Latia." She said changing the subject.

"You talk to Latia?"

"All the time."

"She told you about Mitchell?" My chest was on fire. It's taken all my strength not to tell her what happened. But I wasn't gonna tell her until she told me. That night Malcolm had someone take Melissa home, and I haven't really spoken with her since. I know none of it was her fault or anything, but it's just hard to think about her without thinking about Latia, I'm disappointed.

"They broke up a long time ago, not much else to tell." I could tell Tanisha knew more, if I didn't know better I would've believed she didn't know. But I knew she knew. "Why are you looking at me like that? Is there more?" She asked

"You tell me." I said taking a drink.

Her eyes bounced around, "you guys got any plans or you gonna wing it once you get out there?" I stared at her for a minute. Then she lowered her eyes. "Yussef I gotta lay low. I'm gonna go into law enforcement. I can't directly know about the stuff that happens. You protect me, I protect you. Feel me?"

"Yea" I said not taking my eyes off of her.

"Tanisha?" A barely dressed female was standing in her doorway; it looked like she just woke up.

"This is Yussef." Tanisha said, the girl looked at me, scrunched up her nose and then back at Tanisha. Tanisha exhaled, "excuse me Yussef. She's rude." She said as she went to her room and pushed the girl backwards into her room shutting the door behind herself. I downed my water, went to the kitchen and poured another glass. I could hear them in her room fussing. I was preparing myself to walk down the street dehydrated and all. Tanisha and the girl came out both of their faces were tense. "Where you going?" She said to me.

"You need space, I'm going home." I said

"No! She's leaving, you stay!" Tanisha commanded. I threw my hands up in a surrender type motion. The girl rolled her eyes and stormed out the door. "Go ahead and lay on my bed she said." As she walked towards the door. When Tanisha opened the door, I heard Jennay again. She was screaming at Drew the way I wanted to scream at Shannon.

I laid down and as soon as my head hit the pillow, I was out. Tanisha woke me to tell me she was leaving, and to make sure the door was locked when I left. I laid there for a while telling myself I had to get up. Feeling well enough to get up, I drank some more water. Then I walked out the door, I made sure the door was locked like Tanisha said. Then I noticed I didn't hear Jennay anymore, but I didn't dare knock on the door. When I got to the street level I saw Jennay walking with Amber. They had the same devastated expression on their faces and they were walking slowly but in step with each other. I sighed for Drew; the two people he didn't want to know about his mistake knew and were devastated. I crossed the street and watched them. They mechanically said their goodbyes, then Jennay went up and Amber got in her car and left. I felt horrible for him, but I knew better than to get in the middle of their situation.

****

"Yussef Nighzell Davis!" My class and family cheered for me as I crossed the stage. It was a proud moment for me. Thanks to my sister and Malcolm not only was I graduating but I graduated with honors. I never thought of myself as a bookworm, but Malcolm had a way of encouraging my nosiness that helped me to learn in ways that I never thought were possible. I didn't tell anyone about my Honors, that was my special surprise to them. Shonda said she was coming, but I didn't hang my happiness on whether she was there or not. As long as my Grandma, G-momma, Latia, Tim, and Malcolm were there I didn't care. I was hoping my Auntie Summer, Roz, and Grandmother would come, but I wasn't gonna be torn up if they didn't make it. When I told Malcolm that they only gave me three tickets for the graduation. He told me that Amber made copies of the tickets for Andrew's graduation. He said they had a huge crowd on account of Amber's family being so big. He made enough copies for the others, but Malcolm could've cared less whether my momma and auntie Summer were there. After my ceremony I was saying goodbye to my classmates.

I was telling Tay about my plans to attend San Francisco University when I saw Shannon staring at me. I didn't smile at her, but I didn't frown either. I guess she took that as an invitation to come over and speak. She looked very pretty, her hair was freshly done, and her makeup looked really good. "Congratulations Yussef!" she said extending her arms to hug me. I didn't mind her hugging me; I got mad at myself for smelling her hair as I hugged her. She smelled great, "congrats Tay," she said to Tay who had an uncomfortable look on his face.

"Thanks Shannon, I'm gonna catch up to you in a little bit." He said to me as he walked away.

"Do you have plans for tonight?" She asked me.

"Yes" I said trying to keep my face even.

"What are you doing?" She asked

"Stuff!" I said

"Yussef, don't be like that." She said almost smiling.

"Be like what? And how am I supposed to be?" I asked her

"You're trying so hard to be cold and distant. Its ok for you to be nice to me."

I looked around; Malcolm and Tim were watching me. It was like you could almost see them shaking their heads at me. "What do you want Shannon? My family is waiting for me."

She looked back at her family and there was a guy I didn't recognize with her parents, he was the only one watching. She looked annoyed that he was watching. "I wanna see you Yussef. I am so sorry for what I did to you." Her eyes watered up.

I wanted to believe that those tears could've been real. I wanted to believe that she still loved me, and that she really did have a temporary lapse in judgment. But looking at her, and looking at that guy who didn't look like family to me, I'd be a fool to go for this. I took a step back, "who is that?" I said nodding to the guy who was watching us. She held her breath for a minute, "nobody". But she couldn't look me in my face when she told me that lie.

"Is that the guy?" I asked, my gut told me it was him.

"I don't know what you're talking about." She said looking around the lobby and refusing to look me in the face.

I looked at Malcolm and Tim, and then I sucked my teeth. I walked over to the guy. "How you doing my man?" I said with a big smile.

The guy focused mostly on Shannon I don't think he really even looked at me. "What's up?" He asked Shannon.

"Nothing," she said just above a whisper as she trailed far behind me.

Her mother and father came over. "Hello Yussef how are you?" Her mother said. She seemed surprised but happy to see me.

"Hello Ms. Walters, and I don't think we ever met." I said extending my hand to her father.

"Douglas" He said giving me eye contact

"Yussef" I said, and then I looked at the guy. "And you are?" Ms. Walters looked uncomfortable as she looked to Shannon to say something. The guy didn't take his eyes off of Shannon, so he didn't realize I was talking to him. He was definitely older than us by a few years, but I guess her parents were fine with her dating him.

"Shannon, is this the guy?" Shannon turned pale and her face pleaded with me not to say anything. But how could she think I came over here to do anything but start some mess.

"The guy?" Douglas asked

"The guy she cheated on me with." Shannon's mouth fell open as if she couldn't believe I just said that to her parents. I winked at her and gave her a prize-winning smile.

"What?" Douglas looked surprised, but Ms. Walters didn't.

I put my hands out to explain my innocence. "The only reason she told me is cause she thought I'd pay for the abortion."

Both of her parents turned pale just like Shannon, the guy finally looked at me. But he wasn't looking at me; he was just irritated with her. "ABORTION?" Ms. Walters asked "Or were you really pregnant? I never did looped back around to ask." I looked at Shannon.

"SHANNON! You're having sex!" Her mother said in complete shock.

"Momma," she opened her mouth then she closed it.

Ms. Walters stormed away, "WHAT HAVE YOU BEEN LETTING HER GET AWAY WITH?" Douglas called after Ms. Walters.

Then the guy looked at me and I stared him down, I could see a little fear behind his eyes. He wasn't a real man. I could tell he was a little scared and he didn't want anything to do with this situation. He shook his head at Shannon and walked away. Shannon was crying, she ran behind him. "STEVE! STEVE!" she called out but he kept walking.

Even though I thought that would make me feel better it didn't. I turned to my family who were all looking at this point. "What was that?" My momma asked

"Just some of her skeletons falling out the closet." I said nonchalantly.

"Did you have to do that here?" Grandma asked

"Probably not, are we gonna go eat?" I said looking at Latia who looked like she was looking for Mitchell.

We started walking and I put my arm around Latia. Melissa followed behind us looking like she was pouting a little bit. I hated when she acted all insecure and jealous. And if nobody else she knows what my sister means to me, I don't know why she would act like this. I told her to come on and I put my other arm around her. But her body remained stiff and cold. We piled in the car with my Grandma and G-momma, while my momma and Auntie Summer followed us. Melissa turned to me, "was that your ex-girlfriend?"

I looked at her amused by her sudden charge of guts. "Yes it was."

"Why did you have to act like that? When you act like that it makes it seem like you still have feelings for her."

"I have feelings about her, there's a difference."

"Why do you care who he has feelings for?" G-momma said turning around in her seat.

I smiled at her cause she brought this on herself. "I care about him." She said

"What does that mean? Are you guys dating?" G-momma asked, Grandma looked at us in the rearview mirror.

"Yes" she said proudly.

Latia and I shook our heads at her. "Yussef are you going to get married?" G-momma said

"I'm too young G-momma." I said already exhausted from this upcoming lecture. I looked at Melissa with evil eyes.

"So why are you dating if you're not ready to take a wife? You know that's only gonna lead to trouble don't you? And what happened with Shannon? Did you get that girl in trouble?"

I smiled, "what do you mean?"

"Her folks seemed awfully upset." Grandma said

"Oh well yea I did. By asking a question it shed some light on a truth." I said
"Did you have intercourse with that girl?" G-momma asked
I looked at Latia for help; she closed her eyes and shook her head. We were subjected to a LONG lecture all the way to Shylight. My Grandma and G-momma took turns tag teaming me. I guess it was pay back for telling on Shannon. Before I could sit down Malcolm took me in his office. He and Tim then lectured me about what I did to Shannon. It annoyed me that they felt that I was out of line, after what she did to me, I felt she deserves everything she gets. So I sat there taking it all in not saying anything. When I got back to the table Latia was the only one who was all smiles. After we ordered she and I went on the dance floor. I asked her what was up with her friend. She tried to explain to me that Melissa really cared about me, and she didn't feel like I was feeling her as much as she was feeling me. I explained to Latia that I wasn't gonna blindly jump into an all out relationship with her when she got guys calling all hours of the night even after the quote unquote start of our relationship. Latia asked why would I even halfway claim her if I didn't see our relationship going anywhere? I told her it made Melissa happy, so it wasn't a big deal. She told me leaving stuff like this open would not workout well for me. We had a nice dinner, and then everyone pulled out gifts for me. I wasn't expecting gifts, so the fact that everyone took time out to think about what they thought I would like and used their hard earned money for a gift for me hit me in my chest. As they set the gifts on the table my Grandmother walked in slowly. To look at her you could tell that her coming was still very difficult. Tears streamed down her face as soon as she laid eyes on me. Looking at her and seeing how much she loves my father was always hard on me. She touched my hair, and then she said it gave me my own look, but I still looked exactly like him. Tanisha showed up with a gift from her and Roz. She said Roz sent her regrets she wasn't feeling well. I could tell by the look on Tanisha's face that there was more to the situation than she wasn't feeling well. I could fight Yuri everyday, but if she was gonna stick with him there was nothing I could do but wait for her to be done with him.
Melissa gave me a backpack for school and she filled it with apple and sour apple jolly ranchers. I smiled and thanked her. My Grandma and G-momma gave me a big reference bible that had my name engraved on the lower right hand corner of the front. Grandma told me to always remember my roots. I thanked her for the bible. I knew I needed to read it, but I had too many emotions going on to do that right now. My momma and Auntie Summer pulled their pennies together and got a leather jacket that I would look good on my bike in. Malcolm and Tim each handed me small boxes. Inside Tim's box there was a Rolex and a pair of diamond cuff links. Tim said to wear them whenever I put suits on, which meant when I went to service. I took that as a sign that he encouraged my interest in God, even though he would only listen whenever I talked about him. Tanisha gave me a framed picture of the four of us. My father, her mother, her, and me. I was really little probably eight or something. I knew it was one of those rare occasions where I actually got to go with my father. I thanked Tanisha for the picture. Then my Grandmother gave me a green gift bag that was kind of heavy. When I took out the paper there was a photo album in it. A lump formed in my throat. There were tons of pictures of my father; next to each picture she wrote approximately when the picture was taken and who was in the pictures. A lot of them had family I'd never met in them, then others who were familiar but barely. Latia cried as she traced our father's face. Malcolm came over and looked at some of the pictures then he went back to his seat. I kept swallowing but the lump wouldn't go away. Then Latia was crying which really didn't help my situation either. She wasn't crying out loud but tears were pouring down her face. I pointed at one of the pictures that was kind of close on his face. "You look just like him." I said to her. Why did I say that? She cried

harder. I put the book down and I hugged her. Then our grandmother joined in the hug; we sat there hugging for a long time.

"I wish things could've been different with you guys. I wish you knew me like you know your other grandparents. But my son didn't make the best choices in women." I glanced at my momma who swallowed when my grandmother said it. "He had choices and he didn't make the best ones. I love you guys, and I wish things could've been different." She said crying.

"Alright, alright." Malcolm said looking uncomfortable with the emotion washing over him. "Open mine." I wiped Latia's tears, and then I kissed her and my grandmother's cheek thanking her for the album. I took a deep breath then I opened Malcolm's gift. There was a singular key, but it was a car key. I looked at him with a big grin. "It's within reason, so don't think bigger than you should be thinking right about now. But I wanted to acknowledge how much you stepped up." Then Tim nudged him, "and to show how proud I am of you." He said like it took everything in him to say.

"Aw! Uncle Blackie I love you too!" I said with a big smile demanding all emotion to stay out of my face and voice. Malcolm was not amused by my comment, Tim turned his head to hide that he was laughing. I smiled at him with a toothy grin, and he stared at me. "Is it here?"

"You and Latia are riding with me." He said

I knew that meant Melissa couldn't come, which was fine by me. I couldn't wait to get on the plane with Latia and be away for a while. I love The Bay it will always be home, but I need a vacation. After dinner Latia and I put Melissa in the car with Grandma and G-momma then we got in the car with Tim and Malcolm. "You know she's getting the ultimate lecture about how she needs to be more chase, etc. I wouldn't wanna be her." Latia said

"She should've kept her mouth shut, that's her fault." I said

"Your Grandma means well. And I don't think Melissa had any intended malice against you by saying anything. She really cares about you."

"She's got a funny way of showing it." I said

"You're faulting her for caring for you?" She said

I shot Latia a look, cause I didn't want to discuss it. When we pulled up to Malcolm's house there was a car out front. A woman was waiting in it. Malcolm exhaled when he saw her. Tim looked at Malcolm, and Malcolm was shaking his head. "Talk about a needy female. This one stays in competition." Then he turned to Latia, "don't ever be this dumb!" Then he got out of the car.

Tim exhaled then he told us to come along. Malcolm stood by the driver's side of the car. The woman got out of her car, and slowly walked towards the car. She was focused on Malcolm and trying to read his face. Latia's eyes got wide, and then she mouthed to me "'Torrie!" I shook my head, which was my reaction the first time I met her. Torrie is this high profile singer. She sings, dances, writes her own music, and she's just an all around mega star. On TV they make her seem like she's so sweet and nice, but when you get to know her you realize all she's ever focused on is herself. I don't know how she met Malcolm, but I love to watch him check her. She's always bending over backwards for him, and he could careless. From time to time she tries to throw a fit about Malcolm's shrine to Amber in his house. That's when he kicks her out, and then she's begging him to forgive her. She comes with some ridiculously huge and expensive gift that he accepts, but he still doesn't give her what she wants.

One time we were all drinking and she was completely tore up. She was declaring her love for Malcolm; the look on his face was priceless. Sometimes I try to practice giving that blank of a stare. When he didn't respond with a "I like you too" or anything like that she started crying. Then she fell on my shoulder crying, I looked at Malcolm to tell me what to do. Malcolm just watched. But let me tell you when she came over that night.... Lets just say, she came over dressed like she was on the prowl. Drew and Hubby were there at first, but when she became too touchy feely. They left, which left only me. So she's crying on my shoulder, and when I tried to gently push away, she threw her big and beautiful legs around me and started kissing on me. I couldn't believe it, I pushed her on the floor and I went completely off. I forgot Malcolm was right there. Her tears didn't stop me from going off. Until that night I was a little star struck when I saw her too. But now she looks like any other lap dog.

By the way she's approaching she must've done something else. "Hello Malcolm" she said

Malcolm kept his eyes, which were cold and unfeeling on her. "Latia this is Torrie." Torrie didn't take her eyes off of Malcolm. "Hi" she said unenthusiastically

Latia frowned then she looked at me, and I shook my head like, yep that's how she acts. I looked around I didn't see my car sitting outside. "Kids, lets go inside." Tim said "What's her problem?" Latia asked

"She's so focused on winning, that she can't see she's always been the loser." Tim said Latia didn't understand. I took her to the stairs and I pointed up at Amber's picture. "She already won, there's no competition, that idiot refuses to let it go."

"Who's that?" Latia asked

"That's his baby momma." I said

"Amber's my daughter." Tim said

"Really?" Latia said completely surprised. "It doesn't bother you when he has other females around?"

"I've known Malcolm since he was a child. He's still got some growing to do before he's ready for my daughter. If he tried to hide who he is from me he'd be dead. That's just the relationship we have."

"Does your daughter love him?" She asked

"Very much." He said, "but she's young as well." He exhaled, "they got started too young. They're trying to grow up, while raising children. Not that it can't happen, but those two get in their own way most of the time."

Then Malcolm came in the door with Torrie on his heels. When she came in the door she paused when she saw Latia. "Who are you?"

We all looked at Malcolm, who looked completely annoyed. "You never pay attention. I swear you are so dumb!"

"Malcolm come on now!" Tim said

Malcolm exhaled. "Torrie I just introduced her to you outside." Then his voice got lower. "Don't ever show up at my house uninvited and question who's in it!" Torrie jumped, and then he looked at Latia. "Don't tell her your name again."

Torrie put her coat and purse on the coatrack and then she went in the kitchen. Malcolm told us to come upstairs. We followed him into his TV room. Then he asked Latia where she planned to live after she graduated. She told him that she already has an excellent job offer from a company out here in The Bay when she graduates. He explained that when she graduated he needed to set her up in a house with a car, and whatever she needed. Latia smiled while her eyes watered. Since I was going to school in the city my father's old apartment was available for me whenever I was ready to move. I asked him how was that possible. He told me that our father bought the building and that we were the rightful owners of the building now. We sat up there for about a good hour or so going over everything our father left for us. At certain moments Malcolm would pause and kind of hold his breath. Seeing him emotional was a trip cause you could see him shut down. Latia still asked him questions about our father. He answered to the best of his ability. That lump was back in my throat. All three of us sat there suspended and exhausted as if we were coming up with mathematical equations. The smells from the kitchen were delicious, and then Torrie called up to us from downstairs to come eat. Malcolm told us to wash our hands. I wasn't hungry yet since we left Shylight not too long ago, but I was curious about the smell. When I came downstairs Tim was leaving. I assume he stayed downstairs to make sure she didn't poison anything. Malcolm and Latia were already sitting at the table. When I sat down she served our plates, slamming Latia's plate a little, and then she started cleaning the kitchen. We all tasted our food, it was good but none of us were really hungry. So we all sat there kind of off into our thoughts.

"Thank you for everything Malcolm. I appreciate everything you've done for me." Latia said

Torrie stopped in her tracks; she gave Latia the evilest stare. "What is wrong with you?" Malcolm said to Torrie.

"Who is she?" She said completely pissed.

"What did I just tell you?" Malcolm said

"I'm sick of this Malcolm I'm over here trying to be all domestic for you. Just to make you happy. You act like you don't know who I am!" I could tell it was coming, she was gonna step out of bounds and Malcolm was gonna kick her out again. "I'm sick of putting up with your crap Malcolm. It's bad enough you got pictures of that trick all over this...."

Malcolm moved so fast, she didn't have a chance to react. You could see him restraining himself from slapping her down. He picked her up and she started swinging wild and kicking. "How many times I gotta tell you to keep Amber out your mouth!" Because of all the wiggling she was doing Malcolm dropped her. "Get out of my house!" Malcolm said standing over her.

I looked at Latia and she was taking off her earrings. "What are you getting ready to do?" I asked in disbelief. My sister's not a fighter.

"I'll take her out Malcolm!" Latia said standing.

Malcolm smiled, something he rarely did. "Thank you but no, she can leave on her own." As if he wasn't just mad at Torrie, he walked over and hugged Latia for the first time ever.

Torrie popped up and started to charge at Malcolm and Latia. I hopped over the table. "No you don't! Not today!" I said pushing her shoulders back.

"Boy! Move out my way!" She screamed

"I think they need some privacy." I said to mess with her.

"WHAT???? You expect me to play second fiddle to her and Amber!"

The sound of her saying Amber's name jerked Malcolm's whole body. He started charging at her and she ran. "You better not even dream about Amber! Get out of my house and DONT EVER COME BACK!" Malcolm yelled after her. She ran out the door. Malcolm took her jacket and purse off the coat-rack and threw it to her out the door, and then he slammed it shut. We all stood in the window watching her cry and pick up her things off the front yard. Her purse wasn't closed when Malcolm threw it so everything spilled out. "I think I might be getting too old for this stuff." Malcolm said exhaling.

Latia smiled at him, "Are you talking about the lady in the picture?"

Malcolm looked at her, I expected him to shrug her off like he does me or something like that. "Yea, we're not getting any younger. She broke up with the pretty boy, a woman like that doesn't stay single for too long. I'm getting tired of these idiots."

I stood there in shock; Malcolm has never given me that much information. I couldn't help but feel a little jealous. "Uncle Blackie! How come you don't share with me like that?"

Malcolm looked at me with a serious face. "With comments like that you wonder why!" His face remained serious. "Latia, I appreciate the gesture. But you do know she would've beat you down don't you?" His eyes were glued to Torrie who was crying and still looking for her stuff in the yard.

Latia laughed, "I couldn't just sit here and do nothing. I would've tried my best to do something."

Malcolm smiled AGAIN and put his arm around Latia, and kissed her forehead. "Thanks"

I frowned at Malcolm. He looked at me as if he didn't know why I could possibly be upset. "What?" I kept staring. "You forgot I told you I was proud of you just a few hours ago?" Oh yea! I smiled and made him hug me too, I felt like a big ole kid. We stood there watching a distraught Torrie give up on finding whatever she was looking for in the front yard.

A few hours later we went to my father's apartment, in the garage my father's car was covered by a tarp. That did it, I couldn't help it tears burst out of my eyes. I sat in the driver's seat. I remembered our last drive to Fresno together. I could clearly see my father sitting in this car. I could hear his voice; it was like I could smell him. My reaction to the car told Latia that it was our father's car. She didn't have the reaction I had to the car, but she was there for me. Malcolm couldn't take it; he walked out of the garage. There was no way I was driving this car, except on special occasions. I moved the car to the back of the garage. There was enough room to park my bike and my nice car in front of this car. I would park my buckets on the street. I told Latia about our last trip in that car. She didn't recognize the car, but she listened to my stories anyways. Then we went up to the apartment. Latia said she had only been there once. Everything was covered and you could tell the place had been closed up for a long time. Malcolm was out on the balcony looking out over Lake Merritt. At night it was completely beautiful. We went out on the balcony with Malcolm. "I haven't been here since just before the funeral, this is heavy." He said, "I'll take you to your car, but forgive me for not hanging around here. There's too much history here." His eyes were red.

When we got in the car it was completely silent. "So I leave tomorrow Malcolm. Will you come visit me before I graduate?" Latia asked

"Of course! Hopefully I'll have my lady with me so you guys can meet officially." He said

"You really love her, huh." Latia leaned in on her arm supporting her face.

Malcolm smiled, I tell you he was in rare form today. All these smiles and love expressions were unlike him. "She's always been my heart, since we were kids."

Latia turned into a giggly girl as Malcolm told her the story of how he met Amber, all the reasons why he loved her. I sat there in awe, cause I had never heard any of this before. I guess if a man like Malcolm could have his nose open over a female, there was room for me to let someone in. "How do you know which female deserves to be let in?" I asked

"That's up to you to decide. I can't tell you what will make it click for you. But one day you'll find yourself unable to think about anything or anyone other than her. Until then don't worry about it or stress about it. It'll happen when it happens."

"I can't see it. What do you think of Melissa?"

"Doesn't matter what I think of her, its what you think of her." Malcolm said

"I don't trust her, I can't do it. Sorry Latia, your friend is nice. But I can't be her dedicated man." I said

Latia exhaled, "you know this is gonna affect our friendship. Why would you date her if you knew you weren't feeling her?"

Invisible

"I was feeling her at first, but she became too much. She gave me everything and then started making demands. Who does that?" I asked

"Lots of females do that." She said defensively.

"You better never! You make your demands up front. If he can't meet them, at least you know while you're still intact."

"Now you tell me." She said looking out the window

"Are you dating someone right now?" Malcolm asked

"No, I've been focused on school. I don't have time for another heart break."

Malcolm glanced at me in the rearview mirror. "So do you want to live in the building after graduation? Or you want your own spot?" That was Malcolm's way of telling me to leave her alone.

I sat back in the car and told myself to chill out cause I knew I was emotional from the day I had. When we got to my house, I got my things then I pulled out the bed in the couch because I gave Latia my bed. She came in the living room in her pajamas, slippers, and a robe. She folded her legs as she sat on the other couch. It was like old times, we talked the night away as if we weren't going to spend the next month and a half together. I kept stopping myself from mentioning Mitchell but I wanted to.

In the morning I made breakfast for everyone pancakes, bacon, and eggs. It's been my mission to get more familiar with the kitchen. We sat at the table like a family, and it felt good to look into the faces of my beloved women.

Grandma and G-momma took us to the San Francisco airport mid-morning. Latia insisted on calling Malcolm to thank him again for everything. When I talked to him I could hear a smile in his voice. We boarded our plane, and I had a funny feeling in my stomach and I could feel slight heat on my neck. Fortunately we had a direct flight and I was able to knock out as soon as we lifted. Latia slept most of the flight as well. Almost six hours later we landed in Philadelphia. As we walked through the terminal people were staring at the TVs. They had looks of real concern and horror on their faces. Latia and I both slowed down as we saw Torrie's pictures and footage of Torrie all over the screen. A woman in the airport ran up to the monitor next to us screaming and crying. "What's going on? Is she dead? Please don't say she's dead!" The woman was almost in all out hysterics. The channel we were looking at wasn't giving us details just live news feed from Amber's school. They showed Torrie's car full of bullets and there was another car wrapped around a telephone poll, it was one of Mister's guy's car. I saw Tim and Amber's family in the background. I didn't see Malcolm or Amber. I could hear reporting coming from another monitor so I ran over and Latia and the hysterical lady followed me. "So for those of you just tuning in, we are live on the scene of an attempted murder of the R & B singer and all over sensation Torrie Rowe! The police are reporting that crazed fans shot at her in a drive by fashion in front of The North Star Dance Company, which is owned by her friend and choreographer of all of her best videos Amber Wallace. Torrie's bodyguard returned fire which resulted in the crash you see here." They showed the car all mangled. "There were a total of four passengers in the car. Two died upon impact, and we just received word that another was pronounced dead upon arrival to the hospital. The final gunman is in critical condition we don't know if he's going to make it. We can't get a hold of anyone at the school for an official statement. Torrie has been taken by ambulance to a local hospital, we're awaiting word to know how she's doing." The news reporter said

"Is she hurt?" The hysterical woman screamed at the screen.

Latia looked stressed, I grabbed her hand and pulled her away from the screen. I told her we'd call as soon as we got to her apartment. We got the rest of our luggage and then we caught the shuttle to the train station. Then we caught the train to New Jersey. Everywhere we went people were besides their selves worried about Torrie. Other celebrities were expressing their concerns and best wishes to Torrie. As we were walking in the door Latia was telling me to call. Malcolm didn't answer any of his lines, neither did Andrew. I was starting to feel a little stressed, but I tried to keep my face even because Latia was watching me. I called Tim and he answered. I put the phone between Latia and I's ears so we could hear him together. He said Torrie went up to the school to confront Amber. Malcolm got there a few minutes later. Then Brad's guys struck at them. He said everyone was ok, and that it was good that I was on the other side of the country right now. I gave him Latia's number and told them to keep us up to date.

****

Weeks passed before Malcolm called. When I asked him how things were going out there. His reply was simply, "stressful"! He said this battle with Brad was pretty ridiculous. He asked how our visit was going, and I told him we were having a blast, cause we were. Latia took me everywhere; we were on adventures the whole time. I had to be Lamont Jenkins whenever we went out though. Otherwise I wouldn't have been legal to do anything.

"I need to put you and Latia on assignment, can you do it?" He asked

Obviously if he mentioned Latia it couldn't be dangerous, and like we'd ever say no. "OF COURSE MALCOLM! What do you need?"

He told me he wanted me to be invisible, Amber was in New York with their two youngest. She was going to an awards ceremony, and he wanted to make sure there was someone there who had her back just like they'd have his. He said that he has reason to believe that Brad was going to try to strike at Amber there; and make it look like a fan or paparazzi. I felt honored that he would trust me like that; I know how special she is to him. He explained he wanted us to be as invisible as possible, but it wouldn't be easy cause his "mini-me" would more than likely spot us. The ceremony was black tie so I would need a tux and Latia would need all the girlie stuff as she called it. He told me the room was on my credit card for whatever I needed. He told me to make sure Latia had fun as well. We had a week and a half to get ready. Latia was so excited when I told her we had been commissioned to go to a Black Tie party where celebrities were guaranteed to be. Malcolm booked rooms for us at the same hotel that Amber would be staying in. Latia made hair appointments for both of us to get our locs tightened a couple days before. The hardest part was finding her dress. Latia drug me from store to store. I thanked the heavens when she finally found a dress. BUT THEN, we had to find shoes and all the stuff I could care less about. I thought I was gonna lose my mind! Everything was a big deal. I was so happy when her stuff was done and decided for. So then we go to the tuxedo store and I randomly picked a tux. Of course Latia wasn't having that, she had me try on a few styles to figure out which cut looked best on me. After I stopped fighting her and took notes of the things she pointed out, we all agreed Hugo Boss was the way to go. I looked at my reflection and I loved what I saw. Latia and I started reciting lines back and forth from her most favorite movie "I'm like Jet magazine over here, check it!". The salesgirl even chimed in on the fun. After the tailoring and everything my things would be available for delivery on the day of the party.

The day of the party, we did it up real big at the hotel. After I review the layout of the venue for the event tonight, and all possible last minute exit routes, public transit schedules, different companies for car service for hire, etc. Latia convinced me that facials, manicures, and massages aren't just for women. I went to her room feeling lite as a feather. Our clothes arrived like clockwork. I explained to Latia that there was no room for tardiness in Malcolm's world. And being on time was late. The party started at eight, so that meant that Amber would leave no later than seven-thirty, I told her we had to be ready to go no later than six-thirty to six-forty-five. Latia was ready by six-fifteen, I love my sister. We were in the lobby at seven and our car service arrived at the same time as Amber's limo. She was even more beautiful in person. I hadn't seen her directly since that day outside Andrew's apartment. Even in walking to her limo, you could tell she wasn't like my momma. She loved her boys and they loved her. Malcolm wasn't kidding about his mini-me either. He was checking everyone in the lobby as they walked through. There was no smile on his face, when he looked at me he started with my eyes then down. Like he was taking a mental picture. He did that with everyone and it happened so fast unless you were paying attention you'd miss it. I couldn't tell how old he was or the other, but I could tell he was the oldest of the two. We walked out behind them and got in our car service behind their limo. When we got to the event both of the boys were looking at us. Both of them were on point, and they seemed more like bodyguards than sons in tow. When they observed us walking to the other table giving my name and information they relaxed some, but not much. I couldn't believe I was on their radar that fast. I was impressed by how well they paid attention to their surroundings, Malcolm has trained them well.

We found our table, and as I was pulling out Latia's chair this older white lady came up to me. "Excuse me buster rhymes I presume?"

Latia fell out laughing. I looked at her unamused by this. "No ma'am, my name is Lamont. I saw Busta over there." I said pointing him out to the left.

She turned a little red. "Oh dear! I'm so sorry sweetheart." Then she hurried away. Latia couldn't get it together, she was still laughing. "Alright! Lets see if you're still laughing when someone mistakes you for Whoopi Goldberg."

"Hey, just call me Miss Ciely." She said

Amber was networking the whole evening. I could see why Malcolm liked her; her beauty wasn't even the weapon she was using tonight. But no matter where she went one if not both of her boys were near her the whole evening.

Then it happened, I saw the rapper Comfort giving himself the pep talk to approach Amber. At first Amber wasn't getting it. You could tell she was handling him like she would anyone else. Then he gave her that bashful smile and her eyes softened, you could see the light bulb go off. Her sons picked up on the exchange at the same time, and the oldest came over to shut it down. But not before she gave Comfort her card.

All in all the evening was nice, as they're body language started to suggest their departure I looked for Latia. She caught the attention of this rapper who goes by the name Shameless. He was actually talking and not completely spitting game at her. I walked over to the table, and I told her I would be right back. Then I walked outside and pretended to be smoking a cigarette. There were paparazzi all around. Amber's limo pulled up and you saw the cameras getting ready. I slowly walked in their path to their car so that I could be there when the cameras closed in. One guy stood out as suspicious to me. With a son on either side they walked out the building. Amber took a deep breath when she realized they were coming for her. The guy moved in reaching for his pocket. I reached for mine. The boys kept everyone back, but this guy was moving more determined. He could be aggressive paparazzi, but I decided he was going down regardless. I saw something shiny coming from his pocket, I couldn't tell if it was a knife or not. He was so focused on Amber he didn't look at me once. I sprayed his entire face. The youngest son noticed the guy's scream first and he saw my hand go back in my pocket. He smiled and continued forward. I watched them get in their limo and I got in a car service. I told him to follow the limo but to stay back. I told him I had two hundred if he did exactly what I told him to do. There weren't paparazzi at the hotel. Both of them saw me in the car, I nodded to them and they nodded back as they casually walked inside with their mother.

Chapter 8

"Who are you?" She said with as much attitude as she could muster.

I looked at her, she don't even know me to be acting like this. I looked at Drew and Hubby, "anyways this is Randi, and we go way back."

"Hello Randi, I'm Nicole. And this extremely rude female is my friend Sonya."

"Nice to meet you." Randi said as she sat down.

"Seriously who is he?" Sonya asked Nicole

"What difference does it make? You don't know him is all." Hubby said as the voice to Andrew's irritation.

"Drew is that you?" I said pointing at Sonya as I sat down.

Andrew rolled his eyes, "I'm single!"

Sonya looked embarrassed. Andrew's comment wounded her little ego. I guess she thought a lot of herself cause she was paired up with Andrew but he wasn't interested. It's not enough to be pretty, and she seemed to have that underlying venom that would make you snatch her up. Randi leaned in, "who's your friend?" She had that goofy for Drew look all these females get.

"That's Drew! You interested?" I asked to clarify.

"Is he a good guy?" She asked

"The best! But if you're looking for a relationship you need to give him some space right now. He's rebounding."

The waitress came to clear their drinks. "Did you guys want something?" She said pointing at Randi and I.

Randi looked stuck, "I'll have a Hennessy and can you bring her a Long Island?"

The waitress nodded and walked away. "I Like those shoes, they're real cute!" Nicole said to Randi

"Thank you I was admiring yours and those earrings." Randi replied

Sonya exhaled checked her attitude and then joined in their girlie talk. Andrew leaned into Hubby and I. "Don't bring this girl without someone for her. She runs her mouth too much! I'd hit it, but then Nicole gonna be mad that I ran up in her friend. You know how they do!" Drew's eyes were cold. When he found out Jennay wasn't coming back to Berkeley he's kind of been on the warpath. Hit 'em and quit 'em.

"Your girl seems cool." Hubby said

"Just a friend, she's too fragile. Besides ten seconds in, and she's looking at this pretty boy over here." I said nodding at Andrew.

"I am pretty aren't I!" Andrew said jokingly. "She's fragile?"

"Yea, you would devastate her. I'm talking dang near suicidal." I warned.

"That sounds like some single white female stuff." Hubby said

"I could do crazy." Andrew said like he was thinking about it.

"You already do crazy. But this one is fragile, don't do her like that." I said

"You wanna switch?" Andrew asked

Hubby laughed, "she's that bad man?"

"Her mouth doesn't stop! I said hi and she's almost telling me my whole life story. I'm cool!" Andrew said

"What up?" Andrew's cousin Jeff said.

Andrew stood up to hug him. "You didn't tell me you were coming."

Randi tugged at my jacket. "Who's that?"

"Jeff, Andrew's cousin."

"Andrew's mixed too?" She asked including herself in that equation.

"I guess you could say that." Then she had that look in her eyes again. "You gonna have to figure out which direction you're going in." I said irritated.

"Ok! Ok! I'm sorry. Is he cool?" She asked

"We've hung out a few times, he's good people." I said

"Ok" she said shooting eyes in Jeff's direction.

"Who's this?" Jeff said looking at Sonya and Randi. "Drew is this you?" Andrew gave Jeff the same response he gave me. Jeff laughed at Sonya though. "And how about this little flower over here?" He said to Randi.

"This is Randi, we go way back, but she's unattached." I said

"You wanna dance?" He asked her. By the way she agreed I could tell she wasn't expecting much.

We sat back knowing we were gonna be amused. Her goofy behind started with a two-step. I guess she missed the Oakland accent when he spoke. We all laughed at her when she had complete surprise on her face as he broke her down on the dance floor. Hubby was just about rolling on the floor he was laughing so hard. They stayed on the dance floor for a long time, Randi was thoroughly enjoying herself. "So much for my future wife." Andrew said

Sonya got up and walked away, Nicole shot a look at Hubby. He blew air, when she walked after her friend Hubby turned to Andrew. "You don't like her you don't have to date her. But don't be rude, all that's gonna do is get me in trouble. I'm not letting none of ya'll get between me and my lady!" Hubby said it nicely but he wasn't playing. I thought Andrew was gonna blow up, but he knew he was wrong. He sat back and watched Jeff and Randi. It looked like they were enjoying each other thoroughly. I was happy for her, but I wanted someone of my own. When I looked at Andrew he looked like he was thinking the same thing. Andrew looked around the club, and then he tapped me. "I think I see our dates for tonight."

"You sure you wanna do that right now? You heard what he just said." I said pointing at Hubby who looked pissed off and like he couldn't believe Andrew.

"Did I not just speak? What is wrong with you? Keep this up and we ain't gonna be friends no more." Hubby was serious.

"Alright! Alright! I'll be cool with motor mouth. Where she at?" He said looking around.

"I'm done! Good night Drew! Yussef please take him home if he don't find a chicken head to drive him." Then Hubby got up and walked away mad.

Andrew sat back; I could tell he was struggling with feeling remorse for what he just did. But then I could see it turn off. Andrew was in pain and in destructive mode. "Let's go meet these chicken heads." He said to me looking around the club.

I looked up, and that's when I saw her. She was beautiful! Long curly hair, soft skin, and beautiful smile. Andrew was looking in the opposite direction when I saw her. I saw her about the same time as she saw me. She smiled and I felt lightning hit my stomach. "Whoa!" is all I could muster. I had to go meet this girl.

"You ready?" Andrew said looking in the other direction.

"I'm gonna go this way, maybe we can meet up in the middle in a little bit." I said with urgency in my voice.

"Cool!" I'll take both of them then." Andrew went to the right and I went to the left. As I went to the left my hands felt clammy and I couldn't believe how nervous I felt about approaching this girl. I guess I could understand how Comfort was nervous that night when he met Amber. If the emotion I saw in him matches anything that I'm feeling right now! I completely understand it now. She whispered to her friend as I approached and they both seemed to get bashful, she likes me right? I cleared my throat, be cool! Just be calm and natural. "How you doing tonight?"

She smiled real big, "I'm good and you?" She said blushing

"I'm good now. What's your name pretty lady?" I said

"Sylvia, and this is my friend Monica."

"Nice to meet you, hello Monica." I tried to take all nervousness out of my voice.

"Hello" she said then she giggled again for her friend.

"You wanna dance?" I asked not knowing what else to say to her that would matter to me at that moment. I just wanted to be in her space. I wanted to see her move, I wanted to smell her. I wanted her! This is a first!

"Depends," she said putting her little hand on her hip. My stomach flipped at the thought of rejection.

"On?" I swallowed

"You didn't even tell me your name." She smiled again.

I tried to hide my exhale of almost relief. "I'm Yussef." I said reaching out to shake her hand.

"Yussef, that's Hebrew for Joseph right?"

That did it! My heart was beating out of my chest! No one has ever known anything about my name before. "That's right, so how about that dance?" Be COOL! I kept telling myself. She handed her purse to Monica and we were off to the dance floor. Now, I wasn't a master dancer like Andrew or Jeff, but I did ok. We had a good time, and we were both smiling on the dance floor. We stayed out there almost all night dancing up a storm. Randi looked at us and smiled real big as she seemed to shut down the place with Jeff. Sylvia and Monica went to the bathroom as the club closed. We decided to go get something to eat.

Andrew came over, "I got a hook up." He said pointing at the two girls he was talking about earlier. "You cool or you wanna come with?"

"I met somebody, I'm good." I said with a big smile.

"Alright then. Stay strapped up, and I'll catch up with you later." He said giving me a pound, and then he left.

Randi and Jeff came over, "we wanna go get something to eat. You down?" Jeff asked

"Yea, we were just saying the same thing." I said

"We? Did you meet somebody?" Randi asked somewhat surprised

"Why is that surprising? You think you the only one who can hook up?" I said

She blushed at Jeff, "no. I was just asking."

Then Sylvia and Monica seemed like they were walking in slow motion towards us.

"Whoa!" Jeff said turning his eyes away.

"Are you ready?" Sylvia asked

"Yes, these are my friends Randi and Jeff. And this is Sylvia and her friend Monica." Everyone said hello and shook hands. "Anywhere we all wanna go to eat?"

"Denny's is 24 hours right?" Monica said

"Yes, but there's a National's Hamburger right here in Jack London that's open 24 as well. How does that sound to everybody?" Jeff said

"Good to us." Monica said

Randi shook her head yes as well. "National's it is, did you guys drive here?" I was praying they said no, I wanted as much time with her as possible.

"Her brother dropped us off, we're supposed to call him when we're ready." Sylvia said

My heart jumped for joy. "I can take you guys home if you like." I was trying to be cool, but everything in me felt like I was bursting.

"That would be nice." Then she gave me that smile.

Doesn't this girl know how gorgeous she is! Her smile kills me every time she unleashes it on me. She keeps looking at me like she likes me too. This almost feels too good to be true. I told myself to stop being so pessimistic and just go with it. I opened the car doors for Sylvia and Monica, while Randi and Jeff got in the back on the other side. We decided to take one car to keep it simple. At National's the conversation flowed wonderfully. Sylvia and Monica went to Laney college in Oakland, and they lived in San Leandro. Every time she said my name that slight accent captured my attention. Everything about her is sexy to me, and I know better than to dig her this fast, but something about her keeps pulling me in. Jeff kept looking at me, but he was digging Randi in the same way. And Monica who was equally beautiful was just happy to be out with us. We sat in National's for hours talking. I asked her how she was familiar with the origin of my name. She said as a child she was friends with a Jewish family, they had an Uncle Yussef. We sat in National's so long we watched the sky turn from dark to light. None of us wanted the night to end. Jeff offered his house to hang out for a while longer. So we took him back to his car, then Randi rode with him as we followed him to his house. Monica told him his house was too big for one person. He said his brother stayed between there and LA, while he was in school getting his Master's Degree. Then he shared that he inherited the house from his parents. He grew up in this house. Randi was all smiles as he gave us the tour and pointed Monica to the guest bed where she could sleep. We called ourselves attempting to watch a movie, and one by one we all passed out. I was the last one though. Sylvia laid her head on my shoulder and I sat there staring at her for a long time. She was so beautiful to me; her snore didn't even bother me. This was the start of something great I could feel it in my stomach.

****

"You make me feel! You make me feel, like a natural woman........." Sylvia's voice had me hypnotized I didn't expect that voice to come from her. Her voice was amazing and she sang matter of factly like she wasn't giving her best effort.
"Oh my God girl! Where does that voice come from?" I said when she was done.
She smiled, "did you like it?"
"I loved it!" I said leaning over to kiss her morning breath and all.
"Oh! Baby, don't kiss me like that! You'll get me going again." She said with an evil grin.
That was all the invitation I needed to take her again. This girl has infected my soul, all I think about is Sylvia and I can't get enough of her. The days I stayed away from her, were because I actually forced myself to give her some space. But when I did that she called me back, she wanted to be with me as much as I wanted to be with her. I know I thought I was in love with Shannon, but I was still fooling with Judy and anyone not directly related to her. With Sylvia I don't want to be with anyone else.
I play it cool with Judy though, since she works at the DMV she could mess all my stuff up. My Lamont Jenkins and Jeremy King authentic identifications could be compromised. Even though messing me up could mess her up as well. But I'd rather not even have to deal with a woman scorned. Judy knows I have a girlfriend and she seems to be ok with it most times. When I see her now, its mostly to keep her happy so that she keeps me happy.
"I love making love to you!" She said to me
"I love you!" I said
She kissed me again. "Do you regret letting me move in with you?"
"Not at all! I love waking up to you every morning, and going to sleep to you at night." I said
"And me disturbing your sleep in the middle of the night?" she smiled
"That too!" I said kissing her again.
Then she touched my bruises on my ribs. I jumped when she touched it. "I HATE that you're out there fighting like some common hoodlum!"
"Well what am I supposed to do? I can't leave my boy hanging." I said

"Tell him to stop picking fights. I haven't met this guy but all he does is cause drama in your life. I get nervous every time you go out with him."

Andrew has been an extreme wild card these days. Toya's boyfriend dumped her after his mother met her and told him to get rid of her. Smart mother, but all Toya's done is bring him more drama. Andrew's fuse has gotten so short, and he's fighting and sometimes killing over things I'd rather walk away from. Its like he's lost his mind a little bit. I know he's still hurt about Jennay, but at some point he's gotta change or he's gonna end up with a toe tag. Malcolm has tried to talk to him a few times, but they end up in arguments and almost fights. Thank goodness for Tim, I'd hate to see the day they actually went to blows. I don't know that Malcolm would regard him as his son in that space.

"Why is he so angry?" She asked

"He just is." I said not wanting to talk about Andrew. They hadn't met, and that was on purpose. Andrew is all over the place and something tells me to keep my treasure to myself. We've hung out a lot with Jeff and Randi, who have seemed to take to each other just like Sylvia and I.

"Why don't you ever want to talk about him?"

"What do you want me to say about another man to you?" I said looking in her eyes.

"Nothing, I guess. You guys are close and I've never met him. Are you ashamed of me or him?"

"Maybe I just wanna keep the two of you separate, why would I ever be ashamed of you?"

"I don't know. I haven't met your mother, or your Grandma and G-momma. All these people who are so important to you and your life are separate from me. Why?"

"I don't like my mother, you wanna meet her that's fine. I'll make that happen soon. My Grandma and G-momma are gonna be on us for living in sin. They're very old school. I'm not ready to go through that right now. That's not even about you. And my cousin Drew is going through something's right now. I'd rather that you meet him once he's calmed down. Can't I be a little selfish with my love right now? I want you all to myself." I said taking her into my arms.

She laughed, "I guess so. I just don't want to be your well-kept secret. You've met my entire family."

"Yea and they were so excited to meet me." I said

"I've never dated a black guy, they weren't expecting you."

"What kind of name did they think Yussef was gonna be?"

"Maybe they missed your name when I told them about you. But they love you now. Come on you know that."

"Yea, they warmed up to me." They especially warmed up to me when she could move in rent-free and not have to work. Her family was definitely full of opportunist. Thankfully my baby wasn't like her family.

"Cause you're so lovable." She said twirling my locs in her fingers. "Babe, Monica and I are going to go to the mall today, can I have some spending money?"

"Of course, how much you need?" I asked

"Oh I don't know, whatever you can spare. I wanna get something nice for you tonight." Then she smiled

"Tonight?"

"Yes" she said still smiling

"What's tonight?"

"You'll see!" she said raising her eyebrows

Invisible

"Where you been? Brotha we haven't seen you in a minute?" The MC said. I shrugged to say I've been busy. "I guess that's why you're invisible huh. You appear when you want. Ladies and gentleman, I know we're excited to hear what he's got for us. Give it up for the Invisible Poet!"

Everyone snapped for me. "She moves to the beat of my heart. She sings to the tune of my love. My name drips from her lips like lust and desire. I love to kiss those lips, caress those hips, lick her…" I smiled and everyone cheered me on. "I'm like the moth drawn into her flame. Forever in my heart I want to write her name. She has given me wings so that I can fly, completely spent we lye, in my bed. Only stopping short of my name, what is mine is yours! I love this feeling and I pray it never goes away."

"How come every time I see you, you got that goofy smile on your face?" Malcolm said

"My girl is GREAT!" I said jumping in the air like the fools on the car commercials Malcolm looked at me not amused at all. "Can you focus? This is serious."

I grabbed my composure, "yes of course."

"Brad is gonna get the pictures of Darius and Camille today. Camille won't be there. Knowing Brad he's gonna lash out immediately. The wild card here is Darius, I can't read how he's gonna react. I need you to stay back."

I opened my mouth in complete shock. "Stay back? Why?"

"This is violation of rule number one, its gonna get messy. Brad's already questioning why all the attempts to get at Amber have been utter failures. I really think he thought that paparazzi attempt that you foiled in New York was going to work. We showed him that my Queen is always guarded. He's been making hard but amateur moves. I think a lot of them have been Darius' ideas. Now its time to strike, I gotta get on with my life. Last thing I need is for this to continue on forever."

"But why does that mean I have to stay back?"

Malcolm's eyes pierced me; "I couldn't handle it if something happened to you."

I was so surprised to hear him say that. I wanted to throw a joke out to lighten the moment, but I was stuck. "Ok!" I said swallowing the lump in my throat.

"I got people watching, we will have a play by play of everything shortly." Malcolm said

"We can't watch the camera's?"

"They're going to his house before he leaves, you only mic'd the house." We were quiet for a few minutes. "So what did you find out about this girl?" He said changing the subject

"She looks good on paper. Nothing more than I can handle." I said

"Be careful, cause good on paper doesn't always mean good."

"I hear you, but my girl is good." I said giving him a toothy grin. I can't wait for you to meet her. I think you'll like her." I said

"I'll like her or I'll think she's pretty? Please don't end up like Drew strung out over some no good broad! He drives me crazy with that girl."

"Naw my girl ain't like that."

"Lets hope so, for your sake." Malcolm said giving me the eye.

I wanted to ask him what that meant, but I decided to let it go and get back on track. Malcolm's phone rang and he put it on speaker. The person was giving us a play by play of everything. It was almost like we were there. It had to be someone from Mitigated on the phone, but I didn't recognize the voice. The carrier walked up to the door, rang the doorbell. Brad was just about to go in his garage when it rang. He looked through the peephole for a minute. He took the envelope and signed for it. As soon as he closed the door the carrier ran down the street in double time. Brad snatched the door open pictures in hand. He walked out to his driveway trying to see which way the carrier went. He stood there cursing and grabbing his chest. Malcolm's eyes were evil as he listened to the play by play. Brad went back inside his house, he walked towards his phone, but then he went in his garage. Every door he went through he slammed. He burned rubber coming out of his garage and onto the street. He drove recklessly to his studio. We looked at the cameras inside the studio; Darius was there business as usual. He was sweet talking Camille over the phone. They were saying their I love you's when Brad stormed in the door with two other guys in tow. He threw the pictures at Darius; Darius hung up the phone and stood real tall in front of Brad.

"We didn't want you to find out this way. But since you know. We're in love, and she's going to leave you." Darius said real calm

"Leave me? What makes you think you have the power to replace me?" Brad said in his face

Darius didn't budge. "You have placed everything you own in Camille's name to avoid taxes, child support, you know stuff like that. I helped her get all your debt ratified. I was hoping you'd die on your own really. Your heart has been bothering you for some time and all this fighting with Malcolm has to be wearing you down. Its only a matter of time before you die."

"Speaking of Malcolm, you know she's still stuck on that fool."

"Malcolm is no competition for me. She hasn't seen him since we've been involved." Malcolm and I laughed cause that wasn't true. She was just over Malcolm's last week. Brad grabbed his chest again as he tried to calm himself. "Face it, you're too old for a woman like that."

"Too old? Do you even know how old she is?" Brad asked a little breathlessly

"It doesn't even matter." Then Darius fired on Brad, it looked like it hurt. I grimaced and Malcolm smiled, for an old man Brad held his own pretty well. But Darius was younger and faster. The two guys that walked in with Brad stood there and did nothing. Malcolm shook his head tisking at the whole thing.

Then he pointed at the two of them while talking to the guy on the phone. "The two guys with Brad go down." He said to the person on the phone. The person replied ok. After a while Brad couldn't fight any longer and Darius showed him no mercy. Darius was yelling about all the times Brad hit Camille, and how badly he treated her. Malcolm watched the scene like it was a movie, I turned my eyes cause it was pretty brutal. Brad was hurt and on the ground. The two guys asked Darius what now. He told them to put him in his car and finish him off. Then he told them to find out where Malcolm was. Malcolm smiled and then he looked at me. "These are some of the stupidest some bodies, who makes moves without a plan first. Darius picked up the phone; Malcolm flipped the switch on his control board. We heard Darius dialing as the numbers came up on his screen 415... Then Camille answered.

"We had to implement the plan!" Darius said

"What!" Camille yelled

"Baby he had pictures of us."

"FROM WHERE?"

You could tell the thought didn't dawn on him to think of when these pictures were taken. He looked at the pictures, "I guess this has to be from Santa Cruz, that was the only time we were together like this."

"How is that possible? I thought you swept the room?" She fired at him.

"I did. I'll figure this out. Meanwhile we're gonna figure out how to put this on Malcolm."

"No!" Then she caught herself, "I mean why Malcolm? Why can't it just be a random act?" She said trying to catch herself.

"You think he won't come after me when this gets out? Since its almost impossible to get to him or his woman, he can take the heat for this. Another turn in prison will do him some good."

"Darius can't you pick someone else?"

"Why does it matter who we pick? The point of my call is that we can be together now." He smiled like a lovesick puppy.

"I love you. Let me get back to niecy, call me when it's safe to come home."

"Or I could come see you tonight to celebrate."

"Not yet baby, we need to lay low. But it's on, as soon as the coast is clear."

Then Malcolm's pager went off. Camille was paging him from her cell phone. "I'm gonna lay you out!" Darius said extremely excited.

"Ok baby I can't wait. I gotta go, call me later." She said hanging up the phone cause Malcolm was calling. "Malcolm!" You could hear tears in her voice.

I stood there taking the whole scene in. Darius was convinced that Camille loved him, and he was risking everything for her. She didn't have an obvious sugary sweet tone to her voice, so I couldn't fault him for falling for her game. As Camille told Malcolm everything it hit me, that no matter what you'll never truly know what's going on in a woman's heart.

****

"You don't look so good." This girl in my class said.

I had been running hot and cold all morning. "I'm going home." I said grabbing my backpack. I drove into the city this morning, thank goodness. I got in my car and drove very carefully home. I expected Sylvia to be home, she didn't have classes today, and she was still in bed when I left. When I walked in the door, my head was spinning and there was no sign of life. I took some medicine, took another shower to wash off the sweat. I put on sweats, socks, and a t-shirt and then I got in the bed. I was out before my head hit the pillow. I was awakened by the ring of my phone. I answered and it was my Grandma. She said she was calling to check on me and find out why I hadn't been around or calling. When she heard my voice she told me not to argue with her and that she was bringing me something for my flu. Grandma and G-momma came over with groceries and they made me herbal teas, some concoction to rub on my chest, they made me put on another shirt, and they brought a humidifier. Then Grandma noticed the womanly things around my apartment. They started drilling me with questions, as the drilling was winding down Sylvia came bursting through the door. It was three-fifteen and I usually got home just after four. She looked frazzled, and a little panicked. Then when she saw me she had a busted look on her face. I saw the look as she recovered and smiled at my Grandma. I could tell that Grandma and G-momma didn't like her, but I don't know if they would like any female that I was living in sin with. "Where were you?" I asked her

"School" she said real fast.

"All your school stuff is here." I said watching her.

She got nervous, but she was good about masking it. I don't know why being sick allowed me to see it. "I went to talk to a couple of my professors, sign up for some tutoring Stuff like that, what's with the third degree?" She said defensively.

"She's lying! Son she don't mean you no good, send her away. What happened with Melissa? At least she cared about you." G-momma said

Sylvia got angry, "I do care about him! Why would you let her say that? You know I care about you."

My head was pounding and spinning focusing that much on her was zapping the little bit of energy I had. "Melissa has her own life G-momma. I haven't talked to her in a long time. Sylvia and I are in love, I'm sure there has to be a good reason why she would lie to me as if I wouldn't know the difference. But as for right now my head is spinning and I need to go back to my bed." I said standing slowly.

Grandma and G-momma hugged and kissed me. They told me to come see them as soon as I was feeling better. I had to promise that I would come see them. I went right back to sleep, in the middle of the night Sylvia was kissing on me claiming that getting some would make me feel better. My head wasn't pounding anymore, so I went in. Red flag! Did she really try to stop me from using a condom for round two? I had to put my foot down and tell her nothing was jumping off without a condom. She started pouting talking about for once she wanted to feel me without something between us. "What if I'm HIV positive? Would you want that?" She didn't feed into my what if question, she knew I wasn't. "Sylvia I'm still in school. I'm not ready for a wife and kids." She said she was on the pill so there was no need to worry. "Let me see them, let me see the case that shows you even took it for today." She got up and went to her purse. She brought me a pill container with some of the pills missing. It almost looked legit until I flipped it over and the use by date had passed. What doctor uses expired medication. I looked at her; did she really wanna have my baby that bad? I was almost going to give in and not care, after all I loved her. But I could hear Malcolm's voice telling me to be smarter. I told her I wasn't touching her without a condom!

Invisible

Chapter 9

"Where's that girl?" G-momma asked spitting venom.

"She's going to service with her family." I said not wanting to get into it. When I invited Sylvia to come with me suddenly she had to go to service with her mother. Every time I invited her she had some excuse why she couldn't come with me. "You look really pretty." I said to my G-momma.

"Thank you baby." She smiled really big.

When we got to service I noticed they were saving an extra seat with us. Imagine the surprise on both of our faces when we saw each other. Melissa sat in the middle of my Grandma and G-momma, every once in awhile I'd peek at her. But she was focused, looking up all the scriptures in her bible and following along. After service she said hello and then she hurried away. She was talking to different ones in the congregation, and she paid me no more attention. Grandma said that Melissa was really heartbroken when I dropped her like a bad habit as my Grandma called it. Grandma called her to check on her to see how she was doing one day. She said they had a good conversation about God's arrangement of marriage, which turned into a discussion about the bible. She said Melissa's been coming to service ever since. I watched Melissa float around like a social butterfly. She seemed really happy interacting with her congregation, although she looked at me with sad eyes. I sat there trying to remember if there was any other red flag about her other than the phone calls. Melissa was a good girl, a little jealous at times but she was a good girl. She seemed happy in her new space, so I wasn't gonna bother her.

Besides, the whole time I was wondering what Sylvia was doing. She definitely made sure I never walked out of the house unsatisfied. Ever since the condom discussion, that's the only thing we argue about really. She doesn't want me to use them and I HAVE to. An after one broke on me, I stopped keeping them in the box by the bed. I hopped up so fast; you would've thought she burned me. We argued real hard that night, for the first time ever it was hard to even look at her. In the end I felt like I couldn't trust her at least as far as babies were concerned. I didn't see why it was such a big issue. I love her and I will marry her as soon as I finish with school, she's got me. I'm not going anywhere, I don't understand the issue. I have resorted to popping up at the apartment off schedule and demanding more of her time. I love her but its like my father's voice keeps telling me to back away and I don't know why, nor do I want to. The one time I tried to discuss it with Malcolm, but he was too distracted. He's been running back and forth between here and Southern California looking at real estate. He's slowed down a lot too, females don't pop up at his place as much as they used to. He's not home as much either; I assume he's hanging out with Amber more. Cause although if you didn't know him you'd think he doesn't show emotion, if you pay attention it's there. It's just not like anyone else would show it. Once you realize that then you understand that Amber is his everything, he just gets in his own way. But it looks like he's going to go for it; he's been making moves.

"Are you coming back over for lunch?" G-momma said snatching me from my thoughts. The look she gave me said I better say yes cause she was more or less telling me than asking me.

"Yes G-momma" I said in defeat, I really wanted to get home to Sylvia though. She kept eyeing me. "Good!" She said turning her back on me.

They were not fans of Sylvia, which is why I was surprised that they let Melissa sit with them. Maybe it was different cause Melissa was my past and Sylvia is the now. I told them I would meet them at their house and I hurried out before they could ask me where I was going. I drove down the street to Cutting Blvd, turned right on Carlson,

turned left on Potrero, and parked in front of the blue and White House. I knocked on the door and very slowly I heard someone approaching. Roz opened the door with complete surprise on her face. "Hello sweetheart, how are you?" She said standing in the doorway.
"Is Yuri here?" I asked
"No"
"Then let me in." I said with a smile. She moved out the way and I gave her a big hug. "How are you?"
She still smelled like baby powder. "Oh I'm ok, how have you been?" Then she looked at my locs. "Who's been tightening your dreads for you?"
"I'm ok. I've been going to the Drew's in Oakland. Your books have stayed full lately."
"I'm never too full for my baby. Just tell them your name next time and I'll make sure you're in."
I smiled, "I can't stay long but I wanted to lay eyes on you cause I haven't seen you in awhile." I said
"I think about you every day. Everything ok with you?"
"Yes" I said pretending not to see the bruise on her arm. My insides turned, but I kept my face even. "I'm always thinking about you too. Yuri's still the same?"
"He's better," she said not looking at me.
"Ok, well I got to go to my Grandma's house." Then I looked her in her eyes. "Call me when you need me." Then I gave her my cellphone number.
"Ok Yussef. I love you baby." She said giving me a tight hug.
I walked out the door feeling a knot in my stomach and heat on my neck. I was trying to give her space but I wanted him gone. I drove real slowly to my Grandma's house. I kept seeing Roz's bruised arm in my head and it was pissing me off. There were a few extra cars around my Grandma's house so I sat in the driveway calming my nerves. Melissa came out and knocked on the window. I told myself she was getting kicked out if she tries any dramatic junk, I wasn't in the mood. I unlocked the door and she sat down, she looked at me. I kept looking forward. "You ok?" I shrugged. "Ok well I won't take up too much of your time." I shrugged again; I was praying that she didn't irritate me. Her tone wasn't annoying, but I didn't know where she was going. "So I hear you have a girlfriend, I hear she's really beautiful." I looked at her sarcastically, cause who says that and really means it? If I wouldn't have stopped calling her, she would still be demanding that I put some kind of claim to her. "I am happy for you even if you don't understand it. That doesn't mean it doesn't hurt like crazy." She rubbed her chest above her heart. "I just want you to be happy, and of course I was hoping that the woman who put that happiness in your heart would be me. But as long as you have it is all I really care." Although her face told me she was telling me the truth, I couldn't believe that. I couldn't handle it if Sylvia and I broke up and I heard that she was happy with someone else. "I'm serious Yussef, don't look at me like that." Then I saw the tears on the right side of her face.
I felt like crap. "Thank you," I said as I hugged her. "I hope you find what you're looking for as well."
"I figure I need to change the way I'm going about things. I'm gonna put God first and I know he'll provide the love of my life for me. I just need to be patient and wait on him. Can I ask you something?" She said wiping her face
"Shoot"
"What did I do wrong?"
Ugh! Why did it have to be a hard question? "Honestly, you should've let me have the space to see and appreciate you in the same way that you felt for me. We were together based off of your feelings. Then the phone calls, the last thing a man wants to do is

have second thoughts about his woman. But I don't want you walking away from here thinking that there was something crippling wrong with you. You were good to me, and I appreciate everything you did for me. When the right man for you comes along, let him see you first. He'll see how amazing you are and fall for you just as much as you have fallen for him. If he doesn't fall, walk away. He'd be a fool not to fall for you."
"Does that make you a fool? Even though I jumped the gun, I let you see me."
"I'm fool number one!" I said smiling at her.
She tried to smile back but she broke out in heart-felt tears. I hugged her again feeling horrible about myself. "I still love you! Please don't say anything, I just want you to know that someone not so beautiful in this world is still in love with you when she breaks your heart."
"You're beautiful Melissa, it just wasn't the right time for us." I said still hugging her and occasionally smelling her hair. Her hair always smelled great and I miss that. Sylvia's hair smelled good too, but it was different. "Let's go inside before I get you in trouble."
"What do you mean?" she asked wiping her face.
"Let's go before I'm tempted to explain it." I said unlocking the already unlocked doors. I didn't understand what I felt in that moment. She was purging and then I realized Sylvia hasn't told me she loves me. She says she loves all kinds of things, but the actual me part she hasn't said. She loves it when I do A, B, C, and D; but not me. And hearing Melissa say it from her heart hurt and turned me on all at the same time. When we went inside people were looking at Melissa and I with questioning eyes. Melissa went to the bathroom to grab her composure. I stayed longer than I thought I would, I was eating good food with good people. I had a really good time. When I changed out of my suit in my old room, I had 17 missed calls from Sylvia. When I called her back, she said she was worried sick about me. I didn't know why I told her where I was. She kept hitting me with questions rapid fire. I took the phone off my ear and looked at the name to make sure I was talking to the right person. She's never acted like this. I told her I would be home in a little bit, but I wouldn't commit to a time. She hung up the phone in frustration. I didn't see what the big deal was. She was always with her family, and as long as I knew where she was I was fine with it. Irritated by the whole scene, I made myself comfortable in the living room with my family and friends. I stayed until Grandma kicked me out. She told me to go home, and that I had punished that poor girl enough.
On the drive home, I kept thinking about Roz's arm, Melissa, and Sylvia's changed behavior. I know my father didn't put his hands on Roz, he really cared about her. I even remember him saying he wanted to have a baby with her. How could she go from my father to that guy? It didn't make sense to me. Melissa's comments about her wanting me to be happy were just unnatural to me; if you love someone don't you have to be with them? I didn't get it. Maybe Sylvia's acting weird because she's questioning whether or not I still love her?
When I walked in the apartment Monica was consoling her. Both of them looked at me with evil eyes. "Why would you do this?" She said through tears
"Do what?"
"I was worried about you and you didn't come home!"
"I talked to you. I told you where I was, why are you still upset?"
"Because you didn't come home!" Monica hugged and kissed her and then she left. I went over to hug her, two seconds in she pushed me away. "Who's perfume is that?"
"WHAT?"
"You smell like a female!" She screamed.

"I was with my Grandma and G-momma HELLO! Whom else would I be hugging on?" I said thinking of Melissa.

Sylvia relaxed some, "you weren't out cheating on me?"

I blew air, "where am I supposed to find the energy for that? I swear you send me out of here on empty." I smiled.

"Why can't I have your baby?" She blurted out.

"Whoa! What? Why?" I backed up and cleared my throat.

"Do you love me?" She asked

"You know I do!"

"Then why can't I have a permanent expression of that?"

"Maybe because you haven't told me you love me! You always talk around it, but you don't just come out and say it. Then you sneak around here like I'm stupid. You're up to something, but my love for you blinds me. Until I feel like you regard me in the same light there will be no babies."

"I can't believe you said all of that to me." She said mocking a shocked face.

"Goodnight Sylvia."

****

This trip to No Words was truly an invisible trip. I had so many mixed emotions, and a major case of writer's block! I sat there all night drinking cognac and listening to everyone else's words hoping to gain some insight into my own feelings. I couldn't focus on one single thought. Melissa, Sylvia, Roz, and everyone else danced around my brain like a riddle I couldn't understand. Not knowing what to do next, when Judy called I ran over. I needed something different tonight.

****

"This is Sylvia," I said proudly as I introduced her to Malcolm.

Sylvia held on to my arm for dear life. She was scared of Malcolm. "Hello." Malcolm said

"Hi" she said really nervous.

"Yussef says you sing?" Sylvia shook her head yes. Malcolm looked at me, he was not impressed. "Go sing." He told her pointing to the booth.

Sylvia squeezed my arm, and then she walked into the booth. Monica got excited and clapped her hands in excitement. Not knowing the history she started singing one of Torrie's songs. Malcolm looked at me; I looked at him to say she doesn't know. As she was singing Andrew walked in the studio. Instantly he was eyeballing Monica. "What we got going on over here?" He said

I introduced them, then I pointed to Sylvia and said, "that's Sylvia," I said proudly. Andrew had heard about her but my hand was kind of forced that they had to meet now.

"Nice!" Andrew said looking at Sylvia, and then he looked back at Monica. "How come you're not in there?"

"I'm not a singer." Monica blushed

"Yea right. With that speaking voice you're trying to tell me you don't sing at all? I can hear it, and I've got good ears." He said with a smile.

That did it, Monica was gone. When Sylvia came out she tried not to look affected by Andrew but I could tell she was attracted. Andrew and Malcolm saw it too, and they both got the same look. Malcolm got quiet, that was it, and Sylvia wasn't on his favorite people list. Andrew suggested going to get something to eat. I told him we were linking up with Jeff and Randi. He said he'd meet us there. In the car Monica asked question after question about Andrew. I vaguely answered them cause Sylvia looked like she was taking notes. I didn't say anything cause I wanted to see how she handled herself, even though I had a sinking feeling. When we got to Jeff's, Randi answered the door. She looked really happy to see us. Love made her glow, and it was good to see her so happy. Monica immediately told her that Andrew was coming shortly and then started asking questions. Sylvia was aware that I was watching her so she came and sat by me. Then she asked me what Malcolm thought of her singing. I told her he said she was good, cause he did. But little did she know her glance in his son's direction cost her any help he might've been willing to give. When Andrew got there he went in the kitchen with Randi and Monica. Sylvia waited a while then she went in the kitchen. When she went in Andrew came out immediately. He sat with Jeff and I. He immediately started apologizing for how crazy he's been acting. By his hand gestures and serious face I could tell he was coming from the heart. He was stressing how difficult it's been without Jennay. "So let me ask you something." Jeff said kicking back in his seat. "What if Toya would've said yes? Either way you lost Jennay. I guess I'm missing something."

"No, I think I'd be devastated either way. Especially since the likelihood of that child being mine was very low."

"Why do you still fool with that chick?" I asked

He pointed behind him. "You tell me when you're done with that one. They ain't much different."

I frowned, "say what?"

Andrew smiled, "he doesn't know?" He said towards Jeff. "You don't see it?"

"See what?" I said trying not to get angry.

Jeff put his hands up, "she's not as bad as Toya."

"Not as bad doesn't mean she's good."

I was about to lose it. "Drew! I'm trying to hear you."

"Just sit back and observe, outside of females like Nicole and Randi most of them won't like her. She'll act like she doesn't know why. She'll be lying to your face and you know it, but she's the one person you let get away with it. She's gonna cross the line if she hasn't already and someone you love will put hands on her and you'll find yourself in the middle. Where you will do better than me, you won't let her affect your family."

I wanted to be mad at Andrew but instead I told myself to test the theory. When we sat down to dinner everyone was fine, but I noticed little things. Like when she served Andrew wine before she served me. Or when she offered dessert to me after she offered it to Andrew. Andrew focused his attention on Monica, and even when Sylvia interjected in their conversation he ignored her. When Andrew invited Monica to the movies, Sylvia asked what movie they were going to see cause we might go. I told her I wasn't going to the movies. On our way home we argued again. She said I was acting like an old man because I didn't want to go out. I told her I was going out just not with her. I left her in the lobby of my building. I went to Malcolm's but he wasn't home. It was dark in Grandma's house. As a last resort I called Melissa. She picked up on the first ring. I asked her if I could come by, she hesitated, but agreed.

Melissa had on sweats and a T-shirt nothing like she used to wear when I came over. She looked very comfortable in her skin. She said she was doing her weekly bible reading and preparing for service on Sunday. I went over her reading with her; it was nice to be in her drama free environment. When I leaned in to kiss her she asked about my girlfriend. That was a bunch of reality I didn't want to deal with. I apologized for trying to kiss her. Latia called while I was there, I could hear the alarm in her voice when Melissa told her I was there. I told her Melissa put me in my place, I needed to get away for a little bit but we were on best behavior. When I went home Sylvia was in the bed sleep, for the first time without her being on her period she didn't touch me.

****

"Because you too goofy!" Latia said cracking up.

"Then I got up and walked away." I said cracking up.

Then I looked at Sylvia; she sat there looking unaffected by our story. "So Sylvia, I understand that you go to Laney College, how did you and Yussef meet?"

Sylvia smiled, "we saw each other from across the room. We've been together ever since."

"You look very comfortable here." Latia said looking around the apartment.

"Your brother is very giving." She said

"Where do you work?" Latia asked point blank

"I don't have to."

"Oh? Are you an heiress?" Latia said in a thinly veiled irritated tone.

I looked at her not understanding why her tone changed. "No" Sylvia said looking at me

"What's wrong?" I asked

"Yussef, you got this chick you don't even know living in here like she's your wife. How long before she ends up pregnant? Your are a walking meal ticket for her." Latia said

Sylvia looked at me waiting for me to correct my sister. When I didn't say anything, cause I didn't know how to respond to that Sylvia looked Latia up and down. "You don't know me."

"Nope! But I do know this is all game. You wanted me to come over, so you could act uninterested in getting to know me."

"That's not why I wanted you here. I know you guys are close. Yussef was so excited to have his sister here, I wanted to meet you. But you guys don't talk about anything that interest me, so what am I supposed to do pretend you're an interesting person when you're not?"

"WHOA! WAIT A MINUTE HOW WE GO FROM LAUGHING TO ARGUING?" I said

"She started it!" Sylvia said rolling her eyes.

"Oh, are you the helpless victim?" Latia said

"I didn't say I was a victim." Sylvia said wiggling her neck

Latia looked at me. "I don't like her, and I don't trust her! If I could tell you to kick her out I would."

"Wait a minute Latia." I said trying to control my temper. "When you was with ole biscuit head, I had to suck it up and deal with it. But you can come in here act all nasty like this? You don't like her ok, but be decent for me."

"Fine!" Latia said

"No, how she gonna be in my house talking crazy and that's ok with you?" Sylvia yelled

My body twitched, "this is not your house. As long as you're not my wife, this is my house."

"I live here! So when we are married it will be ok for my brothers to treat you like this?" Sylvia said

"I wouldn't give your brothers a reason to act like this."

"When you get married? YOU PROPOSED TO HER?" Latia was livid

"No, but we talk about marriage." I said

"What do you mean talk about it?"

"Why does it matter? It's none of her business!" Sylvia said while exhaling.

"Sylvia this is my sister and we talk about everything."

"But what we talk about should be between me and you. It's none of her business!"

"So you don't tell Monica everything?" I said, both of them were on my nerves.
"That's different." She said
"There's no difference." I said, "she wants to have a baby. I want to wait until we're married."
"I bet she does. Yussef look at me." So I did. "I'm your sister, I love you. She doesn't love you."
Sylvia got mad and walked in the bedroom. "Latia, please calm down. You're my sister and I love you, but you can't come in here causing problems like this."
"I'm just telling you the truth." She said defensively
"I recall telling you the truth and you didn't want to hear it. I love that woman please be cool."
Latia's eyes turned evil and she leaned in close. "If you love her, why have you been spending so much time with Melissa for the past almost year?" She whispered
Sweat broke out on my forehead. Latia smiled at my reaction, she started to lean back but I pulled her back in. Then I said in her ear, "I'll tell you when you tell me what happened with Mitchell." She had the same nervous reaction. She put her hands up; she ran her hands up and down her pant legs.
Then she stood up and knocked on the bedroom door. Sylvia snatched the door open; Latia seriously humbled herself and apologized. I was impressed and made a mental note of it. I gave Latia the remotes then I went in the bedroom to get ready to go out. Sylvia didn't want to go and I told her that was fine, but I was still going. Then I got in the shower. As soon as I saw her naked body through the glass door I started breathing telling myself to stay calm. It had been a long time since I touched her last. Sex with us wasn't the same anymore, we barely had it. And when we did she didn't seem into it. She was overly concerned with Monica's affairs these days. When I was out she didn't call me, and when I call her she seemed annoyed. So now that she's coming I'm begging my body not to respond. She opened the door, "I'm sorry Yussef, and I know that could've went way better. It just bothers me seeing you having as much fun, if not more, with another female even if it is your sister. I'll go out and apologize to her right away." She said pushing her body up against mine. I tried to act unaffected by her, but my body didn't listen to me. I kept trying to move away from her. Hurry and finish my shower before my other brain took over. I turned my back to her and she reached around me and started massaging me. It's been a minute since she's touched me like this so my body refused to listen to my first brain. She got on her knees and turned me around. Her mouth was warm and inviting, good thing the water was hitting me in the face. I felt like maybe my eyes might've been tearing up. I hated that things had to be this complicated, and everybody was trying to get in my head about my girl. Everybody had something to say, and I just wanted her to be happy. Its not like I couldn't afford a baby. Mitigated pays me very well. Why is it anyone else's business what me and my lady do? When she stood up and let me in I thought I was going to pass out. This felt too right, but it could be because this is my first piece without protection. Right as I started to blow my father's voice told me to abandon ship. Creamy lava ran down the shower drain. Sylvia was trying to hide her irritation but she wasn't doing a good job of it. "Why did you do that?"
"Why is it an issue if I want to wait to have a baby? We've been having this dumb argument for months lets just wait until we're married."
"That's gonna take forever, I want a family now."
I washed off and left her in the shower pouting. When she got out the shower she started getting dressed. "I thought you didn't want to go?"
"I changed my mind." She said trying to change her mood

"Whatever the limo will be here in twenty-minutes, if you're not ready you will be left behind." I said walking out the room.

Latia was on her phone smiling real big. I could tell whenever she talked to him, she'd smile real big and blush. I didn't like the idea of her being all-sweet on a playboy rapper, but she said they were just friends. He wanted more than she could handle, so they've resorted to being friends. Latia and Shameless talk on a regular basis though, so I don't know. As the phone was ringing to tell us the limo was downstairs Sylvia came out the room in a tight fitting dress. She filled it out nicely, but not exactly the look I wanted her to go for tonight. Latia smiled at her and I knew what she was thinking, "this 'female' is doing too much!" In the limo Latia asked me, "what do you think of the building? Should I look for a vacancy when I graduate?"

Sylvia held her breath, "that's up to you. You know I'd love to have you right by me." I said

She glanced at Sylvia, "I'll think about it"

Sylvia's mouth opened wide when we stepped inside the club. I've never been to this club before. We were with Latia so one of the guys at the door greeted her with a smile and a hug, and then he personally led us to the VIP section. The dance floor was full of people and the music was bumping. There were lights all over the place, and pictures of Shameless' new album cover. When we walked into VIP Shameless stood up with a big smile, "here she is. Now I can go out and perform." They hugged. Then Shameless and I shook hands. I introduced Sylvia and a lot of those fools gazed too long for my liking. Latia put Jeff & Randi, Hubby & Nicole, and Andrew & Toya on the guest list as well. I introduced Sylvia to Hubby, Nicole, and Toya. I introduced Latia to everybody and in turn she introduced us to all the people in the room. Everyone kept saying how much Latia and I looked exactly alike. Sylvia rolled her eyes and Randi looked at her like "what's her problem?" Thankfully Nicole, Randi, and Latia hit it off nicely. Toya was people watching, and Sylvia was trying to figure her out. This Club didn't have table service not even in the VIP. So the four of us men went downstairs to the bar. I got a lemon drop for Sylvia and apple martinis for Latia and I. Andrew bought a bottle of something brown and bottles and bottles of champagne. When Shameless went on to perform Latia when down with him. She stayed in the audience in front of the stage. Sylvia was watching for a minute, she mumbled something and then Toya cosigned. I didn't know what she said, but if Toya was in agreement with it, it wasn't good. Andrew was going to town on his drink. He was telling us about his idea to open his own club in Oakland. Hubby asked him to slow down on the drinking he told him he didn't want drama tonight. Andrew put the bottle down and he kept talking. Toya was assessing Andrew from across the room. Then she and Sylvia went down to the dance floor. I was listening to Andrew while watching them dance with random guys in the club. When Shameless finished his set he went down on the dance floor and he danced with Latia only. I shook my head, only friends? Yea right! They like each other for sure. Hubby & Nicole and Jeff & Randi went down to the dance floor, which left me listening to Andrew ramble on, and on about business as the weight of the alcohol he ingested took over. He was drunk, but happily drunk. He did a Michael Jackson spin in the middle of the floor. I told him he was gonna make himself sick if he kept doing that. He said he was ready to dance, I told him I would be down in a minute. Andrew stepped on the floor with some random chick; Toya broke that up not too long after it started. I watched Sylvia and she looked happier dancing with the stranger than she did with me all night. I shook it off and went down to the dance floor. As I walked to the dance floor I felt someone tap my shoulder, I don't know who she was but she was feeling me. I had to catch myself before I yelled out "DANG!" She was definitely a nice consolation to my lady. I

spun her around to take in all her attributes and then we hit the dance floor. Andrew danced by us for a minute, he gave me five saying "DANG!" As he went back to dancing with Toya. She didn't appreciate his comment so she walked away. Andrew seemed drunker than when he was upstairs, but he was having fun so I didn't see any reason for alarm. A random chick found him and they were dancing. After a while I saw Hubby walking Andrew upstairs, they were talking about something and Hubby was laughing so hard, he kept grabbing his stomach. Later I saw Hubby back with his woman. I lost track of Sylvia who for the longest was shooting my dance partner daggers. I took the girl to the bar and I bought her a drink. I thanked her for the dance, and then they announced last call. I didn't see Sylvia anywhere, I even saw Toya talking to some fool. I started to feel heat on my neck as I saw two of Shameless' guys coming down from the VIP by the way they were laughing something was up. Jeff and Randi were all happy and slowly walking in front of me. I threw a jolly rancher in my mouth and continued past them up the stairs. I rounded the corner and I felt like someone punched me in my stomach. Sylvia was straddling Andrew and they were going at it. I couldn't even think, all I could see was red. I grabbed a handful of Sylvia's hair and I yanked her across the room. Jeff and Randi entered as Sylvia's body went flying. Jeff grabbed me as I went in on Andrew. My punch to his jaw sobered him up. At first his eyes turned black, when he stood up and his pants and shorts fell the rest of the way down to his ankles he realized what was going on. His eyes turned from black to remorseful, he told Jeff to let me go and I stayed rapid fire on his face. I couldn't believe this. Toya walked in the room as Sylvia was trying to stop me, and I threw her by her face on the floor. It didn't take a genius to figure out what was going on. Toya and Sylvia started fighting. "YOU CAN, AND DO HAVE ANYBODY YOU WANT! WHY WOULD YOU DO THIS TO ME?" Andrew kept his eyes to the ground, and he didn't say anything. Even in all my anger, I couldn't hit Andrew full force like my broken heart wanted to. He knew I wasn't hitting him like I could've. Someone I didn't recognize stepped forward and handed me a phone. I didn't recognize this guy or know where he came from. But I recognized the style, "hello?" "There's a car outside for you, I'll deal with Andrew." Malcolm said
Sylvia wasn't even the tiniest bit drunk. A guy was holding her back while Toya was still trying to get to her. Sylvia's face was scratched up and red probably bruised. She couldn't even look at me; I wanted to punch her in her face. Jeff put his hands in his pockets, but his eyes begged me not to do it. Randi was crying for me, I went down the stairs. I found Latia on the dance floor. She was blissfully unaware of everything. I told her I was leaving, and I'd catch up to her in the morning. She asked me what was wrong, and I told her I'd tell her later. There was a town car waiting for me. When I sat in the car I wanted to cry, but I refused to shed a tear. I opened my phone and I called Melissa "hello?" she was completely sleep.
"Are you alone?"
"Of course. What's wrong?" She said
I'm on my way." I said
"Yussef! I have a fiancé, you can't keep coming here."
"I need to see you!" I demanded
"Yussef!" She whined
"Melissa please! I need to see you!" I pleaded. She hung up the phone.
I told the driver where to go then I went inside her apartment. She left the door cracked open, and she was sitting on the couch. She had half the place packed up already. She has never looked so clean and angelic to me before. I hated myself for what I was about to do, but I didn't see another way out. She asked me what happened and I rushed her. I kissed her so powerfully I bet she couldn't remember her name let

alone mine. I picked her up and gently laid her on her bed. I made love to her like she deserved me to from the beginning. I didn't hold anything back, I didn't cover myself either. Completely exhausted we both cried ourselves to sleep. In the morning she cursed me out so badly, I think I would've preferred that she hit me. She told me to never come back, to never call her again! I apologized, and I told her I loved her. That made her even angrier, but I knew the anger stemmed from pain. She said I was selfish to do this now that she had a good guy in her life that wanted her. She wouldn't let me tell her what happened, she didn't care. She screamed at me until I left. The driver was still outside and he drove me home. When I walked in the apartment Sylvia was making breakfast. Her face was swollen, scratched, and bruised but she still looked beautiful. "Get out!" I said lacking energy.

"I'm not gonna ask you where you were last night. I'm just happy you're home." She said sitting a plate on the table.

"This is the last time I'm going to tell you, get out. Or else it's gonna get ugly in here." I said with no enthusiasm.

"Sit down, eat some breakfast. We'll talk when you're feeling better."

I blew air and slowly walked to the bedroom. I got my keys to my bucket and then I left. I went to the hardware store and I bought new locks for all the doors. The lobby, etc. Then I called Sylvia's mother and father. I told them Sylvia had thirty minutes to pack her stuff and get out of my place otherwise it was gonna get ugly. Her parents wanted to know what was going on, and I told them the clock was running. I went to the Bakery Merritt I called Melissa and as soon as she heard it was me she hung up. I kept calling back, rapid return. Then the line was busy. I wanted to talk to her, apologize for what I did and explain that I wanted to be with her.

When I got back to my building it seemed like Sylvia's whole family was there. I guess I was supposed to feel some kind of way about all of them being there. I didn't care if I was alone or not this broad was getting out of my place. Her brothers gave me crazy eyes when I walked past them. I returned the stare back at them. Sylvia's mother was screaming at Sylvia is Spanish. I didn't have to speak the language to understand when she called her out of her name. "How come I don't see moving boxes?" I said staring her father down.

"Yussef, please talk to her. She's really sorry, she doesn't want to break up." Monica said

I leaned my head to the side. "Did she even tell you what she did?"

Sylvia cut me off. "I told her that you thought you saw me push up on some guy, you never let me explain what happened." Then she stood up, "it's bad enough that you called them. Can we please finally discuss this in private?"

I shook my head, "no. There's nothing private between us anymore." I looked around her at Monica. "She did Andrew last night!" Monica screamed and covered her mouth. "Yea in the VIP room at the club. He was drunk off his butt, she was completely sober."

"No! I was drunk too!" She pleaded

"No you weren't. Get out of my house!" I demanded

"He was mine! Why do you always do this to me? I saw Yussef first, but you went after him. He didn't even get a chance to see me. You've always done this to me. You had a good guy why couldn't I have Andrew?"

Sylvia's parents and I looked shocked. Sylvia's father said something in Spanish Sylvia hung her head when she responded. Then they all started yelling at her. Monica said something in an evil tone, both of the parents looked surprised. The mother looked like she was pleading with Monica. "She's cheating on you! She's cheated on you the entire time."

If last night hadn't happened, she might've wounded me with this information. But I was numb already. I looked at Sylvia, "if you don't pack your stuff and go! I swear to God I'm not responsible for what happens next!"

"Are you threatening me?" Her father said

"I don't make threats! But this is a bonafied promise! Get her out!" Then it hit me that I was repeating myself and nobody was moving. I went in the room grabbed an armful of her stuff, went out on the balcony and dropped it over. I left the sliding doors open and I started throwing her kitchen knick-knacks out the window. Most of them were glass so you heard them break as they hit the ground. "I don't know who posed for this picture, but Jesus was a Jew. This is a picture of a white guy!" I yelled as I snatched the picture off the wall. They started screaming and finally moving when I threw the picture. Sylvia was pleading with me to calm down; I pushed her out the way. Her father got mad cause I pushed her. He got in my face screaming in Spanish. "You are in my house! If you don't like it take her out."

Sylvia's brothers came in yelling in Spanish. Rod ran up on me, he led with his head. I popped him in the nose. That hurt because I really liked Rod. I know he was responding to the scene, but I wish this didn't have to happen. While Rod was holding his nose, Estephen tried to rush me and I hit him in the throat. Sylvia's father looked like he was gonna blow a gasket. He squared off.

"Parada! (Stop!)" Malcolm's voice rumbled from the doorway. "Que estas haciendo? (What are you doing?)" Malcolm said

"Lo que esta sucediendo aqui? (What is happening here?)" Juan said

"This whole thing has gotten out of hand." Sylvia's dad said

"Oh! When the black man walks in speaking Spanish then you wanna talk in English! I see how it is!" I yelled. "Take your trash out of my house! Including her!" I said pointing at Sylvia

"Yussef?" Rod said still holding his nose.

"Your sister cheated on me man! Apparently she's been doing it all along. Didn't matter that I loved her." I exhaled, and then I stuck my hand out to him. "You ok?"

"Yea!" He wiggled his busted nose. "Thank you for not breaking it."

"I'm not trying to hurt you, make her get out. I'm over it!" I said

Juan started going off in Spanish, all of them moved quickly. But no one said a word. Malcolm asked me if I was ok with his eyes. I looked away. I wanted everyone to go away so I could go back to calling Melissa. In less than an hour they had all of her stuff moved out. Juan left and Malcolm sat on the couch. I wanted him to go too but I guess he needed to talk. I picked up the phone, and I still got a busy signal on Melissa's line. I swallowed the lump in my throat.

"What did you do?" Malcolm asked

The tears burned in my eyes like acid. "I made love to Melissa like my life depended on it last night. She cursed me out this morning and she won't let me talk to her. I messed up!"

"Nobody wants to play second fiddle. Isn't she engaged?"

I thought he only kept track of his sons like that. "Yes."

"I understand but that wasn't right. Now she's gonna have to tell her fiancé and hope he loves her enough to still marry her."

I tried to swallow, "you think she's still gonna marry him?"

"If he'll still have her, yes she will. You didn't appreciate her. Even though she loves you, he's offering her his heart. She'd be a fool to let him go. You're only rebounding."

"YOU DONT KNOW HOW I FEEL! YOU DONT KNOW WHAT IM GOING THROUGH! THERE'S ALWAYS A FEMALE TRYING TO GET OVER! I DONT WANT TO SPEND THE REST OF MY LIFE IN LIMBO! I WANT A

WOMAN OF MY OWN! BETTER LATE THAN NEVER! I can be with Melissa, and we can be happy." I threw my body on the other couch.

Malcolm's face showed no emotion. "You think you're the first man to be ambiguous about a female? You're not the first man to have the wrong kind of momma. You don't know my life! But you've had positive females around you you're entire life. Until I met Amber I didn't have that in my life. I do know how you feel; I know how you're hurting. I completely blew it with Amber! She's walking around looking sick, and I know it's because of me. I don't think I can rebound from this. I blew it, you blew it! Man up!"

I looked at Malcolm and he wasn't his normal brick wall build. He was looking a little sick himself. "What happened uncle Blackie?"

Malcolm swallowed air and he looked at me. We both smiled, "stop calling me that." He chuckled. "She never comes to my house right!" I nodded in agreement, "she came to the house."

I went to the kitchen and I poured us both some brandy.

"What are you going to do?" I hoped he had some amazing advice for me.

He put his hands up, "I'm at a loss."

"What did Tim say?" I was on the edge of my chair.

"That's his baby girl, what you think?" His body tensed. "My boys aren't talking to me. Drew is out of control!"

"That's why he drank so much!" It was like the light bulb went off. "Your relationship with his mom affects him that much?"

"Amber is tight with all of our boys. What affects her affects them. Since Drew's been with her the longest it's like they vibe off each other. He frustrates me! But I didn't have a mother like that so I guess I don't understand the bond." Malcolm exhaled shaking his drink with one hand in a circular motion. "I'm not trying to talk you out of however you feel towards him, you have a right to feel however you feel. All I'm saying is I don't believe he would've intentionally done that to you." Then he looked around the room. "I think he needs to know who you are. This has gone on long enough."

"If you tell him now, will he be remorseful cause I'm family or because of what he's done?" I said, "I wanna know what he thinks of me first."

"You're not tired of this?" He asked

"This has always been my life. It will change soon, but first I wanna know."
****

"Why aren't you taking my calls?" I barked

Melissa jumped so hard she almost dropped her bag. "Where did you come from?" She said with her hand on her chest.

I stared at her engagement ring. "Why are you ignoring me?"

"Yussef, I'm married." She said holding out her hand.

"What? The wedding was six months away!" I felt heat on my neck

"We moved it up. I can't talk to you." She said continuing to walk.

"So that's it? Forget about me? Nobody loves Yussef!"

She screamed a frustrated scream. A few people in the parking lot looked, but this is Richmond no one was coming to investigate. "I almost lost the love of a GOOD man because of you! You had more than enough time to come back to me. It's unacceptable that you try to come back once I find happiness! You broke my heart, and he fixed it. I thought we could be friends, and then you..." She turned around and started walking again.

"I love you Melissa! I'm sorry!" I said

Invisible

She stopped, she turned around her eyes were red and her face was a little puffy. She exhaled and walked back to me. "I still love you Yussef, but I'm in love with my husband. We're moving away, please let us be happy together."
"Why are you leaving?"
"We need space for us as a couple, you know what I mean?" She said wiping my tears.
"I wasn't trying to hurt you. I do love you." I said
"I know," then she backed away.
I smiled at her, "you've gained a little weight. It looks good."
"Thank you, I'm happy. I gotta go Yussef." She said hurrying to her car.
I watched her drive away; it felt like I couldn't breathe.

****

"I tried to vent, but the paper wouldn't let me speak! I tried to scream, but I had no voice to speak! I needed a voice to let out this angst, but she stole my tongue. And you, you plug your ears! If I can't speak it and you cant hear it, my voice has no sound. She cut me, but you took my blood! My body aches all over!" I looked at my journal and closed it in frustration. I can't find my voice. I can't find the words to express what I feel. I'm stuck and frustrated. Its so bad that now even Judy runs from me. She said I'm like the energizer bunny and she can't hang. So I go hang out at No Words and listen to the voices of others as they touch on my life's whoas.

Chapter 10

Ring! Ring! "Ugh!" I looked at my caller ID completely irritated.

"She's calling again?" Jeff asked

"Yea! Seems like as long as I'm arguing with her she's happy." I took a deep breath determined not to argue. "Hello!"

"Yussef I'm pregnant!" Sylvia said

I felt like she knocked the air out of me. I took the phone off my ear, "why are you telling me?" I said as coldly as I could. Then I shook my head at Jeff.

"Come on Yussef! You know why, remember the shower!" She said waiting for me to remember.

"I remember my soldiers going down the drain. You better talk to Drew or whomever else you were messing with. Cause that right there isn't me!"

"After all that time that we were together, this is how you do me?" She said

"After all that time and then I realize you were always after the big fish. You were living well with me; I had all the pussy a man could ask for. As soon as you realized there was a bigger fish to fry, I couldn't touch you no more. You were saving all your juice for a drunken romp in the club. Somehow all of this has backfired on you and you expect me to fall on the sword? NOPE! Not gonna do it! How far along are you anyways? Not that I care, but so that I can make a mental timeline." I said as evilly as I could

She sound like she was crying. "I'm six months."

"Are you crying? Is her majesty crying? Shut up with all that! I don't want to hear it! Where were your tears when you decided you were going after Drew? I refuse to believe that night happened spontaneously." She didn't say anything she kept crying. "What's the other guy's name?"

"What guy?"

"Come on Sylvia we are beyond the whole your innocent and pure phase. What's his name? Be real with me!"

"Carlos"

"Is he Mexican?"

"Yes" she said through tears

"So if the baby comes out Mexican you know its Carlos, if the baby is black you better go talk to Drew. I don't know why you think I would fall for that. I'm not in love with you anymore."

"Yes you are!" She said through tears

"How you gonna tell me?"

"Like I did! If you didn't love me, you wouldn't go so far out of your way to try and hurt me right now. I know I deserve to be treated this way, but don't sit up here and lie to me about how you feel!"

All I could see was RED! I cursed her out so badly all four of her great-grandmothers should've said OUCH! Then I hung up the phone. Jeff watched me as I paced back and forth going off. "I know it hurts man, but you're gonna have to get your emotions in check if you ever expect to go back to work, or even finish school. You only got a little less than two years to go. Bring it back in. Have you talked to Drew yet?"

"NO!" I said still pacing. "I know he's waiting on me. I know he was drunk all of it, but it changes nothing. In the end it still happened."

"Ok! So you wanna change the subject?"

"YES!"

Jeff picked up the paper, "oh wow this is interesting."

"What is?" He had my full attention

"The weather forecast" I shook my head waiting for him to say that there was a storm coming or something like that. "It says that most birds have been flying south for the winter, but there have been reports of storks flying north with little dread loc babies for delivery."

We laughed, "we both know that baby ain't mine."

"How can you be so sure? Nothing is one hundred percent sure. At least get a Blood test once the baby is born to remove any doubt and to make sure you're covered."

I called her back and said I wanted a Blood test as soon as the baby was born. After the results we'd talk if anything pointed to me. Then I told Jeff to prepare his cousin for the test.

****

"This house is nice!" I said staring up at the vaulted ceilings.

"Thanks" Latia said looking like a proud homeowner.

"I still wish you would've moved into the building with me. But Silicon Valley isn't too far away. You might look up and see me sleeping on your couch." I said

"Everybody keeps threatening the same thing. You, Lewis, Tanisha..." Then she got a funny look. "Yussef what happened with Melissa?"

"First, who is Lewis?" I asked confused

"Shameless." She said like I should've known

I did, but I didn't want to show that I did. "Oh, no wonder he doesn't use it on stage." I hoped she didn't go back to Melissa.

"I like his name, what's wrong with it?"

"It just doesn't fit the image he projects. Lewis da rapper!" I laughed

She leaned her head to the side and slightly laughed. "Yussef," she said gently. "What happened?" My heart started racing as I recited that night to her. She had to sit down as she listened. She gasped and covered her mouth when I got to the part about Melissa. "Where did she go?"

"I don't know, Grandma only tells me that she talks to her from time to time. But she never tells me what they talk about. If she asks about anything or me. I'm out here in the dark." I said touching my heart where I saw Melissa do it before.

"She told me about her fiancée he sounds like a good guy. Shoot! He was tolerant of your friendship."

"He knew about me?" I couldn't believe it.

"Yep!"

"How you know she wasn't just saying she told him, but really didn't?"

"When I met him she introduced me as your sister."

"That doesn't make sense to me. I wouldn't be ok with her talking to her ex or hanging out with him. Cause exactly what happened will happen."

"Maybe he was a little inexperienced, but he also loved her enough to trust her to do right by him. You see what happened, she messed up and she ran right to him to make it right. You might be in her heart, but he has it. I don't understand why I got cut off though? I wanna see her and congratulate her on her marriage. Her momma acted funny when I called her too. I was really trying to track her down."

"You want me to find her?" I needed an excuse to look her up.

"Not yet, give her some time. She probably don't wanna see your face so she cut me off."

I couldn't take my feelings off my face. "All I've got is you, Grandma, G-momma, and Malcolm. I want a family of my own. I want to have love in my life."

"The next good girl that comes along pay attention! Don't start treating females badly because Sylvia messed up. She'll be paying the rest of her life for how she hurt you." Then she exhaled. "Go make up with Drew!"

"WHAT? WOMAN IS YOU CRAZY?" I said shaking my head.

"You're not even mad at him. You know he was drunk self-medicating and all. You're not mad at him, go make up with him!"

"NO!" I said like I was putting my foot down.

"Yussef! You can tell him to come here if that will make you feel better." She said It has been months since I've talked to him. I sat there debating. "Fine. But if we start fighting, it's your fault."

He picked up on the first ring, "hello?"

"Hey." I said

"Hey." He said, "I'm sorry man! I'm sorry!"

"Ok" I exhaled, "did Jeff tell you?"

"Yea" he exhaled, "I can't believe this! I wanna say it ain't me, but I don't really remember that part all that much."

"You tell your momma?"

"Heck Naw! Not unless I have to, she's not knowing about this. Nobody's knowing about this! I'm sorry!"

"Toya still mad?"

He blew air, "a good shopping spree and all is forgiven. But I'm trying to slow down. All that was messed up, and that's not me. I don't live under that code. I've been slowing down."

"I hear you. What you about to do?" I asked

"Just finished homework. Trying to get this Master's ASAP! Where you at?"

"My sister just bought a house, I'm at her place. You should roll through."

He hesitated for a minute. I know he's wondering if I'm trying to set him up. "It's cool man?"

"Yea, tell Jeff and Hubby to bring their women. Leave Toya behind though."

We both laughed. An hour and a half later they all arrived. Andrew and I gripped each other's hands like it was life or death to have the stronger grip. Then the men piled in the car and we went on a quest for food and beer. We came back with BBQ, wine coolers, and beer. We played dominos and kicked back. Andrew's eyes kept following Latia around. I shook my head and told him no, this is gonna be a good story once I tell him. When Latia caught wind of it, she didn't think it was so funny.

****

It felt like someone was squeezing me. I felt pressure like I was in a vice grip. I woke up and walked slowly to the kitchen. I drank some water, and then I looked at the clock. It said 4:18am, I wrote it on the calendar and circled the date in red April 10th. I figured if it happened again I would be able to pinpoint when I felt it first.

****

"The results are in Yussef Davis, you are NOT the father!"

I cracked up laughing. "Say it again!"

"Yussef Davis you are not the father!" He said laughing as well.

"Ok, your turn. Andrew Wallace you are not the father!" We laughed. "And that's when she started crying. People who play games get played." Andrew and I high-fived in the air.

"So it was the Carlos guy?" Randi asked

"Nope, it wasn't him either. But you should've seen him. He had something in his hand, looked like he was praying." Andrew said

"So who's the father?" She asked

I shrugged, "beats me. The baby did look a little black though. As long as I know it's not me."

"Was the baby cute?" She asked

Andrew and I looked at each other and then at her. "Who cares?" Andrew said

"Right! If it were mine of course it would be, but it's not so I don't care." Then I looked at my watch. "I gotta get over to Malcolm's, you rolling?"

Andrew shook his head like a little kid. "NO!"

"Why? He's your father!"

His face turned red, I never seen it do that before. "He keeps making my momma cry!" Then he angrily got up and walked away slowly. "If it ain't business, I ain't dealing with him! Period!"

"Your Grand Opening is tonight. It's business." I said

"I told Sophia I was gonna stop by. I was about to head out anyways. As long as you're there I know Malcolm's got it all under control."

"I'm honored that you have that much faith in me, but at least call in and listen over the phone." I said

"I trust you Yussef, you got me. I got you!" Then he opened the door. "See you tonight."

Randi had sad eyes, "the Grand Opening is tonight?"

"Yea, why aren't you out getting your hair done or whatever you girls do?" I asked

"Jeff didn't tell me about it. I think he wants to break up with me." She said letting tears fall.

"Why would you say that?" I said wiping her tear.

"He never wants to do anything with me anymore. After all this time I've never met his sister or his parents. He's met my dad and my sister. I'm here waiting for him to come home."

"Stop waiting on him. Fill your time with something for you. If you guys do break up, at least you'll have something to fill the space. Or maybe he's used to you being here. You gotta let him miss you. Either way you'll be ok." I gave her a hug.

Then we walked out of Jeff and Joseph's house together.

I went home and got dressed; I did my rounds securing the grounds before everyone else arrived. As Mitigated staff arrived, I gave them their assignments. Andrew and Toya arrived. Andrew was too excited, he went in the middle of the dance floor. He started dancing by his self; say what you want to about him. But he could dance; I couldn't dance like that even if I wanted to. Toya seemed unaffected by him. I don't think she even noticed that I was there or maybe she didn't care. "The dance floor has been christened!" He yelled with his arms stretched out, head tilted back, and chest poked out. A lot of the staff laughed. Tonight Andrew's club Elegant Affairs was opening for the first time. I watched how he set everything up. He had a process for everything, even down to how the orders were taken, submitted, and delivered. He made sure every person here was friendly to a point. He kept reminding everyone this is a business and it would be treated like one. He hired a manager after I turned the job down. I didn't want to be stuck in a club everyday. This place was a well-oiled machine, he asked Latia to come. When she said no then he brought Toya. Latia was constantly screaming at me that the situation was gross and he needed to know they were family. Every time I'd start to tell him something would happen, so I let it ride. Tim told me I'd know when the time was right. Between him and Latia my relationship with Andrew was repaired, and it was like nothing ever happened.

When the clock struck eight, the doors opened. Slowly but surely people started trickling in. Amber and her cousin, Jeff's big sister, Sophia came into the club. They were all smiles and thoroughly impressed with the layout. In that moment I understood why Hubby had a crush on her. Amber looked beautiful! And so proud of her son. I watched them interact for a while then I realized how much it hurt to see them so happy. I needed to take some time off, I could feel it. As Malcolm walked in he nodded at me I nodded back. He was all spiffed up. The question was, would it be enough to catch Amber's attention. Yea! She was digging him whether she'd admit it or not. She spotted him right away. Jeff and Joseph walked in with a guy and a girl. She was gorgeous! She made a beeline to Amber and Sophia, that's when I realized she was Andrew's cousin. That was the little girl from the pictures, the one at Tanisha's place and all over Jeff and Joseph's house. The way they talked about her you'd swear she was still a little girl. That has to be her father, she looks just like him. I watched the girl and Amber on the dance floor. They were both all smiles; although Malcolm was dancing as well he was watching Amber like a hawk. As much as he was belly aching over Amber I wondered if he was going to make a move. He watched her walk back to her booth; I could tell he was nervous about approaching her. She was tolerating him, which was a step in the right direction. Malcolm has been throwing back drinks all night. Six is his limit and I think that one is number seven. Andrew went over after awhile and sat in the middle of them. He politely separated them and then he and Amber went out on the dance floor. In between dance partners little miss pretty was dancing alone and having a good time. Finally she saw me watching her and she came over to me.

"How are you?" She said with a smile.

"I'm cool! How are you tonight? Looks like you're having a good time." I said

"I'm having a great time. Who are you here with?" She asked

"I'm working."

"That's cool, guess that means you can't dance huh?"

"Nope." I said

"Ok, well maybe another time." She said

"Ok" I said, not putting much thought into when another time would actually be. She went back on the dance floor and a guy stepped to her to dance. They danced to a song, but she kept looking back at me. The next guy who approached she politely declined. Then she walked back to me and asked, "can I touch your hair?" When I said yes, she gently touched my hair. "I didn't expect your hair to be soft. Your hair really suits you." She said with a smile.

"What's your name?"

"Sasha"

"Why do you say that Sasha?"

"You're standing over here looking like a brick wall, but your eyes say you have a soft heart. Your hair hides your softness." She said still touching my hair

"If you say so Sasha."

"You don't agree?"

"I'm not trying to hide anything. I'm working." I said

"If you say so," then she smiled.

"What about you? I bet you're used to charming people right off the back. You wouldn't know how to handle it if someone you were trying to charm didn't like you." I gave her a serious look.

"As long as you're not talking about yourself, I could live with it."

Yea, I need a vacation. A beautiful woman is coming on to me and all I can think about is she's too pretty. "What's your name?"

"Yussef"

"Nice to meet you. Maybe another time, when you're not working we can have that dance."

"Yea maybe"

****

"Here's your keys, it was a pleasure doing business with you Oscar." The realtor said "Thank you very much." I said taking my keys. Oscar Welch completed this cash transaction. I just purchased this little house right outside Dixon. It has a barn and lots of land surrounding it. The farmland was being leased by another farmer all I had to worry about keeping up was the immediate house and barn. I told Malcolm I needed some time off from work. He was fine with that, he told me to check in from time to time. I commuted back and forth to school, and whenever I wasn't with my Grandma, G-momma, and/or Latia I was fixing up my house and barn. I wanted everything to stay simple, but I didn't want it to look ran down. I didn't tell anyone about my honeycomb hideout, and since I knew how I found stuff on people. I made sure I buried this house that much deeper when I bought it. I didn't want anyone to find me here. I even took my battery out of my phone whenever I came home.

I found peace here! I prayed a lot, I finally found my way around my writer's block, at night I'd go outside and stare at the heavens. The stars seemed like they were in arm's length without the distraction of the city lights. I loved it out here.

It felt like someone was squeezing me. I recognized this feeling it happened before. I looked at my watch it was 4:20am, as I went to the calendar I realized it was April 10th. I scratched my head as I circled the date. I laid back down, but I couldn't sleep. Maybe my internal clock was telling me it was time to return to the land of the living.

I made the journey back to the bay; as soon as I crossed the Vallejo bridge I put my battery back into my phone. Voicemail alerts kept going off. The first one was Andrew, he left it yesterday his breath was heavy and deep. He said Tim was in the hospital. Malcolm's message said the same thing almost exactly. Then Randi's voicemail said Tim passed early this morning. I pulled over on the side of the freeway. Why would she leave me a voicemail like that? She couldn't have thought that through. I kicked my car, I cursed the daylight! I should've been there when he passed! I drove to Malcolm's but he wasn't home. I went to Andrew's and he wasn't home. I was at a loss for a minute, and then I called Tanisha. I got to her house as she was leaving to pick up Sasha from the airport. Tanisha was crying, I hugged her and told her I was sorry for her loss. When we pulled up, Sasha was walking out of the airport. Tanisha hurried out the car and they hugged for a long time. They were crying really hard. I got out and put Sasha's bags in the car. I got back in while they pulled it together. When they got in the car Sasha gasped when she saw me. "Yussef?"

I nodded "hello".

"I was starting to think you were a figment of my imagination." She said

"You've met?" Tanisha asked

"Opening night at EA, I was working she was there." I said with no enthusiasm. I glanced in the rear view mirror; she was looking around with tears still rolling down her face. There were cars all around Jeff's place, I saw Andrew's car in the cluster. Joseph walked up to my car as I was taking Sasha's bags out.

"Thanks man," he said shaking my hand and hugging it out. He looked drained. "This is completely out of the blue." He inhaled like it would stop the pain. "Drew's inside." Andrew was sitting with his Uncles and they had the same drained look on their faces. No one was really talking. Andrew's hands were all banged up, and he had a couple knots on his head. He'd been fighting again, I wondered if it happened before or after all this occurred. "Who's this?" His Uncle Timothy asked

"Yussef" I said shaking his hand, "I work for Malcolm."

"Outside of Hubby, he's one of my closest friends." Andrew said still looking down.

"How you been son?" Frank said

"I was ok until I heard about this." They all nodded in agreement with me.

I asked Andrew where Malcolm was and he said he was with his mother. I didn't know if that meant they were back together or what so I left it alone. Sasha was with her grandmother, Randi, and Tanisha. When Randi finally saw me, she gave me the biggest hug. She was upset with me for being gone for the past year. I told her I needed some space; I needed to shut down for a little while. I told her I was happy she was still here. She told me that she and Jeff kind of broke up for a couple months. When I asked her what kind of meant, she said they didn't speak during that time. She said she was going to move on and to her surprise he came for her. Randi was all dreamy eyed, "he fought for me Yussef."

"I see you've met his mother, and the family." I said gesturing towards everybody.

"Yea, it's better this time. Thank you for always looking out for me. You are a really good friend." She said

"That's me always the loyal friend."

****

"Can you take me somewhere?" Sasha asked

Everybody looked at me, and then at Andrew. "Yussef is good she'll be safe."

"Where you wanna go?" I asked

"I leave in the morning. I need some fresh air."

"You ain't gotta go nowhere special for that Sasha. There's plenty of fresh air in the backyard. Go out there and fill up." Darryl said

Sasha rolled her eyes, "you ready?" She said to me.

Joseph started shaking his leg, "Drew you sure?"

Andrew looked unconcerned; he didn't even look at Joseph. "JoJo when I tell you he's good he's good. I trust him, and you know how often I say that."

Sasha was walking out the door. Randi and Nicole smiled at me as I walked out the door behind Sasha. "How far you wanna go? I'll need to switch cars." I said starting my bucket. "Driscilla is only meant for the city." I said stroking the dashboard.

"I wanna walk amongst the trees." She said closing her eyes.

I knew exactly where to go. "Ok we definitely need to switch cars."

When we parked on the street Sasha paused when she saw the building. "You live here?" She said staring up at the building.

"Yep." I said walking to the garage. I slowed down when Sasha stood still in the parking lot.

"Malcolm used to live here." She said like a memory was coming back to her.

"Did he?" I said opening the garage.

"Yes, when he was staying with his... cousin." She stood there thoughtful for a minute. I pulled my nice car out of the garage. Sasha was still looking up when the garage door closed. She was quiet for a minute, when she got in the car. "How long have you known Malcolm?"

I focused on the road, "since I was young. How long have you known him?"

"All my life. Where are you from?" I could see her brain swishing

"Richmond originally, and then all over." I said

"All over?" She said

"My momma moved us around a lot." Then I remembered I needed to move a dresser for my Grandma. "Shoot, we need to make a slight detour real quick."

"That's fine. Your dad was fine with that? Moving around."

I exhaled, "they weren't together. He didn't like it. It made it difficult for him to see me, which was all part of her plan. It backfired on her when he died. I came to Richmond to live with my Grandma and G-momma."

"G-momma?"

114

"My Grandma's momma."

"My stepfather died when I was young. I thought he was my father for the longest time. My parents were kind of scandalous, who am I kidding they still are." She inhaled real slow and exhaled. "All they've done is dirt, but I'm supposed to be this upstanding lady."

"They just want you to be better than them." I said

When we walked in the door G-momma smiled. "Who do we have here?"

"Sasha ma'am." She said with a smile

G-momma got stars in her eyes. "Aren't you pretty."

Sasha blushed, "thank you."

"She's Andrew's cousin." I said nonchalantly trying to erase any idea that Sasha and I might be a couple from her mind.

"Oh?" G-momma got quiet. "What side if it's ok to ask?"

"Our mothers are first cousins."

G-momma smiled at me. I rolled my eyes, "where do you want me to move it to?" I said walking to her room.

She told me how to move the furniture in her room, and then she went back to talking to Sasha. Grandma came out her room; she said she was on the phone with Melissa. My heart got heavy hearing her name. I asked her how Melissa was doing. She said she was good and baby number two was due any day now. I didn't know she had the first baby. Irritated I found the energy to effortlessly move the furniture I was coddling a minute ago. Grandma saw my change; she came in and shut the door. "Baby you gotta be happy for her. She has a good man and a family. You will have that some day."

"Right!" I said still moving the furniture effortlessly.

G-momma was showing Sasha pictures of me when I was younger. Sasha had a funny look on her face as she followed along. When we got in the car Sasha stared at me with big eyes. I ignored her stare; I was trying not to think about Melissa. "Oh my goodness!" She put her hands over her mouth.

I shook my head but I didn't say anything. I drove over the San Rafael bridge, over to 101 north; I took Stinson beach exit and followed the signs to Muir Woods. Sasha kept staring at me, "what?" I said as I parked the car.

She gently touched my face, "Troy!" I closed my eyes, her touch felt good.

"Let's go walk." I paid the admission and she stared up at the massive trees.

"I asked for trees and you gave me trees. I've never been here." She smiled still looking up.

"We'll take the light trail since you have on sandals." I said walking a few steps ahead.

"Wait a minute. Talk to me." I stopped and looked at her. "Why haven't I met you before now?"

"My father didn't bring me around. He was planning to, but he died before it happened."

"Andrew doesn't know does he?"

"No, and please don't tell him. I wanna tell him myself." I said

"You guys have been around each other for years. When are you gonna tell him?"

"Soon." Then I thought about it. "How do you know how long we've been around each other?"

She smiled, "I asked." She said walking ahead.

"Un huh, why?" I said

"I like you. I was doing my own research." She said

I squinted my eyes at her. "Why?"

"Why what? Why do I like you?"

"You don't even know me." My stomach was turning.

She smiled and reached for my face. I backed away. "Andrew sings your praises. He doesn't do that for everyone. That night at the club, even though you were working you made me feel beautiful. The rest of those hungry dogs were looking for someone to hookup with. My Uncle spoke very highly of you too. This whole time I've been out here; you've given me space to be here for my family. But I see you watching me." She stepped closer to me. "I know about the girl who broke your heart too. We're not all horrible."

"What are you saying to me?" I couldn't really gauge my feelings. Normally I would've been all over this, but I find myself waiting for the other shoe to drop.

"I know you're still hurting. When you're ready come find me." Then she grabbed my hand.

We walked around Muir Woods looking at the trees and reading the signs. Afterwards we went to a pizza place not too far from the park. We talked about her stepdad, her father, and her mother, my mom, my father, and our past relationships. She said her Uncles, Andrew, and his brothers were so protective of her, that she didn't have a boyfriend until she and her mother moved to Concord and she was in high school. She said that relationship lasted until the summer after her freshman year in college. When I asked her about the guy she was seeing now, she asked me what made me think there was someone. I told her I could see it in her eyes. She said that something about me has infected her. She invited me to Southern California to come visit her anytime I felt up to it. I thanked her for the invite, but we both knew I wasn't going. I opened her car door, when she didn't get in I looked at her. She rushed me and kissed me. I thought about Melissa. "I figure this was my only chance to kiss you." I wanted to kiss her back. You know, do something to show I was interested, but my heart hurt too much. I didn't know what to say. "It's ok. I've been there. It'll take a few years. But you will bounce back. When you're ready you call me."

Chapter 11

It was weird being in the Oakland Kiosk as we called it and not seeing Chantel sitting out front with Ms. Lavern greeting people as they popped in. I grabbed mail for Yussef and Jeremy, then I went to Malcolm's office.

He told me to sit and so I did, "I think its time." Malcolm said

"For?" I said not knowing what he was talking about.

"I don't want you out in the field doing all the Mitigated dirty work. I'd prefer that you were in the office like you're father was, but I also can't have you losing sense of what's happening around these parts. That detective has been snooping around since Brad and his crew either came up dead or missing. I don't want them looking in your direction." He said

"But I'm clean."

"I know that, you know that. But they're looking for any and everything to try and bring us down. I have a very important assignment for you." He paused and stared at me. "I want you on Amber."

I sat there for a minute letting his words sink in. She is his everything. "Uncle Blackie you trust me that much?"

He squinted his eyes; "Quit it with the uncle blackie stuff. I'm being serious." He said

"You're always serious." Then I stuck my chest out. "Thank you for trusting me. I really mean it. "

"Don't fail me and we'll call it even. If you need help tell me right away. Its not weak or a weakness to need help."

"Ok"

"Darryl's graduation is tomorrow. Come to Tim's house and get a good look at her, and I want her to at least see you. So that if she sees you around it won't be a shock to her system."

"Ok"

****

"You see all these little girls running around here." Malcolm smiled, "they must think they're players or something."

"The apple doesn't fall far from the tree." I said

"I'm not like that now."

"You've slowed down a lot, you cook your own meals now." I smiled, "but you were worse."

"Aah! They're still young give them time. I don't wish it on them."

Then Amber came out front, she had Tim's eyes it was a trip seeing her this close up and in person. Malcolm waved her over "This is Yussef, Yussef this is Amber. Got her?" Malcolm said with a smile.

"Hello." I said to Amber, while studying her face. "Got her."

Malcolm patted my shoulders and then he asked her if it was time for Bob's. She nodded yes then she excused them. I watched them walk down the street together. I could see that she was holding back, and Malcolm was completely open. I wondered if it was that obvious to everyone when I was with Sylvia that I was all in and she was holding back. I don't think Amber is anything like Sylvia in that regard, but how does the saying go about a woman scorned go? Cant remember right now, but you can tell she's still hurting.

****

"Dark hair, blue eyes?" Malcolm asked

"Yes, the same white guy she's always out with." Amber's eyes turned to fire, and her demeanor turned angry. "Hold on Malcolm something's going on. I'll put the phone

117

on speaker." I said, moving in closer so I could hear the argument. Amber's temper was like lightning most times you didn't know where it was gonna strike. She'd be fine one minute, then something would happen and WATCH OUT! She's coming after you. I got close enough so Malcolm could hear:

He turned red, "no I wasn't. What does that mean any ways?"

She frowned at him. "That you weren't involved in your children's lives, that you didn't provide for them."

He turned his head while shaking his leg. "She wouldn't let me see them, what was I supposed to do?"

"Pay your child support!" His leg started shaking faster. "Look Tag, all I'm saying is. You couldn't talk to them. The only way you could show you cared was by paying for them."

They argued back and forth about his baby momma and his kids. Amber wasn't giving him any slack. You could tell he was regretting whatever took the conversation in this direction, but it was too late it was happening. Every time he spoke Amber's eyes grew colder and colder. I wondered if he'd get the hint that no matter what he said; nothing could fix whatever she was mad about. He reached for her hand, she didn't give it to him. "No, I think I'm gonna go home. I don't feel like dancing anymore."

This guy looked like he was going to throw himself on the floor at any minute and have an all out kicking and screaming fit. They went back and forth some more. If he only knew whatever he said had turned her completely off. Amber stood up.

"Wait a minute! Wait!" He said standing as well. "I'm sorry, I'll fix this. Don't go." He pleaded with his eyes.

"No, I wanna go home. Please take me home.," she said. "If you can't I understand, I'll just catch a cab."

"Yea right! You'll have one of Malcolm's guys take you home."

She smiled, "well at least you know. That actually sounds a whole lot better than riding with you. Have a good life Tag." She started to walk away and Tag was trying to stop her.

That was my queue to make my presence known. "Amber I'm here to take you home."

"Thank you?" She was trying to place me.

"Yussef" I said

Tag kicked the air and swung at it. "I don't believe this!" He put his hands out. "Really Amber? You don't think you owe me more than this!"

"I already paid you, don't you remember!" Then she looked at me to guide the way. Malcolm pushed a button on the phone. I put my cellphone to my ear, "we're leaving." Malcolm's voice was angry, "hand her the phone!"

I gave her the phone. I guided her out of the ballroom to the parking lot. "Hello?" She seemed nervous, she exhaled, "and I'm not talking about this right now!" Malcolm said something to her. "Um! Lets make that never! I don't want to discuss it Malcolm!" She looked irritated, "I don't have to report to you. Were you ease dropping on my whole conversation?" her face lit up a little, "Like what?" She looked disappointed. "No I'm fine. I'm giving him back his phone now." She gave me back my phone as I held the door open for her.

I drove her home in silence. Derrick was coming down the porch when we pulled around the corner. Derrick walked up to the driver's side window before I could get out. "Who are you?"

"Yussef" I said

"When did you get hired?" Derrick asked

"It's been a while now." I said

Derrick opened Amber's door without looking at her. "Malcolm normally informs me of new hires in this division. Who brought you on?"
"Malcolm" I said.
Derrick took out his phone. Kissed Amber on her check and walked towards his truck while talking to Malcolm. I parked in front of the house. I got out the car and walked around the house while she went inside. I made sure everything was secure around the house, before the night shift made their way over in a couple hours. Normally I'd sit out here and watch the neighborhood, and wait for instructions. When Derrick got off the phone with Malcolm he came back to the car. He tapped the window, and then he waited for me to step out of the car. His glare was like Malcolm's more than Andrew's. For whatever reason, Andrew never paid much attention when it comes to me. But Derrick was paying attention to everything. "I've seen you before." I could see him shuffling through his memory. I waited for him to put it together. "You were in New York, the paparazzi." I nodded, "How long you been covering my mother?"
"Since Darryl's graduation."
Derrick's brain was moving quickly, he was calculating and equating. "Malcolm wants to talk to me about you." He said it more like a question. He was registering every facial movement, everything. To say he was sizing me up was an understatement.
"Ok" I said giving him back the same eye contact he was giving me.
Then he started walking away, "I don't want to have to kill you. Take care of my mom!" Then he got in his car and drove away.
I smiled, his promise amused me. If I'm here, then he should know a dumb comment like that wouldn't phase me. I guess if I had a momma worth protecting I might respond the same way.
I sat out there for a while watching cats wonder around the neighborhood then my phone rang, it was Malcolm. "Bring Amber to me and then you can go home." Then he hung up. I smiled at the phone. Uncle Blackie's gonna be in a good mood tomorrow. I watched the lights turn off and on in Amber's house. When she came out the door, she didn't look like herself. She had a wig, red lipstick, and a trench coat. OOH UNCLE BLACKIE DONE UNLEASHED THE FREAK IN HER! I opened the car door for her making sure I showed no reaction to her appearance. Malcolm was standing in the doorway when we pulled up. I could see the surprise on Malcolm's face when Amber stood up. His mouth was literally open as she walked to his door. It's not very often that someone gets a reaction from Malcolm; I chuckled to myself as I drove away.

****

"It's gonna be ok baby. I've lived a long life. I got to see my great grandbaby graduate from college and blossom into this beautiful young man. I'm tired now; I need you to be strong for your Grandma. Tell them not to revive me, I wanna sleep."
"G-momma! "I said feeling helpless.
"Get yourself together. When I wake up I'm gonna be looking for you!"
"Yes G-momma. Find a nice girl and settle down. That thang you been spending time with ain't the one!"
"I know G-momma! We're both just passing time." I said through silent tears.
"Who has time to be passing?" Then there was a knock at the door. Andrew stuck his head in the door, I told him to come in. "Oh yes! Bring your behind in here!" Andrew looked like a little kid being called in for a whooping. He walked slow and pulled a chair next to me. "So you had a good girl, and you broke up with her to get back with that skank!"
Andrew bulged his eyes at me. "When I told her about the baby she made me tell her the whole story."

119

Andrew started slow, "yes ma'am. You see what had happened was...."
"Zip it! I don't know how much longer I'll have the energy to talk so you listen!"
Andrew zipped an imaginary zipper on his mouth. "I don't know what's wrong with
your generation. Ya'll act like the brothel girls are supposed to be marriage material.
Just because she doesn't have her stuff all hanging out doesn't mean you should pass
her by. Both of you, find nice girls, and settle down. Stop playing these games."
"Yes G-momma!" We said in unison.
"Now let me see a picture of that baby." Andrew showed her a picture of his son
Andre. "Does he look like her at all? All I see is you."
"Not really. He's all me."
"What happened with the good girl?" G-momma asked
"She moved on." Andrew exhaled
"It's gonna be harder now that you got that baby. But don't settle for anything less
than a good girl. You hear me?"
"Yes ma'am." Andrew said
"Baby, go send your momma and your auntie in here. I got some more chewing out to
do."
Andrew and I sent my momma and Auntie Summer in the room. Grandma was a
mess; we sat with her and comforted her. G-momma passed away the next morning.
My momma and Auntie Summer asked if they could move in with Grandma. They said
they promised G-momma they would get their lives together.
****
Malcolm and Amber gave me a hug. Amber told me she was sorry for my loss. I
thanked her, and then they left. Melissa came to the memorial service for G-momma. I
felt the weight of missing her as soon as I saw her. Latia cried so hard when she saw
her. "Where are your babies?" Latia asked
"You mean my little people. I left them with my husband." She said
"I was hoping we'd meet them. What are their names?" Latia asked
Melissa shifted. "My oldest is Yesmina, it means right hand or strength. And my son is
a junior." She shifted again, "how about you any kids?"
"Nope, not married yet." Latia continued talking
Melissa was hiding something, she looked very guilty. Latia was so happy to see her
friend that she wasn't picking up on it. I stood there quietly looking at her. I didn't
want to say or do anything that made her go away. After all these years, I was just
happy to be in her presence. "How about you? You married?" She tried to ask without
looking uncomfortable.
"No" I said not turning my eyes.
I was making her uncomfortable, but I couldn't help it.
Andrew came over with his baby. "Hey Melissa how you doing?" He said reaching to
give her a one-arm hug.
Then he bumped me, he could tell I was in a funky mood. "Oh my goodness! Who's
this?" Melissa said touching the baby
"Andre," then he looked down and around. "Where's yours?"
There goes that guilty look again. "I left them with my husband. They would've been
too much of a handful to manage." She looked at me and quickly looked away. "Let
me go talk to your Grandma, it was good seeing you guys."
"Now you know better than that..." Latia said walking away with her. Melissa glanced
back at me. She better not have bruises under that sweater, I imagined her husband
dying a slow painful death.
"Why were you being so quiet?" Andrew asked

"What was I supposed to say? I didn't wanna scare her off. Can't say nothing really she's married. Everybody keeps telling me to respect it."

Melissa still looked uncomfortable at the repast. Latia was talking her ear off, and she kept giving me guilty eyes.

"When are you coming back to work?" Andrew asked

"Probably in a week."

"I talked to Malcolm and if it's ok with you I wanna take you off my momma. I need you for something else." He said

"Talk to me. I need something to take my mind off this." I said moving my hand around.

"Hubby is getting ready to have his second anniversary. They're having a party." He swallowed. "My point!" He shook his head. "Tracy's gonna be there. Nicole told Hubby she's single again." Andrew was trying to seem cool about it, but I know inside he was going crazy. "I'm nervous man!"

I could tell by his demeanor. "You want me to run another check on her, compare it to the last one, and tell you the differences right? You don't have to pull me off your mom for that."

"Yea I want the paperwork, but I need you to check her out for me. Find out where her head is. Read her for me." He said

"Whoa Drew! What if there's something unsavory about her?"

"I'm a grown man! Give me the information, what I do with it is up to me." He said

"You sure you want me on this?" I asked

"Who else can I trust?"

Of course Andrew had everything already figured out, he anticipated my questions before I could ask them. He wasn't sure when he'd tell her about Andre, but he didn't want to scare her off. He told me if he felt the need to infiltrate after the party. He had a plan either way. Andrew was unbelievably nervous about seeing Tracy. I didn't understand why he broke up with her in the first place. He was happy with her, and he calmed down while they were together. "Since when you get nervous over a female?"

"If she'll have me I'm not letting her go! No matter what!"

"No matter what?" I couldn't believe that.

"Yussef I'm so serious."

"Why have me on her if you feel like that? Its kind of like you're spinning your wheels." I looked up and Melissa was watching. "She's hiding something I said nodding towards Melissa

"I saw that, but what?" Andrew said

"I was looking for bruises when she took off her sweater. I don't see nothing physically wrong." I said

"I'd ask her, just walk up to her and be like, 'yo woman! You hiding something, and I demand to know what it is! RIGHT NOW!' But then when she slaps you, you on your own." Andrew smiled

"She's married I don't have no right demanding anything of her. I've said my peace, I just don't understand why she's looking at me like that."

"Maybe she's not really married! If Latia wasn't there who could've been there to witness it? Maybe she wants you to sweep her off her feet and save her from her life of sin. You ready to get married?" Andrew laughed

"I'm glad you're having fun meanwhile, I do wanna know." Latia and Grandma were talking to Melissa. "Lets go over with Grandma." I grabbed the diaper bag. A girl who had been trying to get his attention all afternoon stopped Andrew along the way. You would think the baby in his arms would deflect females, but now it seems like they come at him harder. I sat on the opposite side of Grandma, Melissa watched me walk over. Latia was telling them a story. Melissa was trying to keep her eyes on Latia but she kept peeking at me. I kept my eyes on her, they all laughed about something in the story. "So, where do you live now?" I said to Melissa

She squirmed in her seat, Grandma interjected. "You know that girl ain't right trying to get next to Andrew. You should go rescue him." She said to me.

I looked at my Grandma, and she had guilty eyes. "Its a secret? I can't know where you live?" I said to Melissa ignoring my Grandma's comment.

"I'd rather not discuss it." Melissa said quietly.

I frowned at all of them. "You guys think I'm going to do something? If I wanted to find you, I could. I don't know why you're sitting over there looking guilty and like you're hiding something."

Melissa turned pale, "see Ms. Georgia, I'm gonna go."

"See what?" I said trying to control myself. Why did it seem like my Grandma had her back more than she had mine?

"I didn't want to cause any problems and I should've left a long time ago," she said looking sad

"Melissa sit down!" She did as I told her, but she looked uncomfortable. "You don't have to leave, I guess I can't ask you any questions. Is that what the deal is?" No one said anything. "I won't ask anymore questions."

Andrew came and sat down; he looked at my face and then everyone at the table. Then my momma came up to the table. "Yussef can I get a picture of you and Melissa?" Everybody gave her the craziest look. "What?" She said looking from face to face.

"Why me and Melissa? That's a married woman." I said completely irritated

"Oh my bad! The way you guys keep looking at each other, I thought you were still together." She said

"Shonda go find some way to make yourself useful. You know good and well they ain't together. You like starting stuff." Grandma said

"You act like a big ole kid sometimes I swear!" I said completely done.

****

"And this is where you'll sit." Danielle said showing me to my cubical. She gave me a tour of the building and gave me my ID badges for the doors and garages. "Do you need anything else?"

"I don't think so." I said sitting my candy dish on the corner of my desk full of apple and sour apple jolly ranchers. "Oh wait, the cubical right there has a bunch of boxes in it. Does that mean it's taken?"

"That's Tracy's cubical. She gets shipments regularly, so you will see boxes in there. But the cubical is taken. As the day progresses one by one people will come over and introduce their selves." She stood for a minute smiling at me. "Is there anyone that will come to call on you?"

I sat in my chair and faced her, "what do you mean?"

"A wife, or girlfriend. Would anyone come looking for you outside of business associates that you want let in right away?" She smiled

She thinks she's slick, "no, not at this time. But I'll let you know when that changes." Then I smiled and turned to my computer. I turned it on and then I called Andrew. "She's not here."

"She had to go to the dentist. She'll be there in a little bit. I really appreciate this." Andrew said

"And I appreciate seeing my bank account grow, so hey it works. Its like I'm getting paid triple time and a half just to be here." I said

"You got me, I got you." Andrew said

Invisible

Someone swooshed past me in a haze of browns and black. I heard things dropping on the desk. I told Andrew I thought she was there and I got off the phone. I finished bringing my computer up, then I kept my ear out for her. She was on a conference call, I heard her polite laugh. I heard her blow air after she got off the phone. I heard the sound of her keypad, "heeeeeyyyyy" she started quietly laughing a real laugh. It sounds kind of like a witch but hilarious, it was kind of contagious. "He came over and he made dinner…………. un huh! Yes girl! He is the sweetest man… he didn't bring the baby last night… He's so sweet and lovable, I love when he comes… I gotta go to service this weekend but we could go after that… sounds perfect…ok…. I will… I gotta pee, talk to you later…" I heard her walk out of her cubical towards the bathroom. I peeked my head out into the walkway of our cubicles. All I could see was the back of her. Nice! I could hear her on calls the rest of the day, and then I could tell when she was talking to Andrew. You could hear the smile in her voice for miles. At the end of the day, I listened for the sound of her getting her things together to leave. I needed to leave before her so that I could see her face up close. I heard her coming out of her cubical I put my headphones on, a candy in my mouth for the road, then I stepped in her path as she walked towards the door. She bumped into me, "Oh my goodness!" she said trying to recover from running into me.
"My bad!" I said taking my headphones off. "Maybe I should wait until I get out of the building to put these on."
"No, it was my fault. I'm so clumsy sometimes. I'm sorry." She said, and then she continued on.
No lingering eyes, or any attention to me what so ever. I walked behind her through the civic center to the garage. She got in her car and drove off. Tracy was a cute girl next-door type; she wasn't a stop traffic kind of face. But already she was a million points ahead of Toya. It took me thirty minutes to compile my notes for Tracy's report. I sent it to Andrew at work. He called me with a huge smile in his voice. We went back and forth about how much she gushed over him.
The next day he sent her two-dozen long stem roses. You would've thought he sent her millions of dollars. She cried when Danielle brought them in to her. She sat there freaking out; she called her friend gushing about how wonderful he was. She said she needed to grab her composure before she called him. When she couldn't pull it together she called him anyways. It was cute seeing her genuinely respond to Andrew like he deserved to have a female respond to him. I texted him and told him he made her cry when she got those flowers, Andrew replied with a smiley face.

****

"So I know you want to tell Andrew in your own due time, but I told Derrick." Malcolm said
"Why?" I said
"He was asking questions. Pretty soon everyone's going to be asking questions. You don't think this has gone on long enough?" Malcolm said
"With all due respect Malcolm, I'm not the one who started this."
"I know, but you can end it." Malcolm said
"I want to tell Andrew, but I really feel like I need to know what he thinks of me first. We've been cool but…" I searched my brain for the words. "If he respects me, then he respects me. There's an automatic respect amongst family, I wanna know the difference first." I said
"That doesn't make any sense to me. You should be proud to stand amongst your family."
"I am and I will be."

"You're still mad at him about that girl. You wanna see if he's gonna do it again? If he knows you're family, you know it won't. What I don't understand is why would you set yourself up like that? If you test someone they may not test out to your liking." Malcolm said

"Malcolm I need to know before it's all said and done."

Chapter 12

"OH MY GOD!" Tracy screamed running out of her cubical. I was on my feet and there in one second. This girl was running from a spider. When she ran past me her perfume tickled my nose. "PLEASE KILL IT! I DON'T DO SPIDERS!" She said actually trembling.
Keith one of our cube mates came running too. "What is it?"
"There's a spider, somebody please kill it. I thought they sprayed for bugs in this building." She said her eyes were wide open
"You sure you want him to die? He's a harmless little fella." I said looking at the simple house spider that wandered unsuspectingly into the wrong cubicle.
"He came by me, he must DIE!" She said
Keith rolled his eyes and walked away. "Tracy why you gotta be so dramatic?" He said as he walked away
"Please kill it, what's your name again?" She asked
"Yussef" I said getting a tissue from her box on her desk.
"Thank you Yussef, I'm sorry for disturbing you. I hate spiders!" She said
I picked up the spider with the tissue. "Next time just come and get me, no need to scream."
"Don't play, are you my official bug killer? Cause I will hold you to it." She said
"Yea sure, let me know when you need me." I went out on the balcony and I let the spider go.
When I went back to my desk she walked over. "We never officially met. I'm Tracy." She said with a smile. I had been here for a couple of months now. She barely paid me any attention, but that was a good thing. Daily she was gushing over Andrew, and with every report I could tell he was getting weaker and weaker. At least they were on the same page. Even as she stood here in front of me, I could tell she wasn't really looking at me. She had stars in her eyes, but that was good.
"Right, Yussef." I said shaking her hand
"Have you been with the company long?" She asked
"No, started a couple of months ago. How about you?" I said
"Since I graduated from College. Who do you report up to?"
"Bonnie, on the fifth floor."
"Oh yea, how's that going?" She asked listening for my answer.
"She's ok, but I could probably use more of a challenge."
She was quiet for a minute, like she was thinking. "What's your background?"
"What do you mean?"
"What school did you go to?" She asked matter of factly
"How you know I went to school at all?"
She gave me a sarcastic look. "The way your eyes move. You're too analytical to have not gone to school."
I frowned, "the way my eyes move?" I shrugged, "I went to SF State!"
"What did you major in?" She said like she was drawing me out.
"Business" I said
"Nice! So what kind of challenge are you looking for? I know the world of killing spiders can't be the only stop on your career train." She said leaning against the wall. I focused on her face as I told her I didn't really know yet, but I was open to anything. I heard her talking to someone, who I assume was her boss about needing an assistant the other day. Andrew told me to go for it. She listened intently as I quickly rambled. That was different, most girls only listen enough to know what they're gonna say next. I can see why Andrew would spend hours on hours talking to her. If someone's

listening why wouldn't you keep talking? "Send me your resume." Then she sat in the chair in my cube. She leaned in so she could whisper, "my boss Becca is getting ready to open a requisition for an assistant for me. You interested?"

I leaned back in my chair, "what does it pay?" I asked

"Pull up the listing. Tell me if you're interested, and apply." Then she stood up. "Thank you again for saving me."

"Don't mention it, and I will." I looked at the job posting, applied, then I sent her my resume.

Two weeks and three interviews later I was promoted to Tracy's assistant. On my first day as her official assistant she brought cupcakes and the San Francisco part of our team all came out to meet me. We were in the conference room eating cupcakes and chatting. "So tomorrow, take Yussef with you when you meet with the Spectrum folks. They need to know that if you're unavailable, he's the next best thing." Becca said

"Ok" Tracy said, and then she went back to her conversation with Shirley. Shirley was an older lady on our team. As Tracy talked you could tell she was all dreamy and idealistic about whatever she was telling her. I watched how Tracy interacted with just about everyone. Most people seemed to like her, she was a nice person. She was only dramatic about spiders and things that were directly happening with her. "Yussef, tomorrow morning we'll leave at about nine."

"Do you want me to drive?" I offered

"No, I can drive. You don't know where we're going anyways."

I liked her outfit the next morning. She was always dressed like she had respect for herself and for the work place. Sometimes I would look at the other females in this office and really wonder if they were here to work or just to find a husband. "So you're from Richmond?" Tracy said with a smile

"Yep, Go Eagles!"

"I graduated from Kennedy too, I wonder why we didn't know each other."

"We didn't run in the same circles."

"I wonder if you knew my ex, Steve Turnage? I think he graduated before you came, but he was always around."

"No, he doesn't sound familiar." I made a mentally note to look him up. "So who's the guy who's been sending you all the flowers?"

She blushed real big, "my boyfriend! I could go on for hours about him."

"We got an hour until we arrive in Sacramento, go ahead."

That was all the invitation she needed, she sang Andrew's praises all the way to Spectrum's office. She was definitely in love with Andrew; she had the day dreamy look on her face the entire time she talked about him. She was a little insecure about why he was with her, I could relate to the feeling. Dealing with Sylvia has definitely knocked me off my game. I know I'm not ugly, but I don't feel confident in my ability to keep someone's attention longer than a few romps in the sac. But then again, I wasn't trying either. When we walked into the lobby the receptionist smiled at me real big. Her smile lessened some when she realized Tracy was walking in with me. "Hello I'm Tracy Thomas, we have a eleven o'clock appointment with David Urshkin." She said in her business tone.

"I'll let him know you're here." She picked up the phone. "Would you like something to drink while you wait? Coffee, tea, water?"

"Water" we said in unison

When the receptionist walked away, Tracy nodded in her direction with a smile. "What you think?"

I frowned, "what?"

"I think she likes you." She said

"Right, right! But we're here on business. I might get the digits on the way out." I said
Then David Urshkin came out of his office. He was average height, a little on the skinny side, and thought way more of himself than he should. He looked at me with a question mark on his face. "Who do we have here?" He said looking me up and down
"This is Yussef, he's gonna be your first point of contact from now on." She said with a smile
He sucked his teeth and looked at me. "I didn't sign up for a new contact. I like working with you just fine." Then he smiled.
"Regardless, he will be the person you talk to from now on. But we're here to discuss your company's contract. Maybe you won't have to worry about who you deal with period." She said without a smile.
David straightened up, when we went into his office. I was working on Tracy's computer. The receptionist brought in some chilled fruit after a little while. She made sure to cut her eyes at me before she walked out. I liked the way Tracy handled herself in the meeting, David kept trying to take her off topic, but she wasn't having it. The only time she slightly veered off topic was when he asked her if she was still single. She raved about Andrew for two minutes, and then she went back to business. David called himself flirting with her, but she played dumb. He complimented her on her weight loss, she said thank you and kept it moving. Right before we left I got the receptionist's number on my way back from the bathroom. We stopped at a little restaurant right before the freeway. "I liked the way you handled yourself in there." I said, Tracy frowned like she didn't know what I was talking about. "David was trying his hardest to flirt with you the whole time. You were acting like you didn't notice." She looked surprised, "he was not?"
I looked at her for a minute, she was telling the truth. She didn't pick up on the fact that he was trying to flirt with her. "Wow!" She wasn't used to the attention. "What did he mean about you being fit?"
She took out her phone and showed me a picture of a much heavier her. I knew about her weight loss, but she lost a lot of weight. "You didn't look bad like this." I said
"You're just being nice." She said
"If you say so. How long did it take to lose your weight?"
"A little over a year. I started on my journey before I met my boyfriend. But he really helped me kick it up a notch. He taught me how to run, it was so hard at first. I would be in pain, but he has magical hands."
I frowned at the visual, "TMI Tracy!"
She was embarrassed, "sorry. I just love that man so much and it's only been a few months since we got back together."
I asked her why they broke up as if I didn't know. She said they both had some loose ends to tie up. I could see shame, embarrassment, and hurt all over her face. She got quiet for a minute like she went to a painful place. Then she asked me if I believed in God. Turns out we have similar religious backgrounds. Something we had in common was that feeling of void when we know what we're supposed to be doing verses what we're doing. By the time we got back to the office it was like we were friends from way back. In my report I wrote that Andrew had a good girl, faithful and God fearing. I told him he had a rare treasure and that he should definitely hold on to it.

****

"This is Valerie, Valerie this is my cousin Yussef." Derrick said
The sound of it made my heart speed up, I smiled. "Nice to meet you." Valerie seemed nice enough, but she was no Tracy. I guess each brother had to have his own flavor. "This is my sister's friend Lewis."
"I know exactly who you are, don't you rap under the name Shameless?" Valerie said

"Yes" Lewis said without any real interest in continuing the conversation with her. He stuck his hand out to Derrick. "Lewis, nice to meet you."

Derrick shook his hand, "what's up. I'm Derrick."

Latia and Veronica came back to the table. We introduced them to Valerie, and then Derrick excused himself and disappeared to the back. Valerie and Veronica were star struck with Lewis sitting at the table. "You didn't tell me you knew celebrities." Veronica whispered.

"Does that matter?" I asked almost annoyed

"No" she said backing down.

The spotlight shined on the microphone in front of the curtains. All the conversations at the tables came to a stop. A tall thin guy walked up to the microphone in a black velvet smoking jacket. Only thing he was missing was an actual cigar or a pipe. "Good evening everyone and welcome to The Place Where Jazz is Played." The audience applauded. "We got a special treat for you tonight, for the regulars in the house you know exactly what that is. D-Rick is in the house ya'll make some noise." Everyone went wild. The MC smiled and nodded his head, "that's right ya'll! Give that man some love! Hopefully we can convince him to bless us more often with his gift." The applause were loud, finally the audience calmed down. "So lets get this show on the road. Give it up you guys for Narration!" The MC moved out the way the curtains opened. The band was ready in their places, but Derrick wasn't on the stage yet. When the keyboardist signaled they went in hard. I didn't know what song they were playing, but it sound good to me.

Latia and Lewis kept flashing each other looks. I swear those two are gonna drive me crazy. Latia said his life is too far out there for her. She said she loves him, and she believes that he loves her. But it's all on her as to why they aren't together. Nights like tonight you'd wonder why she drug her feet. She was always his only focus whenever they were together. I could tell he cared about Latia, but she's got Mitchell hanging around her brain.

When the song ended everyone applauded but you could tell they were anxious for Derrick to come out. The lightning changed and the band played a familiar melody. Derrick came out playing the lead vocals on his saxophone. He was so seasoned in his craft that you forgot he was playing an instrument. It was like you heard Stevie singing, "over time, I've been building my castle of love Just for two, though you never knew you were my reason...." We all swayed to the music. When the song was over everyone was up on their feet. The crowd went wild, Derrick smiled and thanked everyone. Derrick took his spot amongst the band, and the keyboardist announced that they were going to be joined by Chantel. The audience went wild again. I knew Chantel the girl, but this was Chantel the woman. She wasn't the little girl who assisted Malcolm anymore. This was Chantel the woman. Chantel came out in a long black dress. She was kind of tall and very fit. She had high cheekbones, and full lips that made you want to bite them. Although her eyes were brown they glowed when the light hit them. She walked straight up with assertion, but you could tell she was down to earth. She hugged each band member on her way to the microphone. Her last hug a long the way was Derrick and everyone noticed that hug went on a little longer than the others. The question was on whose part. Valerie shifted in her chair. Chantel thanked everyone for the warm reception. She said the next song they were going to perform was written and composed by D-Rick! The way D-Rick rolled off her tongue there was no question that there was something there, Valerie shifted in her chair again. The bass line in this song was killer, Chantel sang in a low and sensual voice. Couples were moving closer to each other, people were fanning their selves. If you weren't in the mood before this song, at the end of the first verse you were on board. The way the music changed at the chorus is what got me. I sat there amazed that Derrick put this all together himself. Veronica grabbed my hand, her eyes were all dreamy. I looked at Derrick he nodded to me as if to say "you're welcome". Our table was one of the first to be up on our feet, all except Valerie. When Derrick looked at her, he had no expression on his face but she hopped up. Then Chantel put her arm around Derrick as they bowed again. Derrick looked at Valerie again, and she looked like she was about to fall apart. Derrick and Chantel left the stage and Narration continued to play on. "Your cousin has skills!" Veronica said all smiles.

I smiled at the sound of her saying my cousin. Lewis's mind was turning over, he was deep in thought. Derrick and Chantel came to the table, they were holding hands. Derrick introduced her to everyone and he saved Valerie for last. "And this is Valerie!" He said

"It's really nice to meet you." Chantel said to Valerie

"Likewise" Valerie said looking Chantel up and down.

Chantel smiled and then she looked at Derrick. "Should I leave?"

"No, you stay." He said pulling up two extra chairs.

"I need to get with you. That song has to get out to main stream." Lewis said

Derrick had no noticeable reaction. "You think so?"

"I know so. Can I get your info from Latia?"

Derrick handed him a card. "Really Derrick? You're gonna have her sit at our table?" Valerie said like she couldn't take it any more.

Everybody looked at Valerie with a sucks to be you look. "Derrick I'll leave." Chantel said as she attempted to stand.

"Chantel sit! Valerie if you have a problem with my friend sitting here, then you leave. If you choose to stay, I don't want to hear another peep from you about it. Chantel is just as welcome here as you are, if not more." He said in a low rumble.

Valerie looked stuck and like she didn't know what to do. She looked at Latia like she was asking for advice. Latia didn't give her a reaction either. Then Valerie stood up. She gathered her purse and sweater, and then she left. Derrick didn't appear to be phased by her walkout at all. He pushed Valerie's chair away and pulled Chantel's chair next to him. Chantel was cool, just as witty and laid back as Derrick. Being with Derrick was almost like being with Malcolm, very little got past him. Derrick wasn't as volatile as Andrew either. He handled situations swiftly when needed, but for the most part he was laid back. Derrick leaned in, "we're on camera. You see them?"

"The detectives? Yea I saw them when we walked in. What are they doing here?" I asked

"Detective Dartnell is relentless! Just make sure you watch yourself. What about her?" He said nodding at Veronica

"Female du jour" I said

"Be leery of new friends." Derrick said

I looked at Veronica. She seemed nice enough, but it's not like she'd be my wife or anything.

****

I sat back in the chair, all I could see was red. Sometimes this world is too small. I was shaking my leg, trying to stop myself from falling out into an all out fit. I couldn't believe I even cared this much anymore, I thought I was over all that. Malcolm walked in the office. "What did you find?" He said reading my face.

"Tracy checks out good." I said handing him the folder. "Nice religious background like she said. Standard family, all that. She's good."

Malcolm scanned the folder, "but?"

129

"It's her ex." I blew air, "Steve Turnage" I tossed the printout of his driver's license photo on the desk. "That's the same fool my high school girlfriend cheated on me with." I said standing up and walking to the other side of the office.
"So?" Malcolm said watching me.
"I HATE HIM!" I said
"You know him?" He asked
"Let me put it in terms you'd understand. Dwayne Reed!" I said
Malcolm squinted his eyes.
"How is he like the pretty boy?"
"It's not the same situation, but I care for this Steve fool just as much as you care for the pretty boy. I don't know how Tracy got mixed up with him. She's not like Shannon."
"Maybe Tracy's not who you think she is." He said
"I know you're used to Drew running with females like Toya. But Tracy is the opposite, she's not like that."
"She could be playing you too. You don't know." He said
"I'm working with this woman everyday, I know her."
"Obviously not well enough." He said pushing the picture back towards me. "Did you finish the others I had?"
"Yea, I did those first." I said pointing to the folders.
"Why are you taking this so personally? This is not like you." Malcolm said
"I guess I'm not over that whole thing." I said, "I thought I was."
Malcolm was quiet for a minute. "He'd be more like David than Dwayne." He stared at me. "When Troy told me he saw Amber with David and with my son, I wanted them all dead. Although we all know he could've never replaced me. She was willing to give him everything that belonged to me. Amber is MINE!" His voice rumbled off the walls. "She didn't put Dwayne before me, he was only there because of me. But David.... She put David before me! She still has the ring he gave her that irritates me to no end. Have you talked to Shannon?"
My mouth fell open. "Why? Why would I do that?"
He smiled, "you started falling apart when this girl broke your heart. You don't think you need to talk to her?"
"No! That was high school!"
"As you see Amber and I still argue about stuff that happened in middle school. But ok, get over it. Do something, you're falling apart over here, and it's not even your woman."
Malcolm's words replayed in my head the rest of the night. I was supposed to see Veronica, but I cancelled on her. I sat out on my balcony with some cognac, looking at the lake trying to sort out my feelings. When I saw Steve's picture, I instantly remembered seeing him at my graduation, and how Shannon went running after him. She was supposed to be mine, Sylvia was supposed to be mine, and that's when I realized I wished Tracy were mine. With that realization I started putting my glass to my mouth. I started yelling at myself, "you don't mess with the Boss's woman!" I can't do this! I can't betray myself, or my family like this. Things have been going well with them. It's only a matter of time before Andrew pulls back, I can ride it out just a little longer.

****

"I never thought I could feel like this!" Andrew said taking a shot
"I'm happy for you." And I meant it.
"I wanna do something nice for her, but meaningful."

When I didn't say anything he asked for a suggestion. "Its so obvious, I don't know why you aren't seeing it." I waited for him to chime in, but he stared at me. "Go to service with her."

"Whoa! Whoa! Whoa! Religion, are you serious?"

"You're not religious, why would it matter to you? Its not like you're going against something you have an opinion about. Its only gonna get you major brownie points with her and her whole family. But you could settle for buying her something with all the duckets you have that she doesn't know about. I'm sure something you could buy would mean as much to her and her family. You know something that could be stolen, broken, damaged. Yea that's a better idea. Go that way! Home run!" Andrew gave me evil eyes, and I gave him a toothy grin. He tried to take his next shot and he not only scratched but he ripped the felt on the pool table. I fell on the floor laughing. "You asked!"

"Shut up!" Andrew was so mad he couldn't think of anything else to come back with. "What should I do just show up?"

"That's up to you, you pick the moment. But regardless of when, you'll score big when you do it."

Hubby came back from the bar. Derrick, Jeff, and Joseph were just arriving. "What are we talking about?" Hubby said

"He said I should go to service with Tracy and her family." Andrew said

"Nicole went, she said it wasn't bad. What's the big deal?"

Andrew and Derrick exchanged looks. "You're going so I don't know why you pretend to fight it." Derrick said matter of factly. "Whatever it takes for you to calm your overly sensitive self down."

"I've calmed down a lot already." He said looking at the females at the pool table next to us who started setting up their table. Hubby and I stood there staring at him, until he looked at us. "What?"

"NO!" Hubby said

Andrew rolled his eyes, "its not like she's putting out. What am I supposed to do?"

"She's not putting out?" Joseph said in disbelief. "Why bother?"

"It's not that simple, I love her." Andrew said

"Wait with her!" I said

"Don't make a bad situation worse by adding more females to the equation." Hubby said

"What do you mean?" Andrew asked

"You still hitting Toya aren't you." Hubby wasn't asking he was saying

"NO!" He said like the idea put a bad taste in his mouth.

"WHAT?" Hubby said hysterically, "not even once in a blue moon?"

"NO! I ain't touched that girl since she came up pregnant." He took a drink of his beer, we were staring at him. He smiled, "Ok! One time while she was pregnant, I wanted to know if the rumors were true."

I frowned, "are they?" I was too curious to let my disgust for Toya take over.

Andrew smiled real big. Hubby acted like he was throwing up. "You're disgusting man! You're still talking about Toya. Besides even if its nine months get out of jail free. I heard they lose interest in sex after awhile, and then you're on strict lockdown for six weeks. Then the baby takes over," Hubby frowned. "If Nicole wanna have one eventually I guess that'll be fine, but I don't want nobody coming between me and my woman. Baby or not!"

"It can't be that bad. And plenty of people don't wait the full six weeks. That's how a lot of them end up pregnant at their six week checkup." Jeff said matter of factly.

"Conrad you take sprung to a whole other level, jealous of a baby?"

"At least I'm honest! Nicole is mine! Ain't nobody or nothing coming between us!" Hubby said, "don't call me Conrad. That's my work name!" He laughed.

"As long as you guys are on the same page about it that's fine." Derrick said taking Andrew's pole. "You my friend lack conviction." He pointed to Andrew

"How you figure?" Andrew was offended

"You sit up here subjecting us to hours and hours of your love confessions about this woman. Then some random females walks in the pool hall and you're swaying. If you're gonna do right by this woman, standup and do right by her. If she's everything you said she was earlier why would you jeopardize her for that?" He said pointing at the other table. "If you're gonna do it, do it! You gonna end up like Malcolm if you keep turning your head when ever a female walks by."

Hubby and I stood there smiling. Andrew was angry! If you wanna push Andrew's buttons, tell him that anything about him in anyway resembles Malcolm in a negative light. "Being faithful to your woman gets hard at times, but the pay off is so much more than the guilt you carry from cheating. Step over to the light." Jeff said

"Besides Tracy is a good girl. You know first hand she only has eyes for you. It wouldn't be fair to her." I said

"Just because you work with her, doesn't mean you know her." Andrew said

"I'm with her everyday, I know her." I said

Andrew walked in my face, "You trying to say you know my woman better than me?" I looked at Andrew like he had to be kidding! What would ever make him this dumb? He acts like a little kid throwing a tantrum cause the world isn't yielding to what he wants. "I guess if we're having this conversation, I do know her better than you! You need to check your self!" I said wishing he swung so I could take him out.

"Drew! You got too much aggression! You need to release just not with these chicken heads. Get out of Yussef's face!" Hubby said

I was kind of disappointed when Andrew walked away. Cracking his jaw right about now would've felt great. "I'm not working with her anymore! You guys are fine, I want out!" I growled

Andrew sat on the stool brewing for a minute. Derrick perfectly swept the table. "Lets play." He said

Andrew took out his phone, texted for a few minutes. "I'll be right back!" he said walking out

Hubby shook his head, "he's gonna mess it up! I'm not kicking it with Toya no more!" He took a drink of his beer, "NO MORE! I SAY!" He took another drink, "He finally got somebody who's cool and my woman REALLY likes and he's gonna piss it off again, just like last time! I'm not going back to Toya, I CANT!"

"Oh I don't know, he's making good strides. He could actually make this one work if he can keep his pants zipped up long enough." Derrick said

Andrew was back thirty minutes later and he was a lot calmer. "I'm sorry man!" He said putting his hand out to shake mine. "You're right Tracy deserves better."

He was completely relaxed now; I was irritated at the site of him. "Where did you go?" Joseph asked from the table with girls next to ours.

"I needed a quick release. I'm good now." He said nonchalantly.

"Toya?" Jeff asked with a frown

"NO! I'm not fooling with Toya any more! Drop it, let's play." Andrew said. Then he stood by me. "I was tripping. I apologize. I'll make it worth your while to hang in there a little longer for me."

Derrick looked at me then he looked away. "I guess." I said in a defeated tone.

Invisible

****

"I'm so excited!" Tracy was on the phone talking to a girlfriend. "I've never gone anywhere before... He's been making all the arrangements.... My elevator is here, I'll call you later." She stepped into the elevator with a huge grin. "GOOD MORNING YUSSEF!" She sang in a silly voice. She had a paper bag in her hand.

"Morning" I said almost dryly.

"It's not a good day for you?"

"It's just starting, can't tell yet." I said

"Ok well I'll smile for the both of us!"

Today is gonna be a long day. "Good morning Yussef!" Danielle said trying to get my attention.

"Morning Danielle" I said without looking at her.

I held the door open for Tracy then I went my way and she went hers. I was having a pep talk with myself when Tracy tapped on my wall. "Do you like all things apple or just the candy?" She had an up to something look on her face.

"I like it all, why?"

"Go look on the share table." She looked proud.

As soon as I exited the cube I could smell fresh baked goods. I looked at her and she smiled and walked around the corner. I could hear her talking to Keith. There was a big glass dish on the table and it looked like coffee cake. Suddenly all the early birds were at the table. Tracy told us it was a apple cinnamon coffee cake. Danielle brought plates and forks. I cut the first piece and I didn't care that I cut such a huge piece. It was still warm. She watched as I put the first fork full to my mouth, she looked from person to person. Everyone had the same reaction. It was delicious!

"Aren't you gonna have some?" Someone asked her.

"No, I can't eat it. But watching you guys enjoy it is just as good." She said

"It's a shame cause you're missing out." Someone else said

"Thank you Tracy this is delicious." I said walking back to my cubical. When I heard the crowd die down I went back and grabbed the dish. Maybe I couldn't have the woman, but this dish was mine!

"Ok! For real the pan is gone?" Tracy called out about an hour later.

"I have it Tracy." I told her. I hung up the phone. "I washed it out and my phone was ringing when I was on my way to bring it to you. It was very sweet of you to bring this for everybody."

She smiled a relieved smile. "Thank you"

"What made you do this?" I asked

"I woke up with excited energy this morning super early. I looked at the apples and it happened from there."

"You made all of that from scratch?" I couldn't believe it.

"Yes, it's a hobby that used to get me in trouble. But you liked it?" She asked again

"Loved it! I took the last for myself I wasn't sharing." She laughed, I gave her the dish. She left and I tried my best to get back to work. I knew she was excited cause Andrew was taking her to Vegas. In just a couple more hours I wouldn't have to sit here and pretend I didn't know or I didn't care. I stared at the clock begging it to move faster. Then her instant message window popped up.

TT: can u come over when u have a minute.

YD: is it urgent? Queuing up invoices

TT: when ur done is fine

YD: thanx

I stalled as long as I could. I exhaled took a note pad and pen. I told myself to be cool, and then I walked over to her cubical. Her fingers were flying all over the keyboard. She asked me to sit while she finished her thought. When I sat down her perfume danced in my nose, I told myself to be cool and focus on work. Fortunately she was in a zone, so we discussed work related stuff only. As I walked away it dawned on me that she just gave me a ton of work to do. I laughed to myself at the way she did it though. Very smooth Tracy! Very smooth!

Quitting time! I got my stuff when I heard her coming I started walking. She had the biggest smile as she texted on her phone like crazy. When she got in her car and drove off I felt kind of empty.

Instead of going home I drove to Latia's. We pulled up at the same time. "Hey, didn't know you were coming out tonight." She said giving me a hug.

"Me neither. You got plans tonight?"

"Does eating ice cream in front of the TV count?"

"Sounds like a plan to me." I love my sister and I don't know what I'd do without her. I could've gone to see my Grandma, but the house seems too small with my momma there. One minute she's crying and feeling sorry for all that she's done to me. Then the next minute she's getting on my ever loving last nerve. I can tell my Grandma still talks to Melissa. It seems like they always talking and she stay tight-lipped about anything concerning Melissa too.

"Which movie you wanna watch? Driving like the wind? Or Love in the Summertime?" She held both of them out.

"You know I'm not voting for no chick flick." I said

Latia laughed, "you could've been in a chick flick kind of mood. We'll watch this one next.

We were both stretched out on either one of her couches when her cellphone rang. She smiled when she heard the ringtone. "Hey girl.... Are you guys ok... I was watching movies with Yussef... Um, um... You know he is... It's gonna have to happen... Where are you? I'm on my way..." She hung up. I waited for her to say. Latia swallowed. "Ok so, Melissa and her husband were in a car accident. The other car ran, but Melissa got a couple pictures of the license plate. The tow truck driver who showed up wants to charge them an arm and a leg to tow their car. I'm gonna go so they can use my membership and have their car towed here and then we'll figure out the next step." She exhaled, "can you handle it?"

"Of course!" Melissa didn't seem to ache in my heart as much anymore. And being around Tracy all the time definitely conditioned me for this. "I'm coming with you." Besides, I wanted to finally meet the guy Melissa was so in love with.

When we pulled up Melissa was waiting on the side while her husband and the tow truck driver were talking. Melissa smiled when she saw us. She gave Latia a big hug and she said a calm hello to me. Her husband was about average height, average build, average clean-cut appearance. The only thing he had over me was Melissa's heart. He came with a smile, he gave me a firm handshake while maintaining eye contact. "How you doing man, I'm Jackson."

"Yussef, nice to meet you."

He gave Latia a hug, "I really appreciate you guys coming out." He said

Latia gave the driver her address then we all got in the car and followed the truck by to Latia's house.

"Man! I'm just trying to take my lady out and then all this happened! We can't seem to catch a break." Jackson said halfway laughing.

"We'll get out of you guy's way as soon as possible. I just need to call my momma when we get to the house." Melissa said

"We weren't doing anything, if you guys still wanna go out you can take my car." I said Jackson liked the sound of that, Melissa seemed like she was out voted before she even said. "You sure? That's not gonna be putting you out?" He said

"It was just gonna be sitting anyways." I said glancing at Melissa in the rear view mirror.

"Yussef my brotha! You are alright with me!" Jackson was all smiles.

When we got back to the house, the tow truck driver unloaded the car. I gave Jackson my keys then I went back to my couch.

"That was very sweet of you." Latia said eyeing me. "What are you up to?"

I put my arms behind my head, "nothing." I wanted to see what shape they came back in.

Just after midnight the doorbell rang. Latia had just dozed off and she didn't hear the bell. When I opened the door both of their eyes were red, but Jackson was more tore up than Melissa. I moved so they could come inside. "Latia, girl I'm so sorry. One too many beautifuls and I could barely drive here."

"Yussef you can have the downstairs room, you guys can take the guest room upstairs." Latia said

"Thank you Latia, I'm so sorry. This evening has been full of unexpected twist and turns." Jackson said, and then he turned to me. "Thank you for being so nice. It's makes it hard to hate you when you're nice. Can I rap to you for a sec?"

Panic flashed across Melissa's face. "Don't you want to wait until morning?"

"No, we can talk tonight. If its ok with him." He said

"It's fine." I said sitting back on the couch.

"Go do your girlie thing." He said giving her a sloppy smooch.

Melissa looked like she was gonna cry. Jackson sat down on the other couch with a big grin as he watched the girls go up. "She still loves you." He said still smiling at the stairs where the girls were once walking.

"But she loves you right?" I said

"Of course! I'm her husband. She has shown me how much she loves me."

"How she do that?" I asked

"By leaving you alone completely." He said

I didn't like it, but it was true. "What did you want to talk to me about?"

He looked me in my eyes; he had pain in his eyes. "I really wanted a chance to get a good look at you. Say thank you for letting us have time to work our relationship out. You could've made things more difficult than they had to be."

"I was trying to make things difficult but your wife made her choice."

He smiled and looked at the floor. "Yea" then he looked at me. "Did you love her? Was that night about winning, or did you love her?"

I could see the girl's shadows upstairs as they were listening. "I don't see how I was supposed to win like that? I loved her, and I felt regret for not valuing what I had until that night. In that moment I couldn't think of any other way to show her. I'm not in love with her anymore, she belongs to you. I don't need God to be anymore upset with me than he might already be."

"How do you fall out of love with someone?" He asked

"I don't know, you just do it."

He looked at me, "I just wanted to say thank you. Now I don't have to feel like I'm supposed to hate you." He stood up, "see you in the morning."

The girls scurried upstairs, he looked at me and smiled I smiled back. Latia brought me blankets and sheets, for the futon in the room downstairs. She asked me if I was ok. I told her I was, she hung out with me for a while, then she eventually went upstairs, leaving my door slightly cracked open.

In the morning I heard Melissa creeping down the stairs. I knew it was her, because she didn't walk like Latia and the steps were too light to be Jackson. I didn't move, I laid there listening. She walked to my door; she stood still for a minute. Then she went in the kitchen. She called her mother. She told her she was here, and that I was there too. She started crying, she whispered something to her mother, cried some more then she changed the subject. Then I heard Jackson come down the stairs, his steps stopped in front of my door too. Then he went in the kitchen with Melissa. Both of them sound a little hung over and out of it. I put my shirt back on, and then I went upstairs and got medicine out of the medicine cabinet. I gave it to them then I left and got breakfast. When I came back they were standing around the kitchen trying to decide on breakfast.

"Bless you!" Jackson said opening the containers.

"Thank you" Melissa said quietly with puffy eyes.

We sat at the table to eat. "So I'm still mad at you! Why haven't I met my niece and nephew yet?"

"I'm sorry, please don't be mad at me. It's just been crazy."

Suddenly I felt tension at the table. "How's it been crazy?" I asked

Melissa moved her food around her plate. Jackson put his hand on hers. "It just has been. The kids have their own schedule. It's just a lot."

"That was cleverly vague." I said putting potatoes in my mouth.

She wouldn't look at me and that was upsetting. So I looked at Jackson, "my baby's got a lot on her plate dealing with two kids and me. Please don't hold it against her." He said to Latia

"I'm just saying, I could help with some of that. I got a niece and nephew who don't even know me. We need to meet, and then you guys could have more date nights. I could spoil them rotten and then send them home." Latia exhaled with a smile. "I can see it now. I'd be the best auntie ever!"

"I know you would." Melissa said looking at Latia with sad eyes.

Chapter 13

Drew: RED ALERT! WE NEED 2 CHNG EVERYTHING!

Me: ?

Drew: TOO MUCH TO TEXT 2NITE!

Me: Hit me later

My mind was going a mile a minute. What could've happened? I looked at the time and it was four o'clock in the morning. "Who was that?" Veronica said
"Nobody, go back to sleep!" I said rolling over.
In the morning Veronica was looking at me while I slept. Irritated I turned my back to her. "Oh no Yussef! Who was texting you in the middle of the night?"
I sat up completely annoyed. "You know what, lets stop wasting each other's time! You don't need to pretend like you care whose texting me in the middle of the night. Just like I don't care who's here when I'm not. Its not working for either one of us so lets just cut our losses." I said pulling on my pants.
Veronica sat there with her mouth hanging open. "So just like that you're done with me? I mean I knew you were a little distracted, but like this?"
"And you weren't?" I said putting on my shoes
She blew air and shrugged, "fine! Be gone then!" She said laying back down.
When I got in my bucket, my mind wandered, I imagined all kinds of things happening all the what ifs. I showered and I anxiously waited for Andrew's call. I was in deep thought when my cellphone finally rang. Andrew's voice was deep and panicked. "It's been like a domino affect!" He told me they went over some guy that she knows from Service's house, and it turned out that he knew the sister. He said that was one time bomb, then they run into her ex and Toya. He beat up the ex and police came. "I started feeling guilty man! It was like she was so appreciative of me defending her honor or something. She was trying to get me!"
"What do you mean trying to get you?" I said hoping he didn't mean what I thought he meant.
"Trying to put it on me. I don't understand, she says no sex. I'm getting better at it, but I'm trying to be cool with it too. Now she's changing the rules."
I felt like I was going to be sick. "Women got needs too."
"But this morning I told her how I knew the guy's sister and she flipped out on me. Marched out the door… wait a minute hold on." Andrew started cursing and going off in the background. "WHY IS SHE IN JACK LONDON AT E&J RIGHT NOW WITH SONYA'S BROTHER! DIDNT I JUST BEAT A NIGGA DOWN LAST NIGHT!"
"Who's on her?"
"Derrick" then he kept going off
"DREW! Calm down, she's in a restaurant a public place, it could be worse."
"WORSE! WORSE THAN THIS!!! YOU KNOW MICHAEL IS…."
I took the phone off my ear cause I couldn't handle the heat from him going off in my ear. "DREW! MAN! CALM DOWN!"
"I GOTTA CALL YOU BACK!" He was still cursing and screaming in the background.
I couldn't help it, I smiled to myself. I thought about going to E&J, but there would be no way to justify my being there.

I waited a few minutes, and then I called Andrew back.

"Derrick's bringing her home now, but her ex was trying to get at her. We need to be light on our feet. We'll discuss more on Tuesday."

"Why not Monday?"

"She wants to go get restraining orders."

I laughed, "a piece of paper for real? What's she gonna do show it to him when he comes around?"

"I know, this cat ain't cool. If I wouldn't have been there, he would've hurt her. He was trying to get at her with everything in his body." He got real quiet like he was in deep thought.

"You ok man?"

"No! But I needed to clear the air, you know what I mean?"

"Yea, you think she's gonna break up with you?"

"She can't." He said matter of factly. "I'll talk to you in a little bit, she should be here in a minute." Then he hung up.

Andrew was loosing it. I imagined Tracy's business tone as she ripped him a new one. Then she'd break up with him. I waited, and I waited, and I waited. I kept my phone on me at all times.

Finally Sunday evening Andrew called. His voice was serious and extremely relaxed.

"We gotta ramp up. I'm trying to approach this from all angles. I need a full on security detail on her. You'll still be on point; I need this house locked up like Fort Knox. If Tracy opens a window I wanna know about it."

"You're talking about a lot of man power. Malcolm's gonna have to approve it." I said

Andrew blew air, "I know what his answer is going to be."

"You have a problem with paying this guy a visit?"

"I do when Tracy's watching. She's so innocent; she knows nothing about that life. She'd run for sure." He sounded defeated.

"You know letting him run around is gonna be more taxing."

"I know, but I don't want to affect her with all of this."

"So I take it you guys made up?"

"I guess you can say that. Our dynamics just changed."

"WHAT?" I didn't mean to yell, but the day I understand women is probably the day I die. I just knew she was gonna punish him; try her best to get away.

"Yea, you hear how relaxed I am. But now it's game time. I want Curtis on the house...." He went down his list of the dream team as he called it.

I called Malcolm afterwards and I gave him the list of wants from Andrew. He immediately asked me what was going on. So I gave him the story, as soon as I mentioned Toya Malcolm lost it. He was going off about Andrew being weak and goofy whenever that girl was involved. Andrew knew Malcolm would be mad, but he also knew he wouldn't leave him hanging. I told him he'd have the paperwork tomorrow.

****

Tracy has been really jumpy, the slightest noise and she jumps. She almost runs to and from here now. Whenever a vendor comes she asks me to seat them in the conference room. She doesn't move from her seat until I tell her who specifically was there. If I didn't know what she was going through it would annoy the stink out of me. She's not as happy as she usually is; all of this has made my daily reporting even longer. Her brother came by to take her to lunch and instantly she perked right up. If I didn't hear her on the phone telling her friend he was coming I would've questioned who he was and the reaction she had to him. When they came back he came up with her again. I had a question for her, perfect excuse to be nosey. I tapped on the wall. "Sorry to

138

interrupt Tracy. Quick question, do we have a green light on Mid-Way as a whole yet?"
Then I looked at her brother, "how you doing, I'm Yussef."
Firm handshake, check. Eye contact, check. Loving regard for his sister, check. "How
you doing, Terence. Nice to meet you."
"Likewise," I said turning my attention to Tracy.
She looked so happy in that moment with her brother there. I'm sure that it was for
that brief moment she felt safe. I wanted to tell her that as long as she's with me she's
always safe. But I went to my cubical and I got back to work.

****

"She's ok, she's gonna be working from home for the next week or so." Andrew said
"HOW DID THIS HAPPEN?" I barked
"I keep asking the same thing." Andrew said
"He came into your space and put his hands on your woman! Will she still feel safe
with you?" I was beyond angry. I had been trying to stay out of it and let Andrew
handle it. But all I could think about is how vulnerable Tracy must feel now. "What's
this guy's name?"
"Never mind all that. I need you to stay focused on your part. Make sure everything is
tight on your end."
"NEVER MIND THAT! WHAT DO YOU MEAN NEVER MIND THAT? You
put me on this girl for the past oh I don't know three plus years. How in the world do
you expect me not to care? What's his name Andrew, you know I don't need you to tell
me!" I said
"I know I'm asking you to stay focused on your part." Andrew said
"Either you tell me or I'll look it up. Tracy will always be safe on my watch. I need to
know who I'm looking for anyways." I said
"Steve"
"STEVE TURNAGE!" I yelled
Andrew paused for a minute. "So you know him?"
I dropped the phone, cursed paced. Then my cellphone started ringing. "HELLO!" All
I could see is RED!
"What?" He said
"I HATE HIM! HE PUT HIS HANDS ON TRACY? CAUSE FOR ONCE HE
DONT GET HIS WAY AND HE'S ACTING A FOOL!"
"How do you know him?"
"That girl Shannon." I sat down on my couch. "I've been covering your girl too long. I
need out man."
Andrew was quiet for a minute. "I see that." I heard tapping in the background.
Andrew exhaled, "I didn't finish him because I know Tracy couldn't handle it. Plus
those detectives would've used that in some kind of way." That fast I forgot about the
detectives. "Nobody could be more upset than me. All morning I'm telling her to calm
down, and that she's safe with me, and then the moment I'm not looking Toya brings
him to where we are. I need you right now. I need to be able to focus while I'm at
work, knowing that you're watching over her gives me the space to do that. Give me a
little more time. I'm begging you man." Andrew's voice was low and humble. I didn't
want to leave him hanging, but my mind was telling me to get away. "I know that as
long as she's with you she's covered just like I would."
"Who do you have on him?" I asked irritated that he wasn't getting that I need to get
away from his woman.

****

"I'm going to tell Tracy about you." Andrew said
"You sure about that?" I felt relieved.

139

"You guys have to go to the city over the next three days, and she's freaking out about Steve. The only way to get her to calm down is to tell her about you. You'll have backup, I'm thinking three."
"Make it four." I interrupted
"Four?"
"Two to handle him, one to handle people, one for possible clean up. Four!" I said
"Fine four" he said going on with the plan.
When he was done, "you realize this is gonna change things." I said as a warning.
"I'm aware." He said
I talked to Malcolm, told him who I needed and for how long. That night I could barely sleep. Mostly I wondered if Tracy was going to feel confident that I could protect her. I told myself to be cool. I busied myself by studying the floor plan for our meeting place in the city. I looked at the plans for the buildings on either side, looked at the under ground connections. I was prepared for whatever could come up.
The next morning I got the text that Darryl was rounding the corner. I made my way towards the building, when Tracy got out of the car she kept her eyes on me. I could see question marks all over her face. I opened the door for her; it was business as usual for me. Tracy kept looking for me whenever she thought I was missing. When we had lunch she signaled for me to sit at her table with her and Shirley. You could tell Shirley thought a lot of herself, however the mirror was a constant reminder that she was not as spry as she used to be. So she liked to live through those around her. When she said things she had a hidden agenda. Tracy didn't pick up on it but I did. Shirley felt like she was an authority on everything so whenever Tracy said something she undermined it. Or told her she was wrong, Tracy wasn't picking up on it. It was getting on my nerves so I changed the subject to Shirley's favorite topic, her. She got so excited then she started rambling. That's when I saw the ring on Tracy's finger. Andrew mentioned that he was looking at rings but failed to mention when he planned on proposing. At the end of the day I walked Tracy out of the building without walking with her. When she got in the car I continued on to the Bart station. Shirley was walking ahead of me; her walking sped up when she saw him. My insides boiled over, she hugged Steve and they walked into the Bart station. When she told him Tracy was there today he looked like he was going to run towards the building. He looked disappointed when she said Tracy got a ride home. I put my headphones on and pretended I was listening to something. When really all I could think about was pushing Steve off the platform in front of an oncoming train. Nothing about this fool was better than me. I didn't see what made him so great! I had to turn my eyes, and try to remain calm.

Chapter 14

"Can I touch your hair?" Tracy asked me. I could tell this is the first time that she was actually looking at me. All these years of working together and she was always cordial, and polite. But this time she was looking at me, and seeing me.

My heart sped up and my stomach flopped. "Sure" I said as nonchalantly as I could. When she reached out to touch my hair the perfume on her wrist danced in my nose. I don't know what perfume she wore but I swear I've never smelled it before, and I'm sure if someone else tried to wear it, it wouldn't smell as sweet on them. It wasn't a strong scent, but it always put me at ease. "Your hair is so soft. You got good hair huh." She smiled

"I don't know what you mean. My hair is soft, but I wouldn't call it good." I said

"How long did it take to grow your hair this long?"

"My hair has always been long, when I got it loc'ed the first time it was a little shorter than this. I trim it at this length."

Her eyes were wide, "your hair has always been long. How did that work with service?" she asked

"I would braid it and put the braid in my collar. But if my Grandma and G-momma could've had their way they would've shaved my head."

"Have you ever thought about cutting it?" She asked still staring at my hair like it had her in a trance.

"No, I've always had long hair. Cutting it isn't something I've ever thought about. Why? Should I cut it?"

"NO!" she said real fast. "It suits you, I was just asking." She said still twirling my hair in her fingers. "I like how you always keep your hair neat and clean. I never liked locs until seeing yours. You can tell you take good care of them."

"Thank you" I said staring at her face.

"What do you think Andrew would look like with locs?" She said

I smiled, I didn't want to talk or think about Andrew in that moment. "Naw locs wouldn't suit him."

"You're right, they look very nice on you." She said releasing my loc and taking her hand back. "Where do you want to go for lunch?" She changed the subject.

I couldn't tell if she was feeling me, or just more relaxed in my presence. "Obviously she's still in love with Andrew, she still goes on and on about him every chance she gets. When I bang out those reports at the end of the day, its like my fingers glide over the keyboard. Sometimes Andrew will call me laughing at my word choice. "We could have one of the guys go get whatever, then we can sit out on the balcony and eat. How does that sound?"

"Sounds good, what about Stony's?" She said

I laughed, "you know what's gonna happen. You're gonna order a salad, and I'm gonna order a burger. You're gonna stare at my burger until I cut it in half and we split my burger and your salad. I want my whole burger!"

"Yussef! Come on! Ok, just don't order the burger then. Order a salad like me." She laughed

"Woman! This body needs food. This body needs nourishment. I'll eat vegetables but I want my whole burger." I said with a smile putting my foot down.

"Well where else you wanna order from?" She said in defeat.

"Stony's cause now you made me want a burger." We laughed, "you want your usual?"

"Yes please." She said returning her attention back to her report.

I put the conference room phone on speaker. "Hello?"

"Hey Todd, we need lunch."

Todd laughed, "Let me guess Stony's?"

"You know it, you know what she wants right?"

"Yep got it. What about you?" He said

"I wanna try the Ostrich burger this time."

"WHAT?" Tracy's face flushed

Todd and I cracked up laughing. "Ostrich for real brah?"

Tracy shook her head no. "Yes!" I said shaking my head yes. "And all the fixings like normal. Sweet potato fries, you know the drill." I said

"Danielle there today?" Todd asked

"Man you better call her and do that on your time."

"Alright man. I'll have her call you when I'm in the lobby. Food delivery guy at your service." Then he hung up.

Tracy looked disgusted, "Ostrich? You could've just said no I can't have none of your burger." She mocked

I smiled but didn't say anything, when Todd delivered our food he hung around the receptionist desk for a while flirting with Danielle. She was completely eating it up. I took the food then I told Tracy to come on. We went out on the balcony that looked out over downtown Oakland. She looked at my bird burger in disgust. "Do you want me to cut it in half?" I asked with a smile.

She sucked her teeth. "Sometimes you can act just like Andrew. No I don't want your bird burger!" She said rolling her eyes.

"Suit yourself," I said picking it up and taking a bite.

She frowned, "how is it?"

I chewed for a minute. "It's good, it's like a turkey burger with more oil. Which makes it juicy."

I loved moments like this, where it was she and I. I know she's in love with Andrew but I enjoy the time we have together. I wonder if this is how Melissa felt when I was with Sylvia. Matter of fact I know it is. I wish I would've paid attention. I could've had a good girl who loved me before everyone else. Saved myself from heartache and pain. Or maybe I should've went to Hubby's engagement party instead of belly aching at home. Maybe I would've met Tracy first. All the woulda, coulda, but did nots. Now I sit here savoring stolen moments with my family's woman. I don't know how my so-called life could get any worse.

"Hello? Earth to Yussef!" I looked at her. "Where do you go when you space out like that?"

"I was trapped in my own brain. What's up?" I said

"I asked you if you were going out with Andrew tonight?"

"I haven't decided. I need to check on my family, haven't popped by in a minute. So no working this weekend for me."

"That's fine. Oh! I need pepper I'll be right back. I have some at my desk." As she got up and walked away, I watched her body sway to unheard music. She looked at me in the glass and then she turned around like she knew I was checking her out. I put my eyes on her face and she had a question mark on her face. I gave a "what?" look.

I put in my report I needed to be reassigned. To be so smart, it's beyond me why he always seems to miss the mark when it comes to his closest acquaintances. Toya's the number one offender, it's like there's no line for her to cross she does what she wants when she wants to. Andrew doesn't make her stop; his compassion for her goes too far. I don't pretend to know all that goes on in his life. But he's never extended much thought to me as a person. I mean we're close, but one day I appeared. He's never asked where I came from or why I'm here. I know how much trust he has in me to keep me on his woman this long. But he's not listening, I'm asking for out and he's not getting it.

Todd gave me his report and I slumped in my chair. Toya was hanging around the Civic center today. It could be a coincidence, but I doubt it. I erased my request for a reassignment; I couldn't live with myself if something happened to Tracy. I sent Andrew my report then I debated whether I felt like seeing his face tonight. I decided to pop up on my Grandma since it had been awhile since I've dropped by. I hoped my momma wasn't home or on best behavior. Last time I walked out and it took me a long time to calm down.

When I pulled up to the house Auntie Summer was there, she was cleaning the dishes. She looked startled to see me like she was sneaking. "Boy! You scared me!" She said putting her hand on her chest. The tan line from her engagement ring stood out on her soapy bubble dripping hand.

"Didn't mean to scare you. Why are you washing so many dishes?" Grandma was a stickler for a clean kitchen. I knew they couldn't have been dishes from the course of the day.

"Momma had company. I call myself being nice by offering to clean the kitchen for her." She said nervously

"When is she coming back?" I asked

"Oh um", she looked around for her phone. "I'm not sure, let me text her." She dried her hands, which were now a little shaky. She smiled at me nervously. "You coming from work?"

"Yes", her unusual nervousness was starting to annoy me. "What are you hiding?" She nervous laughed. "Stop reading me Yussef you know I hate when you do that." She said picking up her phone again waiting for a response.

"You're not making it hard. What's to be nervous about?"

"FINE! But you can't tell anybody you know. Promise?" She said, "Do you remember Arthur Prasad from Momma's congregation?" I nodded yes. "Momma's dating him."

"WHAT?" My eyes got big, not what I was expecting her to say. "The only person not dating in this house is my momma? She has to be hating that!" I chuckled.

"Oh she is fit to be tied!" Auntie Summer laughed

"But why is that a secret?" I said watching my auntie's face, turn nervous again.

"Cause momma wants to tell you herself."

"And?" I gestured with my hands for her to spill it.

She exhaled, "and Melissa and her husband came out to chaperone them tonight. They had dinner here, then they went to the movies."

"I've met Melissa's husband before, but why do they know about this before me?" I said

She was surprised, "you have? Were you nice? Was he nice? When did this happen? Tell me!" She said leaning in like I had juicy gossip to give her, and ignoring my question.

"They came by Latia's and I was there. He's fine enough, but they're hiding something." I watched auntie's face change. "Spill it!"

"What makes you think I know?" She was trying to keep the lid on whatever it is.

"I know you know! Nobody's telling me, do you know how upsetting that is?" I said watching her face.

She touched my hand. "Baby, she's still in love with you." She watched my face for a reaction.

"Why did she marry him then?" I said irritated. "I was trying to show her I was ready, and she ran to him."

"The way I understand it, she felt you were rebounding again. Jackson loves her, and he still wanted her after you guys did what you did. Who would choose uncertainty over consistency? But...." She took a deep breath. Then she looked at me, "this conversation stays between us you hear me!" I shook my head yes. "He's sick."
"What do you mean?" He looked fine when I saw him.
"He has sickle cell anemia, and lately it's been giving him more problems than before." She took a deep breath. "He's been in the hospital a few times due to crisis flare ups. That's a lot for anyone to deal with. Sometimes Melissa has to be momma and daddy, and then you know everyday life whoas. Sometimes she calls momma in tears just from the stress of it all. She loves her husband, don't ever doubt that. But she's still in love with you." Auntie rubbed my hand then she went back to finishing her dishes. I sat there letting her words sink in. Her phone chimed, then she said, "they're on their way back. You get to meet Momma's boyfriend."
Then we heard the front door. "Yussef you're here?" My Momma's voice called out. I rolled my eyes. "I'm in the kitchen."
"Hi baby" she said giving me a kiss on my cheek.
"You went shopping?" Auntie Summer said looking at all my Momma's bags.
"Mind your own business." My momma said throwing her bags in her room
"I'm not covering your rent tomorrow, and if momma say you got to go then you got to go this time." Auntie said
"I got my rent for your FYI! Can you get out of my business, I'm trying to visit with my son." She said wiggling her neck.
Summer picked up her phone and texted again. Then she rolled her eyes at her big sister. "You haven't been paying your rent?" I asked
"Work has been slow lately. But I got a part time job waitressing so I got my rent. I had a little extra so I went shopping, that's not a crime!"
Grandma didn't need the money, Malcolm paid for the house and he pays the insurance and taxes on it. He still gives her money monthly for her utilities and she gets a little money from my grandfather's social security. But I told her she needed to charge them rent or they wouldn't respect the gift of being in the house my father provided for her.
The front door opened auntie's phone vibrated. "Yussef?" Grandma called out. I came around the corner and my Grandma and Brother Prasad were standing in the living room looking proud. I looked him up and down. "What's going on?"
"Yussef you remember Brother Prasad don't you?" Grandma said all proud
"Un huh. Still don't explain what he's doing here."
"How you doing tonight son?" Brother Prasad said sticking his hand out and giving me eye contact.
"I'm good, and you?"
"I've got no complaints. Can I wrap to you for a minute?" He said
Grandma smiled real big, "I'll go put on some coffee." She said as she floated to the kitchen. You could hear them whispering in there.
"I'm gonna be straight with you." I motioned for him to sit on the couch, while I sat on the couch next to his. "Me and your Grandma have been getting close. I care for her a lot, I wanna marry her."
"Whoa!" He wasn't beating around the bush. I frowned, "how long have you guys been dating?"
"Oh I'd say about. Three months, but you know I've known your family since before you were born."
"How long ago did Sister Prasad die?" I asked. My Grandma wasn't gonna be nobody's bed warmer. Anything less than three years was too soon.

"Five years ago. I told myself I wasn't gonna remarry either, and that's the way I've been living. But your grandmother is an exceptional woman. She makes me feel alive again. I would never try to replace your grandfather, just like she doesn't try to replace Gillian. But I tell you, I couldn't imagine my future life without her." He said pouring out his heart.

"Have you asked her to marry you already?" I asked

"No, but we've talked about marriage. I feel pretty certain that she will accept me. I wanted to talk to you first though."

"So you guys have been dating all this time unchaperoned?" I asked looking around

"Oh no, he shook his head. Everything with us has been on the up and up. Tonight we were out with that young girl your Grandma is close to." He snapped his fingers trying to remember her name. "I think you know her, her husband has a last name for a first name."

"Melissa and Jackson?"

"Right! I'm terrible with names. We went to the movies with them and their kids."

"Why didn't they come in?" I asked

"You gotta talk to your Grandma about that. I don't know."

I could tell he wasn't in the "know" about Melissa and I's past. But that also meant he wasn't a busy body. That worked for me. "Are you healthy?"

"As an ox!" Then he laughed. "I've got a little high blood pressure, and arthritis in my knees. But I'm in good health, I plan to be around for a long time." He said proudly

"You seem fine to me. If she wants you. She can have you." I said

He smiled and shook my hand. "Thanks son. Now you know us old folk don't move slow like you young ones. We could be married in the next three months."

"If that's what she wants that's fine too." Then I stood up. "Excuse me." I said going to the kitchen. I heard chairs scooting as they tried to act like they weren't ear hustling. "Ya'll some nosey some bodies." Grandma hugged me and kissed my cheek. "Can we talk?"

"Sure honey." Then she turned to Summer. "Baby will you take this coffee out to him?"

We went in her room and shut the door. Grandma sat on her bed blushing real hard. I sat in her chair across from her. I smiled real big, "my Grandma's got a boyfriend."

"Oh get on boy!" She said blushing real hard. "You like him?"

"I like him if you like him." I said, "why didn't you tell me?"

"You've got your own life. I didn't want to bother you." She said still being bashful.

"I'm never too busy for you Grandma. You and Latia always have my undivided attention."

She smiled, "thank you baby. Momma used to say he was watching me. But I never paid it no mind. I knew he was hurting from losing his wife. All those women were constantly trying to get his attention. That wasn't gonna be me. Imagine my surprise when he asked me on a date. I thought we were just friends." She smiled as a couple tears ran down her face. "I haven't felt like this in years. I never thought I'd feel like this again. Not only does a man want me, but he knows about your momma and all her craziness and that didn't scare him away."

"What are his kids like?" I asked

"They're nice. Two boys and a girl, they're much older than your momma though."

"And they're ok with you two courting?"

She told me that the daughter was having a hard time at first. Apparently he discussed the idea with his kids before he even approached Grandma. She said they'd probably live in her house cause she wouldn't feel right changing things in his wife's house. And there was no way she was leaving my momma in her house. I smiled at her thinking. I asked why Melissa and Jackson left, and she started fidgeting saying they needed to get the babies home cause they were tired. Then she asked me if I would give her away in her wedding. I told her I would be honored.

****

"Why they always over there whispering?" My momma said waiting next to me.

"Maybe they don't want your big mouth in they business!" I said, Charlotte my soon to be new auntie laughed.

"What are you laughing at?" My momma said full of attitude.

"You! Leave them alone, and let them have their private moments." Auntie Charlotte said

My momma stared at Charlotte like she wanted to say something smart, but she couldn't think of anything. Grandma, auntie Summer, and Latia were over to the side whispering about something but I didn't care. We just finished picking out Grandma's wedding dress. I felt like THE MAN paying for it, and her eyes doubled when I told her there was no limit on the dress. Whatever she wanted she could have. But being the Grandma that I know and love she fell in love with a very reasonably low priced dress. They picked out bridesmaids dresses, Latia cried when Grandma told her she wanted both of her grandbabies in her wedding. I naturally assumed that both of Melissa's kids would be in the wedding. But Grandma said Arthur's grandchildren were going to be in the wedding.

"Thank you baby." My Grandma said planting a kiss on my cheek.

I blushed and then Latia snapped a couple pictures of our moment. Then we posed for some pictures.

Latia and I rode with Charlotte to the restaurant. I liked her; Charlotte was a real person, not a fake female. She said her dad waited a year before approaching my Grandma just so she could adjust to the idea of him being with someone new. She said the fact that my Grandma wasn't one of the women that tried their hardest to push up on her dad or even try to get his attention was a major plus. Charlotte said once her dad pointed Grandma out she started watching her and interacting with her. She said once she liked her then she became fearful that Grandma might not like her dad and she had already set her heart on her. She said she was relieved when Grandma finally caught on that her dad liked her and she was open to it. "No disrespect but that's some momma you got." She said

Latia and I chuckled, "I know." I said

"I can only imagine how you guys grew up with her." Charlotte said shaking her head

"Shonda's not my mother, we have the same father though." Latia said

"GET OUT!" We pulled up to the light and Charlotte looked back and forth between both of our faces. "You guys look exactly alike! Do your momma's look alike?"

"Nope not at all, her momma is light skinned too." I said

"Wow! He's got some strong genes."

"Our grandmother actually, he looked just like her." Latia said

When we got to the restaurant Brother Prasad was there. He told us to call him Arthur since we were family now. Grandma looked so happy, and everyone there was happy for her. Everyone except my momma of course. She chose this dinner to ask Grandma where she was going to live after the wedding, and when Grandma told her they were going to live in her house momma asked what Arthur was going to do with his house. Grandma said one of his kids was going to take that house. My momma got mad and asked where she was supposed to go. Grandma was trying to be nice and tell her they would talk about it later, but my momma had to cause a scene. I was listening but then I wasn't, and then I saw Grandma stand up with her finger pointing in my momma's face. She had her neck wiggling and her lips clinched. My momma started crying, saying that she wasn't even married yet and she was putting everybody before her. I could tell Arthur was annoyed with the scene but he was trying to let Grandma handle it. But when momma kept on with the tears Arthur stood up, "look here little girl. You are disrespecting your momma, yourself, and the whole evening. If you can't pull it together get on, start walking. But your mother has said her peace and it's done. Deal with it or move on, but we ain't gonna have all these tears and carrying on. Not tonight!" Arthur stood next to Grandma like he was confirming he had her back. I sat back and smiled. My momma looked around the table and realized it was a long walk from Crockett to Richmond so she sat down. She sat over to the side the rest of the night looking like someone stole her blanket. No one felt sorry for her, not even one of the kids went to her rescue.

****

"Are Andrew and Tracy coming today?" Latia asked

"Naw, they had something to do with Tracy's family already. But Jeff and Randi are coming." I said

"I like them, they make such a cute couple."

"I guess," I said. "Derrick is bringing Chantel."

"Are they dating or what?" She asked straighten my tie

"I don't know. Chantel just got back. But I don't know that they label their selves as anything really. You know Derrick, he don't talk in detail about anything emotional." I looked in the mirror, "Lewis coming?"

Latia sighed, "yea he's coming. I only invited him because Chantel mentioned the wedding in front of him."

"You didn't want him here?" I looked in her eyes and I saw fear

She opened her mouth then she closed it. "I care about him…. I really do! It's just… scary." She took another deep breath. "He wants us to be together, but I don't know how that would work."

"Why?"

"What rapper gets married?"

"There are plenty of married rappers." I said

"Happily married?"

"The ones who keep their relationship out of the limelight. Why do you keep running from the man? It's been years, I'm surprised he's held on this long." I said still staring at her.

"I guess I have unfinished business. I wanted to ask you for a favor."

"Shoot"

"I wanted to know if…."

Charlotte came in the room. "We're about to start. Yussef your Grandma is ready for you."

"You guys look amazing!" I said smiling to the two of them. They both blushed

"You look pretty amazing too nephew." She said

I popped my collar, "Hugo Boss!" I smiled then I walked next door to the library. I knocked on the door as I opened it. Grandma was admiring herself in the mirror. SHE LOOKED AMAZING! "Grandma!" I put my hand over my heart, "you're breath takingly gorgeous!"

She blushed, "Thank you baby." She put her arm around mine. "You look amazing yourself."

Grandma's friend tapped on the door and told us it was time. When we stepped out into the congregation it was PACKED standing room only. Cameras snapping like crazy and people were going ooh and ah when they caught a glimpse of Grandma. There were too many people to look for anyone specifically, so I looked straight ahead.

Arthur shook my hand and anxiously took my Grandma's hand. I sat next to my momma who was kicked out of the wedding because of all her drama. She cried during the ceremony but I'm sure those were tears of uncertainty about her future. After everyone cleared out the wedding party stayed behind to take pictures. Latia and I sat back and watched Grandma look so happy with her new husband. I was happy somebody was getting a happily ever after. When we got to the reception Melissa was sitting at the table with Lewis, Jeff, Derrick, Randi and Chantel. Melissa looked beautiful, it made my stomach hurt to look at her. I was looking around for Jackson, but it appeared he was nowhere to be found. And once again neither were these so called kids. I'm starting to believe they were made up kids. I've never seen them or even pictures of them. Latia went to their table, I was talking to Arthur junior, and Melissa kept peeking at me. I smiled to myself the locs, and Hugo Boss on my back…. I mean how could she not look at me? When Latia and Melissa left the table I went and sat down to say hey to my people. Randi told me I was wearing my tux, Jeff shot her a look playfully but I knew that was also a warning. I think Randi understood it as well she backed down. We were laughing about something when a female put her fingers over my eyes. "Ok who's this? Latia?" although I knew it wasn't my sister, it didn't smell like her. The person shook; I guess she was shaking her head no. That's when I recognized the feeling of those large breast on my head, and I recognized the smell. My smile dropped and it seemed like everything was moving in slow motion. I grabbed her hands, but I had to remind myself not to grab her too firmly, and I pulled her around to my face. "What are you doing here Shannon?" My heart started beating really fast. She had the NERVE to be here looking beautiful.

She smiled, "my mother is friends with your new aunt. Charlotte invited us." She smiled bigger, "how have you been?"

"Honestly I was doing fine until you showed up. Why do you think I would want to talk to you?"

"Shannon?" Latia said in complete shock, Melissa stood next to Latia giving Shannon evil eyes. "What are you doing here?"

"I was just telling your brother that my mother and your auntie are good friends, she invited us." Then she looked at Melissa who didn't change her face, "do I know you?" Melissa started to say something to her, and Latia pulled her away by her arm. "Is that your girlfriend?"

"No" I said

"Then what's her problem?" Shannon said disregarding Melissa before she got an answer

"What do you want?" I said completely irritated

"I wanna talk to you."

I sucked my teeth, "fine!" This girl had been asking to talk to me every since we broke up in high school. Fine! I'll talk to her now. I stood up and I followed her. Latia was trying to calm Melissa down when we walked past her to exit the banquet hall. Melissa's eyes got big like she couldn't believe I was going to talk to her. We stepped right outside the doors. "What is it?" I said sounding exhausted already.

"I wanna apologize for what I did to you. I know I hurt you, you trusted me. I know I betrayed you." She said trying to look genuine

"What makes you think I care about that now?" I said matter of factly.

"Come on Yussef, you're talking to me. I know how much you cared about me." She said

"I know how much you didn't care about me. I don't have time to rehash this with you. Speak your peace and stop asking to talk to me." I said flatly

"Can we start over as friends?" She smiled

"What? I can't hear you? My hearing aide must've went out." I said tapping my ear as I put the other one closer to her mouth.

"I said can we…" I put my hand up to her mouth.

"That's what I thought you said. I don't keep tricks as friends! You've got some nerve showing up here like this. Stop disrespecting my Grandma with this nonsense. There's nothing left for us to talk about. You cheated on me in high school with a joke of a person, we broke up. The whole time you're begging me to talk to you, you were still with him. You eventually did have his baby and he left you hanging. Now you come in here see me looking good and happy with myself and you wanna press up. What I felt for you died a long time ago. Now all I feel for you is anger and disgust."

"How do you know all that?" She said in shock

"People talk" but I found it in the cross reference I did on Steve's background check. He owes her thousands of dollars in arrears/back child support, he's left her hanging completely. He had at least one more child last I checked.

She looked like she wanted to cry. "I'm sorry Yussef! I was young and dumb, I didn't realize what I had until it was gone."

Now I'm wrestling with myself. I definitely know the feeling, but I don't want Shannon back in my life. "Ok" I sighed, "we're even."

"Really?" she said as a tear ran down her face.

"Yea", but I don't want to be your friend, but I won't hate your existence anymore." I said feeling weak for giving in.

She pressed her breast up against me as she hugged me tightly. "Thank you!"

"Alright." I said letting her go and turning on my heels.

When we walked back into the banquet hall I did feel like a huge weight had been lifted from my shoulders. Shannon rejoined her mother's table and I took my seat at the head table. Latia and Melissa came straight to me. "What did she want?"

"She wanted to apologize." I said

"Did you forgive her?" Latia asked

"Yea, that was high school." I said

"So what, now you guys gonna start dating again?" Melissa spit

Latia and I looked at Melissa who was not masking her jealousy. "What does it matter to you? You're a happily married woman." I said

Melissa rolled her eyes and walked away. "This just got interesting! I had to remind Melissa today is Grandma's day, that was the only way to get her to calm down. She's a little bit pissed off right now." Latia said

"Why?"

Latia put her hands out, "Melissa hates three people. Sylvia, Shannon, and Mitchell! Although I don't know how she would respond if Mitchell walked in here right now, but those other two…. yea. How much you wanna bet the evening doesn't end without Melissa getting in Shannon's face?"

"Doubt that, why would she do that?" I asked

Latia laughed and walked to Lewis, they went out on the dance floor. Pretty soon Jeff and Randi joined, then Derrick and Chantel. Melissa kept shooting me looks, and I smiled at her. I couldn't believe how jealous she was acting. My momma was watching from the other side of the room. I could tell she was getting a kick out of this dramatic scene. I decided to find someone to dance with when Shannon approached me. "Can I have this dance?" she said, I figured what the heck I could dance with her. Melissa got up and stormed out when she saw us heading to the dance floor. Shannon and I had a good time. Grandma danced up next to me and asked where Shannon came from. I told her real quickly. Grandma didn't smile at Shannon she just shook her head, then you could tell she was looking for Melissa. She spotted her sitting at her table with my momma talking her ear off. Grandma and Arthur said their thank you's to everyone for helping them put today together. Then they left their party, I cringed when Jeff made a joke about me having a new Uncle or Auntie soon. Shannon tried to stay by my side even after we stopped dancing. I was enjoying the attention I was getting from Melissa so I endured Shannon just to keep it going. Auntie Summer came over to our table and I introduced her to everybody, but she already knew who Derrick was. She got quiet after she said Derrick's name at the same time as I did. "Do you remember me?" She asked him

"Yea, you worked for my mom at the center." He said

"How have you been?" she said

"Fine" he said staring at her like Malcolm would, "this is Chantel"

"Didn't I see you on TV?" Auntie said

Chantel smiled a modest smile, "performing with Shameless, yes you did."

"THAT SONG IS AMAZING! I LOVE IT!" Auntie said

"Derrick wrote and composed it." Chantel said proudly.

"Really wow! Derrick the song is beautiful!"

"Thank you" Derrick said with no emotion in his face or tone.

Auntie's new husband was waving her on so she said her goodbyes and she left. "I thought you guys looked familiar. Yussef I didn't know you ran with celebrities." Shannon said with stars in her eyes.

I changed the subject cause no one at the table wanted to discuss it. I guess Melissa had enough of my momma talking her ear off, cause she came to our table. A lot of the guest left shortly after Grandma left. I expected Melissa to leave then too, but she stayed put. "Do you have a son or daughter?" I asked

"A boy" Shannon said showing me a picture

It was Steve's alright, he looked a lot like Shannon but I could see Steve in his face as well. I asked her if she was going to have anymore. She said she would like to after she was married of course. Melissa got up putting her purse on her shoulder then she stopped and came back to the table. "You know what, I hope you two get back together. She's only going to hurt you again."

"Get back together? Whoa!" I said

"Why do you care what he does with me? Who are you?" Shannon said

"Don't worry about who I am!" Melissa said, "You're nothing but a hoe. I don't know what you said to get your foot back in the door, but she's gonna do it again don't you see that?" she said

"People mess up, but they can change Melissa." I said talking about myself

"Some people can, but this trick hasn't!" Melissa said

"Who are you calling a trick?" Shannon said

Melissa looked at Derrick, and he looked like yea she asked you that. I saw my momma scooting closer with her chair so she could hear everything. Melissa walked around the table and just outside of Shannon's circle of space. "You're the only trick I see in here. You were just pushing up on some other guy until you got stars in your eyes watching Yussef walk down the aisle. You're still a tramp trick playing high school games!"

"I don't know who you are, or why you're so concerned about my business but Yussef and I are grown. We can be friends if we wanna be. What's it to you anyway? Who are you?" Shannon said "Naw! Naw! Somebody tell me who this hoe is. She's all up in my business but she don't wanna say who she is."

"That's my best friend. Latia said pleading with her eyes with Melissa asking her to calm down

"You're best friend huh?" Shannon looked her up and down, "sounds to me like she got a crush on your brother.

Invisible

Everybody at the table kept going back and forth from person to person like it was a tennis match or something. Melissa sucked her teeth, "I'm going home I don't have time for this. I've got my own kids and a husband to get home to." She said taking out her keys, she hugged Latia bye and then she walked around Shannon and hugged me. Our first embrace since that morning in the parking lot, my heart sped up. Then Melissa looked at Shannon as she kissed my cheek. Shannon pushed Melissa, Melissa stumbled backwards three steps. Then she laughed a wicked sarcastic laugh, "you know you messed up right? You put your hands on the wrong one!" Melissa said storming off

"Ooh! I'm scared!" Shannon said mocking Melissa

Latia went outside then she came back she put her hands up. "She left!"

"You'll call her later?" I asked

"Why do you care? She's married let her husband worry about her." Shannon said with an attitude

"You know what Shannon bye! Leave my friends and me alone. I just remembered another reason I don't like you. Your mouth runs away with you. I'm cool! Peace!" I said turning my back to her

"Yussef?" She sounded like she was going to cry.

Everybody was staring at Shannon. Shannon walked away towards her mother and her friends who all had their backs to us. Melissa was shoeless and she crept up behind Shannon with her hand behind her back. I should've known by the smile on Derrick's face this was not gonna end well. Melissa tapped Shannon's shoulder. When Shannon turned around Melissa bopped her up side the head with a mini baseball bat. Shannon went down like a sack of potatoes. "Don't you EVER put your hands on me again!" Then Melissa walked over to Latia hugged her one more time while staring at me the whole time. I smirked at her, and she kept her face even. Even though there was a crazy look in her eyes I knew she was lucid cause she only popped her once. Melissa walked out while everyone else tried to figure out what just happened to Shannon.

Chapter 15

Over the past few years I've learned to take April 9th - 11th at least off. April 10th just after four am I'm waking up feeling like the life is being squeezed out of me. It normally stops when I wake up. Awhile back I asked my Grandma if she had any idea why this keeps happening to me. Best we could come up with is that maybe since it is around the time my father died that my body subconsciously reacts. Sounds stupid, but it was the best I could come up with. I go out to my place and unplug from the world. I write poetry to calm my soul, I go out at night stare at the stars in the heavens, contemplate my life and reflect on myself as a person. I hate my situation; whenever I meet someone I now compare her to Tracy. Who really stands a chance when someone is thinking that way? At the end of the day she happily goes home to Andrew. I finally came to terms with my feelings towards him. Really this isn't his fault either. My momma kept me away from my father, my father never made a real effort to introduce me to my family. I think he was so excited to see me that all he could really focus on was the time he had with me. When he wrapped his mind around the fact that I needed to know my family he died before he could do something about it. Malcolm has his own life; I can't blame him for not doing what my father should've done in the first place. Now that so much time has passed how do I say who I am? Do I even care anymore? Sigh! Then I think about Melissa, she's wicked! I smile because I didn't know she had it in her. I keep thinking about her sneaking up on Shannon like that. Her behavior that whole day was out of the norm if you ask me. I pretended like I didn't notice her following me home that night. She parked across the street and watched my apartment for a long time. I wondered what she was thinking, but smashing married women is not how I get down. I got enough reconciling to God to do as it is. No sense in adding to it for something that would never workout starting that way. She's hiding something and every time I sit at that computer to run a background on someone, I have to restrain myself from looking Melissa up. Something tells me to let that one alone, and to let it go. Its not like I have the right to know everything that happens in her life anymore.

****

"Hey stranger." Randi said opening the door. "Welcome back."

"Hey yourself, and thanks. Where's everybody?" I said looking around the empty living room.

"You know them, backyard. Tracy and I were making margaritas you want one?" She asked

"Sure" I said giving her a hug.

Tracy had on one of Randi's aprons; she looked all-domestic in the kitchen. Andre brought his cup in to her and she poured him a "veer sheen Rita" as Andre called it. I wasn't expecting it but Tracy hugged me and told me it was good to have me back. She told me we had a ton of work to get done. When I came back to work on Monday. It never fails; I think I come to grips with my feelings. I feel firm in my resolve, and then I see her. Randi looked at me funny after I hugged Tracy, but she turned her head.

"Go ahead and join the men outside. I'll bring your drink to you when it's ready." Randi said

Andrew, Darryl, Jeff, and Joseph were playing dominos. Aleisha one of the performers from EA was sitting next to Joseph. I said hey to everybody then I sat down to watch the game play out on the opposite end of the table from Andrew. As soon as he had his bones it seemed like he knew where he was playing next. But they all looked that way. Their game moved fast, if you aren't quick on your feet these were not the people to play with. Andre was looking at his father's hand observing the game like he understood the rules. Another female now accompanied Tracy and Randi. They were walking carefully with drinks in their hands. Randi gave her extra drink to Aleisha. Tracy told the girl with them to give me my drink. Tracy was so busy watching us, she missed that Andrew was waiting for his. He shot her a look and she snapped out of her smiling trance. She apologized and handed Andrew his drink. He accepted her apology, but I could tell he wasn't letting it slide.

"Yussef this is my friend Madelyn, Madelyn this is Yussef the guy I was telling you about."

We all kind of paused and looked at Randi. "Oh really? And what have you told her?" Jeff said not looking amused at all.

"Just that he's a good guy. Mandie was saying there weren't any left, so I told her about him. Then I invited her." Randi said matter of factly.

"But did you ask him if he was open to hooking up with anybody? He might not be in a good guy space right now." Jeff said irritated, Randi shook her head no. "I know you're Yussef's hype man. But you can't put people in these embarrassing situations."

"Did I embarrass you guys?" Randi asked defensively. Madelyn and I shook our heads yes. Darryl grabbed his stomach laughing extremely hard. Andre laughed at his crazy uncle. Randi sighed, "I'm sorry you guys. I know you both and I thought you'd be good together."

Now I know Randi had good intentions. But if she ever paid attention to the women I date, not one of them has been skinny. And Madelyn was SKINNY! Not unhealthy skinny, but very petite. She had short neat hair, and I mean she was alright, but not my type of female. Andrew was watching my reaction to Mandelyn. He didn't say anything; today he was a man of very few words. Tracy was trying to help her friend out and said, "I've thought of a couple people that I thought he would mix well with as well. She was only looking out for her friends."

Andrew shot Tracy a look, Tracy looked confused but backed down. "Yussef is a grown man, he don't need you guys to help him find a woman. No disrespect Mandelyn, but you two need to stay out of that man's personal business." He said

"Well, it was nice meeting you. I'll let you guys get back to your afternoon." Mandelyn said setting her drink down and walking away.

I could tell she was embarrassed, I was too. But I'd have felt bad letting her walk away like that. I put my drink on the table and I followed after Mandelyn. "Mandelyn! Mandelyn!" I had to light weight jog to catch up to her. "Hold on girl!" She was crying. "I apologize for that whole scene."

"That was hard!" She said embarrassed by her tears.

"I know!" I said hugging her cause I didn't know what else to do.

"You're not my type either." She said smiling

"PLEASE! I'm everybody's type. I have no girlfriend right now just to prove my point." I smiled back, "let me take you out for a drink or something."

"There are free drinks inside." She said

"I don't wanna hang around here. Do you?" I said

"Nope"

"Let's go say bye, and then go somewhere." I said

"I said bye already." She said

"Ok well let me go say bye and then we'll go. You're gonna wait for me?"

She smiled hard revealing dimples. "Ok"

Darryl was walking towards the living room as I came through the door. "She alright?" He asked

"Yea, just a little embarrassed." Darryl looked out the window at Mandelyn then back at me. He raised his eyebrows. "You interested?"

"Only if you not." He said

I put my hand up to my chin. "How should we do this? She's gotta think she's choosing you and not like we passed her around. AND I don't want to go back out there and be the seventh wheel with all those couples."

Darryl nodded, "tell them you're gonna take her out. I'll go out and test the water. If I feel like she's digging me, I'll tell you she's coming with me. Then you can bounce."

"Alright! That works." We shook and I went back to the backyard. Tracy was watching me as I walked over. Andrew was watching Tracy. "I'm gonna take off."

"But you just got here." Tracy said

"You're friend is kind of embarrassed, and I don't want her day to end on that note so I'm gonna take off." I said, "I'll catch up with you guys later."

"Let us know what you're doing later. We'll try and catch up." Randi said

"No we won't!" Jeff said looking at Randi in disbelief. "Is this everybody rally around Yussef day?" Andrew put his hand up and Jeff gave him a pound.

"You team Yussef too?" Joseph said to Aleisha.

"I don't even know him like that." She said shaking her head

"It's not like that. We just know that Yussef is a good guy, and he deserves to be in a relationship." Randi said

"RANDI STOP!" Jeff said irritated

"What?" She said

"I'm gonna go!" I said walking away.

I had that sinking feeling, I looked back and Tracy was watching me walk away while Randi and Jeff argued. Andrew was glaring at Tracy. I popped candy in my mouth and walked back into the house. I looked out the window, Darryl had Mandelyn laughing. She even touched his arm, yea she was digging him. I walked out prepared to give a disappointed face.

"Hey Yussef, we wanna go to Golf, Carts, and Stuff." She told me not asking me. I looked at Darryl and he was all smiles but he wasn't saying he wanted to bounce.

"Darryl's coming too?" I didn't have to fake surprised, I was.

"Yea, if it's cool." Darryl said, then he hurried over to open the passenger side door for Mandelyn. "Here you go sweetness."

When Mandelyn got in the car I bucked my eyes at him. He shrugged as he got in the back seat. So now I went from being the seventh wheel to being the third wheel. I told myself to make the best of it. I was third in line when this pretty little girl unknowingly cut me in line. The little girl was so cute how could I be mad that she cut me? Her curly hair was pulled into a long ponytail. Her little outfit was neat and clean. She wasn't plastered in name brands like most of the kids running around here. I actually didn't see one label on her. She held onto her five-dollar bill like it was all the money in the world. I could tell she was really excited about being here, so much that she didn't notice me or the people behind me. Her little voice was so cute as she told the cashier she wanted nachos, popcorn, and an ice slush drink. The nachos by their self were $4.50. Uh oh! The cashier told her that the total was twelve dollars. The little girl proudly handed over five. She had the biggest smile as she focused on her ice slush. The cashier looked frustrated, I waved my hand to tell him I'd cover the rest. The little girl gathered everything in her arms spilling the popcorn a little then she hurried away. I ordered a pizza, a beer, and sour apple candy. I paid for everything, and the cashier gave me number eight to put on my table so that when my pizza was ready they'd find me. I put the number eight down on the table. Darryl and Mandelyn came to the table. Madelyn said my beer looked good, Darryl popped up and said he'd be right back. "So you two seem to be hitting it off." I said

She smiled, "please don't be mad."

"Why would I be mad?" I asked
"I don't know cause...." She looked past me and smiled. "Hey! What are you doing here?" She said getting up to hug someone.
"Sydney's been saving her money to come." My heart dropped I immediately recognized the voice; there was no need to turn around. "I was coming to thank your friend. The cashier said he paid the difference for her purchase." I took deep breaths to calm myself. "Yussef this is my friend Sylvia and her daughter Sydney."
Sylvia lost her air looking into my face. "Oh my God!" She said putting her hands on her mouth.
"Sylvia" I said with a blank stare. Then I looked at the cute little girl who was staring up at her mother with a question mark expression. She looked like Sylvia a little bit, but she had her own look. She probably looked more like her father. "So your name is Sydney. That's a very pretty name." I smiled
"Thanks" she said blushing
"Oh my God! I'm sorry I didn't know. The cashier said that the guy with the number eight paid. I wouldn't have come if I knew." She said apologizing.
Sylvia wasn't the Sylvia I dated. Her face looked tired, she was a little heavier than when we dated. She didn't look bad, but her clothes covered her body. There was no trace of the sexy vixen; I was once in love with. She cut her hair to shoulder length; she looked like a tired mom. "It's not like I knew she was your daughter." I said nonchalantly
"How do you guys know each other?" Mandelyn asked.
I looked at Sylvia, she lowered her eyes. It looked like she wanted to cry. "We used to date."
"How do you guys know each other?" I asked
"We work together." Mandelyn said watching Sylvia's demeanor.
"You work?" I said in shock
She didn't look at me, "I have to support my daughter."
I wanted to ask who her father was, but I didn't think it was appropriate to ask in front of the child.
Darryl came back with two beers and the kid from the kitchen was following with our pizza. Darryl set the drinks down on the table, and then he looked at Sylvia, "who are you?"
"Sylvia" she said reaching for Sydney's hand. "We're gonna go." She said
Sydney's eyes were fixed on the pizza. "Do you want a slice or two of pizza?" I asked Sydney.
As she started to shake her head yes. Sylvia told her no, cause she still had nachos to finish. I told her it was ok; I pulled up an extra chair. I sat on the opposite end from them. "Thank you Yussef." She said looking like she wanted to cry. "You look good by the way. Exactly the same." She looked like it pained her to say it.
I said thank you, but I wasn't gonna lie to her and tell her the same. I imagined her kicking herself right about now. I wanted a family and everything with her. She messed up, not me; and from the looks of things her life was a reminder of how she messed up. I sat a little taller in that moment.
I saw the light bulb flash across Darryl's face just as little Sydney ran off to play.
"You're Sylvia, Sylvia?"
Sylvia peeked around Mandelyn. "I guess so?"
"You're the skank that tried to come between my brother and my boy?" Darryl said matter of factly.
"Darryl!" Mandelyn said taken by surprise by his frankness

Sylvia put her hand up, "it's ok." She said to calm Mandelyn. "What I did was really wrong. I deserve that, and more!" Then she looked at me. Tears started pouring out of her eyes. "Yussef!" She took a breath, "nothing I could say will ever take back what I did to you." She exhaled trying to catch her breath. "You loved me," then she couldn't breathe because she was crying so hard. "All I cared about was money and what I could get next." She cried harder, "I get it now! I'm sorry! You don't ever have to forgive me, I deserve that. But you should know how sorry I am." Then she stood up and walked away.

Mandelyn looked at me like she expected me to chase after Sylvia. Then she looked at Darryl. "WHAT?" Darryl said defensively

"You're gonna let her walk away like that?" She said to me.

"NO! Mandelyn you need to mind your own business on that one. You don't know what she did." Darryl said in protection of me.

"She said she was sorry Dang! What you want her to do crawl?" Madelyn said in defense of her friend.

"You heck of dumb! You don't even know what she did! You heard her say she deserved it and you still talking! Delete my number! Don't call me!" Darryl said turning his back to Mandelyn and facing me shaking his head.

Mandelyn gasped, sucked her teeth and stood up. "That's fine! I didn't want your number anyways I was trying to be polite!" She said hurrying away to catch up with her friend.

Darryl watched her walk out. He shook his head then he looked at me. "Maybe I should've hit that before I kicked her to the curb." Then he chuckled. "Lets go get real drinks and some freaks." He said standing up.

"I'm with you on the drinks, but I'm cool on the freaks part." I said. As we walked towards the exit I saw Sydney looking lost and scared. "What's wrong baby girl?"

"I can't find my mom." She said with red cheeks and tears in her eyes.

I looked at Darryl and this little girl had him emotional. He tried to check his emotions. "You want me to help you find her?" He said taking her hand. She shook her head yes as she wiped the tears from her eyes with her free hand. I smiled at Darryl, "I don't even wanna talk about it! I'm not a monster!" He said chuckling to his self. We walked all over the inside of that place no Sylvia anywhere. I looked outside and Sylvia was sitting outside the door on a bench crying her eyes out while Mandelyn comforted her. I told Darryl and Sydney to come on cause I found her mom.

Sydney screamed, "MOMMY!" When she saw her and took off running to her. "I COULDN'T FIND YOU!" She said crying

Sylvia swept up her baby girl, "I'm sorry baby." She said through tears.

By the expression in Mandelyn's face, Sylvia just told her everything. Mandelyn looked like she wanted to apologize, but Darryl flipped her off and kept walking.

****

"So you're gonna be on the soldiers team. Its gonna be us against them." Darryl said too excited as he gave me my uniform.

"Everybody is gonna be there?" I asked not wanting to watch Tracy and Andrew suck face.

"Almost, my momma and Tracy are not gonna be there. They gotta work. But I'm sure they play like girls anyways." Darryl was planning a baseball game against Malcolm's dream team.

Invisible

With everything going on right now I didn't know if it was the smartest thing for us all to be out in the open playing baseball. Seems like there was drama around every corner. Toya and Steve were one thing. This guy Kevin and whatever his vendetta against the Wallace's is. This guy Phineas Cobb who's on a whole other level. And then the Detectives who seem to watch the falling bodies and wait for us to slip up. Darryl said we all needed to do something to shake off the stress and come together for something good. Which I'm sure meant he wanted to beat Malcolm at something. I told Darryl I would be there, and again I was studying floor plans and mapping out escape routes just in case.

I needed an outlet, I needed to scream to the world about what I was feeling. I put my pen to the paper and my work flowed through me. I needed to get this out before the game tomorrow.

I made my way to No Words, when I walked in the door there she was; as usual she's beautiful! When I saw them I thought about leaving, but I needed to do what I needed to do. I blessed the crowd with my words, Sasha took in every syllable. I hugged Tanisha, Carina, and lastly Sasha, I couldn't believe they found my little honeycomb hide out. Little miss never available for me, but always wants me confuses the life out of me. Sasha was eager to talk to me, but where I am right now! If I could take her and run, as long as she promised to always love me and no one else I would do it. I'm tired of all these unavailable women. But I could see the love of another man all over her. I hated the look! So I kept the evening pleasant and tried to keep my mood as even as possible while Sasha and I put a nail in the coffin of the possibility of she and I. In the end she's my step sister's sister, but cousin's cousin. It was too complicated to sort out.

****

"No events? Really? Nothing?" Andrew said sounding irritated.
"No, it's been quiet here." I said matching his irritation
"What's going on with you?" Andrew said
"What do you mean?"
"Darryl told me you saw Sylvia a few months ago." He said
"So!" I said
"You've always been down for the family. Lately you've been distant." He said
"That's been you! I'm still me." I said
"How you figure?"
"You the one who got your panties in a bunch whenever I'm around. I've been giving you space."
"Why haven't you been clocking the time you spend watching Toya or Steve?" He asked
"I got the hours, just kept forgetting to turn them in." I lied
"You only need to be concerned with any of them when you're protecting Tracy. When she's with me, you don't need to worry about none of this." He said firmly
"What's wrong with me doing recon?" I asked
"I'm not paying you for recon. I'm paying you to make sure she's safe while she's at the office ONLY! You're spinning your wheels needlessly." He said firmly. I laughed.
"What's funny?"

"Seems to me if you did more recon they wouldn't keep getting so close to her." I barked

"It's not your job to evaluate how I protect my woman. I pay you to do your job. Not to follow Toya and Steve around."

"Help me understand what the problem is?" Andrew took a deep breath but he didn't say anything. "Oh I see! You're scared!"

"WHAT?" Andrew barked

"You heard me. Thinking about all that Sylvia stuff makes you feel insecure about me being so close to your woman."

Andrew blew air, "Trust! No one over here is insecure!" He said lowering his voice

I lowered my voice lower, "so then you tell me. Why are you on my phone? I'm doing what you asked me to do. And I'm doing it quite well if I do say so myself! Tracy never has to worry when she's with me. Isn't that what you pay me to do?"

"Are you plotting on me?" He said point blank.

I took the phone off my ear. "Just because we saw that trick, you're doubting me now? Shouldn't I question you for the rest of my life! You've got this whole thing twisted up!"

"That wasn't a yes or a no!" Andrew said

"It's beneath me to answer such a stupid question. If you're looking for me to kiss your butt telling you things to tickle your ears" I blew air. "We've never got down like that!" I looked around the room, "I do my job and I do it well! I asked you to reassign me and you wouldn't. Now you wanna sit over there scared! I don't have time for this! Tracy is safe when she's with me! Get over yourself!"

"Don't cross me Yussef!" Andrew's voice was heavy. I imagined him looking crazy and disconnected.

"Andrew!" I said low and determined, "Don't cross me!" Then I hung up!

Chapter 16

I looked at the clock, it said five thirty in the morning. I looked at my tracker Tracy was still home. I answered the phone, "hello!"

"You quit?" Malcolm barked at me

I slowly sat up. "Yea" I said looking around the room.

"You have any idea how that looks?" Malcolm was heated

"First of all you should ask me if I care." I said stretching.

"What happened?"

"Nothing." I said nonchalantly

"BOY!" I could hear him grabbing patience out of the air. "If you two don't stop acting like kids! Lets squash this!"

"I left the assignment how is that acting like a child? I bowed out. He's so afraid I'm gonna do something he can't see straight. He had Curtis put somebody on me. ON ME!" I stood up and started pacing. "First he's telling me I'm the only person he can trust. Now he acts like I'm Steve! What I look like making a move on his woman? Family doesn't do that!"

"But you're feeling her."

"I wouldn't say that."

"No! That's not a question. It's obvious Yussef! Why else would you leave?"

"Maybe because the situation was becoming too hostile." I said

Malcolm exhaled, "talk to me like a man. Don't beat around the bush with me!"

"Malcolm I've asked him more than ten times to reassign me. I kept asking for an out." I plopped down on my bed.

"Why didn't you tell me? I would've moved you." Malcolm said, I didn't respond. Malcolm blew air, "you're coming back in the office?"

"No." I said

"Excuse me?"

"Not until I know she's safe. Toya's striking at her left and right. Todd's good, but without me that whole team is gonna fail him."

"How can you be so sure?" Malcolm said

"Cause every time I was the one telling them what to do to be stealth like. How to foil her plan when she got close. Nobody has laid a finger on her under my watch, I know she trusts that."

"Andrew has always been too soft with that one. Although, I don't think he'll choose Toya over Tracy. He'd be a fool!" He exhaled. "Andrew wants you gone."

"I know!" It hurt to hear it.

"I won't let that happen, but I need you to talk to me. Stay back as much as you can. Once she's secure, you walk away!"

"Why would I hang on after that?"

"Ok well then let's speed this up." Malcolm said

****

"So mister???" She waved her hand.

"You can call me Jeremy." I said amused by her attempt to hide her attraction to me.

"Jeremy, this car is a late model vehicle, but the mileage is surprisingly low. It may need a little work but it runs."

"Yea, but it's not pretty." I said looking at the car. I could see her in the car window checking me out. When I looked at her, she tried to keep her face straight. "I need to test drive it."

"I'll go get the keys." She said. I watched her walk away. As she walked up the stairs, she looked back at me. She looked surprised to see me watching. When she came back out she seemed nervous. "Ok mister..."

"Jeremy" I said taking the keys from her.

"Thank you," then she touched my arm. "I'm sorry I will get your name right."

I smiled at her hand, and she quickly removed it. "Aren't you coming?" I said opening the passenger door for her.

She looked surprised. "You want me to come with you? I don't have to go, but I will need to hold on to your keys while you're gone."

"Or you could get in. Tell your boss I'll agree to the terms you guys set within reason if you ride with me." I smiled

She walked back inside. Her boss stuck a camera out the window and took a picture of me. I was laughing and she came out of the office laughing. I closed her door and we were off. I drove around the Richmond, El Cerrito, and Kensington Hills. Angela was nervous and she kept nervous laughing. So I talked a lot. I pulled in front of a mom and pop deli in Berkeley. I convinced her to get out and have lunch with me. I hated myself for doing it, but I found myself comparing her to Tracy. But I liked the comparisons. She didn't assume anything; she didn't even assume that I liked her. She was more like Tracy than anyone I've met in a long time. Once she relaxed our conversation started flowing. I started feeling butterflies in my stomach. The more she talked the more I listened, I liked the way she thought and the things she was talking about. When she called me Jeremy that jarred me back to reality. In the car I asked her for her number. She looked surprised that I was asking. It surprised me that she didn't realize I was into her. At the dealership I gave her boss five hundred over the asking price. I told them I would come back the next day to pick up the car.

When I came back the next day Angela had a little more spunk to her whole presence. I liked it. I sat in the office with her and her boss chatting the day away. In the early afternoon a customer showed up and Ken went out to greet them.

"Jeremy do you have a girlfriend?" She asked me point blank

"I wouldn't have asked for your number if I did."

"Is that a yes or a no?" She said

"No I don't have a girlfriend." I said

"There's somebody though, I can see it in your eyes."

It was an interesting feeling being read. "I could say the same for you."

"What?" She said turning her eyes.

"There was somebody even if he's not a factor now, didn't make you feel good about yourself. So much that you couldn't believe that I was looking at you. I like you; I don't have a girlfriend, no kids. But I do work a lot. Once I finish my current assignment I hope to be able to take you out." Her eyes got big. "I'm sorry is that too direct?"

"Um, no..." Her eyes danced around. I smiled at the affect of my words. "I guess I started that." I could've came across my chair right then and kissed her. But I told myself to be cool, cause she wouldn't have received that well. So I stared at her, which made her blush. Then she asked me if she could touch my hair. OK! SHE WANTS ME TO ATTACK HER!!!! I said yes, and continued staring at her face. "Your hair is soft!"

"You are beautiful!" She blushed and moved a little closer. Then my alarm went off, I looked at my phone. Tracy was getting off in an hour. I had to go. "I gotta get to work." I stood up.

"Thank you for everything Jeremy." She said it like she wouldn't see me again.

"Angela, I like you. As soon as this assignment is over you will see more of me. I promise!" I said

Invisible

She smiled and stuck her hand out to shake my hand. I smacked her hand and made her hug me. She was my new smell.

****

"Thank you for meeting me baby." She said kissing my cheek. "This is Jarvis, Jarvis this is my son Yussef." She said proudly

I shook his hand then I turned my attention back to her. No fake sugary sweet tone, nor did she have fear in her eyes. INTERESTING!

"So, what's this?" I said pointing between the two of them.

"I love your momma and we're gonna get married." He said matter of factly. "She said you and I needed to meet first."

"Ok, if that's what you're going to do regardless, why meet me first?" I asked

"I wanted you two to meet first is all. We're going to Reno next weekend. Can you come?"

I couldn't afford to be that far away from Tracy. "No!"

"Fine! Momma and Arthur are coming." She said

"Good then you're covered." I saw a couple of Mitigated guys watching me out the corner of my eye. "What about Auntie Summer?"

Momma rolled her eyes. "I didn't invite her! She's all-uppity since she married him. No since she got engaged."

"You're just jealous!" I said waving my mother off.

"What she got to be jealous about? Summer ain't finer than Shonda! I got more money than that fool will ever have! And I know I look better than him." Jarvis said

"Yes you do baby!" My momma said leaning over the table to kiss him.

I sat there with my mouth hanging open. My momma smiled and asked me why I was looking like that. "Oh my God! There are two of you!"

They both erupted into laughter. I guess this was a high fiving moment for them.

"Amen!" Jarvis said. "She's like my twin soul!" He said looking at my momma with stars in his eyes.

"What do you do Jarvis?" I asked

"A little of this a little of that. But my family owns a gas station, a liquor store, and a hamburger joint. What do you do?"

"I work for Mitigated Staffing Solutions in the city." I said

He smiled, "you're a temp."

"Yep" I said

He laughed, while my momma smiled. "How's the temping game treating you?"

I didn't see what was so funny. "It's good."

"I bet it's real good when you're waiting in between assignments." He said still laughing.

I looked at my momma and she was laughing right a long with him. Latia walked in with a smile. "Nope." I said standing up. "We're not staying. Not gonna have you go through this headache. You've met my momma, Jarvis act just like her. They'll entertain each other while trying to kill each other."

Latia nodded and turned on her heels. "Come on Yussef don't be like that. Sit down, Jarvis is paying." Then she laughed again. Instead of making her a better person he just enhanced what was already there. I didn't have to see either of them again. We started to walk away. "Oh Latia, I think I figured out you guy's little secret." She said using her finger to make a circle.

"Secret?" Latia asked

"Don't play dumb. The little secret your little friend has. As soon as I have confirmation, I'M TELLING!" Then she laughed.

"We're not little kids." Latia said

"Play innocent if you want to. What's done in the dark always comes to light. And the fact that YOU!" She said pointing at Latia, "didn't say anything is gonna be the worse part." She pointed to her watch. "Time is ticking. Every minute that passes makes it worse to be you. YOU WERE THE TRUSTED ONE! The betrayal! The scandal!" She dramatically grabbed her hair. "You guys can sit up there and judge me all you want, but I never sunk to such a low level of evil secrecy. Like it or not my stuff has always been out on the table. I don't know how you sleep at night!"

Latia swallowed, and then she turned and walked away. Jarvis leaned in to get the juice. You could hear them hooting and hollering as we walked out.

****

The tracker started glowing and humming. Tracy was leaving home. It wasn't like her to leave this early. I popped out the bed showered in thirty seconds. Threw on clothes, and ran to my bucket. She went to the office but this was still beyond early for her. I went up the elevator and I got my old badge out of Danielle's desk, and I let myself in. Tracy was sitting at her desk with her head down crying her eyes out. She was upset because she and Andrew ran into Jennay. She was upset about his reaction to her. In true Tracy form she dramatically ran away from Andrew. Poor guy didn't know she was gone yet. I talked to her for a few minutes calmed her down like I normally did. Then I decided to hang around. I spotted Todd in the courtyard. He had no expression as I approached him. I told him she was in the office already. He had a busted look on his face. I told him it was ok, and that she was off script. But he needed to look lively I had a feeling something was gonna happen today. Todd thanked me for the heads up then he went to his post.

Sure enough, Tracy walked out the building and Todd, Sam, nobody was on point. She had her purse so she was leaving, if she was coming down for lunch she'd only have her wallet. She walked right past me, without seeing me. I exhaled these fools needed to get it together. I got in my car and once she came out of the garage I followed her. I felt a little relieved when I realized she was going to Andrew's office. I parked at the far corner of the lot. She got out the car with a smile. Then she froze and her smile dropped. Andrew and Jennay walked out of his office together. I shook my head, Andrew is dumb in love. I followed Tracy and I watched her face as she watched them eat lunch. The lunch was innocent enough, but I knew Tracy was hurt all the same. She was gonna run again it was just a matter of figuring where. She let Andrew finish his lunch and she let the two of them go back inside his office. I didn't recognize the walk she used as she spoke over the phone and walked inside. When she came out she was crying. She sat in her car for a minute, when Jennay came out the office I expected her to try and run her over. When she jumped out of her car, I felt a little nervous. I wasn't expecting Tracy to hold her own against Jennay. We were in a business park in Hercules. All she needed was for someone to look out their window and see them fighting. The police would be there in no time. I hopped out the bucket; Tracy's clothes were all ripped up. But I was impressed with the way she handled herself in that fight. I grabbed her threw her body in the passenger seat of her car. It took her a minute to realize that I had her. Andrew came out as I sped past him, with Tracy screaming profanity at him as we drove past. Great! Now he's gonna look for whoever she's with, all roads were gonna point to me. Oh well! If I was gonna die it was gonna be worth it. The only safe place to take her was my home away from home. Tracy cried the entire way to my place. She barely looked around.

When we got there I took the battery out of her phone. I gave her clothes to change into, while she changed I went back out to the barn and I unplugged the battery in her car. Just in case Andrew was tracking her car as well, I couldn't risk him showing up out here. We made dinner and we talked she cried, I comforted her. Although she was upset, we both knew she was going back.

As I washed the dishes I heard her coming. She put her arms around me, and her breast against my back. I had to tell my inner self to be calm. I had to tell my hands to stay inside the dishwater. I wanted to lay her on the kitchen floor. She thanked me for everything, and then we agreed I would sleep on the floor in the room.

We talked for awhile laughing, joking, clearing the air. She confirmed that she was digging me just like I was digging her. Receiving confirmation that the woman I loved, loved me even if it could never work out was all I needed to keep me moving forward and to do the right thing. But first… My heart started racing, I figured we only had tonight "Can I kiss you?" If this night got me killed, it would be worth it for one kiss. "What?" She popped up

"I'll never ask again, but I know this is the only time if ever that you would say yes. I PROMISE it won't go any further!" I put my hands up.

"Ok" she said right away. I expected her to say no.

"Ok? Really?" My voice cracked.

"Yes" she said very deliberately.

I sat on the edge of the bed, my heart was pounding. I've wanted to kiss her for a long time. I kissed her slow at first and she melted into the kiss. My body wanted more, and Tracy wasn't fighting me as she kept melting. I broke free from our kiss, and I retreated to the floor before she noticed my salute. "Ok! I'm good! Gotta stop there!" We both laughed. "I SHOULD'VE NEVER DONE THAT!" I yelled cause now my body was begging me to keep going. We both laughed again.

"Good night Yussef!"

"Good night my love!"

Once my body calmed down I blew air, and she laughed. "I thought you were sleep." I said

"Nope" then she sat up. "Why aren't you sleep?"

"Yea right!" We both laughed. "Andrew better be happy that we love him." I said

"You love him?" She asked, "you mean like family?"

"Yea" I sat up. I wanted to tell her what he did to me. But if I told her it would taint the way she saw him. If Andrew messed up with Tracy I wanted that to be all on his head. I got back on the bed and I spooned her, she snuggled into my arms.

"What if I didn't go back to him? What if I stayed here?" She said

I put my arms around her. "That's your pain talking. We both know you're going back even if you decide not to go tomorrow. Don't waste time lying to yourself."

She sucked her teeth. "Has anyone ever hurt you like this?"

"My situations were different." I told her about Shannon, but I left out Steve's name and the kid they had together. I told her about Melissa, and then Sylvia minus that it was Andrew that I saw with my own eyes, and then back to Melissa. Then her, she rubbed my hand then I felt her tear drop on my arm. They kept dropping. We talked about Angela, her, and Andrew. We talked about everything.

"What if I stayed and never went back? You wouldn't make me feel like this." She said still crying, and then she kissed me. The kiss went on for a long time, but she was still crying.

"In the end I'm not Andrew and we both know that's who you love. Andrew loves you more than he's ever loved anyone, I couldn't be that selfish." It killed me to be the bigger person here. I wanted to cry myself. "Don't make me weak. I'm trying to be a good guy here."

She laughed then she silently cried some more as she fell asleep. I laid there thinking about what life would be like if she stayed. No matter which way I tried to spin it, I ended up hurt and angry and dead because Andrew wouldn't let her go, and she knows she's not letting him go. She was in love with Andrew, her heart belonged to him. In the morning I told her she could tell Andrew whatever she wanted about last night, she just couldn't tell him where. I told her my life depended on it, and then I made her promise. I made breakfast; we ate knowing that moment meant closure. No more could we, should we, and what ifs. She belonged to him, and I had to move on. I reconnected her battery before she came out to her car. She told me to be good to Angela and then we kissed one last time. All those years of wondering what it would be like to hold her, and to kiss her. I loved this moment, but it was better in my mind. In my mind she belonged to me, and she wanted only me. This was it, after this I'd never touch her like this again. I screamed at the weakness in my soul as I released her. I told her how to get to the freeway then she went her way and I went mine. I was sure Andrew was looking for me, but ask me if I cared. If I had it to do all over again, I'd do it every time.

I cleaned up, locked up, and walked the ten plus miles back to civilization.

****

"Yussef what did you do?" Malcolm's voice almost sound like he was pleading, a sound I never thought I'd hear from him.

"I didn't do anything, she came back didn't she!"

"I'm outside, come out." He said

"How do you know where I am?" I asked standing up.

"We'll talk about it after you come out." Then he hung up.

I grabbed my backpack and I walked out of the bookstore across the street from Tracy's office. Malcolm was out front like he said. Malcolm had on shades. The windows on his car were all tinted black; the sun obeyed him and only illuminated the day. Even the sun knew not to penetrate his cabin. "What's with the shades?" Malcolm locked and unlocked his jaw. "You two are gonna be the death of me. What did you do?" He said driving away.

"I had to get her out of there. Andrew could've lost his job if he was linked to their little scuffle." I said

"Why didn't you take her home?" He spit

"She didn't want to go." I said

"Why didn't you call Andrew, or me?" I didn't answer. "What did you do?"

"I didn't sleep with her if that's what your thinking."

"I can't protect you like this!"

"I'm not asking you to do anything."

Malcolm's foot got heavy on the gas. "You're not asking...." He locked his jaw again. He opened his mouth to speak, and then he shook his head. We were driving so fast on the freeway the other cars started looking like flashes of light.

"How did you know where I was?"

"When it's comes to you, I ask myself. What would Troy do? Where would he go? How would he react? Until that stunt you pulled you've always been predictable in that way. Your father protected Amber for me, sometimes history repeats its self."

"Are you telling me Amber was in love with my father?"

"BOY! HECK NAW!" He shook his head. "Your generation is twisted! A man's Queen cannot be compromised. I'm not saying Drew handled this right, but after this doesn't he have a point? You gave him justification!"

"I don't care!" I said

"You don't care about Drew or you don't care about me? What happens between you and Drew affects me. It affects Amber, and I can't have that."

Invisible

I sighed. "Without me his protection for her is weak. If Toya was just a little smarter Tracy would be hurt maybe even dead. I've walked in Tracy's house. Even with the dogs, security cameras, and guys outside. I can tell you where she keeps her panties." I said

"Don't you think that right there is crossing the line? Even if you could do it! Why would you? Although those other fools have been trained, no one has been trained like my boys. You guys will always lead! But we can't have you guys turning on each other. You two will destroy everything I've worked so hard to build. I know about your cameo appearances all over the place. Stop taunting Drew."

"Where are we going?"

"Latia's"

"Malcolm, Toya's gonna hurt her. I couldn't live with myself if that happened." I flexed and unflexed my fist.

"Drew doesn't want me to put her down. You're the first person that he's been attached to that he's wanted put down." Malcolm shook his head. "I can't let that happen."

"So what if I die! Only a couple care anyways!" I felt angry.

Malcolm looked at me. "I care!" Then he gripped the steering wheel. "I can't lose you twice." He said like it pained him to say. Then he changed up. "All this Toya irritation ends this weekend. After we put them down you back off! Understood?"

I agreed. My mind stayed stuck on Malcolm's emotional state. "Uncle Blackie you really love me don't you?" I smiled real big.

Malcolm clinched his jaw, but he didn't respond.

When we pulled up to Latia's house she was walking out. She had her office attire on and she looked shocked to see us. She gestured to me to ask what was going on. I shrugged cause I didn't know either. Malcolm told Latia to call whomever at work and tell them she was taking the rest of the day off. When she got off the phone she joined me on the couch. "Your grandmother is sick." Latia and I didn't move. "I know Troy didn't handle a lot of things right. I know you guys are mad, and you have every right to be. But she didn't do it. I know she clocked out when you needed her most, but she's been through a lot. Your father should've explained all this. I'M AT CAPACITY FOR EMOTIONAL CONVERSATIONS! I got my own issues! I'm asking the two of you to let this woman die in peace. Momma Shuga, her mother was evil! Of all her kids, your grandmother is one of the few who didn't follow in her footsteps. Even if you feel nothing for her, please you guys. Do this for me."

"That's why you're wearing shades?" I asked

"Why do my shades bother you so much?"

"Malcolm it's overcast outside, there's no sun. I just wanted to know why."

"Are you guys coming or not?" He asked

I looked at Latia, and then we looked at Malcolm. "Of course!" Latia said, "Let me go change my clothes."

Malcolm walked over to the flower arrangement sitting in the middle of her table. He read the card, and then he put it back. "I'm gonna bring my car." She announced.

"Ok" Malcolm said.

"Why?" I asked

"I'm going over Melissa's afterwards." Then she rolled her eyes, "nosey!"

Malcolm pointed at the flowers, "he doesn't know we're connected does he?"

"No, it's not like I've been taken around the family. So why would I tell him about all this family I allegedly have?" She said sitting on her bottom stair tying her shoe.

I could feel Malcolm's glare through his shades. "Allegedly?"

I could tell she was gonna say something else smart. I shook my head no at her. If she pushed anymore I was out of it. "Sorry, there's a lot going on." She said deflating.
"Like?" He asked crossing his arms.
"He wants to get married..."
Malcolm threw his hands up and spun around. "WHY DOES EVERYBODY HAVE TO GET MARRIED? WHY CAN'T WE JUST AGREE TO BE TOGETHER? If I want to leave some little piece of paper isn't gonna stop me!"
Latia and I exchanged looks. "Amber still wants to marry you Uncle Blackie?"
Latia gasped and covered her mouth, but she couldn't pull back the giggle. Malcolm was about to say something when I said that. He started to smile and chuckle a little. Then his face turned serious again. "You better NEVER call me that! I don't know why I let him get away with that! I've dang near killed people for less."
"Yes sir!" Latia said saluting him.
"Baby girl why don't you want to marry him?" Malcolm said sounding defeated.
Latia was stuck, tears poured out of her eyes. She cried out loud violently. I backed up from her closer to Malcolm, was her head about to spin around? I couldn't say. Malcolm now looked stuck too. "My father! My father!" She couldn't get it out she was crying so hard. As if he understood, Malcolm rushed over and hugged her up. They were both crying and I was standing there uncomfortable. Uncle Blackie ain't supposed to cry. He's a brick wall; at least I thought he was. He rocked Latia back and forth rubbing her locs, which made her cry more. "My father called me that!" She said in between sobs.
"I'm sorry!" Malcolm said
I pulled out a chair at the table prepared to run. Now this fool is apologizing, where's the real Malcolm? They sat there a good twenty minutes before they spoke. "Why did he hide us? Was he embarrassed? Was he ashamed of me?" Latia asked
"I don't think he was intentionally trying to hide you. It just happened that way. I know that doesn't make it better, but it's the truth." Malcolm said
"Lewis wants to marry me. He wants to be with me. I'm scared." She said
"Marriage is scary." Malcolm said agreeing. "Do you want to get married?"
"Of course I do. But what if I become his best kept secret? I don't want to exist my entire life that way." She said
"Does he treat you that way now?"
"No, he always wants me with him. I always decline.... BECAUSE I'M SCARED!" She said crying again.
"Of?" Malcolm asked
As if she felt like she was talking too much. She shook her head no. "There's too many secrets in this family." Her eyes darted by me.

Chapter 17

"Do you have her?" Malcolm's voice was serious and deep.
I had Toya up against the wall by her neck. Her eyes were big and she looked like she couldn't believe I had her. Tears were streaming down her face as she listened to Malcolm's voice over the phone. You could tell she knew this was her final moment. Through clinched teeth I said, "I got her!" I've never wanted to snap someone's neck so badly before! She mouthed the words "please! Please!" to me. As if I should feel some compassion for her after all the trouble she's caused. "You're on speaker!" I said out loud
"Toya! You have been nothing but a PAIN in my side! You've played on my son's compassion for you for the last time!" I heard the echo of his voice, as he got closer to the room. Toya started panicking, kicking, and scratching anything she could do to try one last time to get away. Her tears became heavier when she laid eyes on Malcolm; she knew her demise was here. "Let her go!" The look in Malcolm's eyes was unlike any I had ever seen before. His voice rumbled the room and Toya cried uncontrollably. He asked her what she promised the police. She tried to play dumb, like she didn't know what he was talking about. He told her he knew she had been talking to those nosey detectives. He named them by name, and she still tried to play dumb. One of Malcolm's men by the door came in the room. He had a knife, He grabbed Toya's hand and he brought the blade in to take one of her fingers, Toya pleaded. Before she answered any questions she needed to know that Steve was still alive. Malcolm told her whether or not he lived depended on her. Then she started talking, when she tried to lie Malcolm raised his phone to call to tell them to kill Steve. Once she understood what his hand raising meant she sang like a bird. She had nothing strong to give to the police. Malcolm drilled her backwards and forwards. The way he asked her questions quickly any and all lies she spouted were uncovered quickly. Sparky put tape over Toya's mouth. Then he taped her arms behind her back. He made her sit in Indian style then he taped her legs together so she couldn't move. They brought a moving box in on a cart then Sparky and Nate put her in the box and taped it up. The box had "Misc." written on the sides. Malcolm asked me if I was ok. He knew I wanted to do more to her. Then he looked at his watch, "Do you think you can make it there in an hour?" He asked me.
"I have to!" I said bolting out the door.
I took the stairs since Sparky and Nate had the elevator. We arrived at the ground floor at the same time. I walked past Sparky and Nate as if I didn't know them. The girl at the hotel counter asked them about the box. They told her it was blankets and old decor. She waved them on as she went back to her phone conversation. I held the door open for them; they went to a white van on the right. I went towards the parking lot on the left.
I drove like a crazy person to Blackhawk from Oakland. I made it there in record time. I drove around the back and I spotted Steve's car. I changed my clothes behind the trunk of the car. I put on black slacks and a white shirt. If nothing else I would blend in with the staff. I walked into the back door, and the kitchen was humming. Everyone moved with efficiency, and urgency. I glided through the crowd and around the back. I saw the profile of Steve's face as he walked into the main banquet hall. My heart dropped into my stomach, not only was I late, but I let Tracy down. I hurried my steps but it was too late he was pulling her out to the dance floor. All I could see was red! Enraged by my failure I kept telling myself to keep it together. Tracy looked like she was about to lose it, Andrew was nowhere in sight. Then she saw me and her breathing somewhat returned too normal. When Andrew entered the banquet hall he looked at

me then the anger that flashed over his face as he saw Steve dancing with his woman. Once I saw Andrew had Tracy, I slipped out the side door into the kitchen. Curtis and a couple other Mitigated guys were there. "Yussef! Drew wants you!" Curtis said, signaling for me to come over.

I turned and walked in the opposite direction. I took out my phone and I texted Malcolm "911!"

He responded, "grey sedan northeast corner". My car had been compromised. I exited the kitchen and ran up the stairs, which took me out to the top of the room above the banquet. Tracy and Andrew were gone. I walked very quickly across the top of the room, and then I ran down the stairs and out the side door. I crouched down and moved very quickly between cars. When I saw Curtis and his team come out of the building I moved quickly. They couldn't see me above the cars. It was only a matter of seconds before someone got on the ground and looked for my feet. I hurried next to a van that had a foot rail. When I saw Marcos go down I stood on the rail still crouching.

"Curtis!" Someone whispered as Steve lightweight ran around the corner. He was running from the Mitigated staff towards the front of the building. He basically ran into Curtis. I made my way to the grey sedan. The keys were taped on the inside of the tire on the rear driver's side. I got in the car and calmly drove out of the parking lot, I didn't look back to see who saw me. I called Malcolm and I told him they had Steve. He told me to go to his house and wait for him. He said he needed to talk to Drew. I asked him what he was going to say. He told me he was going to bargain me for Toya and Steve. I didn't like the sound of that, what if Andrew had a change of heart and wanted everyone dead? I drove around the city for a while hoping that anyone looking for me on the freeway would be long gone by the time I got on it. After about forty-five minutes I got on the freeway and drove quickly but not fast enough, a car hit the back of me causing my car to spin out on the 24 highway. The tire flattened and the car stood still facing the wrong direction in the middle of oncoming traffic. Curtis had his gun out and he told me to get out of the car. I was tired of running anyways. I got out the car, and I got in the backseat of Curtis's car. He drove away leaving the sedan in the middle of the highway. We got off the freeway, crossed over and drove back to the 680 freeway. We got on the highway 4 junction towards Richmond. Then we descended down into Crockett. The city of Crockett was a little town next to the Vallejo bridge. We drove through the town on the winding road to the secluded and closed regional park. Curtis parked at the top of the hill close to the gate, and he told me to get out. When I got out I looked up at the sky, there were all the stars again. I asked God what to do; I knew I could take Curtis if I needed to. But I didn't have any more fight left in me. If Andrew wanted me dead then he would have to answer to God for my life. But I wasn't gonna fight. I was tired. Curtis walked slightly behind me quietly, he kept calling Andrew, but he was getting no answer. When we got to the pier at the bottom of the hill, I stood there waiting to hear either Andrew confirm my death, or set me free. What did I do that was so horrible? You reap what you sow right? I hadn't directly killed anyone. But its not like I saved too many either. My Grandma, Latia, Auntie Summer, Malcolm, Roz, and Angela would be heart broken. I doubt they'd tell my grandmother; she was on her deathbed already. This would just push her over. We were out there for a little over an hour I guesstimate when my phone started going off. Malcolm was texting, but I didn't answer. Then he called, and I let the phone roll over to voice mail. Maybe an hour later Andrew called Curtis, he almost sounded like Malcolm. He asked Curtis if he had me. When Curtis confirmed he had me, Andrew told him to put me on speaker. "I talked to Malcolm. Stay away Yussef!" Then he hung up. Curtis and I walked up the hill. I had him take me to my apartment. I prayed real hard that night, I thanked God for saving me. I turned off all my Tracy tracking devices. At this point a desk job was looking pretty good.

****

I knocked on the door, excited about what the day would bring. I had the perfect location picked out. The perfect lunch packed. The perfect wine, and book of poetry. During one of our late night conversations I told her about this book of poetry that I happened to stumble across. During one of my downtime moments I found this book "Pleasures of the Unknown" by Jamila Gomez. I scanned through a few pages and decided to purchase it. I told Angela I could relate to the writer, as it seems she strives to hold on to the values she was raised with, while dealing with the fires within. We talked about poetry a lot after that, so I thought it was only fitting that I bring this book.

Angela's mother answered the door. "Hello Jeremy, Angela will be right out. Come in." Her mother said. I now know why Angela was so sweet, loving, humble, and appreciative. Renee is a wonderful mother to her. Sometimes I come and sit with them for hours talking about nothing, which is always something. At first I could tell that Renee was looking for something to be wrong with me. Honestly I was looking for something to be wrong with her and her daughter. But as far as I can tell they're just good people who've had their fair share of bad things happen to them. "So you have a special surprise planned for the day?" Renee asked with an approving smile.

"Yea, its nothing fancy." I looked around to see if Angela was ear hustling. I whispered, "I'm taking her on a picnic. I saw this huge weeping willow tree inside one of the picnic areas within Tilden park. Do you think she'll like it?" I asked

Renee's eyes glazed over, "sweetheart, she'll love it. Thank you for being so good to my baby. She's been through so much!"

"Renee, she has been good to me. I can't help but reciprocate." I said

Angela cleared her throat as she stood in the hallway waiting for us to notice her. She had on a nice little summer dress, with a big white flower in her hair. She looked beautiful! I smiled to match her smile. She blushed, "Angela. You look beautiful sweetheart." Her mother said

I couldn't stop smiling, "you are breath taking!"

She blushed again and humbly said, "thank you".

We said good-bye to her mother and then we walked out the door. Her eyes got really big. "WHOA!" She said looking at my car. "Jeremy this car is BEAUTIFUL!"

Angela would be the first person to ride with me in my father's car. This morning when I took the cover off the car, I stood there for a good maybe thirty minutes pulling myself together. Over the years I've started the car up, driven it around the block and then put it back in the garage. All of that was done on autopilot at that. This morning I saw my father, and he looked just like me minus the dreads. Instead of fighting it, for the first time ever I forgave him. I forgave him for waiting so long to free me from my crazy momma. I forgave him for not telling me I had a sister. I forgave him for being young and not knowing how to handle anything personal in the right way. In my mind I imagined him asking me if Angela was a lap girl or did she belong in my mind. I proudly told him not only did she belong in my mind but my whole mind, body, and soul was hers for however long she wanted to have them. The whole scene played out like a real conversation. I imagined my father liking Angela and approving of her. "Thank you. This was my father's car." I said proudly. On the car ride to my honeycomb hide out I told her about the car. She quietly listened which I loved. When I stopped talking she thanked me for sharing this moment with her. It was stuff like that! Her appreciation for the small things. Sylvia was always in my ear about buying an expensive brand new car. She only rode in my nicer car, she refused to ride with me in my buckets. She barely road with me on my bike, Angela proudly did it all. As long as she was with me, I was enough for her. A feeling I've never had. Even though Melissa showed the same kind of appreciation for me, I didn't have it for her until it was too late. She knew me before I got a chance to explain myself. So I always felt like I was trying to catch up to what she knew. Even with all of her appreciation there were the late night phone calls that never stopped. That always stopped me from completely taking her seriously. Angela started snapping pictures of me as I drove on her digital camera. She loved taking pictures and then she'd scrapbook most of the pictures at home. When I parked the car she showed me the pictures, I looked just like my father. I could see it so much that it reminded me of being younger and looking at him while he drove. "I think I might cut my dreads." I said

"Why would you do that?"

I opened her door. "I've had long hair all my life. I think I've been trying so hard not to be my dad that I've made a lot of the choices he would've. Which makes me just like him. I might as well embrace that I look like him and see myself without the long hair for once in my life."

"I understand, and it's your choice. But I do love your hair and all its glory." She smiled.

"It will be a while from now, but I think its gonna happen." I said taking everything out the trunk.

Angela snapped pictures of everything. When she saw the weeping willow she gasped and said how beautiful it was. I smiled because I knew she'd like it. I laid out the blanket under the tree and then I told her to sit. I took the food out, I researched online appropriate picnic foods, and then I searched until I found something I could actually make. The simplest I could come up with was chicken salad sandwiches. Angela took pictures of everything. Then she'd look at the pictures and smile really big. Angela had beautiful brown eyes that used to be full of sadness. Now every time I see her less and less of that sadness exists there. I love her full lips; she said as a child she hated them. Kids would tease her all the time; she said her features were awkward and too big for her growing up. I told her I loved her full lips and slanty eyes. I loved everything about her; it just killed me that she knew me as Jeremy and not Yussef. I knew I had to fix that, I just didn't know when. We sat under this tree for hours talking, laughing and carrying on. Half way through the second bottle and listening to her sultry voice read "Daddy's little Devil" from the book; I couldn't deny my yearning anymore and I kissed her. The shared passion in this kiss, told me she was ready for the next level. But I couldn't go there with her in good conscience with her believing my name is Jeremy. So I backed down from the idea of laying her down in our honeycomb hideout. We packed up our basket and went back to her mother's house. We shared the remaining items in our basket with her. And just like her daughter she was very appreciative.

My cell phone rang, it was Malcolm. He said it was time. I told Angela I had to go because my grandmother was dying. Angela asked me if I wanted her to come with me. I wanted to say yes, but I said no. Everyone there would call me Yussef. I needed time to explain.

When I walked in the room Malcolm was there and my cousin Bernadette. Bernadette asked me where I had been, and that she hadn't seen me in ages. Malcolm focused on my grandmother. Bernadette told me I needed to come by her house. She said I had a ton of cousins I needed to meet. I shook my head in agreement but I didn't say anything. Malcolm said he tried to call Latia but it seemed like she turned her ringer off. I gave my grandmother a kiss while she was sleeping. I told her I loved her. The nurse said it would be a little longer. Bernadette stared at me with misty eyes; I knew she was seeing my father. She asked me to go down to the cafeteria with her. She said she was hungry enough to eat two cows. When I chuckled it startled her. She said even my laugh was like my father. The elevator stopped on the third floor and a little girl and a little boy got on the elevator. The little girl's hair was LONG and thick. She had long ponytails all over her head. She was brown and just the cutest little thing. Her little brother decided it would be fun to push every floor button on the panel. The little girl fussed at him and threatened to take him back to their mother if he didn't behave himself. They stepped out of the elevator before us, and she made her little brother hold her hand as they walked to the cafeteria. "She's a bossy little somebody." Bernadette said

I couldn't help but watch these kids. The big sister showed her little brother the things he could choose. Then she let him choose, he chose an apple and apple juice. She told him it didn't make sense to get an apple and apple juice. But he insisted that he wanted both. The little girl picked out chips, sour apple candy, and orange juice. When they went up to the cash register the cashier gave her the total. The little girl took her money out of her pocket and handed the cashier six one-dollar bills to cover their $5.45 total. When the cashier gave her, her $0.55 change. She stood there counted her change. And then she smiled and thanked the cashier. Her little brother asked her how much money she got. He didn't understand the concept of change. I smiled at the pretty little smart girl. I bought Bernadette's food even though she protested, and then we sat at a table over from the kids. The little girl noticed me watching them, her eyes got big. Her brother asked her why I was staring at them. She whispered she didn't know, and then she reminded him that they aren't supposed to talk to strangers. Ignoring his sister he looked and me and said hi. I said hello. The little boy smiled at his sister. He was amused by his defiance. "You know it's really not safe for little kids to talk to strangers. You should listen to your big sister. I don't know why you guys are down here by yourself. You're too little. Where is your mother?" Bernadette said

"Our daddy got sick again." The little boy said

The little girl flashed her brother a look telling him to shut up. "She's very responsible though. Look at how well she takes care of her little brother. I'm not saying its right but I understand why her mother would be comfortable with them coming together." The little girl frowned, she looked just like Latia when she did it, and.......... this little boy looked like Melissa. I could feel heat on my neck as I stared at her face. "He's hard headed! He makes everything difficult." She said shaking her head.

"I DO NOT!" He yelled, "momma says I'm a good boy!" He said sticking his tongue at her.

"I'm gonna tell her what you did in the elevator." She said

"Ok, I'll be good." Then he took a bite of his apple, "can I have some of your candy?" He asked her

"I'll think about it, you know these are my favorite." Then she thought about it, "I'll save these for later if you don't get on my nerves too much Jack, I'll share some with you."

There was even more heat on my neck. It couldn't be! I stared at this girl long and hard, seeing everything that looked like Latia to me only meant she looked just like me. It was like I put my thumbprint on her face. Uncomfortable behind my staring the little girl told her brother to get his stuff so they could go. I told Bernadette I would be back or meet her upstairs whichever came first. She had a huge question mark on her face, but she agreed. I walked ahead of the kids to the elevator. I pretended like I pushed the button to call the elevator. I could see them peeking around the corner to see if I was gone. When an elevator came I stepped into the elevator. When the doors closed I pressed lobby right away. The kids were right there gasping when the doors opened and I was standing there. I apologized for scaring them. The little girl put on a big girl front and she held on to her little brother for dear life. I pressed the third floor, and they exchanged looks. When we arrived at their floor I told them I would go after them. They walked very fast to the waiting room. No one else was in there. I took a seat in a chair on the other side of the room while I analyzed everything about this little girl. I hoped I was just having a weird moment, like the dreams I would have where I was talking to my father and they seemed so real. But something told me this was cold and hard reality. I heard footsteps approaching the room. "I got here as fast as I could…" Latia said rushing into the room just to find me sitting there staring at the kids. My Grandma was right on her heels and stopped in her tracks as soon as she saw me as well. I COULDN'T BREATHE! ANGER BLAZED THROUGH MY BODY! I FELT LIKE THE ROOM SPUN! I didn't want to scare the kids; I tried to pull myself together.

"Yussef!" Latia said as she covered her mouth to mute the scream and loud out cry. Both of the kids look scared once they saw Latia's reaction to me. Grandma pulled out her phone and told Melissa to come to the waiting room, then she sat three seats over from me, and she made Latia sit between us.

My heart started pounding. I looked at the little boy, "Jackson?"

"How do you know my name?" The little boy said with a smile.

Yesmina looked a little nervous. "I know your parents Melissa and Jackson, its ok. You won't get in trouble for talking to me. I'm not a stranger, I'm family." I said, as everything in my body wanted to strangle Melissa! How could she do this to me! You could hear Melissa in full run to the waiting room. When she rounded the corner, she screamed out loud. Lil Jackson ran over to his mother and hugged her. "What's wrong momma?"

"Yussef! Um, um…." She said hurrying over to the seats by her children. "Baby," she said to Yesmina in complete tears. "Can you take your brother to the room. I need to talk to Yussef."

"NO!" Everybody jumped. "SHE STAYS!" I said. Melissa made Yesmina sit next to me, and then she took Lil Jackson to his father's room, her eyes were red and she was trembling when she came back. Yesmina looked scared as she looked at everybody's faces. I touched her hand and rubbed it. "How could you do this to me?" I said looking at Melissa as my tears burned my face. Then I looked at my sister and Grandma, "all of you! How could you hurt me like this?"

"I couldn't tell you. She said she'd tell you something else I really didn't want you to know. My hands were tied." Latia said through tears

I looked at Melissa, "you blackmailed her with a secret you already told me!"

"You didn't?" Latia cried harder

"Grandma?"

"Baby the situation was complicated. Melissa please tell him the truth that I was always on your case for not telling him. I didn't agree with this whole thing." Grandma said

Melissa was looking at the floor crying, "she did. Yussef its not like they were ok with this or condoning it. I would threaten to move away or keep Yesmina from them if they told you."

"Baby, what was I supposed to do?" Grandma asked

"YOU TELL ME ANYWAYS! THERE'S NOWHERE SHE COULD'VE HIDDEN THAT I WOULDN'T HAVE FOUND HER! I CANT BELIEVE ANY OF YOU!" I looked at Yesmina; her eyes were glassy and big. "Do you understand what we're talking about?" She shook her head no. Melissa's eyes got big, like she was pleading with me not to. But I didn't care; I would never be invisible to her again. "My name is Yussef. I'm your auntie Latia's little brother. I'm your daddy."

Yesmina frowned at me looking just like me. Then she looked at her mother, "is he joking?" Melissa shook her head no, while crying. Yesmina's eyes got big, and she looked confused.

"Jackson is your stepfather. Yussef is your real father."

She looked at Latia and Grandma, "are you my real auntie and G-momma?"

"Yes baby." Latia said still crying

"Oh so EVERYBODY GETS TO EXIST BUT ME! I CANT BELIEVE THIS!" I spit at them!

Yesmina looked at my tears. "I'm sorry."

"You didn't do ANYTHING! They lied to you just like they lied to me." I said

"Does this mean I get to come over your house and eat ice cream?" She smiled

My body was shaking I was so upset, but her innocent question calmed me. "Is that what you want?" my voice cracked

"Yes!" She said with a HUGE SMILE

"What kind of ice cream do you like? I'll make sure I have a ton of it when you come."

"Coffee!" She said excitedly

I stared at her smiling. "Why are you here?" Latia said

"Our grandmother is taking her last breath upstairs. I went down to the cafeteria with our cousin. I couldn't take my eyes off of this little girl." I said pointing to Yesmina, she laughed. All my anger melted, and my heart pounded as I looked at her. Then I looked at Melissa, "this is far from over!"

"Yussef please let me explain!" Melissa pleaded

"Explain what? Why would you intentionally make history repeat it's self? How could you do this to me? YOU know first hand how it was for Latia and I! When do you think she would start noticing that she was different." Then I turned to my sister and Grandma, "how could you let her do this to me? No secret could be so big that you'd let this happen to me. Whenever Mitchell is involved you get stupid Latia! Every time! I'm done!" They both gasped, "I've always protected both of you! And you let this happen to me! I'm DONE!"

Yesmina tapped me, "what do I call you?"

I took a deep breath, "What do you want to call me?" I asked

"Daddy!" she said with a smile

"I like that." I said

"Daddy, please don't be mad at them." Her big brown eyes were melting my heart. SHE WAS ALREADY WORKING ME!

"Yezzy!" She giggled at her new nickname. "I cannot ignore what they've done. You thought I was a stranger! I thought you were just a pretty little girl."

"You're putting them on time out?" She asked

"Yes! On time out!"

Chapter 18

I couldn't sleep! I had too many things on my mind. My grandmother peacefully passed away in her sleep. Malcolm had everything planned out and executed in record time. The only thing left was to get up and get ready. Malcolm's face turned to stone when I told him about Yesmina. He asked me what I was going to do. I knew I was going to have her with me as much as I possibly could even if that meant fighting Melissa in court if she tried to be like Latia's mother and mine. Malcolm seemed more upset than me, as if that was possible; needless to say he fueled my anger instead of calming me down. But I didn't know how to tell Angela about Yesmina. I don't think she would have a heart attack about Yesmina, but sometimes you never know. My main worry was whether or not I invite Angela to my grandmother's funeral. Jeremy would be nowhere to be found. How do I explain to her that the name she's known me by is made up? I couldn't come up with an answer that didn't make me look bad. I know Malcolm was going to have family at the funeral; they were at my father's. But this time I know for a fact the pot would be stirred. I decided that I wouldn't invite her. Angela didn't question me about why I didn't invite her. She just made sure I was taken care of for the next few days. She called me regularly to check on me, she brought me food. She even asked me which suit I was going to wear and then she took it to the cleaners for me. I didn't ask her to do that, and I even tried to protest a little bit, but to my delight she insisted. It was definitely different to be with someone who looked out for my other needs and not just the physical needs. Angela and I hadn't slept together yet. Which in my heart just made everything sweeter, everything she did for me touched me.

Latia keeps calling me, but I can't even talk to her. Now I understand my mother's words, "you were the trusted one!" Say what you want about my mother, but she was right. Her drama and mess was right there in your face not hidden and secretive. I couldn't believe she hurt me like this. She knows more than anyone else what we went through with our father. She knows how disconnected and disjointed we feel from our whole huge family. I couldn't make my mind or my heart understand why she would betray me like this. There really wasn't any way she could spin it to make me understand either. Latia broke my heart more than ANY female ever could. How could they be so stupid?

I picked up the phone, dialed the number. "Hello?" Melissa said

"I'll be there in three hours to pick up Yezzy for the funeral."

"How did you get this number?" She said in shock

"Like I said there's nowhere you could go that I wouldn't find you. If you fight me I will make your life a living HELL! You don't wanna mess with me! Have her ready in three hours." Melissa blew air. "Melissa! Don't test me!"

"Yussef! We need to talk." I could hear her voice quiver.

"Not right now! Today is too much as it stands. Have her ready!" I hung up.

I stood in front of my spare bedroom; it was no longer a spare. This is Yezzy's room, and we could decorate it anyway she wanted to. Anything she wanted! My heart started pounding thinking about her. It was a mixture of love and pain. I didn't know her, I missed all her first. I felt so robbed. Even my father knew me when I was in diapers.

I drove to San Leandro, and I parked in front of Melissa's mother's house. Melissa stood in the doorway; her face was stressed and sad. I stood there staring at her with evil eyes. I still wanted to strangle her. My glare made her cry, but I didn't care. Yezzy came to the door in a pretty little dress. Her hair was nice and neat. She had a little purse, jacket, and a backpack. Melissa said there was a change of clothes in the backpack in case she wanted to get out of her dress later. Yezzy hugged her mother and then she happily came to me and hugged me. I melted when she hugged me. "I like your car." She said as I opened the door to my nice car. She sat in her booster seat, fastened her seat belt.

"Thank you baby girl." I said closing her door.

Yezzy was all smiles, which made me smile, even though my heart was heavy. She told me about school, and how she was so happy she got to miss it today to be with me. She was sad that her best friend would have to be without her today though. Then she asked me if she and her best friend could have a sleepover at my house. She said her best friend was happy for her when she told her about me. I told her we should give ourselves a little time first, but I was ok with it if her friend's parents were ok with it. There were a few cars in the parking lot when we pulled up. There were men standing outside with shades on who looked like they were taking the day hard. I grabbed Yezzy's hand and then we walked in I nodded at them as we passed, they did the same. Inside the mortuary Malcolm and Amber were sitting in the section for family. Amber asked me how I was holding up as she hugged me; I told her I was fine. Then she greeted Yezzy with a hug and a smile. Yezzy smiled to match hers. "What's your name pretty little girl?" She asked

"Yesmina Davis" Yezzy said sounding proper. Amber was too tickled, I screamed inside. She gave Yezzy my last name, which is good. But none of this made sense to me. Why would she do that if she didn't intend for me to know? Yezzy walked over to Malcolm who hadn't said a word. "Hi" she said with a big smile.

I thought she'd be scared of Malcolm. He didn't look approachable in that moment, and kids are supposed to be good judges of character. "Hello", he said looking at her with no expression.

"What's your name?" She asked

"That's Uncle B..."

"DON'T YOU DARE!" Malcolm said firmly to me while cracking a smile at Yezzy. "I'm Malcolm".

"Uncle Malcolm?" She asked with a smile

"If you want, but you can call me Malcolm."

"Really? Cool!" She said giving him a hug. Malcolm was stiff about hugging her, and he looked like he was trying to reject her cuteness. But he was as weak as I am. Amber stood there misty eyed as she watched their interaction.

Amber took a deep breath, "so the wedding is almost here. Are you coming?" She looked at me with sad eyes. I shook my head no. "I don't understand everything that's going on. But I hope it gets ironed out as soon as possible."

Then Derrick and Darryl walked up. They hugged their mother and said hey to their father. Derrick chatted with me for a minute, Darryl stood back and watched me. I know he doesn't understand any of this. Amber asked him where Andrew was. He told her that he was trying to get here as soon as he could; he had a meeting at work that he had to attend. Malcolm shot Amber an evil look, she sat next to him probably defending Drew.

I introduced Derrick and Darryl to Yesmina. Darryl had been staring at me so hard he didn't even notice her. Yesmina flashed those brown eyes and smile, I could see Darryl melt.

"Where did she come from?" He asked keeping his eyes on her.

"It's a long story." I said

"Melissa right?" Derrick said as he analyzed Yezzy's face.

"Right." I said wondering if he knew about this already.

"You could tell she was hiding something. That part was obvious" Then he looked at me, "Are you ok?"

I appreciated the question, but I didn't know how to answer. "Yea I'm good". I said because I didn't know what else to say.

Yezzy let go of my hand and she took off running to Latia as she walked into the mortuary. Lewis, my Grandma and Arthur were with her. Latia had sad eyes as she looked at me. Lewis looked completely shocked when he saw Amber and Malcolm sitting together. Amber smiled sheepishly as she acknowledged Lewis. Malcolm's face was stone as he looked at Lewis. Darryl watched the interaction for a minute then he said hello. Derrick said hello as well. I nodded at Lewis and I shook Arthur's hand. Then I sat down next to Amber as I glared at Latia and my Grandma. Derrick sat next to Malcolm and they were talking about something. Darryl sat next to them ear hustling on their conversation. Yezzy excitedly sat next to me. She asked Latia to sit next to her. Latia quietly sat down. "Yussef I'm sorry!" I shook my head and refused to look at her. She was trying to melt the ice around my heart. "Yussef!"

Malcolm snapped his fingers at her. "Hey! Stop that! Do that on your own time. This is about your grandmother show some respect!"

Yezzy looked at her auntie's reaction to Malcolm then she smiled at me. "Is Uncle Malcolm Auntie Latia's daddy?"

"No, we have the same father and he died a long time ago."

"She acts like he's her daddy." Then Yezzy went back to people watching.

Roz and Tanisha hurried in with the last of the people, right behind her was my momma and Jarvis. When Malcolm saw Roz trying to sit in the back he stood and told them to come to the front, and he told someone who had to be family to scoot over and make room for them. Everyone did as they were told. Malcolm didn't acknowledge my momma and her husband. I didn't feel good about seeing her; I could feel the drama coming. During the service they went over the obituary. Yezzy pointed to a picture and whispered what happened to my hair. I told her that was my father not me. She looked confused like I was trying to trick her. Darryl looked at the picture then at me. His mouth was open like he couldn't believe it. Then when they read our names, Malcolm even made sure Yezzy was acknowledged I sat taller. I was invisible no more. After the ceremony tons of people approached us, introducing their selves. Malcolm and Derrick sat on the side with the same expression watching us. Some of the little ones even knew Yezzy from school. She had a huge smile on her face as well. We rode in the limo with Amber and Malcolm to the burial site. They seemed completely smitten with Yezzy.

"You don't like Lewis?" I asked Malcolm

"I don't care about him." Malcolm said shrugging off my question.

"He's good friends with my ex, that's all." Amber said nonchalantly.

I wanted to ask another question, but I chose not to cause Malcolm wasn't in the most conversational mood. "Thank you for everything." I said watching Malcolm's eyes.

"You have a ton of family. It's time you knew it." He said looking out the window.

"Me too! I can't wait to see all my cousins at school." Yezzy said excited. I imagined feeling that way if I would've met everyone when I was young.

At the burial site I could tell Malcolm was looking for Andrew. He looked more and more annoyed with each moment that passed and he wasn't there.

Back at the reception hall I was talking to one of Bernadette's brothers. He said he had to touch me to make sure I was real. We had a good laugh as he went on and on about my father. Everyone said he was a good man, which made me feel good.

I was so happy to see Roz; she looked one hundred percent like the Roz I used to know. She told me she broke up with Yuri. She said she's been working on getting her head together. I promised I would bring Yezzy by often so that they could get to know each other. She liked that, and then she stopped smiling when she noticed my momma looking at her like she was crazy. I ignored her and kept talking to Roz. No matter how hard and how crazy she looked at Roz, it wouldn't change anything. My father was in love with Roz when he died. I heard him with my own ears refer to forever with her. No matter what my father didn't love my momma and she needed to get over it. Amber signaled for Roz to join her outside.

My momma stared at Yezzy as she approached us. "This is her!" She had tears in her eyes. "I'm not old enough to be a Grandma!" She said

"But you are!" Jarvis laughed

Yezzy frowned, and then she looked at me. I hated to break it to her. "This is my mother." Jarvis cleared his throat. "And her husband Jarvis."

"That's right cause I'm not old enough for anyone to be calling me grand daddy."

"You don't ever have to worry about her calling you that." I said glaring at him.

"How did they tell you?" My momma asked like she was ready for the drama.

"Momma not now." I said trying to shoo her off.

"Boy! Don't you talk to your momma like that!"

"WHO ARE YOU CALLING BOY? NIGGA YOU DON'T KNOW ME!" I spit at him.

Jarvis smiled, "oh the temp got heart! Check it out! You don't know me either! You can't disrespect my woman in my face and think I'm not gonna have something to say about it!"

I walked up on him. "A wise man would shut up when he doesn't know what he's talking about! You got point five seconds to get out of my face before you get...." Derrick hit him, he went completely unconscious.

Derrick looked at me with no expression. "Too much talking for me." Then he looked at some cousins. "Can ya'll take him outside."

I looked at my momma expecting to see her worried or concerned for her husband. She looked completely amused by what happened. When she realized I was looking at her, she tried to straighten her face. "I guess we'll get to meet some other time." She shrugged at Yezzy. "Bye baby," she said getting on her tiptoes to kiss my cheek.

When she walked out Derrick asked me if I was alright. I shrugged, and then I looked at Yezzy who was unphased by what just happened. She wanted to play with the other kids. I got her backpack out the car and she went to my Grandma and asked her to go with her to the bathroom.

Darryl walked over to the table with two red cups. He handed me one. "The man of many secrets." He smiled. "How come you never said anything?"

"My father never said anything and it went from there." I said matter of factly.

My Grandma sent Yezzy back to me changed. Yezzy handed me her backpack and then she went outside where Malcolm and Amber were talking to Roz and other family. Darryl looked at my Grandma's sad eyes. "What's up with her?"

"She knew about baby girl and I had to find out." I said still visibly angry.

"Same thing with your sister?"

"Yep!" I said shaking my leg.

Darryl whistled, "that's too bad." The he stood up. "I wonder how my brother's gonna feel when he finds out about you." He let his question ride on the air, and then he walked away.

I took a swallow of my drink, was he trying to say this was the same thing? My mind was racing, and I was completely in my thoughts. Lewis sat next to me. "I'm sorry for your loss, both of them." He said

"Thanks man, at least one of them can be fixed." I said

"I know this is not the time, but whenever it's good for you. I wanna talk to you about your sister."

I looked him in his eyes. "Is that right?"

He maintained eye contact, "yes".

"Why?" I said like I couldn't understand.

"I've always wanted to be with her. But she was the one dragging her feet. I'm sensing a change and I'm jumping on it."

"Like what?" I asked

"The fact that I'm here for one. She's got so many protective layers. She called me upset and I dropped everything to be here. I've never met anyone like her, and I doubt I ever will again." He took a deep breath. "I didn't know you guys were linked to Malcolm, but frankly that's my boy's problem not mine. I don't care!"

"Who's your boy?"

"Dwayne Reed, you know him?" He asked

"Aw! The pretty boy!" I said. I remember him quite well. "The football coach turn actor right?"

"Yea" Lewis said watching Latia's face as she talked to my Grandma and Arthur.

"Everybody messes up Yussef. Your sister loves you!"

"I know, but I don't like her very much right now." I said taking another drink.

****

"So..." She sound upset, "why haven't I heard from you Jeremy? Did I do something wrong?"

"No Angela, in a matter of a few hours my life flipped upside down. We need to talk, but I can't do it right now." I said still searching for words.

"Do you want to be with someone else?" She asked

"No!"

"Jeremy I think we can be strong together, but I need you to talk to me. I'll try to understand if you can't do it right at this moment. But I can't sit over here waiting for you to remember me."

"Baby I know! Please know that I want you. There is nobody else for me. I need a minute to present this to you. You may not want me after we talk. That's what is blowing my mind right now. I don't want to lose you." I said from my heart.

"You won't lose me as long as you come to me first. I don't like finding out from other people things I should know from you." She said firmly

The buzzer for the door downstairs sounded. "I hear you." I said looking out the window and seeing Melissa's car parked on the street. I buzzed her in, then I cracked the door so she could come in. "I promise we will talk as soon as I get a handle on something's."

Her breathing got heavy, "if you don't hurry up!"

Melissa walked in the door, I pointed to the couch for her to sit. "I love you! I promise I will." Angela hung up. When I looked at Melissa, jealousy was all over her face.

"What's wrong with you?"

Melissa rolled her eyes. "Thank you for letting me come over." I pulled out a chair from the table and sat down. "I wanted a chance to talk to you alone."

"We're alone, talk." I spit at her.

I know she was searching my face for a trace of the loving feelings I used to carry for her. Little did she realize love has left the building. "Can I explain how it happened?"

"I was there I don't need a play by play."

She took a deep breath. "You never took me seriously! I was IN LOVE WITH YOU!" She jumped out of her seat like it burned her, and she started pacing. "I put myself on the line for you. I even tried to be happy for you while you were with Sylvia. I didn't like being your friend while you went home to her. I could've told you how that was gonna end, but I wanted you to choose me. When I FINALLY give you up,

FINALLY give Jackson my heart, I feel better." She sighed, "I'm engaged and preparing for my new life then you kissed me. I FORGOT MYSELF! I told Jackson right away, I don't think you were in your car before I had him on the phone crying my eyes out. You were just rebounding from Sylvia, I honestly thought you guys were going to get back together even though." I sucked my teeth. "I promised Jackson I would stay away from you, and that we would marry as promised. When I found out I was pregnant I was devastated and overjoyed all at the same time. Jackson told me I had to choose. I chose the only man who's ever chosen me."

I mimicked her like I was playing a violin. "Still doesn't explain why I had to be a stranger to my child!"

"Yussef it was always all about me. Every time I see you I wanna be in your arms! You have no idea how much I love you! You don't get it!" She said still pacing and now crying.

"The sad part, is if something would've happened to Jackson. I would've come for you.... Until I found out what you've done! You did the unthinkable, and you forced my Grandmother and sister into your web of lies. You know I can't stand Shonda, and you go and forever change my perception of you by doing this. I would've left you alone to have your marriage. I would only come for my child. Every year on the day she was born I wake up in a sweat feeling like the life is being squeezed out of me. I didn't know what it meant, I thought I was sick!"

"I'm sorry Yussef!" She said crying

"I loved you! Yesmina is here behind me showing you! You were supposed to choose me! You had me walking around here lost." Fire burned in my stomach. "I never thought you were capable of being this selfish!"

"I'm sorry!" She said dropping to her knees in front of me and kissing me. Everything with her was familiar, no explanations, and no newness. "I'm sorry!" She said kissing me deeper.

I'm not gonna lie, my mind went blank for a minute. So blank that the caress of her warm mouth taking in my head jarred me. I looked around the room trying to gather my strength to make her stop, my sweats were down and I felt none of this until now. She wasn't here for this; I needed this to stop even though it felt good. My eyes misted up as I told her to stop, but that only made her go faster. I tried moving backwards in my chair but she followed me bobbing faster and faster. I couldn't move her.

"Melissa please stop!" I managed to get out even though I had no air in my lungs. She continued moving and more determined than before. She wasn't going to stop until I blew. I didn't want to, but my body disobeyed me.

She backed away from me crying her makeup ran down her face. "I love you! I'm sorry! I'm sorry!"

"Woman! What are you trying to do to me?" I said catching my breath. She moved like she was going to come back towards me. "STOP!" I put my hands out, "I can't trust you to do anything right!"

She was still crying, "Yussef! I love you! I couldn't be around you because I can't trust myself when you're involved."

"You don't have to worry about trusting yourself cause you will never do this to me again!" I said angry and standing up to fix my pants.

Melissa screamed, "why won't you love me? WHY?"

"I did love you! You chose Jackson, now we've both moved on." I said

"I haven't, I was waiting for Jackson to die. Every time he goes in the hospital I prepare myself for them to say that time his crisis was too great and he succumb to his illness. Please wait for me."

"What?"

"Don't love whoever you were talking to, love me! Please Yussef! You know I love you!"

"You have the most ridiculous way of showing someone that you love them." I could feel steam rising off my body. "If you loved me you would've told me about the baby even if you still chose to marry Jackson. If you love me like you say you do, you'd want me to be happy even if it meant finding happiness with someone else. You are selfish!"

"I messed up Yussef! I'm human!"

"You turned my family against me! There's no way I could choose you!"

"I'll make it up to you, I promise! Please Yussef I love you!"

Her makeup was still running down her face, she looked completely crazy. I didn't want a hostile environment for Yezzy. And I didn't want Angela walking away because of Melissa. I took a deep breath. "Melissa I'm already in love with someone else."

"No! No! You love me!" She cried

"No I love her." She cried harder, "but who knows what the future holds. My girl could mess up just like Sylvia did. Whether or not I forgive you depends on how you conduct yourself while I'm with my girl." She was still crying but she was listening. "Don't ever in your LIFE even think about keeping my daughter from me. I will be respectful of your family plans, but be respectful of mine. If we can be civil about visitation and everything else I won't take you to court or fight you for custody."

"But what about me?" She said

"You have Jackson and little Jack to fill your time. When Jackson dies, hopefully that won't be any time soon if I'm free we'll see. If I'm not, give me space like I gave you." I said hoping that would satisfy her.

She sat there thinking for a minute. "I need you to do something before I agree."

I shot her a very irritated look. "WHAT?" I said through clinched teeth

She stood up, walked over to me and straddled me. I screamed at my body not to respond to her. Then she kissed my neck, "make up with your Grandma and Latia." She said kissing me.

"Honestly Melissa you could've said that from across the room. You didn't have to come over here for that." I said allowing her to kiss me. My heart missed her smell too.

"I know." She said still kissing on me.

I had to think of something to get her off of me. "You wanna see Yezzy's room?"

She looked at me, "I thought you guys were going shopping this weekend?"

"We are, but maybe you can give me some pointers. Yezzy's gonna pick everything out, but I don't know how to guide her. You did most of the decorating around here."

"You gotta agree first." She said sounding happy.

"Fine! Whatever, get up!" I said grabbing her hips to make her move. I looked at my pants and she made them wet. I needed a shower anyways.

Chapter 19

"I'm not in it, but you guys need to talk. Tracy thinks you're dead. Talk to Drew." Derrick said

"How do you know?" I asked

"I was there. It was awhile ago." Derrick said, "I want this to all be over."

"I hear you. I'll call him." I said. Derrick hung up. I expected him to say something else. I guess he was done talking.

The wedding was this weekend; I guess it was now or never. "I dialed Andrew's number. I imagined him staring at the phone like he didn't know what to do with it. He answered on the final ring, his voice had so many question marks when he said hello. "Drew we need to clear the air," I said in response to his hello.

"Where you wanna meet?" He said

"Can you come to my place?"

"I need to come now, I gotta pick up some family from the airport in awhile."

"That's fine man! Just come on."

"Where am I going?"

"I'm in Troy's place by the lake."

Andrew paused for a minute. "I'm on my way."

I didn't have a speech prepared in my mind or anything. It seem like Andrew flew to my place. I stood on the balcony watching him. When he got out the car his demeanor told me he was upset. He had on shades and he kept inhaling and exhaling. He walked in the door as one of my tenants walked out. I cracked the door for him, and then I stood back. When he walked in the door he didn't take his shades off his jawline clinched and unclenched. "Hey!" He said. He took deep breaths as he looked around the apartment. "I used to live here."

"I heard the story, do you wanna sit? Something to drink?"

"I need a drink for this!" He said plopping on the couch

I brought back two glasses of single malt and the bottle. "Do you have questions cause I do?"

"Why didn't you tell me?" He said

"At first you weren't concerned. Its not like Malcolm brought me around right away. When we met you weren't concerned with who I was. When Malcolm decided it was time, I asked him not to."

He picked up his glass and took a drink. "All this time, all these years!" He growled "I wanted to know what you truly thought of me. Everybody else seemed to see me for who I am. Everybody except you!"

Andrew didn't like the sound of that, we went back and forth. He felt the need to go all the way back to Jennay. Each time I reminded him how I've always had his back. "Spending the night with my woman was not having my back!" He spit

"You wanted me dead already, in that moment I struggled with holding back." Andrew took his glasses off and there was nothing but PAIN in his eyes. He stared at me long and hard. He was debating with asking me about that night. I could tell. I waited for him to decide, "I didn't know you were family. But you knew! You forgave me based upon that alone didn't you?" I nodded, "although Tracy is very tight lipped about that night, I know certain connects were not made." His glare could've burned a hole in me. He was looking for the slightest indication that there was reason to believe other than he did already. When I had no reaction he exhaled like he was relieved. "I'm not about to sit up here and cry like no little girl!" He exhaled, and then he tossed his shades on the table. "YOU SHOULD'VE TOLD ME! SOMEBODY SHOULD'VE SAID SOMETHING! You guys let me dang near fall in love with my cousin! If that isn't messed up on so many levels! I couldn't understand why she wouldn't give me the time of day."

I cracked up laughing, I had forgotten about his crush on Latia. "Even if she didn't know, you aren't her type anyways."

Andrew blew air, "Please! I'm everybody's type!"

"Not anymore, you're almost an officially married man."

His smile dropped, "I'm still mad at you man!"

"I'm mad at you!" He raised an eyebrow then he sat back on the couch. I let it all out. How tight we were to a point. How he always disregarded me. How he has his head so far up his own butt that he barely notices the people around him. I told him it was amazing that he even noticed Tracy with all his constant distractions. I told him if it wasn't for me his woman would be dead! He flinched when I said it, but he knew it was true. We went back and forth for a long time.

"I hear you've got a daughter. How are you holding up?"

"I'm definitely looking at you and Toya through different eyes." I said shaking my head "It's not so black and white is it?"

"But you still have no excuse you knew she was crazy when you knocked her up. Melissa…." My stomach turned with fire.

"Tracy thinks you're dead." He said matter of factly

"So I hear." I said looking at him. He shrugged. "Seriously Andrew? You guys are in Berkeley, I'm right here. You don't think at some point our paths would cross?"

"I'm expecting you to make sure that doesn't happen." He said matter of factly.

I smiled at him. "You really wanna spend the rest of your life wondering if you got her by default?"

Andrew got up, he was pacing and he was angry. I leaned back in my chair; Andrew was no threat to me. I wasn't going to pretend like I needed to watch my back in regards to him anymore. He growled and paced for a long time. I knew he was going over all the options, playing chest against himself in his head. "Fine!" He stomped, "FINE!" Then he picked up his shades, "I can't even deal with you right now! The wedding is Saturday. I guess I'll see you at some point." He said then he left.

I felt lighter already.

****

Of course Andrew didn't tell anyone I would be coming. He wasn't gonna make this easy for me. But I was pushing his insecurities to the limit, so I understood. I was asking him to let her choose, although she and I know she already made her choice. The fact he felt the need to let her think I was dead, means he wasn't convinced of her choice. Andrew had Mitigated staff on her everywhere she went. I hated that we had to come down to the night before the wedding to have this whole scene. I was sitting in the lobby when the wedding party came back from their rehearsal dinner. I called Angela and I told her I needed to come by, she exhaled and told me she would wait up.

After I talked to Tracy, I got in my car feeling almost completely free. I raced from San Francisco to El Sobrante in record time. The light was on in Angela's room. She turned it off as soon as she heard my car. She came outside, that sadness was back in her eyes. I already felt horrible. I caught myself before I threw out a defensive attitude. She leaned against the car and folded her arms. Her sad eyes burned a hole in me as she waited for me to spill it. I took a deep breath; I asked her if she would ride with me. I didn't want her to be able to run in the house. But I think she thought of the same thing when she declined. I took another deep breath. "My name is Yussef Davis." Her mouth fell open. I know that wasn't what she thought she was going to hear. But I felt almost completely better after it came out of my mouth. I explained that my job sometimes required me to use aliases. I showed her the three different authentic driver's licenses that I had. She said that wasn't what she thought I was coming to talk to her about. With a heavy heart I assured her there was more. Her defense went back up, I asked her if she wanted the detailed version or if she wanted me to get to the point. We had been outside for a little over two hours at this point. She told me she needed to understand the entire story and to start at the beginning. I told her about Shannon, and how Melissa and I got together the first time. I told her about Sylvia, and that night with Melissa. When I got to Yezzy she had no visible reaction, she just listened. She told me before that she couldn't date a man with a child. I remembered feeling relieved that I didn't fit that description. Now I wondered if there was an exception for a man who didn't know he had one.⬜ Since I was purging and I had nothing to gain by lying I told her about the "conversation" gone wrong with Melissa as well. She made a wounded sound but she kept listening taking everything in. I stared at her face looking for an indication of how she felt. Or what she was thinking.

"Is that everything?" She looked me in my eyes like she was reading me. I told her that was everything. "This is a lot to process. I need sometime."

My heart sank; I knew that was the right answer. But it still wasn't what I wanted to hear. "I don't want you to think about it. I want you to ride with me. I want you to still want me. I want us to be ok. I want you!"

"Every time I attempt to say your name my mind screams at me! That's not even your name!"

"I can be whoever you want. You can call me Jeremy. It's just a name, it's still me." I pleaded

"I need to think about this. I need to understand how I honestly feel about all of it." She said putting her hands up.

"I wanna believe that no good deed goes unrewarded, but that's not the world we live in. Sometimes you're punished for the truth. But you said as long as I came to you and you didn't hear it from some one else we could work through it. I'm here! I'm begging you to work with me! Please Angela!"

"I know Jere... See! I don't even know what to call you! I need to think about this! Please let me go!" She pleaded.

Feeling defeated, I exhaled. I reached in my pocket. "I don't know how long you'll need. When you're ready, if you ever are, come to me." I handed her a keychain with the keys to my place on them. "This one is to the main door," I showed her the key. "This is to my front door," I showed her that key. "My schedule varies, but I'm normally home from work around three. My schedule is every other weekend with Yezzy, I have her tomorrow, and I have dinner with her on Tuesdays and Thursdays." I said putting the keys in her hand.

"Did you make up with your sister?" She asked me staring at the keys.

I exhaled; I started walking to the driver's side of my car. "Kind of! We've talked on the phone a couple times. I don't feel like I can trust her anymore."

"You've asked for forgiveness twice in one week, but you can't forgive them?" Then she walked away.

Chapter 20

Melissa had a funny look on her face when she opened the door. "Sylvia's here." She said searching my face.

I froze in place. "What do you mean?"

"Yesmina said you wanted to meet her best friend's parent. Sydney is her best friend."

"You knew about this?" I asked her.

"I knew her best friend was Sydney. I've met the little girl at the school, but I'm just finding out like you are." Her face turned evil, "I don't think they should be friends anymore."

"You can't take her best friend away from her. How do you think that will make her feel about you? Is Sylvia inside?"

Melissa rolled her eyes. She called out to Sylvia. When Sylvia saw me she jumped. "You're Yesmina's father?" Her mouth was hanging open.

I backed away from the door. "Yes"

Sylvia stepped out the door, then she looked at Melissa, "you know who I am don't you?" Melissa didn't respond she continued to glare at Sylvia. "Why don't I know who you are?" Melissa didn't respond. Her chest kept moving up and down like she was trying to control her temper. Sylvia looked at me, "what's going on?"

"When was your daughter born?" Melissa said through clinched teeth.

My stomach started turning, Sylvia and I looked at Melissa in disbelief. "What are you saying?" Sylvia asked

"WHEN WAS SHE BORN?" Melissa barked

"April 11th, what are you getting at?" Sylvia looked at me, she was clueless.

"Yesmina was born the day before." Melissa spit

I was trying to remember if we had a blood test or a DNA test done when Sydney was born.

Melissa called the girls to the door. When the girls came to the door she told them to stand side by side. I took two steps backwards. Yezzy looks exactly like me, Sydney looks just like Sylvia, BUT the girls favored each other. Sylvia put her hand over her mouth, Melissa started crying. The girls looked lost. "You guys go get your stuff together. Sydney make sure you grab your mother's purse." Melissa said staring Sylvia down.

"We had her tested. In court and everything." Sylvia said looking back and forth between us.

"Was it a blood test or a DNA test?" I asked

"I don't remember. I didn't know there was a difference." Sylvia said

"There's a huge difference." I said, as my brain started hurting.

Sounding panicked Sylvia asked, "what do we do?"

"I'll schedule DNA testing for all of us so we have everything in writing. The girls will come with me this weekend. We should know by next weekend." I said

"You think that's necessary?" Melissa asked looking like she was gonna lose it.

"You saw them yourself. I need to know!" I said

The girls came out blissfully unaware of anything. Sylvia got Sydney's booster seat out of her beat up bucket. I chuckled to myself. When she was with me, she was too good to look at a bucket. Now a bucket was all she had. "Did you move?" Sylvia asked

"No I'm in the same place, let me give you my number." I said taking out my cell. Melissa went inside and slammed her door. I got her number and then I looked in her eyes. "Get in your car fast, and don't ever come back here. I'll bring Sydney home on Sunday."

Sensing the urgency Sylvia waved bye to Sydney. She started up her bucket and took off. I watched her drive away, Melissa watched out the window. I got in the car and drove off.

At the stoplight I turned around and looked at both of them. With the two of them together I saw glimpses of me in Sydney's face. I wanted to curse, but I smiled instead. "Wait until you see my room. I picked stuff I knew we'd both like." Yezzy said, Sydney made and excited sound just like Latia does. I CAN'T BELIEVE THIS! I gripped the steering wheel.

I told the car to call Latia. "Hello?" She answered on the first ring.

"I need you to come to my house immediately! It's an emergency!"

"You aren't going to the wedding?" She asked sounding confused.

I huffed, "what part of emergency don't you understand?"

"On my way!" She hung up

When we got to my building I hoped to see Angela's car, but she was nowhere to be found. In that moment I accepted it was over, and I tried to exhale. The girls were excited when they went in the room. In that moment I was glad we got the bunk beds Yezzy wanted instead of the day bed I was trying to convince her to like.

Latia got to my apartment in record time. Her eyes were big, "what's wrong?"

I was sitting at the table staring at my hands. "Yezzy's here." I said drained

"Is she ok?" She said listening to the girl's laughter in the other room.

"She's fine, but... You gotta see!" I said

"Stop being scary!" She said

"Yezzy your auntie is here." I called out

Yezzy came running out the room excited. She jumped in Latia's arms. "You're off time out?" She asked her auntie

"Yes, I am." She said examining Yezzy to understand my words.

"Auntie! This is my BESTEST FRIEND IN THE WHOLE WIDE WORLD SYDNEY!" Yezzy said as Sydney peeked out the door.

"Hello sweetheart." Latia said then she looked at me with a question mark.

"Syd, can you come stand next to Yezzy? I wanna show my sister something." I said in a tender voice.

Latia smiled at the girls as they positioned themselves next each other. Latia looked at them and shrugged. "Look at their features." I said

Latia looked at them. She wasn't seeing it at first then she turned her head to the side and her eyes got big and her mouth fell open. "What?" The girls said in unison

"You guys have the same noses, and the same eyes!" She smiled real big, "have you guys been operating on each other?"

They both touched their noses, "really?" Then they hurried to the bathroom to look for their selves.

Latia plopped down at the table with me. "Sylvia?"

"Yea"

"I thought you got tested?"

"I did too, I don't remember if it was a blood or DNA test. I will get to the bottom of it by the end of the week." I said staring at the table. "If Angela was on the fence before. This has definitely sealed my fate." I exhaled. "If Melissa wouldn't have pointed it out, I don't think I would've seen it either." Then I told her how it all happened.

"Thank you for calling me." Latia said through tears.

"I needed my sister. The only person who wants to be with me is proving to be crazy. She's probably melting down right now." I said shaking my head

Latia put her hands over mine. "Yussef before I lose my nerve I have to ask you. What did Melissa tell you about Mitchell?"

I exhaled, "that you were pregnant, he beat you up." I looked at her, "why would you hide that from me?"

"You tried to warn me, I didn't listen. I thought you'd be mad at me. Then I didn't know what you'd do. It was my fault, I thought I knew him. I thought he loved me."

"I guess you didn't think about what would happen when he'd unknowingly walk up on me in Malcolm's spot ready for my retaliation." I said staring at her eyes.

She swallowed, "no".

"Melissa told me while he waited for me outside. Malcolm heard everything." She looked down then she looked at me. "There's no reason to be afraid. Stop tormenting Lewis, Mitchell can't hurt you anymore." Latia started crying really hard. I put my arms around her and I rubbed her back.

"I love you Yussef! I'll never hurt you like this again. I promise!"

The girls came out their room, "what's wrong with auntie?" Yezzy said

"Nothing baby, I'm just so happy!"

The girls smiled. "Yezzy, should we let Syd pick our early dinner spot?" Yezzy smiled a knowing smile. "Syd where would you like to go?" I asked

She looked at Yezzy and smiled, "The Cheese!"

I blew air and both of the girls giggled excitedly. "You're coming right?" I said to Latia.

"Yea, I feel for you when they get older." She said

"You're sure that's me?" I asked

Latia looked at both the girls smiling wide-eyed at her. "Project twins for sure!" She said

I exhaled and accepted my fate. We took the girls to The Cheese and they had a blast. On the way there Sydney shared how she always asked her mother if they could go, but her mother couldn't afford it. While the girls played Latia and I discussed my plan of attack. I would have to provide for Sydney just the same as I provide for Yesmina. Nothing more and nothing less. Hopefully I could have both of them on the same schedule. Then the girls drafted us to play with them. We chased them through tubes, dove in ball pits, played skee ball. They had so many tickets that when we were done they both had big stuffed dogs and little trinkets. In the car both of the girls thanked me for such a fun day. Running around with them took away some of the pain in my heart. I didn't bother looking around for Angela's car when we got to my apartment. When I opened the door Angela was sitting on the couch watching TV. Her smiled dropped when she saw Latia then it resurfaced when she looked at our faces. "Hi I'm Angela." She said coming over to hug Latia.

Latia squeezed the life out of her. "It's nice to finally meet you! I've heard so many wonderful things."

"Thank you," she said then she looked at the girls. "Who do we have here?"

"This is Yesmina, and this is Sydney." I said watching her face.

"Nice to meet you ladies, I'm Angela."

Both of the girls very shyly said hi to her.

I felt like I was gonna burst. "Latia can you hang out with the girls? I need to talk to Angela in the other room." Latia smiled and said of course. I couldn't get her in my room fast enough. As soon as I closed the door I squeezed the life out of her. She laughed, "you had me thinking you weren't coming." I kissed her, and then I remembered the whammy. "I have an update."

She sat on the bed, "shoot."

I talked as fast as I could, "I need to get a DNA test done for Sydney I think she might be mine."

"What?" Angela looked at me like she hoped I was joking. "Why do you think that?"

"If you look past color and look at them side by side, they look a lot a like. Being around her today I see similarities. It could be coincidences, but I gotta be sure. And it wouldn't hurt to have it on paper that Yezzy is mine too."

Angela shook her head, "we went from a family of two to four in no time. Are there any more baby possibilities?"

"Those two are the only time I had unprotected sex. My last HIV test was good, haven't had sex since before you."

"And the other day." She said

I exhaled and hung my head that fast I forgot. "Yea and that".

"So now what?" She said looking at me.

"You're gonna ride with me?" My heart fluttered

She smiled big at me, "yes sure. Why not?"

I rushed her on the bed. We laid there on the bed kissing. "You gonna spend the night?"

"Not tonight, when do the girls go home?" She asked

"Tomorrow" I said excitedly.

She smiled and laughed a little. "I can come back tomorrow, spend the day with you guys and then spend the night if that's ok?"

"If that's ok?" I sat up, "do you have any idea how hard it's been not to tear your clothes off?" She laughed. "Tomorrow can you do me another favor?"

"Me spending the night is doing you a favor?"

"A shared experience, but yes. You agreeing to ride with me is doing me a favor."

"Momma is over due for a tune-up so I think we'll settle on shared experience. But what's up?"

"Will you cut my hair?"

"NNNOOO!!! Really? Why?"

"I'm starting over. I don't need to hide behind my hair no more. I may want my locs back later. But for now, it's time for a new me."

She took my hair out and released my locs. She touched them, "I'm gonna miss you!" She said touching my hair. "It's so soft, you sure?"

"Yes!" I said staring into her eyes. "I love you! Thank you for choosing me!"

"You chose me first! I love you!"

MORE FROM THE AUTHOR

Thank you for allowing me to entertain you. I hope you have enjoyed reading my current release. If you have not read Volumes I – VIII of the Wallace Family Affairs series, please do so. Click here for a list of all the background stories. Once you have read the background stories, please checkout the current date series Together We Are Strong. Stay tune for more to come shortly.

Wallace Family Affairs
At Last (Click here)
Tracy's Complications (Click here)
Distorted Mirrors (Click here)
Sometimes Love Isn't Enough (Click here)
Love Is Just Enough (Click here)
Just A Friend (Click here)
Invisible
Look Beyond Your Eyes (Click here)
No Regrets (Click here)
First You Laugh Then You Cry (Click here)
A Heart That's Taken (Click here)
Abandoned (Click here)
Last Words (Click here)

Together We Are Strong
Season 1 Present (Click here)
Beyond The Wallace's ~ I Knew You When (**TBD**)
Season 2 What Comes Next (Release **TBD**)

Standalones
Secrets & Lies ~ (**TBD late 2016 release**)
Anthology **Short** Story (Where Love May Find You Collection) ~ (Click here)
Waiting (**TBD**)

Hopefully you've enjoyed all of the background stories for our lovely Wallace's and Latour's. Please tune in for more from the "Together We Are Strong" Wallace & Latour Family Episodes on Amazon.